EDEN REVEALED

EDEN REVEALED

Fourth Novel in the Eden series

LEXI POST

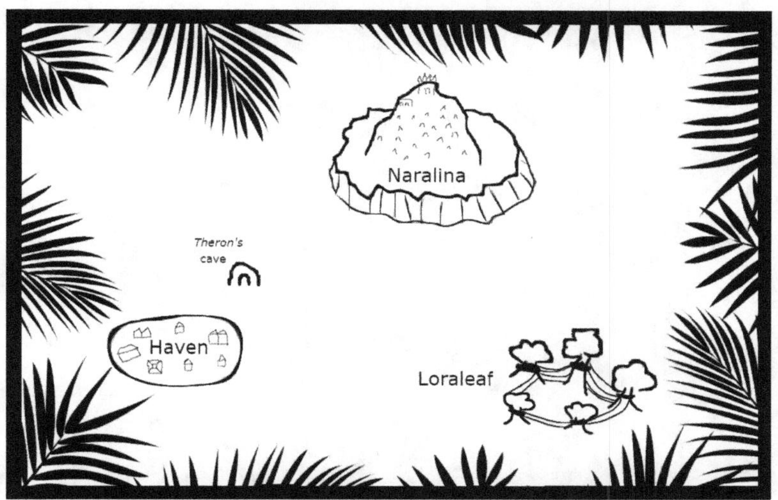

Naralina
Theron's
cave
Haven
Loraleaf

EDEN REVEALED

The Eden Series, Book 4

By Lexi Post

A female spy, an Eden monk, and a man with no memory must reveal a corrupt leader while keeping their hearts safe—an impossible task.

Former stunt woman, Toni Reid, has adopted Eden as her new home. What's not to like with naked hunks walking around and women being worshipped by them? She doesn't mind the distraction of spying on one of the leaders of the Ruling Circle too much, but just as she discovers his secret, she's caught.

Akasha is next in line to ascend to the Triad panel, those who determine which men are morally good enough to receive a portal chip. His connections to people have been minimal to keep his future judgements unbiased, but when he discovers Toni spying, he has no choice but to capture her and discover what she knows.

Sandale is busy learning about who he was before his memory wipe. Traveling to Naralina to rescue Toni is a good excuse to meet his family and find himself again. He discovers Toni is more than a task, she is a force to be reckoned with, and his focus quickly shifts.

Akasha and Sandale are soon embroiled in a plot that could well send Eden back into another world war over women. The only way to stop it is to work together with Toni, but working to stop a world war is easy when compared to laying siege to Toni's heart.

Acknowledgments

For Bob Fabich, the man who proved to me that men really could be like my Edenists.

For Paige Wood who supports me in more ways than I can count!

Thank you to my critique partner, Marie Patrick, for tackling my rough pages and keeping the pressure on. I couldn't have done it without her.

I also want to thank Lori Hammons, Carolyn Derrico, and Lisa Fishback for taking the time to review this story with a fine-tooth comb. I know how hard that is to do.

THE FAMILIES OF EDEN

Naralina:

Toni Reid – Former stuntwoman – Cythera in a Pleasure Temple

Akasha – Triad member-to-be – Kindred of Light (Controls color spectrum)

Loraleaf:

Serena – Former explosives expert for movies – Beloved of Jahl and Khaos

Jahl – Kindred of Eden (Controls all nature that is not alive)

Khaos – Kindred Unknown (Foresees the future in parts)

Sandale – Kindred of Heart (Calms people)

Jaelene (Serena's sister) – Former interior decorator and an animal lover – Beloved of Theron, Konala and Rekah

Theron – Kindred of Light (Creates reflections)

Konala – Kindred of Eden (Communicates with animals)

Rekah – Kindred of Heart (Senses others' emotions)

Haven:

Erin – Former IT expert – Beloved of Wareson and Nassic

Wareson – Kindred of Air (Pushes air)

Nassic – Kindred of Mind (Forces people to tell the truth)

Author's Note

Eden Revealed was inspired by Emily Dickinson's poem, *The White Heat* which was first published in 1891.

This poem speaks of what pain and suffering the soul must go through to become pure. It is not for everyone. Even to see someone else's is to be in such intensity that you must stand back by the door, away from the fire of experience. The fire's color is red, but when it heats the iron at the forge, the iron turns white because it has been purified, a symbol for the soul. This purification is available to anyone who would willingly step into the red fire until even the source of the fire is obliterated.

So what if a man followed a calling to judge the morality of other men? Could he reach this white heat, even if his own light is red? What about the man who at the age of thirty has suffered the heat? Is his soul now pure white? And can a woman who has the black stain of the forge on her soul reach for such purity? Would she? Would those who are pure accept her?

The White Heat

Dare you see a soul at the white heat?
    Then crouch within the door.
Red is the fire's common tint;
    But when the vivid ore

Has sated flame's conditions,
    Its quivering substance plays
Without a color but the light
    Of unanointed blaze.

Least village boasts its blacksmith,
    Whose anvil's even din
Stands symbol for the finer forge
    That soundless tugs within,

Refining these impatient ores
    With hammer and with blaze,
Until the designated light
    Repudiate the forge.

For free books, updates, sneak peeks, and special prizes,
it's easy to sign up to receive the latest news from Lexi at
http://bit.ly/LexiUpdate

CHAPTER ONE

That bastard. Toni Reid stood in shock, her ear glued to the peephole into the next room, trying to digest the fact that the leader of Naralina planned to abduct women from Earth. Lots of women.

Grandall's voice had her listening intently. "If only there was a way to open a portal that was large enough to transport groups of women, then we could fill the Pleasure Temples and every filoz would finally have their agapayto."

"Am I not enough for you?" Jasmine's purr was probably accompanied by pouty lips.

"Ah, my sweet. I worry about others. For myself, I need only your honeyed richness to satisfy me."

The jerk. He had his own wife sitting at home. Hearing nothing else from inside, she took a peek. Ugh, watching Grandall humping Jasmine was not for sissies.

Luckily, Jasmine probably thought Grandall *dreamed* of bringing hordes of women to Eden, but that was crap. Toni had been spying on him for months, and he never revealed his entire plan, but now all the pieces fell into place. She had to get word back to Loraleaf immediately!

Someone grabbed her arm from behind. She instinctively balled her other into a fist, but that one was caught too and twisted behind her back.

"Do not make a sound, understand?"

Sure, she understood. She understood she was going to relieve one Edenist of his balls the minute her arms were released. The man pulled her backwards, away from the peephole usually used for voyeurs and not for spies like herself. Yeah, she was toast if she didn't get out of this.

Every ounce of her being wanted to fight against the hold on her, but she gritted her teeth and pretended to be meek. She'd *never* been meek. Her friend Serena always told her she turned aggressive when she was afraid and she "needed to keep her head"—whatever that meant.

She took a deep breath as they stopped while the man behind her kicked a door open and inhaled a scent like clove. Clove? She wanted to see who it was so she could gauge her ability to talk herself out of this one…after she brought him to his knees. Not only didn't she like being restrained, but aggression toward women was strictly forbidden on the entire planet. She doubted this Edenist would want to go before the Ruling Circle with Grandall in charge.

The man turned her toward the bed then pushed her away, slamming the door behind him.

She spun, her foot already headed for his groin as she glanced at his face. The air left her lungs in appreciation, even as his arm came down to knock her leg away from her intended target. As she turned, barely keeping her balance, her libido sighed in relief, but her ego wasn't so happy.

She stopped her movement and stood facing him, her weight

on the balls of her feet. She tried to keep her anger up as she stared at the tall man with the long dark hair, light blue eyes, side-shaved head and the only tattoo she'd ever seen on Eden. This was her kind of male—just her luck.

He stood silent, studying her.

She didn't mind at all. She had on a green satiny halter and hip wrap while he was in all his naked glory like every other Edenist she'd ever met. She enjoyed the moment and took in his large defined chest, ripped abs, big cock and sinewy thighs. She liked the tell-tale feel of sexual tension growing in her stomach.

She'd always gravitated toward the bad boys on Earth. On Eden, there was no such thing unless a man was a lawbreaker, and they were far too dangerous.

This hotty definitely deserved a story from her. She'd much rather talk her way out of this and have sex with him, than make his junk unusable. "I'm Toni. I've never seen you here before. Who are you?"

"Akasha." His bass level voice pinged every female erogenous point in her body.

Fuck.

She waited for him to elaborate, anxious to hear him speak again, but he remained silent. She gave him a side glance. "So are you interested in taking your pleasure with me? I'd be happy to help you with that." She could tell by his age that he wasn't an Edenist who needed to be taught. There were a few women in every Pleasure Temple who were experts in that area. She preferred men who knew what they were doing.

He shook his head, his brows lowering. "Why were you spying on a Ruling Council member?"

So he'd figured that out, did he? She sauntered to the bed and sat, exposing her long toned legs. She worked hard to stay in shape since arriving in Naralina. While the men enjoyed physical activities, the women were put on such pedestals, they were lucky if they were allowed to walk from one house to another.

She met Akasha's gaze with confidence. "Why do you have a tattoo across your collar bone?"

His brows lowered further, impeding her view of his gorgeous blue eyes. "Answer my question."

The sternness in his tone excited her and pissed her off at the same time. Who the hell was he to question her? She was a woman. Edenists didn't speak like that to women unless they were protecting them.

"What do you think I was doing? I was watching. That's why those peep holes are there. Don't they have those at the Pleasure Temple you usually go to?"

"You weren't watching. You were listening." That extra deep voice stroked her in all the right places, keeping her anger at bay, which considering the circumstances was probably a good thing.

But the man was like a dog with a bone. She gave him a sultry smile. "Don't you know that hearing is as much a part of voyeurism as seeing?" She cocked her head. "What good is watching if I can't hear their heavy breathing, her soft whimpers, or his hard grunts? I like it all."

She ran her hand lightly from the juncture of her thighs to her knee and back, never taking her eyes off him, making it seem as if she did it absently, instinctively.

His gaze flickered as if he started to believe her. His brow rose a bit. "I heard the sound of words."

What? How could he hear anything without listening at a peephole? The stone walls in all of Naralina were practically sound proof. She scanned him for his Kindred birthmark, but it wasn't anywhere on the front of his body. She couldn't take the chance he didn't have some special hearing ability.

She nodded slowly, keeping her body language sensual. She wanted him to think she was turned on by what she heard and saw. She didn't need him to know *he* was reason her libido had just jumped into second gear. "You're right. Jasmine said 'yes, please, more, oh more' and the man with her said, 'I will take you as if I had eleven women, over and over again. Have no fear.' Or at least that is what I heard before you rudely pulled me away." She pouted for good measure.

Akasha crossed his bulging arms over his large chest, clearly doubting her story. "Do you deny that you knew who was in that room?"

She widened her eyes, feigning surprise. "I only know that he has a big ass and short black hair, but I think he dyes it. I could see gray when Jasmine grabbed his head to get him to suck her nipple."

He didn't bat an eyelash at her bluntness. "That was Grandall." He peered at her, watching her every move.

Who the hell was this guy? "That's Grandall? Wow, I've never seen him before, not that I would necessarily recognize him by his butt anyway. Isn't he *the* leader of the Ruling Circle?" She raised her eyebrows. She was well aware there was no leader, but Grandall, the ass, thought he was. She'd learned a lot in a few months.

Akasha dropped his arms. "Why do you lie?"

Great. He must be Kindred of Mind and be able to figure out she wasn't telling the truth like Nassic did. That meant she needed to distract him in a big way. Rising from the bed she made a show of smoothing the satiny green cloth over her hips.

The Edenists believed wearing clothing was rude, but she'd been able to convince a half-dozen that some clothing could make sex even better. It had taken her a while to figure out how to sew a few things through trial and error. The halter and hip wrap she wore now was the easiest as the top just crossed in front and tied behind her neck.

She gave him her best sultry smile. "Not lie. I just don't care. With someone like you standing here, all I want to do is have sex." She punctuated her statement by pulling the shiny material taut beneath her breast to show off her hardened nipple.

His gaze moved to her breast and his eyes darkened, but then he raised his head. "No."

"No?" Shocked, she dropped her hand. "What do you mean 'no'?" She'd never heard of an Edenist turning down sex. With the population being only male, except for the women brought from Earth, sex with a female was always considered the ultimate life experience. "Isn't that why you came to our Pleasure Temple?"

The hotty standing before her just shook his head. "It matters not why I came here. Your actions force me to take you with me."

"Hold on. Just slow down a minute, Akasha. Where exactly do you want to take me? As a single female, I must stay here or join a filoz. I know that much. You aren't allowed to take me anywhere but shopping." And she seriously hoped he didn't plan to take her before the Ruling Circle or she would be found guilty and sent outside the city walls. That wouldn't be good if she couldn't get word to Jahl and Khaos beforehand.

But if Akasha planned to take her before Grandall only, there was a very good chance she could disappear without a trace. It was whispered that one woman who had sex with him had vanished after she told his wife he'd been with her. He was a snake, hiding behind a façade of caring. He'd burned his own son's kindred birthmark until it was unrecognizable. Who knew what he'd do to a woman he thought had figured out his plan.

"I am taking you to my home." Akasha scowled. "Or I can take you directly before the Ruling Circle."

She shook her head. She couldn't go before the Circle until she could send a note out and Akasha's "directly" sounded ominous. However, going to his home and meeting the rest of his filoz had interesting possibilities, especially if they were all as hot as him. Maybe he was even one of five. Just the thought had her getting excited. "I'd much rather go with you. Could we stop by my rooms so I can pick up a few things?"

She sauntered toward him as if she'd open the door, but his hand came down on her arm. He held her tightly, but not so it hurt. "Unless you want to tell me the truth about your spying now."

He seemed to really *not* want to take her home. Now that was odd. She'd never met an unattached Edenist who wasn't attracted to her, except for one short man. She was tall for a woman, so she couldn't blame *him*.

Maybe Akasha had a wife. If her going to his home made a little trouble for him, she was fine with that. After all, he was the one who insisted on taking her.

"Well?" He expected her to spill the truth to him as if that was a better option, but he was wrong.

With Grandall being at the very top, she had no idea who was in league with him. "I'm happy to go home with you. I just hope this is all legal. I don't want to get in trouble. Can we go to my rooms now?" *So I can leave a note for the elseire bird and let Loraleaf know what's going on.*

The man went back to frowning as if she'd disappointed him greatly. Why did she suddenly feel like she used to when confessing to Father Anselm back in high school? No matter how many made-up sins she'd told that man, he always expected more. Probably because the real ones she kept to herself.

Finally, Akasha nodded and opened the door for her, but his hand didn't leave her arm.

She stepped through and led him upstairs to her condo, at least that's how she thought of it. It was more like a luxury suite, but since she'd never been in a luxury anything on Earth, she preferred to think of it as a condo.

Once inside, he allowed her to move about freely, but remained in front of the door. She quickly went to her bedroom and packed some of her more tantalizing creations, as well as her favorite lube, what they called shilla on Eden, and her scent. She'd had it made up especially for her.

She'd discovered some Edenists had an exceptional sense of smell and could enhance a person's natural scent. This was usually done at an early age, but she'd come late to the party. She really liked the cinnamon scent they concocted, so she assumed they got it right. Her newest acquaintance, on the other hand, smelled like clove.

She grinned. All they needed was apple and they'd be a pie.

"It's time to go." Akasha's words from the other room put a damper on her mood. She loved a new adventure as much as anyone, and on Eden, within city walls, she wasn't afraid of anyone but Grandall. There were far too many laws to protect her. Unfortunately, Grandall didn't give a rat's ass about the laws. He thought he was above the laws.

"I'm almost ready." She grabbed a small square card and wrote a short note in code. PROJECT IS TO BRING WOMEN HERE BY THE TRUCKOAD AND SELL. GOT CAUGHT. TAKEN BY AKASHA. The shortness of the note was typical in their communications, but the message should light a fire under Loraleaf's leaders. Luckily for her, every man in Naralina had a different name, so she actually might get a little help escaping—*if* she needed it.

Footsteps across her living area had her folding the note quickly and slipping out onto her seventh story balcony. Dropping it in the planter of a small tree, she continued to the railing where she could actually see three of the cobbled streets below, the other four were obscured by buildings. The white and gold city of Naralina reminded her of a city in one of those hobbit movies, the way it was tiered and built into the side of a mountain and made of stone. Not a city by modern Earth standards, but an amazing feat. It did also make for beautiful views of the jungle at her level and those higher.

If Akasha had a similar set-up, she should have no problem getting away on her own. But if he didn't have a balcony, she'd need help. Unfortunately, she wasn't sure when Konala's bird would come by next to pick up a note.

Akasha's footsteps came through the doorway and out onto the balcony. "Why do you delay?"

She turned to face him. "I just wanted to enjoy my view one more time. Do you have one, too?"

She couldn't be sure, but he appeared to soften a little. Seriously? Because she was nostalgic for a view?

He nodded. "I have a view. Come." He held out his arm to let her leave first.

She looked over her shoulder once, then back at him and sighed. She didn't mind making him feel bad in the least. She let her shoulders slump and shuffled by him to pick up her bag of items.

Once she was inside, he strode past and waited for her at the door. "If you tell me the truth about what you heard, you can stay here." His gaze held sympathy and for the first time she sensed interest in her on his part, but he seemed unhappy.

Hell, it made her want to tell him more than any threat did, but not knowing what job he had in Naralina, she couldn't risk it. "I already told you."

The man sighed, one of those disappointing ones a parent might give—if a girl were to have a *real* parent. Then he opened the door and taking her wrist, ushered her into the corridor.

She closed the door behind her, the click sounding so final that it made her catch her breath. Now who was being stupid? It wasn't as if she'd expected to live there forever, and she could always come back after Grandall was caught. She quickly swallowed the lump in her throat and joined Akasha.

He took hold of her wrist and led her downstairs.

Akasha tried to ignore the spicy scent that filled his nostrils as he escorted the woman through the Pleasure Palace. He would let one of the Temple Protectors know that Toni had been taken for other purposes, leaving the message as vague as possible.

Though he had the right to take her, he skirted too many rules to be completely comfortable.

Why couldn't she just tell him the truth? His gut said it was because whatever the truth was, she wasn't supposed to know it. If it had to do with Grandall, then it might put her in danger.

She completely baffled him. He'd never met a woman like her. On one hand beautiful, but also obviously strong, based on her physical condition. He didn't like the way his body reacted to that fact. Sex was simply required by nature, but to be attracted to someone who was not morally correct, was not good for someone in his position.

Toni's uniqueness was far more than her physicality, though her height and brilliant green eyes were not as well known to him. She also seemed to welcome confrontation, goading him by telling her lies. Even her name was different from other women's.

He was an *ithio* for taking her home, but his need to discover what she was involved in, outweighed his discomfort in having her around. His body wanted her, probably because it had been nearly a cycle of Selene since he'd last had a woman. He would simply take another to avoid her.

As they walked out into the bright light of Helios, Toni's stride lengthened. The men she passed openly admired her.

How could he have forgotten? "Do you wish me to suppress your pheromones?"

She glanced back. "Shit, no. I haven't had this much male attention in months." She continued on, her walk continuing at a quick pace.

His curiosity required satisfaction. "Are you in such a hurry as to rush to my home?"

She looked at him almost as if she'd forgotten he was with her, though he still held her wrist. "No, but it's good exercise to walk fast, especially uphill like this. Gets the blood pumping and the heart racing. I can slow down if you want."

Scanning ahead, he could see the stone road that wound up the mountain city was sparsely populated. "No, you may continue as you are."

"Good." She grinned and increased their speed a bit more.

He held back a smile. He could sense her need to compete, but he refused to go any slower or faster than she did. He did tug her in the right direction as they continued upward. Naralina's buildings took advantage of every bit of space on the mountain's sides, making for many cobbled dead ends.

His abode was near the top, one reason why he'd hadn't been to her Pleasure Temple in almost six cycles of Selene. He was careful to slake his need in a different one each time, so as not to form attachments. As the next Edenist to take a seat on the Triad Panel, he had to avoid relationships at all cost.

"Either you are someone really important, or your family has been here since the Crius stole humans from Earth." Toni's words were clear despite her exertion.

"Everyone is important in Naralina." He guided her toward the base of a set of steps, five levels high.

She slowed to a stop and looked up. "You're important. Got it." She dropped her bag and pulled her hair tie out, quickly retying it before she grasped her bag again. Then she faced him. "Are you Ruling Circle, too?"

He shook his head. "I did not say I was important."

"Which is how I know you are." She waved off his comment.

"You ignored your own value, which is a refreshing trait. I already know I'm important because I'm a woman, and let's face it, we are a rare commodity on this planet. I just don't know of any other important positions besides the Ruling Circle and the High Poetess, and you are definitely not her." She smirked, her gaze raking over his body with interest.

How could she not know about the Triad? Every woman who entered Naralina was given lessons on the oligarchical government structure, the history of the planet and the city, the Crius and Dickinson Laws, and the natural habitat and customs. She should know about the Triad. "It appears that some of your training is lacking."

"Trust me. I've had all the most important training." She winked at him, giving him a sly smile.

Holy Bendis! The woman had his stomach tensing with just a look. This was not good. The sooner he could discover the truth, the faster he could get her back to the Temple, or before the Ruling Circle, whichever was appropriate. "Come. My home is at the top."

Her grin surprised him. "Great. Race you to the top." She pulled away before he could react and ran up the stairs.

Fool woman. She was under his command. He took the steps two at a time and caught up to her quickly.

She laughed as he matched her step for step. When she slowed near the top, he also slowed.

A strange exhilaration filled his veins. He hadn't done anything together with another person to accomplish a goal, since his days as a young boy, before he decided to become a Triad member and forgo friendships altogether. Even when at a Pleasure

Temple, he didn't reach his climax at the same time as his bedmate. It was a given that the woman must find her pleasure first. The unusual euphoric sensation he felt now had to be the novelty of the situation.

When they came to the top at the open square before the Triad building, Toni bent over, dropping her bag on the white and savinstone tiles, and took deep breaths. He waited patiently as she regained her normal breathing, still fascinated by the strange happiness he felt that was beyond simple contentment.

Finally, she lifted her head and looked up at him. "That was great. I'd love to do that twice a day. Talk about a workout."

Though familiar with much of Earth's customs, he did not understand what she meant beyond her pleasure in it and an interest in doing it twice a day. Perhaps that could be an enticement to get her to tell him the truth. "We may be able to make that possible."

She finally stood straight, her hands on her hips, her breathing still heavier than normal, showing the muscles of her bare midriff contracting and loosening. He stared in fascination.

"Wow, some place you've got here."

He moved his gaze to her face to find her leaning back to look at the Triad building. It was two levels high with white round domes and savinstone spires, or gold spires as Earth women called them. "This is not just my home but home to the Triad members and members-to-be."

Her green gaze met his. "Triad? What's that?"

Why hadn't she been schooled on the Triad? "The Triad is a panel of three who evaluate each Edenist based on his morality, or level of goodness if you will. If he is found to be worthy, he is given a Crius chip which is implanted beneath his arm so he can open a travel portal."

"Oh, I know about the portals. Love those things by the way. I didn't know Edenists had to earn them though."

He shook his head. "They are not earned. They are awarded. They are a technology far beyond what our civilization has achieved yet, so we only allow those of good moral standing to receive them."

Toni pulled her head back in a strange imitation of a henny bird. "How exactly do you determine that? Are you some kind of mind reader? Oh wait, are you Kindred of Mind?"

"I am not." He latched onto her wrist again, not willing to risk her running off now that she had her breathing back under control. "Come. We can discuss this more inside."

"Sure." She retrieved her bag, hooking it over her shoulder. "Lead the way."

That had been his plan, but when she said it, it felt like she commanded him and not the other way around. It must be because she didn't yet understand the Triad. Everyone deferred to the Triad and its future members. Shrugging off her lack of deference, he led her through the two-level archway at the center of the building.

Once inside the arch, they continued down the long, wide hall, another open arch at the end.

She slowed halfway through the corridor, twisting to look at the opposite wall. "How come there are only three doors on that side and a gazillion on this side."

He barely kept his smile in check at her observation. "There are not a gazillion on this side. There are eleven."

"Okay, so eleven. Why eleven here and three there?"

He stopped, pointing to the door opposite them. "That side is where the current Triad live. This side is where the Triad members-to-be live."

She took a step closer to the members-to-be side, or was it she stepped back from the Triad? "Which side do you live on, Akasha?"

For the first time since meeting her, he sensed unease. "I am a member-to-be."

Toni simply nodded, but didn't say anything.

He took that as a sign that she understood and led her down to the final door. Opening it, he stepped back and let her enter. As he expected, she immediately scanned the room then strode toward the archway to his sleeping area.

He closed and locked the door behind him. If she looked for a way out, she wouldn't find one. His outdoor patrio was on top of a cliff.

She came back into his living area. "Can we swim in that pool at the end of the corridor?"

He raised his eyebrows. "Swim? No. That is the meditation pool."

"Meditation?" She looked around the room. "And this is your entire home?"

He nodded.

"But you have nothing on the walls, no mementos. You don't even have a meal room, as you call it. Seriously, are you a monk?"

He had to think back to his school days to remember what she spoke of and when he did, he smiled because this was a subject he enjoyed immensely. "No, I am not a monk."

As she visibly relaxed, he moved into the room, close to a cabinet where he kept libations and some light food. "We have no type of 'religion' here in Naralina. Our Triad is a judgment panel, if you will, but it is not based on a god so much as on the natural order. We realized early in our civilizational development that the Greek gods were simply a reflection of man's emotions and we focused our standards on ethics, ideals and reality instead after the great philosophers Socrates, Aristotle and Plato."

He quirked his lips. "We retain many of Plato's teachings regarding the ideals. The Triad members simply seek to obtain the ideal state, or rather as close as we can get."

"Oh, hell. You *are* a monk." Toni dropped onto his longseat as if she'd been inflated with air and had suddenly had it all sucked from her.

He shook his head. He'd have to teach her the basics of Eden life before he could discover why she lied. He also needed to discover how she came to be in a Pleasure Temple without having learned about Eden.

Nothing about the woman conformed to the way things were, and she wasn't going anywhere until he had the whole truth from her.

~~*~~

Yelling outside had Sandale standing up, just before the door to his room burst open.

"We need you." Khaos, the former brother of his heart was anxious, so anxious Sandale could feel it.

"You know I don't have full control of my ability yet."

Khaos shook his head. "That doesn't matter. Cordtz is so

angry he's going to hurt someone. Even if you send him into an unconscious state, he will be better off."

His own tension eased. *That* he could do. He nodded and followed Khaos outside to their front landing. "What is wrong?"

"We don't know. He and the brother of his heart left Loraleaf to hunt a feroon. We aren't sure if he saw something the lawbreakers left behind, a Boarox or something else. We fear for his mind."

Sandale's need to help multiplied tenfold. Though he remembered nothing of his life before his mind was erased of all memories, he'd been told of his own anguish. He'd even read his own words as taken down by Khaos. His mental pain had been so great, he'd asked for the ultimate procedure.

Now, living with the consequences of his request, he hated his decision. He'd lost everything. Except for instinctive behaviors like eating, speaking and moving his limbs, his life as he'd known it was a blank. He'd do everything he could to save another man from his limbo.

Instead of taking the lift down, Khaos grabbed an infragile vine and swung from their third level tree house to the jump-off ledge across the way on the second level.

Sandale grasped another vine and followed. Once on the second level, Khaos did the same to reach the first level.

The yelling escalated. *Fury.* Sandale sensed it now that he drew closer. Grasping a vine, he landed on the first level and immediately grabbed another to swing across the open expanse between the walkways to land beside Jahl, the other former brother of his heart.

Jahl and Theron held Cordtz, whose rage seemed to escalate at Sandale's arrival.

He ignored it, far too used to the hesitant and pitying looks of the inhabitants of Loraleaf to be bothered by Cordtz's hatred. Instead, he immediately put his hands on the man's chest and calmed him.

Cordtz crumpled to the walkway.

Jahl nodded to two Edenists who stood nearby. "Take him home. When he regains consciousness, send for Rekah. If he isn't sane…"

Scrat, Jahl would have the man's mind wiped. Sandale interjected. "Then send for me. I will bring him down slowly so he can speak. He was too agitated now to do so."

The men nodded as they lifted Cordtz by the arms and loaded him into the lift.

Jahl grasped him by the shoulder, drawing his attention. "Thank you." While Jahl's gratefulness was sincere, there was still sympathy in his gaze.

Sandale kept his irritation hidden. "It is what I am supposed to do."

"Yes, but I know you struggle with your own issues." Jahl removed his hand. "Even if you did not, it is important that we appreciate the abilities each of us possess."

Jahl's understanding added to Sandale's irritation. "I will be at Libations if I'm needed further." Turning on his heel, he strode down the walkway attached to the trees, his patience gone.

He had no right to be upset with Jahl, or anyone else for that matter. His problem was of his own making.

Actually, that wasn't entirely true. The fact was, one of the lawbreakers had implanted the thoughts of an evil mind into his own. He had not asked for that.

He turned the corner on the walkway only to find himself face-to-face with the image of himself as he was before. The savinstone statue they had made to give him a burning ceremony when they thought him dead stared at him accusingly. It was as if it shouted "You are not me!"

It *was* him, or at least it looked like him only with shorter hair, the golden color of the stone just a shade brighter than his real hair. It had the same full lips, straight nose, and high forehead. Only his violet eyes were nothing more than unseeing holes in the stone. Lifeless.

No! He wasn't lifeless. He had life. He just needed to find it again.

Turning away from the statue, he stepped into the lift and had to unclench his hand before throwing the lever. As he rose, he concentrated on calming himself, taking deeper breaths and clearing his mind, but it was no easy feat.

Stepping off on the third level, he forced himself to a stroll. When he reached Libations, he was only slightly calmer. He stepped to the counter.

"Apple Fire, Sandale?"

Of course. He was known for enjoying Apple Fire, but that drink revved him up. He must have been much calmer before the wipe. Right now, he needed one to slow him down. He shook his head. "No. I'm in the mood for a Bendis Blender."

He ignored the surprised look from the liquidator and raised his eyebrow in expectation. The man gave a quick nod and made him the concoction. Taking the blue drink with him, he found a table in a quiet corner. The scene on the wall at the moment was a blue ocean with no land in sight.

He took a sip of the melony drink and savored it. More and more he found himself in Libations, seeking outside help for his inner turmoil. If he continued, he'd soon be dependent on the drinks. He didn't want that. Still, he took another sip.

"May I join you?"

Having ignored his surroundings, he looked up in surprise to find Khaos there with a hopeful smile on his face.

How could he say no to a man who had been a brother of his heart? He opened his palm toward a seat across from him.

Of the two Edenists he had been bonded with, he preferred Khaos, but it wasn't because of a strong affection. It was simply that he wasn't as abrasive as Jahl. He took another sip of his drink, not in a hurry to start a conversation.

"I could tell Jahl angered you. He doesn't mean to. He just doesn't know how to act with you now." Khaos stared at him with his enigmatic grey eyes.

"I know, but I get tired of the condescension from him and the pity from others."

Khaos smiled. "Trust me, it's better than fear. Everyone here used to fear me."

That caught his attention. Khaos was one of the most relaxed men he knew. "Why?"

The man gave a self-deprecating chuckle. "They thought I didn't have a Kindred birthmark and I let them believe that, thinking it was for the best. But then Toni, that's the woman we saved when we brought Serena here, told a group about my odd shaped birthmark and the fear went away." Khaos shook his head. "Turned out they were fine with my birthmark being an aberration, but deathly afraid of my not having one at all."

"Pity or fear, it is the same. At least with you, their reactions changed. I'm not sure that will ever happen for me." He took another swallow, wishing the drink would do its job and take his tension away.

Khaos took a swallow of his own, a blue one as well. Then he opened his mouth, only to close it.

Sandale's patience hit an end point. "Just say what you want, I won't break."

"You are right. You were always strong. No one else could have held on to his own mind despite the other thoughts sharing it." The man paused then met his gaze. "You will not be at Loraleaf much longer."

Excitement skittered through him. He'd been thinking of requesting acceptance at Haven, the other jungle settlement outside the city of Naralina. If Khaos foresaw his leaving that had to mean he would be accepted…and there, no one knew his past self. "I am pleased to hear this."

Khaos lowered his brow. "You want to leave?"

He rubbed the droplets of condensation from his glass with his thumb, searching the blue liquid for the right words. "I do. Here, there are expectations of how I should act, what I should want to do." He held up the glass. "What I should drink. All based on who I was. If I am somewhere else, I won't disappoint so many, nor will I receive the looks of pity. I can take time to discover who I was without hurting anyone. Like you, once Toni told the others of your birthmark, everything will change for me."

"I see. Yes, that is true." Khaos nodded. "I had not considered that. I guess like everyone else, I wanted you to resume your old life."

He shook his head. "I cannot. You and Jahl have bonded with Serena. I am without a filoz now. I have no brothers of my heart and every man here is already in a filoz. I am alone." As he said the words, he finally understood the underlying sadness he felt.

Khaos grasped his forearm. "You are never alone. We will always be here for you."

He nodded, but Khaos could not understand. He barely understood it himself. "When do I leave?"

"I don't know exactly, but soon." Khaos removed his hand and took another sip. "I do not see you coming back, but that does not mean you won't. Only that my visions only reach so far ahead, depending on their mood. So you can see, I too am still learning my ability." He raised his glass. "We must celebrate your next step."

Sandale held back his retort about learning abilities and raised his glass as well.

"May you find happiness and peace."

They tapped the glasses to their foreheads and drank. When Sandale lowered his glass, he smiled. He didn't know when, but he now knew there was hope, and that's all he needed…for now.

CHAPTER TWO

Toni threw off the clear blanket the Edenists called a hesta and sat up, her long legs swinging around so her feet touched the stone floor. Luckily, only one moon was out and it was not very full, so she had enough light to see, but hopefully not be seen.

She rose and quickly donned her halter and wrap. Picking up her homemade bag, she tiptoed out of Akasha's sleeping area and into the living room. He lay on his stomach, one arm having fallen past the couch, his hand resting on the floor. His long dark hair covered his face as he slept.

She had such high hopes for him. Her own bad boy, but he was the farthest thing from it! Though he insisted he wasn't a monk, that was the closest he came to on Earth. Dedicated to morality. Staying away from developing any relationships. Living simply. None of which interested her. Her sexual drive toward him had died a slow death.

Focusing on her goal, she continued to stealthily make her way to the door. She grinned. Akasha's apartment wasn't the first place she'd sneaked out of before dawn. When she reached the door, she lifted the wooden latch and pulled but nothing happened.

Hell, she'd forgotten he locked it somehow. Very few homes had locks on their doors in Naralina. What good were they when two Edenists with chips could easily teleport anywhere? Which begged the question, why did Akasha have a lock?

Kneeling on the floor, she examined the contraption. There was no metal on Eden, so the mechanism was made with infragile vine, stone and wood. There was also something shiny deep in the door, but she had no clue what it was. Infragile vine was impossible to break once cut from the live plant, so there was no way to cut that. Besides, she had no idea how it all worked. When she first came inside, she hadn't expected to want to leave so soon, so she hadn't paid much attention.

She stood and glanced at Akasha before looking at the patrio outside the floor-to-ceiling windows. She'd gone out there after her lonely dinner, Akasha having left to have it with the other Triad members upstairs. He said it was expected, and no women were allowed. That had been the final evidence she needed to be convinced he was an Edenist monk.

While Akasha's patrio had a magnificent view that was far more spectacular than her own balcony's, it hung over a cliff, making that route an impossible escape plan. She turned back to the door, wishing she'd paid more attention to it earlier.

Stepping closer, she studied the hinges in the dim light. They seemed similar to the way her own door worked back at the Temple. If she could push the wood peg from the loops of infragile vine, she could move the door...hopefully. It all depended on that lock. The problem was, she couldn't be sure without more light.

As if she was magic, light flooded the room. She spun to look for the source, but it shone directly at her, and she had to cover her eyes with her hand.

"Did you need light?" Akasha's deep tone held a hint of humor.

Well, hell. "Yes, I did, but could you tone it down?"

The light dimmed until it disappeared altogether. The room appeared pitch black until her pupils readjusted.

Akasha sat on the couch, one arm on the back, the other resting on one of his hunky thighs.

She couldn't help but think it was such a waste he wasn't in a filoz. "Now I can't see anything."

He turned the hand on his thigh over, and a small ball of golden light formed. At first it was no bigger than a golf ball but it slowly grew until it was the size of a cantaloupe. It brightened the room, but was far less bright than a moment ago.

"You're Kindred of Light." She dropped her bag and stepped closer, the round ball of light more than just utilitarian. Within it she could see golden sparkles that moved constantly.

"Toni, if you want to leave, all you need to do is tell me the truth." Akasha's deep voice enveloped her as she stood mesmerized by the ball of light.

She blinked and looked away. "I just wanted some air."

His chuckle sent her gaze to his face, but if he had smiled, it was too brief. "With your bag?"

She looked back at her tell-tale bag then at him and shrugged. "That was to put at the bottom of the stairs, so after running up once, it would force me to go down again."

His laugh caught her by surprise. Were monks allowed to laugh? Weren't they supposed to be solemn all the time? He had a great smile and his teeth were perfect, like the Hollywood stars she did stunts for back on Earth. *Used to do stunts for.* She wasn't ever going back to Earth. She had it made here.

"Toni, do you never tell the truth?" Akasha set the ball of light on a wooden statue of a tree she'd admired earlier before he rose.

She cocked her head. "Will you always doubt everything I say?"

He stepped closer until he was less than a foot away. "It appears we have a lot to learn from each other."

There was that clove-like smell again. It had to be his natural scent enhanced. It made her think of the mulled wine she'd had on a shoot in Colorado—while it was cold outside, it was warm, relaxing, and sensuous inside. Once again, her stomach tightened with sexual need. The man was just too hot to be a monk.

She placed her finger tips on the scrolling tattoo that ran across his collar bone and traced it lightly to its end. "We can start here. What does this say?"

His hand caught her own and held hers in place. "That is something you are definitely not ready to learn yet."

She frowned. "Now why in the world would I need to be ready for a tattoo? It's just ink embedded into skin."

He shook his head. "Maybe on Earth. This tattoo is part of my essence."

She moved her gaze away from his light blue eyes and stared at the tat. She'd only heard the word "essence" used in whispers and that very rarely. Her best definition for it was the word "soul," though that wasn't exactly it. "Do other Edenists know what it means?"

He pulled her hand to his lips and spoke against her fingertips. "Only a few."

She stared at her hand as a shiver raced over her skin. Hell, if she didn't know better, she'd say he was seducing her.

"Come." He brought her hand down and pulled her toward the couch. "Since you are awake, we can start now."

Start what? If he thought she'd have sex with him, he was greatly mistaken. She never knowingly slept with married men and though she'd never had a rule about monks, she'd definitely place them in the same category.

"Sit." He looked expectantly at her as if to refuse would be rude.

She pulled her hand from his and took out her hair tie. Leisurely, she redid her ponytail. She didn't like feeling that if she resisted such a simple command she was being silly, but she also didn't like being told what to do either. When her hair was back in place, she gestured to the couch. "After you."

His brow furrowed in confusion, but he shrugged and took a seat.

She moved to the other end of the couch and sat. "Now what?"

"Do you know there are two sets of laws on Eden?"

Huh? What did that have to do with sex…unless he was planning to accuse her of spying. The tension she felt moments ago shifted. "Of course. There's Cruison Law and Dickinson Law. I'm much more familiar with Dickinson Law since it was created by the Earth poet Emily Dickinson." He didn't need to know she'd never read a poem in her life, never mind a great American poet who was worshipped on his planet. Poetry wasn't her thing.

He nodded. "Good. We can delve into the depth of your knowledge on that subject later. And what about the colonization of Eden? Do you know about that?"

Why did he make her feel like she was back in high school, only at a private school run by monks? "Sure. I know the Crius stole a number of people from Earth's early civilizations and planted them here on your planet. Then they left, leaving a few of their advancements behind, but not many. They even left the High Hall here in Naralina, which was integral in the Fullamush." She smiled slyly. "It's amazing what women can do when they want to, isn't it?"

Akasha swallowed hard, his Adam's apple catching her attention. Now why would the Fullamush cause him to do that? Maybe he didn't like women in general. That would explain a lot of his behavior besides his monkish lifestyle. But she had yet to run in to a gay man in Naralina. Maybe they had their own city. On a planet of only men, there *had* to be some gay filoz around. Didn't there?

"But you have never heard of the Triad." His deep voice had softened as if he couldn't imagine anyone not knowing about his group.

She shook her head and shrugged. "It could be I did, but I wasn't paying attention. I get distracted easily." *Especially by hunky Edenists*. She smiled to hide her thought.

He rose, placing one arm behind his back and walked to the door before turning around to face her. "Do you know what we do with lawbreakers?"

She jerked her gaze from his hard abdominals to his face. Uh-oh, this line of questioning couldn't be good. "Of course, they are exiled beyond these walls." *The best defense was a good offense*. She'd heard one of her many foster fathers say that during basketball season. As a strategy, it might work.

"Who decides who gets exiled? Is that the Triad's job? That would make sense based on what you've told me." But if the Triad determined who was guilty and who was innocent, Nassic and Wareson, former Ruling Circle members and now of the Haven settlement, would never have been exiled. Akasha didn't need to know she knew all that.

He sighed as if he was exasperated. "You know that's not the Triad's task. We only determine who receives the chips as that can be a long process."

"How do you know if I know that or not? It's not like you are of the Mind Kindred." And for that small favor she was very thankful. As it was, the man had called her on every lie, and no one had ever done that before.

Akasha studied her until the silence grew long.

Well, hell. Now what was she supposed to do? Maybe some actual sleep would help her regroup. She was done being interrogated.

Rising from the couch, she stalked toward Akasha. When she reached him and that entrancing smell of clove, she bent and retrieved her bag. "Since I can't get some exercise tonight, I might as well go back to sleep. But I expect to be able to do those stairs tomorrow. I'm used to a lot of physical activity." With a scowl at him, she turned and sauntered back to his bed.

Unfortunately, she had a feeling she was in for some hot sex dreams that included one hunky, dark-haired monk with light blue eyes.

Akasha didn't take his gaze from Toni until she disappeared around the corner, and even then he had to keep himself from following her. He wasn't sure what he was more attracted to, her healthy body or her constant hiding of the truth. That in itself made no sense.

He strode to his cabinet and poured himself a glass of ambrosia. Taking a sip of the citrusy-coconut drink with a spicy after taste, he leaned against the wall. Why did he find Toni's lies so intriguing? He should be frustrated, even angry over her immoral conduct, but he wasn't. Her lies flowed so easily from her lips and when caught, she just created another, never admitting anything.

He grinned. That was part of it. The refusal to admit she lied. He'd never encountered someone who so steadfastly continued their story despite all the evidence to the contrary. It was like a game of wits to him and probably her too. She created and adapted and explained on a second's notice. Her mind fascinated him.

He pushed away from the wall and strolled to the door of his patrio. Opening it, he walked out into the silver light of Selene. The night temperatures were comfortable, as usual. The quiet, this high in the city, was rarely disturbed. One reason why the Triad compound was placed so high on the mountain Naralina was built upon.

The only higher structure was the Ruling Circle complex. Toni's words flitted through his brain. *Who decides who gets exiled? Is that the Triad's job? That would make sense based on what you've told me.* It did make sense, and to hear his own thoughts on the matter spoken aloud for the first time made him uncomfortable. It was that very thought that had urged him to take Toni. She spied on Grandall, a Ruling Circle member, so how could the Ruling Circle be unbiased in their judgment of her? The Triad remained unbiased because their members and members-to-be remained separate, apart from the rest of their society, which made them the most objective.

He took another sip of ambrosia as he meandered toward the end of his balcony. Gazing beyond the city walls, he appreciated the wildness and beauty of the jungle, his mind more at ease now that he understood his interest in Toni. She was an intellectual curiosity.

He chuckled silently. He was a fool if he believed that was it. Her eyes, as bright as the jungle after a rain when Helios came out, were captivating. Her long dark hair, always pulled back and away from her high cheek bones, made him long to run his hands through it. What he found most odd was that her clothing, which he usually found offensive, made him all the more curious about the areas it hid.

Above her outlined abdominals, she covered full breasts and below her birth-scar, her wrap hid the entrance to her pleasure. That she enjoyed sex with Edenists was obvious by the fact she was a Cythera, one who lived at a Pleasure Temple where men like himself went to enjoy the ultimate pleasure of life. These women were revered on an even level with the Triad. Only wives were higher, equal to the Ruling Council.

He took another sip of ambrosia as he contemplated that fact. It was the only element of Toni he knew to be true. How could he get to what lay beneath the lies, especially why she spied on Grandall? More importantly, why would she need to spy on one of the Ruling Circle? She called Grandall the leader of the Circle and though that was not true by law, it did seem to be so in practice.

That gave him pause. Were Toni's lies actually true observations if dissected?

A shout from inside his rooms had him dropping his drink and sprinting inside.

"I'll rip you a new asshole you touch me again!" Toni's voice came from his bed.

He scanned the room, but no one was there. Quickly, he bathed it in blue light to reveal anything his eyes couldn't see. Some Light Kindred could blend in with their surroundings, but his light revealed no one in the room.

"Get the fuck off me!"

Akasha created another yellow light ball and threw it onto the corner table as he sat on the bed. Toni's eyes were closed, but her hands were everywhere - a night-terror. He'd read about them in his studies.

He had no colored light to calm her down. He didn't even know if he should.

"If you touch me again I will kill you." The last was said with such conviction that he flinched.

The hatred behind the words was far beyond anything he'd ever seen except once in a lawbreaker. His gut told him to restrain her would make matters worse. Carefully, he exuded his red light, keeping it soft and almost weightless. He let it cover her in gentle strokes, far gentler than he could do physically.

At first she swatted at it, so he kept it to her hair, arms and face. Though still restless, she did calm somewhat.

Then she sneezed. Her eyes opened and her brows drew together, reminding him of her look just before her foot started flying toward his cock when he'd first caught her.

"It's me, Akasha. You were having a night-terror."

At his words, her face relaxed and she batted at her nose.

He withdrew his red light.

"What was that?" She grabbed his hand where the light had re-entered his body and she stared at his palm.

"That was my red light. It has a light physical feel my others don't."

She rubbed her nose again. "I think I'm allergic to it."

He gave her a kind smile, like he would to a child. "There are no allergies on Eden."

Toni rolled her eyes. "I know that. There are no diseases whatsoever, not even sexual ones, which I definitely appreciate. I said I was allergic as a joke. Your light tickled my nose." She turned his hand over to look at the back as if she expected to see his light there. "So how many different colored lights do you have?"

He ignored the pleasurable feeling of her hand holding his with effort. "Seven."

Her gaze snapped to meet his. "Seven? Like the colors of a rainbow?"

"The colors of Eden rainbows."

She cocked her head. "I don't think I've seen an Eden rainbow since I arrived here."

That didn't surprise him. "You sleep late, don't you?"

She nodded.

"It usually rains in the early morning, which is one reason why the jungle outside the walls is so lush and the gardens within the walls so healthy. It is also why there are few foods we must trade for with other cities. We can grow almost anything we need."

She squinted her eyes at him. "Except sugar."

At her comment, his curiosity about her grew. That was not in the basic education of women entering Eden. "Do you like sweets?"

Shrugging, she looked back at his hand. "Not really. I prefer healthier foods and the ones here in Naralina are exceptional. So what about your colored lights?"

That she shied away from the sugar topic wasn't lost on him, but he let it go for the moment. "An Eden rainbow is split because our water is different than Earth's. The colors in order are red, orange, yellow, white, purple, blue, green."

"And you can produce all of those?" Her eyes were wide in astonishment.

It reminded him of his family's reaction after his transition. They looked at him in wonder ever since, as if he was high above them. It had hurt at first, but he soon learned that it was for the best that a distance develop between them and himself since he planned to be a Triad member.

Still, at Toni's look, he steeled himself for what would follow. Reverence, distance, and a severing of their limited connection.

"That's seriously cool." She smiled, then lifted his hand as if in a toast. "Show me."

He blinked. That was not what he expected. "Show you?"

She dropped his hand and waved off his comment. "I've already seen the yellow balls of light and now the red light. Show me the other colors. Do they all have a different function? The only Kindred of Light men I've met don't produce colors like that. They do other things with their light ability."

Of course, as a Cythera she would have had a great opportunity to learn about the different Kindreds. Is that how she learned about sugar? "And did you ask them to show you what they could do?"

"Of course, though some used theirs before I even asked. You have to understand, on Earth, men don't have these extra abilities, so I like learning about them."

For the first time since he'd met her, he felt he was hearing the truth. Could it be she had started to relax around him? That thought had him more willing to share, but he wanted something in return.

"I will show you my blue light. It reveals what the naked eye can't see."

"You mean like the blue fluorescent light crime investigators use to check for evidence like blood or semen?" Her voice had risen in her excitement.

A strange wish to please her had him swallowing hard. That was not his purpose. He must remain detached. "It is somewhat similar, but we will see what we need to see without any special goggles."

"Go for it."

He raised his brow at her expression then held his hand palm up and emitted the blue light.

"Wow." She rose from the bed and studied the room, peering into corners and examining the chair, table by the bed, and the bed itself. "I don't see anything."

"Look under the table."

She bent over to investigate. "Ugh. What the hell is that?" She snapped to a standing position and pointed.

"That is an amobe. His kind are why my rooms are so clean."

"Does it bite?" She bent over again to stare at the flat blob that moved across the wall.

He chuckled. "Only if you are dirt of some kind."

"Do they ever crawl on humans?" She rose to look at him, clearly uncomfortable with his creature.

"No. They are quite harmless and very helpful. In fact, you probably have one in your rooms at the Pleasure Temple. Most homes and buildings have them. The bigger the space that needs to be cleaned, the larger the amobe." She opened her mouth, but he raised his other hand to forestall her comment. "No one can see them because you need blue light to find them, but everyone knows they are doing their job because their homes are clean."

She closed her mouth and seemed to ponder his words. "Do they like eating the dirt?"

He pulled the blue light back and closed his palm. "Yes, it is what they eat to survive."

She looked toward the table. "Then I guess amobes are good things."

He rose from the bed. "I used the blue light when I first heard you yelling to see if a Light Kindred had somehow entered my rooms."

"Yelling?" She sat on the bed, not looking at him.

"Yes, you yelled in your night-terror. Tell me why you threatened to kill someone."

She didn't look at him, but he saw her shoulders tense at the word kill. "I have no idea. I don't even remember what I dreamed about."

Liar. Killing was serious. He wanted the truth. "I believe someone was touching you and you didn't like it."

Her gaze snapped to his and in that split second her eyes reflected the terror he'd heard in her voice before she lowered her lashes. "I was probably just remembering one of the movies I worked on."

She pulled her hair tie from her hair and retied it within

seconds then lay back down on the bed. "I should probably go back to sleep. It's going to be morning soon and I haven't had much rest." She looked accusingly at him. "It must be the strange environment."

His irritation at her withholding the truth firmed in to anger, and he forced it down. Anger had no place in judgments. "We will talk tomorrow."

"Of course we will. You're going to show and tell about your colored light." She rolled onto her side, away from him.

He remained where he was, the feeling of frustration new and uncomfortable. He needed to meditate, calm his emotions and determine a course of action. Turning on his heel, he headed back outside into the silver light of Selene. Standing with his feet more than shoulder-width apart, he raised his arms and tilted his head back. Staring at the night sky, he focused.

~~*~~

Sandale strode from Cordtz's tree home, having left him with Rekah, Loraleaf's designated counselor and a Kindred of Heart. Cordtz was in good hands and Sandale was determined to keep it that way.

He headed for Khaos and Jahl's. He still didn't think of it as his home, though it had been before the wipe of his brain to a clean slate, or B.W. *before wipe*, as he referred to it. Now he had only one purpose, to keep Jahl from ordering the wipe of another man's memories.

The only problem with Cordtz was he swore he saw a Dirgon, and no one believed him, which sent him into a rage. Those mythological creatures had never existed, though the oldest text of the first settlers on Eden described them as if they were real. Even if they had been, they would be long extinct since they hadn't been seen in over two thousand years.

Most likely, it was a lawbreaker who was Kindred of Light who used the illusion to scare away the hunters. Or as Rekah thought, a Kindred of Mind lawbreaker had implanted the vision in Cordtz's head. Either way, the lawbreakers were too close and Loraleaf needed every man they had to protect their home.

As Sandale passed Libations, feminine laughter filled the air and slowed his step. That had to be the most pleasant sound on all of Eden. Looking ahead, he found the source. Serena, with Jahl and Khaos, hung over the lift as it rose from the first level. "Jae, get back in your house and put some clothes on."

Jaelene, Serena's younger sister, stuck out her tongue before responding. "Don't be such an old fart. Get with the times." Jaelene was the first woman to shed her clothes in Loraleaf. She was also the first person to have a Tigran pet. Princess, otherwise known as Meowser, sat at her feet, the young cat only reaching Jaelene's waist.

Serena laughed, and Jaelene waved before Theron pulled her to him and gave her a kiss.

For the first time, Sandale felt truly alone. Serena had been his chosen one and Jahl and Khaos his filoz. He was supposed to be part of that family, but circumstances had taken that away when he was shot on Earth. He may have resented the bonding of Jahl and Khaos with Serena while he still had half his mind, but now he felt nothing more for the three than for any others in Loraleaf. Their history together was gone.

But seeing Jaelene's love for Theron and her happiness at living near her older sister, pulled at his heart. Maybe it was because he liked Rekah, another Kindred of Heart like himself. Rekah could feel people's emotions, while he could calm them. They made a good team. But Rekah was part of Jaelene's filoz along with Konala, a Kindred of Eden who could communicate with animals, and Theron, who could create reflections, so Sandale was still alone.

Not exactly. Jahl had told him he had five brothers, and of course, his parents. According to Jahl, he had a good family life and only left Naralina because Khaos and Jahl had families who were abusive. So to be fair, he did have a family who loved him. He just didn't remember them…at all.

He watched as his old filoz walked off the lift and entered their home. Part of him wanted to lose himself in the blue drinks at Libations, but he quickly remembered his purpose and continued in their direction.

With any luck, as Khaos said, he would be leaving soon.

He opened the door and found the three enjoying ambrosia at the bar in the living area.

"Sandale, please join us." Serena's soft gaze bothered him far more than it should.

"Are you celebrating something?"

Jahl grinned. "We are. We are celebrating the news of a new addition to Loraleaf."

"Who?" He accepted the glass Khaos handed him.

Jahl laughed as if the joy inside him was too much to hold, which in itself was odd. Jahl tended to frown more than smile. "My dear friend, I am happy to share the news that my beloved's sister, Jaelene is with child. Soon this treetop settlement will hear the cries and laughter of a baby."

Happiness, like he hadn't felt since he woke after the wipe, filled his soul. Instinctively, he recognized the enormity of such an event. This would be Loraleaf's first baby. He raised his glass and smiled naturally for a change. "To Jaelene."

The others raised their glasses as well and after tapping them to their foreheads took a sip.

"I just can't believe it." Serena set her glass on the bar. "My little sister, a mother. My parents will be thrilled."

Khaos wrapped his arms around Serena from behind. "I'm sure you will follow soon."

She pushed away and turned to look at him. "Is that a vision?"

Sandale didn't need Rekah's ability to sense emotions to figure out Serena feared being pregnant.

Khaos shook his head. "No, just thinking of the odds."

Serena had confided in him that she had some chemical in her body that would prevent her from becoming pregnant for at least a year and that was two months ago. Surely, she'd told her agapaytos as well.

She looked relieved as she lifted her glass and took a large swallow. She put her glass down. "Good, because Wally still needs me and I'd hate to be distracted." She winked at Sandale before her gaze found the pen outside with the rather fat welchet inside.

In his opinion, the welchet was big enough to be released, but the critter probably loved being spoiled.

A banging on the door had them all turning toward it.

Jahl yelled. "Come!"

The door burst open and Konala, one of Jaelene's agapaytos, ran in. From the look on his face, he wasn't there to join in their celebration of his impending baby boy.

From instinct, Sandale touched Konala's arm, helping him calm down and catch his breath. The man smiled gratefully at him before turning toward Jahl and Khaos. He held up a small piece of paper. "Toni has discovered the secret project, but she's been caught."

"Caught?" Serena stepped forward. "How? By who? Where is she?"

Jahl took Serena's hand, but spoke to Konala. "Is it Grandall?"

Konala shook his head. "It's a man named Akasha. I do not know him."

"We have to save her." Serena shook off Jahl and faced him. "We have to find her. She was helping us and now she's in danger. I don't want your father anywhere near her."

As Serena's voice escalated, Sandale stepped next to her. At Jahl's nod, he placed his hand on her arm, smoothing out the edges of her agitation. He'd mastered light calming and unconsciousness so far. The middle ground was still uncertain for him. Losing his control over his ability had been as frustrating as losing his memories.

Jahl moved Serena to a cushioned chair and Konala sank down onto the longseat opposite her. Since Jahl and Khaos stood on either side of their beloved, Sandale sat next to Konala.

Konala opened a small piece of paper. "Let me read you the note."

Jahl nodded.

"Project is to bring women here by truckload and sell. Got caught. Taken by Akasha." I'm not certain what she means by 'truckload.'"

Serena gave them a half smile. "That means a whole lot at a time."

Khaos shook his head. "I don't understand how the Ruling Circle could bring that many women to Eden at once. If two men stand too far apart, the portal becomes unstable and even farther would make it inoperative."

Sandale addressed Konala. "Didn't you say that they had stopped working on tracking portal openings outside the city walls so they could work on this one?"

When the man nodded, he continued. "Then it probably means that they are building a large portal of some kind to bring many women at once."

Khaos widened his eyes. "Bringing dozens of people from Earth at one time was banned over a century ago, when humans turned their sights on space as an explanation for the disappearances in an area they called the Bermuda Triangle."

"You did that?" Serena looked at her beloved in shock.

He shook his head. "No, but one city on the planet did many years ago."

"And Grandall wants to do this again only this time sell these women?" Serena looked up at Jahl. "Who would he sell these women to, or more to the point, who would buy them?"

Jahl growled. "My father would deal with only the worst kind of Edenists, those who skirt the laws. Maybe even lawbreakers."

"No." Konala surprised them. "I don't think even Grandall is that cruel."

"I put nothing past my father." Jahl rubbed at the scar over what used to be his Kindred birthmark.

Sandale's instinct was to calm everyone, but sometimes heightened tension helped productivity, so he made himself remain where he was. "Who is this Akasha that has caught Toni?"

Since he, Jahl, and Khaos had originally brought Toni to Eden with Serena when both women were being held against their will on Earth, and since he now resided in what was built as a room for Toni, he felt a certain obligation to help.

Jahl shook his head. "Akasha was not one of the Ruling Circle while we lived in Naralina, but Wareson and Nassic were two members before being exiled, and we do not know who replaced them."

"So this Akasha could be a Ruling Circle member and he has Toni." Sandale did not like the uncertainty.

Jahl's hands curled into fists. "And if she is held by a Ruling Circle member, it is only a matter of time before she's brought before my father."

Serena grabbed Jahl's hand. "We can't let that happen. She's done so much for us, for both Loraleaf and Haven."

Sandale stood. "Let me go to Naralina."

Four gazes focused to him, but it was Khaos who spoke. "You? Why do you wish to go?"

"Ever since you told me you saw me leaving here, I have been thinking about doing so. My initial thought was to go to Haven." Jahl scowled, his distrust of Ruling Circle members, even if they no longer ruled, was well known and Haven had two.

Sandale held up his hand to forestall any forthcoming argument. "But today, I had begun to think that I should first finish finding out everything there is to know about my life before the wipe, so any of my future decisions are based on facts. To that end, I think I should visit my family."

"Oh, Sandale. Of course. We should have suggested that months ago." Serena's eyes were misty as she gazed at him.

He understood. She was very close to her family and she and Jaelene visited their parents often with their agapaytos.

He shrugged. "I think it's better that I came to the decision on my own, when I was ready to consider it. I feel ready now and Toni needs help."

Jahl shook his head. "I don't know."

Sandale fisted his hands, but remained calm, more certain than ever that this was what he needed to do. "As our first High Poetess said, *Dare you see a soul at the white heat? Then crouch within the door. Red is the fire's common tint; but when the vivid ore has sated flame's conditions. Its quivering substance plays without a color but the light of unanointed blaze.*"

Khaos stepped to him. "You are right. You have suffered and gone through the white heat. This is your time."

Jahl looked around the room. "Fine, but we need another to open the portal with Sandale."

Khaos stepped forward. "I will go. Konala has a baby to prepare for."

Jahl nodded. "I agree. Find Toni and bring her back. We will need her information to create a plan to stop my father. If he succeeds in this, we could be looking at another Eden-wide war of cities."

Serena looked up at that. "Why do you say that?"

"This plan of my father's goes against every Dickinson Law there is. To have a leader of any city disregard these laws gives silent consent to everyone else. It also places Naralina above others as having the most scarce commodity on the planet. The balance between cities will be broken and everyone will seek to recreate the technology or try to steal it. And with so many women disappearing from Earth, humans will eventually figure it out."

Sandale frowned. "Do you think your father realizes all these implications?"

Jahl snorted. "I doubt so. Even if he did, he would not care as long as he saw himself as benefitting and gaining power."

Khaos stepped to the side of Sandale, just far enough away to allow two men to pass between them. He addressed Sandale. "Have you opened a portal since…"

"Since my mind was wiped? No. How is it done?"

Khaos motioned to the distance between them. "This is the ideal spacing, though closer works too. Any wider and the portal loses its integrity."

"Ah, so that is why Grandall is trying to build something bigger."

"Unfortunately, yes. But he hasn't succeeded yet." Khaos looked away a moment, his grey eyes turning silvery. When he looked back, his eyes were normal again. "I've searched for any hint at this portal being complete, even for long term fall out, but I see nothing…yet."

Serena sighed. "That's a relief. It means we have time to stop it."

Khaos lifted his right arm and put his left finger beneath it. "Sandale, reach beneath your arm and you will find a small hard chip against your ribs. Press it."

He reached beneath his right arm, but felt nothing. "Could it be beneath my other arm?"

Khaos frowned. "I can't remember. Try it."

He repeated the action on his other side. "There is nothing. Are you sure I have one?"

Jahl practically growled as he stomped toward Sandale. "Of

course you have one. You received yours long before Khaos and me. The Triad was convinced of your goodness even while you were still just past your transition." He stood on Sandale's right side. "Lift your arm."

Sandale did.

"Holy Bendis. It's gone!"

Sandale looked to where Jahl pointed and could just see a small jagged scar that ran perpendicular to the ground.

Khaos elbowed Jahl out of the way. "It can't be." He studied the scar then turned to Jahl. "Lawbreakers."

"By the Bowels of Bangley!" Jahl spun away and punched his hand into the table next to Serena's chair. The wood shattered.

"Ow." Serena grabbed her hand. "That hurt. Please stop punching things."

Instinct had Sandale stepping to Jahl and grabbing his shoulder, calming the former brother of his heart.

Jahl took a deep breath and stepped aside. "Thank you." He gave Serena an apologetic look for her pain before he moved away from them and stood facing the large window that gave a view of Wally's cage. After a few tense moments, he turned to face them. "We now have more than one crisis on our hands. The lawbreakers only need to catch one more Edenist with a chip and they will have full rein to portal anywhere, to Earth, into Loraleaf, to Naralina."

"And to Haven." Khaos stepped next to Jahl. "We must stop all patrols and confer with Nassic and Wareson."

Jahl scowled but after a moment he grudgingly nodded.

Khaos turned to Konala. "Take Theron and portal directly to Haven. Tell them only as much as you need to, but have them come back here with you." Then he stared at Serena, the love in his gaze so strong, Sandale looked away, feeling as if he intruded on a personal moment.

"Serena, my beloved, we must wait to rescue Toni. This is far bigger than her plight right now, but I promise, we won't delay more than a day."

Though she opened her mouth to protest, she closed it again and nodded. "I understand."

Khaos' gray eyes turned silvery causing everyone to look away. The man was seeing something. Sandale could only hope it wasn't the end of Eden.

CHAPTER THREE

Toni waited until Akasha left then she jumped out of bed. She'd bet a million dollars he was going to breakfast with the other members-to-be. Now was her chance.

She strode to his cabinet and opened it, searching for anything like a knife. She found a flat stone that looked like a chisel without a handle, but there was nothing like a hammer.

Closing the cabinet, she scanned the contents of the rooms. The only doors were the one that led outside and the windowed one that led to the patio, or what Edenists called a patrio. Even the bathroom just had an archway instead of a door. She shrugged. It made sense. If she lived alone and never planned to have anyone over, she wouldn't need any doors either.

Though she could see the entire living area, there wasn't anything that she could use with her newfound chisel. Even if she just had a nice sized rock, she could make do.

Rock? Hell, the whole city was built on rock. She ran to the patrio door and opened it. Outside she walked along the half-wall that portioned it off from the mountainside. Finally, she found what she needed. Reaching high above her head, she grabbed a rock that was bigger than her hand and hefted it. "Perfect."

Running back inside, she planned her approach. Nudging the chisel stone beneath the head on the stone peg and above the infragile vine that held it, she hit upwards with the rock.

Nothing happened. Maybe she needed to hit it harder. Taking careful aim because the head of the stone peg wasn't that large, she gave it a good wallop. Something whizzed by her and she examined the peg. "Well, hell." Part of the lip of the stone had chipped off. That wasn't her intention. How could she wiggle that stone out of the vine if the head chipped off?

She repeated her effort but gentler and again nothing changed, so she hit it hard and another piece winged by her. This wasn't working. She looked over at the locking mechanism. That appeared far too complicated, so she gave the stone peg another hard hit. A huge chunk came off and the peg itself cracked.

"Just great." She smacked it with her hand in frustration and the stone separated. Was it her imagination or was the vine a little looser. She hauled off and hit the peg hard with her rock. It broke into three pieces, one piece falling to the floor. "Yes!"

Jubilant now, she hit the peg with all her might. It broke more and pieces fell from within the confines of the infragile vine. All she needed to do was pull out the pieces and the hinge would be free.

Setting the rock on the wooden chair nearby, she started to scrape at the stone bits. One in particular wouldn't come out, so she picked up her rock again.

Just then, the latch that opened the door moved upward and Akasha stepped in.

He looked at her, her hand with the rock, and the door. He scowled. "What are you doing to my door?"

"It was an accident." She tried to look guilty, though she felt no guilt at all. He could hand her over to Grandall at any moment and despite how hot he was, she had to get away from him.

He raised both eyebrows in disbelief. "An accident?" He stepped closer to examine the hinge, his spicy scent filling her nostrils. "It appears purposeful to me." He looked her in the eye. "Were you trying to break the hinges on my door so you could escape?"

She shook her head to break eye contact. "I hadn't even thought of that. I told you, I like to stay in shape. Since you left without taking me down the stairs, I found a rock and I was working out with it." She raised the rock above her head with one hand. No need for him to know that it was a much smaller weight than those she used in her rooms. "I was just moving to a different position when it slipped from my hand and flew against the door. I'm very sorry."

Akasha stared at her with his bright blue eyes, and she almost forgot he was a monk. Seriously, what a waste.

He sighed and stepped away. "Come eat. I brought you warm baka buns and two cups of kafez."

Monk? Shit, the man was a saint! She loved baka buns. The citrusy filling was a great eye-opener in the morning. "Thank you." She moved to the small table that could fit two people if they didn't have much food and sat.

Akasha didn't say a word. He just placed a basket in front of her.

The smell of the strong hot coffee drink had her lifting a large mug out. After taking a sip, she sighed. "I owe you one."

He took the seat opposite her. "Good. Then tell me why you were spying on Grandall, and don't tell me it was because you like to watch. I've spoken to Jasmine and watching is not your way. You'd rather be watched."

She grinned over the mug. "Well, you know what they say. If you've got it, flaunt it." She winked, thoroughly enjoying his undivided attention.

"Then why were you spying on Grandall?"

She dug into the basket and took out a baka bun. "Why wouldn't I? He's the leader on Naralina. Anything he did or said would make me in the know." She took a bite and let out a satisfied groan as the lemon tang hit her tongue.

"In the know?" Akasha shook his head. "What does that mean?"

She finished chewing and swallowed. Then she took another sip of kafez. "It's like being privy to important information and then telling friends."

He frowned. "You mean a gossip."

"You make it sound so distasteful. It's more like being popular."

He studied her, so she took the opportunity to have another bite. They didn't get baka buns this good in the Temple. Being a monk must have a few perks, and she'd say breakfast was one of them.

"You're lying again."

She widened her eyes at that. "Why do you keep asking me things if you aren't going to believe me? If I'm lying, then you tell me why I was supposedly spying on Grandall."

He leaned back in the straight-backed chair and crossed his legs, setting his ankle on top of his knee. "You do not trust

Grandall. You wanted to know what he planned and for who, and thought by listening to him while he was taking his pleasure, you would learn something important."

Holy shit, the monk was far too smart. She waved off his comment. "Why wouldn't I trust Grandall? He's our fearless leader."

"You keep calling him *the* leader of Naralina when you know the city is ruled by five men, each of different kindred equally. Why?"

She shrugged again. "I don't know. He just acts like the city leader. Or maybe it's because I see him all the time since he uses Jasmine like a mistress even though he has a wife. I don't think that's fair to the Edenists who need pleasure who have no one at home to get it."

"Finally." Akasha smirked. "Truth comes from your words."

Fuck, what did she say? "I always tell the truth."

He started to smirk then stopped. He dropped his leg and leaned forward. "Tell me why you spied on Grandall."

She had to give it to the man. He was nothing if not persistent. "What's in it for me?" At his questioning look, she dropped the slang. "What will you give me if I tell you why?"

He stared at her, but she didn't drop her gaze.

If he wanted to negotiate, she could do that. It would help her stall for time. She had to escape or get rescued. There was no way anyone from Loraleaf would open a portal this deep into Naralina. That would cause way too many questions. Of course, that was assuming Konala's birdy actually picked up her note.

"I will show you my orange light."

Oh, he was good. He caught on to her fascination with the kindred abilities of the Edenists. Learning what his orange light could do would be very helpful in understanding how he might keep her from escaping, but it wouldn't aid her in actually doing so. "That's a start. Okay, you show me your orange light and what it does and you let me run down and up the stairs twice a day."

He didn't even flinch. "Once a day and you tell me what you heard."

"I'll tell you *why* I spied in return for seeing your orange light and running the stairs once a day."

"Done." He sat back and lifted his hand to indicate that she go first. "So why were you spying?"

She took another sip of kafez. "First, you show me the orange light." She had no doubt that he, of all Edenists, would keep his word, but she didn't want him to know that. "Not that I doubt you, but…" she let her words trail off.

He stiffened at the insult before he rose. At first, she thought he might actually flip the table over on her. Maybe she needed to take insulting his integrity out of her arsenal. That obviously was of no help.

Akasha lifted his hand and every instinct in her body yelled at her to move out of the way. He did not treat her like most Edenists, and if she was wrong about him, he may well do her bodily harm.

A small orange beam of light issued from his finger and blasted apart her baka bun, splattering lemon jam everywhere.

"Fuck, what was that?" She stared at the scattered remains of her breakfast.

"That was the burn of my orange light."

She glanced up at him. Every element of his face looked like the bad boy she'd expected him to be when they first met.

Unfortunately, instead of scaring her, it turned her on, and she was pretty sure that was not what he wanted.

His sky-blue eyes seemed to glow as he stared at her. "Your turn. No lies."

Oh yeah, bad boy all the way. She rose as well, not wanting him to think he had the upper hand with his little show of power. "I spied on him because I don't trust him. He is only about himself and not the caring ruler he wants others to see. He is cruel, vindictive and willing to stop at nothing to have his way."

He raised his brow. "Continue."

"I'd heard from a reliable source that he had stopped work on the machine for tracking portal openings outside the city walls, though why Naralina needs that, I have no clue. It's not like lawbreakers have Crius chips, right? I mean if they did, that would mean your Triad wasn't doing a very good job."

"Stay on the topic."

Seriously? If he wanted to play hardball, she'd be happy to. "As it turns out, our fearless leader did stop work on that project."

"And how do you know this?"

She rolled her eyes. "Because I heard him tell Jasmine. I told you, I had a reliable source."

"And did you not think that Grandall may be feeding Jasmine stories that aren't true to make her feel special, like she was 'in the know' or maybe even did so to test her loyalty?"

She snorted. "That requires the man to think about someone else, and I guarantee you he doesn't do that…ever. Do you think he cares how his 'beloved' feels knowing he's having sex at Pleasure Temples. It's not like the poor woman has any other agapaytos since Grandall was so selfish as to accept the waiver for Ruling

Circle members to have a beloved all to themselves. Do you know who else on the Ruling Circle has taken advantage of that waiver?"

He shook his head, his brows now lowered.

"No one. Yes, that's right. No one." The more she thought about the slimeball, the more she had to move, so she left the table and started to pace. "Need more examples? How about what he did to one of his own sons?"

Akasha opened his hand toward her once again, signaling her to proceed.

Good thing because he was going to hear it whether he wanted to or not. "He didn't like his son's Kindred of Eden ability, so he had the other boys hold Jahl down while he burned the birthmark beyond recognition. And don't ask me if that is really true because it is."

She kept pacing, her anger now taking over. "And you know what else this pillar of society did? He trumped up charges against two Ruling Circle members then threatened the remaining two to side with him to get rid of them." She stopped and looked at Akasha. "You know why? Because one of them had started to ask too many questions and the other was a Kindred of Mind and could make Grandall tell the truth. Can you imagine what that vile joke of a ruler would spill if that happened?"

Shit, she was so angry now, she saw red. Everything really looked red, like the sparse furniture, Akasha, and even the sky outside. Even as she recognized that fact, the sensation of her hair being stroked caught her attention, and she spun around to find no one there.

"It's just my red light. You appeared agitated."

She looked at Akasha, who had his hand lifted again and red

light flowed from it to her. She waved off his help, but her curiosity was piqued. "Do you have to raise your hand to use your light?"

He blinked as he lowered his hand, the red light retreating into him at his palm. "If I need to direct it, yes. I did not want to hurt you."

She glanced at her burned up breakfast. "Really?"

He actually looked a little uncomfortable. "Thank you for being truthful."

"It feels good to finally tell someone the truth about Grandall. It burns me up every time I see people fawn over him or hear them sing his praises. The man's a weasel." And she knew a weasel when she ran in to one. She'd had a number in her life, but Grandall's fake social exterior reminded her too much of her worst nightmare. A nightmare she didn't plan to relive again.

She stilled. Was that why she had the nightmare last night? She shook her head as if she could clear it of the scum in her life. "Can we go run the stairs now? I'm so wound up. I need to release some energy."

When Akasha shook his head, she lost it. "We had an agreement!"

"And I promise I will honor it. We cannot go outside right now."

She placed a hand on her hip and glared at him. "Why?"

"It is time to meditate alone, so I must stay in here. Later, I can visit the meditation pool if I wish, but going outside is not allowed now until Helios is at its peak."

He had to be kidding. "Just great. Then I'm going to shower." And if he had a problem with that, he didn't have to look. He could do his meditation thing.

She turned on her heel and strode into the bathing area. She didn't care a wit if he saw her naked. Hell, everyone here was naked.

As she undressed, she tamped down the urge to invite him to join her. She could show him *her* type of meditation.

Just her luck, she found the only bad-boy monk in all of Naralina.

Akasha could not move his gaze away from Toni as she strode out of the living area and into the bathing area. It was not until she passed through the archway that he finally looked away, but he wanted to follow her in.

Everything about her was different from any woman he'd had contact with, including his own mother. Toni fascinated him, and now that she'd told him the truth, he was even more intrigued.

She had strong convictions despite her lies, and there was history behind that. With each piece of her that was revealed, he found eleven more he wanted to learn about. But he couldn't keep her with him forever. It wasn't exactly against a particular rule, but having her stay with him was definitely questionable.

He forced himself to move away from the bathing area and sat at the table again. He couldn't let her leave yet. After all she'd revealed, his gut told him he needed to protect her, mainly from Grandall.

Despite being raised to respect the Ruling Circle, he'd always had concerns about Grandall. He had met the man when he was a boy and took an instant dislike to him, but had never shown that. Now, everything Toni said, even without knowing her sources, was too easy to believe. But as a Triad member-to-be and the next in line to sit on the panel, he couldn't afford to simply take her at her word.

He needed to learn more. As part of the Triad membership, he had kept apart from the daily life and concerns of Naralina, but for the first time, he questioned that strategy, a strategy all members followed.

Toni had opened his eyes to much, but she needed to reveal more. He only had three colored lights left to bargain with and that was obviously not enough.

Singing came from the bathing area, and he grinned. The tune was terrible but no less passionate. Unable to resist, he rose and meandered toward the archway.

In the open rainbox with the clear wall, she had her back to him, her long, wet hair plastered to her skin, well past her shoulder blades to her waist. Her hips flared out just slightly from there and her naked ass was as tan as the rest of her. Obviously, she enjoyed being naked as much as any Edenist, so why did she wear clothing?

As she moved her hips back and forth with the beat of her song, the muscles in her toned thighs and calves flexed and relaxed. She was a perfect specimen of an Earth woman. He looked down at his hard cock. He usually had better control of his needs than this.

She turned around and lifted her face up into the spray.

As the water washed away the lather of soap, he stared at her full breasts with large areolas and nipples. His balls tightened. He let his gaze roam down her defined abdominals to the juncture of her thighs where she was shaved clean.

Holy Bendis! He had to find out all she knew and soon because he wanted to bury himself deep inside her. She would meet him thrust for thrust. Everything about her hinted at—

"Like what you see?" Toni's question brought his gaze to hers. She winked. "I so wish you could have sex. I wouldn't mind having that between my legs."

His cock jumped as if it heard the longing in her words. He stepped into the bathing area, but did not move too close to the rainbox. "Why do you say I cannot have sex?"

She cocked her head, water splashing from her long hair to the side of the box. "Because you are a Triad member-to-be. Ever think of going in to another profession?"

At her assumption, a plan formed. "No. I have known I was meant to be a Triad member since I was a boy. As a member-to-be I *am* allowed certain…pleasures."

That caught her attention. She stepped out of the spray and looked at him from around the corner of the clear wall. "Really? Like what?" From the way her gaze roved over his body with appreciative lust, it was obvious she meant every word about wanting him between her legs.

"I am allowed to pleasure a woman and be given certain pleasures in return."

"Oh, I'm liking the sound of this. Let me just dry off."

He strode forward. "No. You have missed quite a few places that need to be cleaned."

Toni spread her arms wide and stepped back into the water. "Please. Show me what I've missed."

~~*~~

Sandale looked up at the two level walstone and savinstone

structure embedded into the side of the mountain next to dozens of other homes made of the same material. It had taken him awhile to find his home, after being portaled in next to the north wall of the city.

The people he'd asked for directions were very nice and none recognized him, so that made him feel a bit more comfortable. After all, he was a stranger to himself as well as to them.

He banged on the door and waited. In those interminable seconds, his stomach turned as hard as the walstone his home was made of. A hundred questions sped through his mind, the most important being, would he remember anything?

He stood rock still. The silence, due to the thick stone walls, made it difficult to know when someone might open the door. If it was one of his fathers, he wouldn't know who was who. What if one of his brothers was there and opened it? Or they could all be out. Then what? Should he go to the market and come—

The door opened slowly, as if it was a bit too heavy and a woman faced him. She was far shorter than himself and wore a wrap much like Serena's. Her hair was as blonde as his and showed no sign of graying. Her violet eyes, so much like his own, seemed confused. Was this his mother?

Recognition dawned just before she shrieked. "Sandale!" Tears immediately filled her eyes as she threw herself at him.

Her joy and love flowed over him, a balm to his hurting heart. He hugged her tight, breathing in her sweet fragrance that reminded him of the pecone rolls they made in Loraleaf. This *had* to be his mother. He had hoped her scent would remind him of his childhood, but it didn't. Still, everything about her was welcoming…but would that change once she knew of the wipe?

She finally pulled back to look at him, but still held tight to his arms. "We thought we'd never see you again." More tears flowed down her cheeks as her gaze ran over him. "You let your hair grow. I like it."

He grinned at that. At least she approved of that small change.

"What was all that screeching—Sandale?" The tall naked man with light brown hair and light blue eyes that came into the entryway halted. "Son?"

His mother nodded at the man. "Ulik, he's really here."

His father strode forward and gave him a strong hug, then stepped back, moisture shining in his eyes. "We thought…" his voice trailed off as he looked at his wife.

She wrapped her arm around Ulik's waist. "We didn't think you'd survive in the jungle."

He found his own throat closed with emotion and cleared it to speak. "I have survived, but I'm not the same." On one hand, he dreaded telling his parents, but on the other, he wanted them to know as soon as possible.

"Oh, you must come in and tell us everything." His mother took his hand, letting go of Ulik to guide Sandale farther into the house.

He was thankful she had because nothing seemed familiar. He had held out a tiny hope that coming home would bring back some of his memories, but it didn't.

His mom bustled off to get drinks for them as he and Ulik sat. He scanned the room, hoping something would trigger even the hint of a memory.

"If you search for Baruch, he will return shortly. He will be as shocked as we are. Fripp will arrive when he arrives. Have you been well? I mean, did you have a place to live or did you wander?"

Sandale returned his gaze to his father. Jahl had warned him that people in Naralina thought the jungle was a death knell. No one had ever left voluntarily until he, Jahl and Khaos brought their group of men out. Certainly, no one had ever returned, as far as he knew. He gave his father a small smile. "Yes, we have a beautiful place to live that is hidden from lawbreakers."

His mother returned, full of energy and quick to hand out drinks. As she gave him his, he held her hand for moment to help her calm down. Her eyes watered. "Thank you, Sandy. You always did know when I needed you."

He let her go and took a sip. "I was just telling Ulik about where I've been living."

"Ulik?" His mother frowned. "Since when do you call him Ulik? He's still 'dad' to you."

He swallowed and attempted to smile. "I am sorry. It has been so long."

"I know." His mother held up her hand and spread her fingers. "Five years, eight months, two weeks and four days."

He and his father stared at her.

"What?" She gave them both a reproving stare. "Of course I'm going to remember how long it's been since I last saw my second to last son."

He wasn't sure why, but his mother's counting of the days gave him a shred of peace that he had not felt since the wipe. That kind of love had to be special enough to—

The sound of the front door opening interrupted his thought. He stood and faced the archway, knowing this had to be another father. He had no idea what his relationship had been like with all of them. Did he get along better with one than the other?

"I only found enough henny for—By the Crius! It's Sandale!" Baruch dropped the bag he held and grabbed Sandale to him.

After hugging him hard, Baruch let go and slapped a hand on his shoulder. "Scrat. I never thought I would lay eyes on you again." His dad's deep blue eyes did more than water and tears flowed down his cheeks into his dark beard. "Are you well? Is Jahl and Khaos here too? Do you have a beloved to introduce us to?"

Sandale smiled at his father's enthusiasm. "I will tell you everything. I promise."

His mom had already risen and picked up the bag from the floor. "Really Barry? That's our dinner." She looked at Sandale. "You will stay for dinner at least, right?"

He nodded. At her relieved look, his gut tightened. How could he have left such a loving family?

"Sit, sit." Baruch motioned to where he'd been and then sat next to him. "Tell us everything."

He looked at each dad in turn and then his mom as she returned to snuggle next to Ulik. "I will."

He took a sip of the kafez his mom brought him. "The most important thing you need to know is that back a few cycles of Selene, I had my memory wiped clean. I had no choice, but now I do not know anything about who I am."

His mother's intake of breath gave voice to the shock in all their faces.

"I do not remember you, my brothers or this house. I did not remember Jahl, Khaos or our chosen one, Serena. I even have had to relearn the control of my Kindred abilities." He gave them a self-deprecating smile. "And I am still not that good with them."

Baruch laid his hand on Sandale's arm. The feeling of being loved flowed through him bringing him to the edge of tears. He looked at his father in question.

"I am also Kindred of Heart and I can flood anyone with whichever emotion I feel."

He nodded, his throat too closed to speak.

"I am Kindred of Mind." Ulik gave him a shadow of a smile. "I remember everything I see, read and hear. When you were small, I used to play a memory game with you by showing you where I kept various items in the house and then quizzing you on their placements."

Sandale swallowed against the hurt he inflicted. "Thank you for telling me that. I wish I had some of that knowledge now." He looked at his mother. "I was hoping I could stay for a while and learn from my family who I was."

Baruch put his arm around his shoulders and pulled him against him. "Of course, you can stay. As long as you like, right, Pam?"

His mom nodded, the tears still flowing down her cheeks. He couldn't stand to see her hurting so much on his behalf. He reached across the space that separated them and put his hand on her knee. "It is okay, mom. It had to be done."

Ulik frowned. "Perhaps you should start from when you left Naralina."

He sat back. "Of course. First, we found a place to settle deep in the jungle and thanks to Jahl's ability to control anything of Eden that is dead, he quickly built homes high up in the trees with walkways and lifts." He wouldn't tell them about the encounter with Haven. It wasn't his place to reveal another settlement.

"Once we developed an impenetrable shield that also hid our homes from view, we made ready for bringing our chosen ones, or in the case of some filoz, they began to look for one. It was at this point that Khaos sensed our chosen one, Serena, was in danger. He was right, and we portaled to Earth to save her and her friend, but I was shot in the escape."

His mother gasped and Ulik interrupted. "With a real bullet?"

"Yes. I was then taken by the lawbreakers. I do not remember what happened while with them, but Khaos did record some of my own words from before the memory wipe. I read them and know that my mind was not my own anymore and my torture was excruciating. I begged them to free me from my memories. They still cared for me despite everything."

He swallowed down the self-disgust he felt when he remembered the acts he'd committed according to the notes Khaos had taken at his own insistence.

"Oh, my poor boy." His mom reached her hands out to him and he took them. There was no remembered closeness, but it didn't matter. He felt it now and it felt good.

"And so you came home to find yourself again. Great idea." Baruch's smile was big and brash like him.

"What about your chosen one?" Ulik's concern for Serena was sobering.

"She had already bonded with Jahl and Khaos before they even knew I lived. The lawbreakers went out of their way to make it look like I died."

Ulik frowned. "I am sure you nearly did. These lawbreakers must have a very strong healer to have saved you."

He had never given that a thought.

"I cannot believe it, but it appears we must be grateful to lawbreakers that you are here with us today." His mother's confusion mirrored his own.

Baruch removed his arm and slapped his knee. "We must have all your brothers come and help too. Your oldest brother has a beloved and one son. The next brought his beloved to Naralina a year ago, but no baby yet. Darret and his filoz have two women they are considering. Haldone hasn't even begun looking for a chosen one yet, but your younger brother is very close to bringing his to Eden."

"And my younger brother's name?"

Baruch's smile dimmed. "His name is Vectar."

"I know my questions like this will be painful, so if you prefer I do not stay, I can leave."

"No!" All three parents yelled the word at the same time then laughed.

Sandale smiled. "Thank you. I can tell you that already I feel more grounded. Unfortunately, learning about myself is not my only task while here."

Ulik raised his brow in question, though no one spoke.

"Serena's friend, Toni, has been living in a Pleasure Temple and yesterday she was taken by a man named Akasha. I must find her and bring her back to the jungle." He wouldn't tell his family more than they needed to know. The last thing he wanted was to put them in a position of having to lie for him.

"Akasha? I haven't heard of anyone by that name. Have you, Ulik?"

His other father shook his head. "But it shouldn't be hard to find him. I can check at the Hall of Records tomorrow. For now, I think we should show Sandale his childhood home and then send for his brothers."

Sandale frowned. Until he knew who Akasha was, Toni could be in danger. As much as he wanted to learn more about himself, first, he had to make sure she was safe. Every woman should be safe in Naralina, but after what she'd discovered, he could well see her jeopardy. "Would it be possible to go to the Hall of Records now? Toni could be in danger and I need to find her."

"A woman in danger in Naralina?" Ulik gave him a searching look. "What has she done?"

"It is not so much what she has done, but what she has discovered. Her very life could be at risk." He'd heard enough about Grandall from Jahl to understand the urgency.

Baruch rose from the longseat. "Then we must find her immediately. Come Ulik, the three of us can search faster than one." He moved his gaze to his beloved. "And in the meantime, your mother can tell Fripp his son has come home and to fetch your brothers."

His mother rose. "I agree." She held her hands out to him. "But first I need another hug from Sandale. My mind understands you are here but my heart still needs convincing."

Willingly, he wrapped the petite woman in his arms and inhaled her sweet scent. *Home.* The word rebounded through his brain and seeped into his heart. He spoke against the top of her head. "I will return shortly."

She finally pulled back. "Oh, I know. Just a bit emotional is all."

He held her hand and calmed her again, wanting more than anything to take the ache from her heart, but had a critical task to accomplish. "I look forward to seeing my old room." He gave her an encouraging smile, and she brightened.

"Well, if you want to see your room, then you better get going." She practically pushed him and his fathers out the door.

Chapter Four

As they strode up the hill toward the Hall of Records, people they passed who knew his fathers looked at him with wide eyes. "Why do they stare at me so?"

"We had to explain your disappearance somehow." Ulik looked to Baruch.

Sandale's other father shrugged. "So we told them you had gone to live in another city."

"So why would that engender such shocked stares?"

Ulik grinned. "Because son, usually when people move to another city, they don't return."

"Why not?" If they all had portals, it seemed fairly easy to visit family members in other cities.

Baruch grimaced. "Because many Naralinians believe they live in the best city and generally do not welcome return visits from those who chose to leave. To them, those who move away have betrayed them in some way."

Sandale slowed to a stop and looked at each of his fathers. "I do not think I truly realized, even when I had my memory, how hard it would be for you."

Ulik set his hand on Sandale's shoulder. "No, you probably didn't, but five years ago you were young and completely loyal to your filoz, which we all understood. Do not worry. We are not so arrogant as to believe our city is the best on this planet."

"Speak for yourself." Baruch shouldered Ulik and tried to hold a scowl, but he failed quickly and burst into laughter.

Sandale smiled, enjoying the freedom of emotion his loud father had. It was obvious Ulik was the serious of the three, while Baruch was the boisterous one and Fripp was what? He hoped to find out soon.

Maybe he was a little of all three? It certainly gave him a place to start regarding who he was.

"Here we are." Ulik pointed to a long two story building while Baruch opened the tall door.

Sandale entered and inhaled. The two-level hall with arches on each side was filled with the strong scent of the sherry flower. Looking to his left and right, he discovered why. Two round levitating circular gardens on each side of the entryway were filled to overflowing with the flower. The windows above gave them plenty of light and a caretaker must water them daily to keep them alive. They were a very delicate flower. "Have these flowers always been in the hall?"

Baruch laughed. "No. It is a little overpowering, if you ask me."

Ulik nodded. "I have to agree, but it is an improvement. The committee in charge felt the entryway was not inviting enough, and the agriculture committee was looking for safe places to grow these since there were very few plants left in the city. The thought was to welcome visitors."

"I think the initial idea was valid, but I agree, the scent is too much." He tried not to take deep breaths so close to the flower beds.

"Come." Ulik motioned to the right. "The room with male names beginning in A is down at the end."

Sandale followed. "And where are the female names?"

Baruch pointed to the second floor walkway, but behind them. "All the female names are in the last room on the left upstairs."

"Does that mean that not every man finds his beloved?"

Ulik nodded. "Unfortunately, that is the case. It's one reason why the Pleasure Temples are so important. If those men could not be with a woman, I fear we would have our beloved stolen every time we turned our back."

"That makes sense. In my home in the jungle, we did not have a Pleasure Temple, but Jahl, Khaos, and I guess, myself, required every man who followed us into the jungle to be part of a filoz, so they could find their beloved on Earth." He sighed. "Unfortunately, I am no longer part of a filoz, which was another reason for my coming here. I really do not belong there anymore."

Baruch stopped before the archway of the final room. "You mean you may stay in Naralina?"

He thought he would go to Haven, but maybe being in a large city would be better. "I do not know. My first loyalty is to my jungle home. First, I must help Toni and make sure she is safe. Then I will figure out what to do with my life."

"You can always find a position with the—"

"Baruch, the man just arrived." Ulik frowned. "Let him have at least a full twenty-two hours before you start making plans for him."

His father smirked, but nodded. Then he leaned in and whispered. "I can be a little enthusiastic. Just tell me to stop when I go too far."

Sandale smiled, before he turned his attention to the room. "Scrat. What happened here?" The room was lined with cabinets all neatly labeled according to their ancient Greek alphabet, but in the center where long tables stood, were piles and piles of square cards.

"I'm afraid the Hall of Records is no longer kept up since the Depoteese died. No one has stepped in to take over in more than two years." Ulik opened his arms to encompass the room. "The Ruling Circle has received requests to do something, but they don't see it as a priority. As long as every birth is recorded and placed in the correct room, which they think is occurring, they have not pursued finding a new Depoteese."

He picked up a card recording the birth of a boy three months earlier. "So these on the tables are just births? If that's so, then we can ignore the tables."

Baruch looked at another card across the table. "I wish that were so, but it isn't. This card has added a beloved." He picked another card. "This man was added to a filoz."

"This could take days." He didn't have days. "We need a system. Baruch, you take those tables. Ulik, you take those tables. I'll go to the cabinet and hope no one has had any reason to change this Akasha's card."

Baruch laughed. "He still has your leadership attitude, Ulik."

He had already headed for the cabinet, so he stopped and turned. "I apologize if I have overstepped."

Ulik's smile held only caring in it. "You haven't. Please, proceed."

A bond began to form in his heart for his fathers, one he wanted to pursue, but Toni had to come first. If anything, his family had only motivated him more to finish his task so he could discover who he had been.

Stepping up to the open cabinet, he skimmed the labeled drawers until he found the one with names beginning with AKA. He opened it and moved his fingers through the cards swiftly, his heartbeat racing with his quest.

Within seconds, he found the card. Triumph barreled through him. "I have it." He pulled the card out and brought it to show his fathers.

Baruch read the residence. "The Triad Building."

Sandale looked at him. "Do you know where that is?"

"Yes, we do." Ulik's voice sounded concerned.

That just made Sandale's need to go that much stronger. "Then we must go, now."

Ulik shook his head. "That will not be so easy."

"Why? Is it far?"

Even Baruch frowned, which was not a good sign. "It is high in the city, but that is not the problem."

"Then what is it?" He hated not having his memory.

Ulik shook his head. "No one is allowed in the Triad building except guests of the Triad members and those scheduled for their Crius chip panel."

~~*~~

Toni kept her arms opened wide, breathless at what Akasha might be able to do with her. Thank God the monks on Eden weren't like the ones on Earth. Eden rules were definitely more to her liking. The question was, exactly what pleasures was Akasha allowed to enjoy?

As Mr. Tall, Dark, and Handsome stepped into the shower with her, she had to remind herself he was no bad boy because with the water sluicing over his tat and plastering his hair back, he looked like a motorcycle gang member, not a Triad member.

He reached behind her and came back with a handful of the soap she'd already washed with, the scent that so enhanced his own dark clove smell. "You have done this before?"

Seriously? She spotted the slight quirk in his lips as he spread his hands out and took her own, washing her finger tips. Since he was a bit taller, his arms were longer than hers, but his mounded chest was only an inch from her nipples. Hell, if they got any harder they'd reach out and touch him.

Since he asked, it was only polite to answer. "If you mean have I had an Edenist wash me before, the answer is no. But if you meant have I been in the rainbox with another Edenist before then the answer is yes."

He paused for just a second, but then continued to wash both wrists, then forearms, then elbows. He took his time, rubbing the lather against her skin. When he reached her arm pits, she held her breath.

Instead of cupping her breasts like she wanted, he moved his hands to her shoulders, lightly massaging them. She wanted to be irritated that he disappointed her, but his hands were like magic, loosening her muscles beneath the warm water.

It was a given that all Edenist men had healthy sexual appetites, but Akasha was not a typical Edenist. "And have you done this before?"

"No." His succinct answer was followed by his hands running along her neck, causing her to drop her head forward as his thumbs gently rotated against her skin.

"It feels like you have."

His chuckle surprised her. Then again, even when he smiled it surprised her. She obviously needed to readjust her assumptions about Eden monks.

His hands moved to her chest, and she lifted her head to watch his face as he smoothed the soap over her breasts. His gaze was intent, his light blue eyes now almost cobalt as he circled her areola before running his fingers over her tips.

She held her breath, waiting for him to pinch them at least, but his hands left her and he reached for more soap.

She inhaled and exhaled, trying to relax, but everything about the man hit all the right buttons in her libido. Relaxing, despite his soft circular motion across her stomach, was not going to happen.

He washed beneath her breasts and over her ribs, but didn't return to her nipples. Obviously, he didn't know how this was supposed to work. Unless he wasn't excited by her. It wasn't like she had small bones like Serena, which a lot of men liked. Probably because it made them feel more manly. Her friend actually called her an Amazon.

She glanced down to find his cock hard and stiff. He moved back from her as his hands reached her hips, so his body wasn't touching her. Was that one of his limitations? Shit, she hoped not.

As he washed across her pelvis, her sheath contracted with excitement. He *did* say she missed a few places.

He reached behind her again and loaded up on soap, then he knelt down before her. "Spread your legs."

"I thought you'd never ask." She winked at him, but he wasn't looking at her face. His gaze was riveted to the juncture of her legs.

His hands smoothed the lather around her thighs, lightly massaging those muscles, too. That wasn't where she wanted her massage.

Finally, his fingers traveled up her inner thighs until they reached her pussy. His fingers gently washed through her folds. When his thumb and index finger stroked over her clit, she couldn't keep from rising up on her toes. Fuck that was good.

He slid past and continued to wash her, his hands moving down to her knees. Her disappointment after that one single thrill was too much. "Are you sure you got every spot between my legs? I think you missed one."

He didn't even look at her. "No, it is all clean."

Well, hell, it was clean before he started. That wasn't the point…or was it? Suddenly, an awful thought occurred. What if he wasn't allowed to make her come? That would suck.

"Lift your foot." He tapped her right ankle, and she raised her foot as he washed between her toes with the same attention he'd given her pussy. Seriously?

When he finished with her right, he tapped her left ankle, and she lifted that foot. Now she just wanted the torture to end. Obviously, she wasn't getting any satisfaction from him today.

He finished with her foot and rose. He stood close, looking down at her, his hair slicked back behind his shoulders. She couldn't help moving her hand to touch his tattoo, but before she made contact, he caught her wrist. "You're not done."

She balled her fist, her frustration getting harder to tamp down. "You seemed pretty thorough to me."

He shook his head and dared to smile at her. "I need to wash your back side."

She swallowed her expletive as a zing of pleasure raced down her back and into her ass. This was crazy. She had sex every day she wanted at the Temple with many skilled sexual partners and this man, this monk, had her more wet and more frustrated in minutes than her longest dry spell on Earth.

She should just say no. That's what they taught her in school about drugs, but no one ever said anything about using the same strategy with a hot hunky man with a cock the size of the Vegas Strip.

Akasha raised an eyebrow. "Do you not want to be clean?"

There was a hint of deviltry in his gaze, and she had the distinct feeling he was enjoying her frustration. She pasted on her best sultry smile. "Of course."

"Good. Then step against the clear wall and put your hands over your head."

Her sheath contracted at his request. Oh, shit. It was as if he read her mind. That position had her melting in minutes. "Are you sure you're Kindred of Light?"

He frowned. "You've seen my light."

"Right." She would have sworn with his ability to tell when she lied and his uncanny request that she take the position that turned her on the most, he was Kindred of Mind, or rather mind-reader.

Maybe he wanted her like that because he enjoyed the position just as much as she did. Just the thought of his cock sliding into her from behind had her moving away from the rain spray. She lifted her arms and rested them above her head, only her hands to elbows actually touching what she referred to as glass.

Seconds ticked by and he hadn't touched her. Was he turned on? She had to sneak a peek. She turned her head, but before she could glimpse him, both his hands caught her jaw.

His hold was gentle, but firm. "Face the room. I do not want to miss an inch, and if you keep moving like that, I will."

She wasn't sure if it was his words or his hold that sent the thrills cascading across her skin, and she wasn't sure she cared.

A few more seconds went by before she felt him lift her hair and secure it on top of her head. That's why he hadn't touched her. He must have been untying the small leather tie she'd seen around the lever. He probably used it in his own hair.

Then his fingers began their magic again, kneading gently into her neck before moving across her shoulders.

She let her head fall forward as it was too hard to hold it up, and rested her forehead on the glass.

His hands made their way down her shoulder blades, massaging her muscle, relaxing her as if he wanted her to be open to anything. Well, hell, that thought didn't help. The moisture seeped from her sheath. Good thing he'd already washed there.

She wanted to use the glass to help her stay upright, but it would be a lot cooler than the heat in her body. Still, as he continued his washing to her waist, she kept catching herself sagging and her nipples touched the cold glass, sending spikes of need to her core before she pulled back.

Akasha held her hips and his breath passed by her ear. "Move your pelvis closer to the wall."

She swallowed hard. That would mean her breasts pressed against the cooler surface.

"Unless you want me to stop." He hadn't moved at all, his

hands still resting on each side of her hips as if he planned to plunge inside her.

Taking a deep breath, she moved so most of her body touched the glass. Her nipples pressed into her breasts as she flattened herself. The rush of heat from the cold wall flew through her body like a flying fish through the Caribbean Sea.

"Good." Akasha moved his hands to the middle of her back and washed her ribs and along her spine.

She wanted to arch her ass toward him, basically what she would do with any man in this position, but Akasha was different. For some reason, maybe because he was a monk, it felt as if any overt sexual move on her part would stop his attentions. Yes, it was all in her head, but she didn't want to test her theory right now, not with his hand smoothing its way over her ass.

He kneaded as he washed, his fingers finding every tense spot, relaxing her, until he spread her cheeks and washed between them, his finger moving down her crack and across her anal star.

Instinctually, she arched back.

He stopped.

Oh, shit. She was afraid of that. She caught her breath when his hands latched onto her hips and pushed her against the glass.

Every nerve-ending he'd relaxed came alive with hunger. Yessss.

"You must stay in this position."

Did he sound out of breath? With the water still pouring down behind her, it was hard to be sure.

"Okay." It was the best she could do. He better bring her to orgasm after she was sufficiently cleaned according to his specifications because her turn-on level had reached an all-time high.

He finished with her ass and paused.

Now would be a great time to—

Akasha took that moment to press his entire body against hers, flattening her against the glass, his hard cock pressed upward, partially in her crack.

Her heart raced as her sheath tightened in anticipation while relief that he wanted her gave her hope for satisfaction.

"Toni." Her name on his lips was a whisper of desire.

She slid her hands down, anxious to encourage him, but he grabbed them, moving them back above her as his weight held her in place. "No."

No? No, she couldn't touch or no, he didn't want her? Or no, he did want her and wasn't allowed to? "Um, you need to be more specific. I'm on the verge of coming so either you do it, or I will."

His chest vibrated against her back with his silent chuckle.

What the hell was so funny? She was completely serious.

He let go all at once and stepped away from her. At her release, she turned to find he'd rinsed himself in the water and was stepping out of the shower.

Seriously? That was as clear as mud. She placed her hand on her hip. "Are you going to satisfy me or not?"

Akasha's grin was one she hadn't seen before on him. It was pure seduction. She sucked in her breath as tingles raced across her skin to the juncture of her thighs.

"First, I need to see if you are clean."

She rolled her eyes. "I don't see how I can't be." She stepped into the spray and rinsed off the last of the soap he'd used then shut the water down and stepped out. "Ready for inspection." As she said the words, she couldn't help hoping he would inspect with great detail.

Instead he shook his head. "You need to dry off first."

She gave him a sultry smile. "Why? I'll just get wet all over again." She licked her lips. If he could get her hot as the asphalt in Vegas on a triple digit day, then it was only fair she return the favor.

He lost his smile. "When you are dry, come to the sleeping area." With that, he turned and walked out.

Talk about mixed messages. She shook her head. On one hand, his words excited her, but his look was like cold water on a hot grill.

After drying off, she sauntered to the sleeping area and found him leaning against a wall, arms folded, legs crossed at the ankle, and worse than that, his cock relaxed. "Dry?"

She nodded, now thoroughly confused, not to mentioned frustrated.

"Good." He pushed away from the wall and raised his hand.

Blue light flooded the room. It wasn't bright at all, but what did that have to do with climaxing? He'd said he used blue to see what couldn't be seen with the naked eye. "What are you looking for?" She scanned the walls, searching for the invisible amoeba cleaner, or whatever it was called. It still gave her the willies.

"Turn around."

She did as he requested, searching the wall behind her for the critter, but there was nothing. The blue light went out. She turned back to look at him. "What were you looking for?"

"I was checking to be sure you were clean."

Huh? "Are you serious? Well, hell, you *are* serious. Is this some type of ritual you have to perform before having sex or something?" If it was, she should probably feel honored. He probably only had sex like once a year or something. Poor guy.

Akasha barely kept his lip from twitching. Though he found Toni's lies frustrating yet entertaining, hearing her true thoughts fascinated him far more. The way her mind worked was like an intricate painting. On initial glance, it may seem very simple and straight forward, but beneath were depths he found himself anxious to explore.

Unfortunately, he was anxious to explore the depth of her body as well. Giving in to that meant losing his perspective, and for her sake as well as his own, he couldn't do that.

He chose to ignore her question and instead opened his arm to the bed. "If you would lie down, I can finish checking you."

He didn't miss the dilation of her green eyes. It was like watching the elseire bird open its green wings only to appear purple in flight—very obvious.

She gave him that sexy grin that had him regulating his breathing to keep from reacting to her.

He couldn't let her know how difficult it was for him to not reveal how much he wanted her. He had no doubt she would take advantage of that fact to manipulate him into letting her go, an action that could put them both in danger.

As she lay down, he steeled himself. He had to find out what she'd learned from Grandall, no matter how difficult it might be. "Spread your legs."

"Now you're talking." She grinned broadly.

Kneeling between her knees, he held up his hand and shined the blue light at the juncture of her thighs. "Now, don't move at all."

By the rapid rise of her stomach at his words, he could tell that excited her. Good. He needed her desperate for release. Gently, he used his other hand to spread her folds and reveal the entrance to her very core.

His cock responded despite his control. Ignoring it, he explored her entrance with his finger before examining her folds and finally moving her clit to the side and back then up and down, the moisture around her entrance making it easy to do.

Her whole body was tense, made obvious by the way her strong legs were pressing against his hips.

There was actually no need to be doing any of this. He was free to take his pleasure with any woman at any Pleasure Temple, but her ignorance would be his advantage. His only requirement was that their essence be acceptable. He let his finger glide from Toni's clit down over her entrance and further to press between her cheeks to her anal hole.

When he had completed his route, he removed his hand, settling it on top of his cock to keep it from her view. "You are clean. I can give you pleasure."

"Well, hell, I hope so. You've got me ready to come in seconds."

He raised his brow as if disbelieving her, but he was well aware of how ready she was. He hadn't even touched her breasts, yet her nipples were hard, looking almost as swollen as her folds. "But before I do, I need to know that you are free of all encumbrances. Tell me what you plan to do now that you learned what you wanted to learn from spying on Grandall."

Toni's head snapped up. "Now? You want to talk about that

now?" She squinted at him. "Oh, you're good. Get me all hot and panting then ask me what you want to know." She leveraged herself up on her elbows. "This little stunt will cost you though."

"Cost me? You mean like in rancels?"

She shook her head. "I don't need rancels. That Eden money is worthless in a Pleasure Temple anyway. No, I want to see two more colors from you, and you promise to fuck me at least once a day."

His cock jumped beneath his hand, but he kept his face impassive. Shaking his head, he offered a counter proposal. "I cannot have intercourse with you every day, but I can offer to bring you to your climax once a day and show you one color."

"I don't think so. If you can't have intercourse with me then you have to make me come with your mouth every day, show me three colors and get some ale in here. That ambrosia is nice but it's kid stuff."

He moved off the bed. He could wait days to get the information from her, but he was fairly sure she would prefer he brought her to climax rather than herself. It was a risk, but well worth it. "No. I can offer you two colors, the ale and for me to bring you satisfaction once a day as I choose. I know what I am allowed and not allowed. That is my offer. If you don't want it, you are free to please yourself. Now I need to go out on the patrio to meditate, which is what I am supposed to be doing." He shrugged for good measure, wishing his cock didn't make it obvious how aroused he was.

She stared at him, her brows lowered, her legs now crossed at the ankle.

When she didn't respond, he turned away to walk outside.

"Wait."

He didn't turn back, but he slowed.

"Fine. Two colors, ale and satisfy me once a day. You play hardball, Akasha."

It wasn't his balls that were hard. He grinned. "Good. This afternoon you can tell me what you plan." He stepped toward the archway.

"This afternoon? Oh, no you don't." Toni jumped out of bed planted herself in front of him. "We do this now."

He stared at her, forcing his smile to stay hidden. Finally, he frowned. "I cannot. I have wasted too much of my meditation time as it is. Later." Giving her a curt nod, he strode toward the door.

"Fucking-A." Toni's voice held a mixture of frustration and real anger.

He hoped he hadn't pushed her too far. As he opened the glass door to the patrio, a head puff from his bed hit him in the back of the head. Slowly, he turned and scowled at her before continuing outside.

At least it hadn't been a table. He had no doubt she could and would, if provoked, hurl an entire table at him if she wanted to. That she hadn't gave him hope.

CHAPTER FIVE

Sandale paced the center courtyard of his boyhood home. Learning that he couldn't just walk into the Triad building, render Akasha unconscious and walk out with Toni, had raised his anxiety. He may be able to calm others, but not much worked for himself, at least not that he knew. In his past, he may very well have figured out what to do when agitated, but he was a blank slate now.

Anger and frustration boiled in his gut. He wanted to lash out. Picking up a chair set against the courtyard wall, he raised it.

What are you doing? What will that solve? His own inner voice came to his rescue and he stopped. Slowly, he returned the chair to its resting place.

"I'm glad you didn't throw that. Mom is really partial to that Earth dolphin fountain." A tall man with short dark hair and the beginnings of a beard strode toward him. In his almost black eyes was humor and warmth.

Sandale had to guess that this was one of his many brothers.

The man stopped in front of him. "You don't know who I am, do you?"

"I'm sorry, I do not."

"Mom told me, but I didn't actually believe her until now. Scrat, Sandale, they need to be punished for what they did to you."

He laid a hand on his brother's arm and calmed him. "I'm fine. I asked my own filoz to wipe my brain. It was my choice."

His brother's hands, which had curled in to fists, slowly loosened. "You don't know how many times I have missed that in the last five years—missed you."

He couldn't be sure, but he would guess from what his mom had told him about his brother's personalities that this was Haldone. How interesting that she didn't describe what they looked like except to say they were all handsome boys. "Haldone, I know I must have missed you as well."

Haldone's lips quirked upward. "I wouldn't be too sure of that. Mom always said you were born after me to temper me, otherwise I would never have lived so long."

That he had helped his older brother in some way appealed to him. "Why did you need to be tempered?"

Haldone laughed. "It would be shorter to talk about when I didn't. As a baby, mom said I never stopped moving, and as I grew up that just intensified until I was in trouble with everyone, inside the family and out. Or rather, everyone but you."

Sandale glanced toward Haldone's hip, to the same area his own soft-edged heart birthmark resided. His brother had three dots with two above. Kindred of Air. "What is your ability?"

His brother frowned. The change in his appearance was quick and harsh. Haldone obviously only knew strong emotions. "This is wrong. That you do not know your own family…Sandale, we need to make them suffer as you have."

His brother's loyalty to him, when added to the warm welcome his parents had given him, helped him feel like he was a part of something. That he had a connection to others. "I told you. It is not the men I lived with that are to blame. In fact, they saved my mind. If you want to be angry with anyone, I suggest the lawbreakers who kept me from dying only to force an evil mind into my own. My friends only know of some of the things I did."

He looked away from his brother. "I'm thankful I cannot remember all that I perpetrated while among the lawbreakers. Though the wipe took my past from me, even my family, I am glad of it. I do not want to know what I did. I *do* know that the atrocities I participated in were fracturing my mind."

Haldone grabbed him by the shoulders. "Then we need to find the lawbreakers that put you through such torture and take our revenge."

Sandale placed his hand on his brother's chest, slowing the fast beat of his heart. "It is too dangerous. The lawbreakers live in the jungle and they answer to no one. I would rather focus on reconnecting to my world and my life."

"I understand that, brother."

Sandale removed his hand and stepped away. He was not convinced that was the end of the revenge topic, but at least he had been able to set it aside for a while. Maybe it was time to shift Haldone's attention. "Mother says that you have not begun to look for a chosen one on Earth yet."

Haldone shook his head but his smile returned. "My guess is that mom said something a lot less diplomatic like she has given up on ever seeing any baby boys from me."

He nodded.

"As I suspected." Haldone rolled his shoulders before sitting on the stone edge of the courtyard fountain. "She has three other sons who are well on their way to making babies. I see no reason to think about a chosen one now. I'm too busy for a relationship."

That got his attention. "Too busy?"

"Yes, I am on the team that creates all the windows and rainboxes for the city. We used to have a discoverist with us as we were working on how to make the windows more sturdy, but he was called away to work on a special project of the Ruling Circle."

It took all his will, but Sandale kept his face from showing any emotion at Haldone's remark. "Will your discoverist return?"

"Who knows? Nothing is certain anymore. In my opinion, the city has changed since we had Nassic and Wareson on the Ruling Circle. It is hard to explain. It is not as if we have terrible rulings that cause harm. It is more that no rulings are coming down, as if the Ruling Circle has forgotten what and who they rule." Haldone shook his head. "But I don't get involved in that. If you want to know all there is on that topic, ask our dad, Fripp"

"I will." And the sooner, the better. "What does the rest of your filoz think about you being too busy to search out a chosen one?"

Haldone rolled his shoulders again and didn't meet his eyes. "I don't have to worry about that."

Understanding dawned. "You don't have one."

Haldone rose. "Mom has probably been serving you ambrosia. Would you like an ale?"

He opened his mouth to comment on Haldone's lack of filoz then closed it again. Who was he to comment on such a situation when he was in the same place? Naralinians usually formed their filoz before finishing school. Even going before the Triad for their chips together.

Sandale looked at his brother. Did he have a chip? Was the "trouble" he was in enough to keep him from receiving one? "Thank you. An ale would be good right now."

"My thought exactly." With those words, Haldone strode back into the house.

Sandale resumed his pacing. Did he pace before the wipe? Not knowing who he was would destroy him if he didn't control his anxiety. The pacing felt right, so he would do it. It helped him think and he needed that right now.

He had already started feeling bonds to his three fathers, mother and brother. Though the house brought no memories, he felt comfortable in it. More comfortable than in Loraleaf with Jahl and Khaos. Could that be because the bonds he had with them came from shared experience and the bonds with his family were strengthened by blood?

He paused, staring at an infragile vine that grew up the back wall of the courtyard. It seemed out of place in Naralina, like it should only be in the jungle outside. He'd begun to feel the opposite as if he belonged in the city more than the jungle.

"Look who has returned with good news." Haldone held out a mug of ale, but remained next to Ulik who nodded.

"My friend has invited three of us to go to his son's chip review."

Finally, progress. "I am relieved. When do we leave?" Sandale took a sip and set down his mug, ready to go immediately.

His father raised his hand. "It is not until the day after tomorrow."

He couldn't help it. The frustration over his lack of memory combined with the constant hurdles put in his path to finishing his task had him balling his hands into fists.

"Stass, brother! This is *good* news. I am the one who's supposed to be the first to anger."

Sandale widened his eyes. "I apologize if my reaction was not what you expected." He turned to his father and forced his hands to relax. "Thank you for making this possible. I meant no disrespect."

Ulik laid a hand on his shoulder. "What is it that has you so angry?"

Sandale stepped back. "I think it is everything, but mostly the delay. I want to find out who I was—am, but I have a duty to fulfill first. Toni, the friend of my former chosen one, is in danger and my gut tells me I need to find her sooner rather than later. In addition, I do not feel comfortable learning more about myself, which I need to do to make me whole again, until I rescue Toni."

"I understand." Ulik nodded. "Emotionally, you feel it wrong to pursue your own goals while a greater goal you have been tasked with is yet incomplete."

It was a bit more complicated than that, but it was enough. He nodded.

"I believe that since there is no way we can enter the Triad building without this invitation due to the Crius shields around it, you have no reason to feel guilty about not getting to Toni immediately."

Haldone set his empty mug on the fountain wall. "And unfortunately, I can't pierce that shield. That one was made with Crius technology. I don't think even the Triad members know how it actually works. The good news is, I doubt any harm can come to her from within the Triad building itself. They are all very distant creatures." He made a grimace. "Since it is a Ruling Circle member who is the threat, what if we set up a watch over all who enter and exit until we can gain access?"

Sandale could feel his frustration dissipating with Haldone's idea. "And if a Ruling Circle member were to enter?"

"Then whoever is witness to that immediately sends a messenger, and we can all wait for the member to leave. If he leaves with Toni, we attack."

Ulik scowled. "That would be a great risk."

Sandale looked at his father. "I do not want to put any of my family at risk. If it comes to that, you must let me go alone."

"With your brother, of course." Haldone grinned as if that was a foregone conclusion.

Sandale wanted to deny his brother as well, but a strong desire for Haldone's company held him back. "Of course."

"I will set up the watch immediately." Ulik turned to go then looked back. "Will that put your mind at ease?"

Sandale nodded. "Yes, thank you."

"So, brother. What do you want to know about your life here?" Haldone settled his arm over Sandale's shoulders.

"Everything you can tell me. Start with your ability."

Haldone stepped away and grinned. "That's easy"

A slight brush of air swept by him, but he didn't see anything. "So?"

Haldone crossed his arms over his large chest. "Walk by me."

That was an odd request, but he was happy to oblige. He took a step forward but as he moved his foot to take a second step, he hit an invisible wall. Putting his hands in front of him, he moved them over it. "Is this solid air?"

Haldone nodded. "It is how we create the windows and rainboxes, though for those I must combine my ability with others and the energy rock, eyllen, so that they will last. This box is just temporary. You can still have your ale."

Sandale moved to the fountain and picked up his mug. "How far does it go?"

"I just made that one around you and part of the fountain."

Air brushed by Sandale and he put his hand out again to touch the wall and found it gone. "I can see where that could be of benefit."

"I can also make sharp objects or big bulky ones. All of them invisible to the naked eye." He dropped his arms and shrugged. "That is one of the reasons I was in so much trouble when I was younger."

At the image of a young Haldon throwing invisible balls at other boys, Sandale laughed.

"It is good to hear you laugh." Haldone grinned. "You need to do it more."

"Did I laugh often while growing up?"

Haldone scowled. "These questions are wrong. We need to find the ones who are responsible for you losing your life."

He laid his hand on his brother's shoulder. "If you cannot help me without turning angry, I will have to seek out other family members."

Haldone crossed his arms and sighed. "I cannot help how I feel, but talking to the others may be worse. I will tell you that you laughed a lot more until you joined Khaos and Jahl. I think because they both came from cruel families that you may have felt a need to tone down your happiness."

That was a far more insightful conclusion than he had expected from this brother. It made him all that more interested in getting to know Haldone. "I hope you will continue to share any memories."

"I will. Now my mug is empty. Let us go inside and see who else may be coming to see you. I hope mom told you, you have a big family."

"She did. They started for the inside door when he stopped his brother. "Were you ever awarded a Crius chip?"

Haldone laughed. "Are you sure you don't have any memory? I was the last in the family to receive one, but I finally did."

"I'm glad."

Haldone grimaced. "Not sure everyone else was." He laughed before continuing inside.

Sandale followed Haldone, happy his brother wasn't considered so similar to a lawbreaker that he didn't receive a chip.

Had his going to Loraleaf forced Haldone to learn to control his own actions? He would have to him how he did so because he definitely had a hard time with his own control. He smiled as he stepped through the doorway. Now he had family who he could ask those tough questions.

He had wondered about them and his life with them after Jahl and Khaos told him about theirs. When they said his was perfect, he didn't know what that meant. But if having brothers like Haldone and supportive fathers like Ulik, Baruch and Fripp plus a mother who constantly pulled him in for a hug was perfect then he had to agree with them.

~~*~~

Toni moaned one last time then let her hand flop to the bed. Her entire body relaxed as her breathing slowed. If Akasha wanted to play tough then so could she. Her damned libido had her giving in to him. She wasn't about to let that happen again. Pleasuring herself without a toy was usually a long process, but he'd had her so close, it didn't take long. He did, after all, invite her to do that very thing. Too bad he hadn't watched.

She interlocked her fingers over her stomach and stared at the blank white ceiling. The man lived like a monk, or what she imagined a monk would live like, but he pushed every one of her pleasure buttons. How did he know so much about sex? He must have learned at a Pleasure Temple before he became a Triad member-to-be.

From what she'd seen of his Light Kindred abilities so far, there wasn't a single one that could hold her if she broke away and ran when they walked outside. She'd just have to avoid his strong arms.

Despite her plan to escape as soon as he brought her for a stair run, she wasn't quite ready. Maybe one stair run without trying to get away would lull him into trusting her and give her a chance to enjoy his sexual expertise.

The problem was she now had to tell him the truth about her plan after she'd figured out Grandall's scheme. That would be difficult. She couldn't mention Loraleaf or the people there without endangering them. They hadn't been ridiculously careful about portal openings for this long only to have her spill the beans. She'd just have to choose her words carefully.

Comfortable with that, she swung her legs over the side of the bed and walked naked to the bathing area. After a quick clean-up, she sauntered over to the cabinet where Akasha hid all his goodies. As she walked by the glass door to the patrio, she stopped.

Outside, Akasha stood with his legs spread apart farther than his shoulders, knees slightly bent, his arms straight out to each side and his head back as if he stared at the sky, but even with his back to her, she could see his eyes were closed. Every one of his muscles was tensed as if he did muscle isolations, only all of them at once. She always thought of meditation as a relaxed state, but from his position, it was anything but that.

Shaking her head, she continued to the cabinet. Inside, she found just what she needed, a couple fruits, three biscuits and in the mini-fridge, or what they called the cold box, she found a hunk of tyree, a dairy product like cheese, but with far less salt and always with spices. This one reminded her of oregano.

After setting everything on the single plate Akasha owned, she poured herself a mug of ambrosia and sat on the couch. She always worked up an appetite when she came. Though Akasha's food wasn't as fancy as what they had in the Pleasure Temples, it was definitely high quality.

After arriving at the Pleasure Temple, she'd gone to the markets with a couple of the other women. She picked out a few items to try, but her choices were far inferior to those chosen by the men who stocked the Temple pantry, so she stopped going after the second time. As she bit into a biscuit, she decided Akasha's providers were also good at what they did.

She hoped Grandall wasn't as close to getting his Eden-made portal to work as he sounded. After months of eavesdropping on him, she'd discovered his pattern. It was like deciphering clues. Whenever he had success, he talked about how wonderful something *would* be. When he had a setback, he complained about the limitations of the discoverists' abilities.

What made her nervous was when he talked as if the future had already occurred. That was how she'd figured out he planned to amass money and favors from other cities in return for women. He mentioned his untouchable position on Eden and offered to grant Jasmine's most outrageous wish.

When she requested a trip home, he'd become irritable and cut their session short. Something about going to Earth bothered him. Could that be his Achilles heel? Toni bit into the fruit. Maybe Jahl and Khaos could sneak up on Grandall and portal him to Earth to make him talk.

But that wouldn't reveal his crimes to the city. Toni wanted the bastard to pay. She'd met Erin and her agapaytos, Nassic and Wareson, and it was obvious those men really cared for Naralina. They had been falsely accused by Grandall and sentenced to exile but had escaped to the jungle before their chips could be taken from them.

She wanted the whole city to be witness to Grandall's downfall. She smiled at the thought then took a sip of her drink. When she'd first volunteered to spy for Loraleaf, she hadn't known anything about Grandall except what he'd done to Jahl and how he'd exiled Nassic and Wareson.

Now, having watched him for months, he reminded her too much of one of her foster fathers who looked like the pillar of society in public and then perpetrated horrific acts on his household. That particular "father" had paid, and she wanted Grandall to as well.

Unfortunately, she was too aware of how difficult it would be. The populace of Naralina put the Ruling Circle on a pedestal and had complete faith in them. From what she'd gathered, there was good reason to until a few years ago. Grandall had been on the Circle for decades, so something must have changed.

Taking a bite of the tyree, she chewed it and savored the spice with its reminiscent flavor of pizza. That was her only complaint in Naralina. No one made pizza. Breaking off another piece, she added it to the biscuit and bit into it. Now that was even better. Too bad Akasha didn't have any tomatoes or what was similar to tomatoes.

She turned her head so she could look at him. He was still in the same position. What was he thinking about? Probably how to get her to tell him what she'd learned from Grandall. She had no doubt that would come. He only had one color left to bargain with and he'd already played his sex card.

She almost wanted to stay to see what else he would come up with, but she couldn't. She had to get more specifics to Loraleaf and the only way to do that was to write another note and get back to her balcony so she could leave it there for the elseire bird.

Washing down her snack with the ambrosia, she rose and placed the dish on the counter. She had to admit, Akasha treated her differently than most Edenists. The Eden men always put their women on pedestals, which she had completely enjoyed…at first. She'd never been treated that way. She was so tall and strong that on Earth no one treated her like a delicate flower to be worshipped. Far from it.

But on Eden, they all had. She walked toward the patrio door and admired Akasha. *Except him.* Was it because he caught her spying? Because he was such a good boy? Or did it have to do with a lack of interest. She shook her head. No, he *was* interested. She'd witnessed the physical manifestation of that twice.

As an idea formed, she strode back to the bed area and grabbed her bag. Rummaging through it, she found what she wanted. Quickly, she slipped on the too short boy shorts she made that showed just enough of her ass. Then she pulled out the cropped top she'd sewn together that revealed the underside of her breasts. At her condo in the Temple, she worked-out nude, but here she wanted to entice a certain monk—not to break his vows or whatever he was committed to, but enough to turn him on.

Payback was a bitch. She chuckled as she put the bag back in the corner. She never thought there would come a day when she put on *more* clothes to entice a man, but in this case, it was warranted. She walked back to the patrio door and opened it.

The quiet outside reminded her of exactly how far up Naralina she was now. She closed the door so it wouldn't make a sound, then sauntered past Akasha. She positioned herself so he would see her when he brought his head back to a normal position. Then she began to stretch. First, she spread her legs and bent over, touching the stone with her palms then grabbing her ankles and trying to pull her head between her knees.

She forgot for a moment that she tried to tempt Akasha and enjoyed the stretch to her back and neck. She moved her body to lay her chest along one leg and stretched the back of her hamstring, then moved to the other. By time she rolled up to a straight position again, she felt great.

Pulling her elbows back, she began to twist at the waist, first right then left, taking furtive glances at the hunk behind her, but he hadn't moved. She would have been disappointed, but it felt too good to be moving and exercising. Her enticement plan didn't seem so important anymore. After stretching the back of her arms by lifting them over her head and towards her back, revealing her breasts to the sunshine, she was ready for muscle work.

As a stunt woman, she'd worked out at the gym five days a week, minimum. In addition to that was gymnastics, Tae Kwando and practice stunts. On Eden, where women didn't have to do anything they didn't want to, there were no gyms or fight instructors, so she'd had to make do.

She started with basic squats and push-ups. When she lay down on the patrio, she glanced at Akasha who hadn't moved. Seriously, he was missing some great peeks at her body. Then again, since he'd already washed and inspected every part, he'd seen all there was to see. Lacing her fingers behind her head, elbows out wide, she worked on old-fashioned crunches, twisting every other one to mix it up and work more muscles. Between her movements and the sun, she worked up quite a sweat. It felt awesome.

When she finished those, she jumped up and this time turned to face Akasha. He remained in the same position, but she noticed he also had perspiration beading all over his body. That had to be excruciating to hold the same position for so long. No wonder he was built and so tan. Were all the Triad members-to-be as dark or did they do their meditating inside?

In her opinion, Akasha was smart to do his thing in the open air. The weather on Eden couldn't be beat, or at least in this part of Eden. The Eden way of keeping track of temperature completely eluded her, but she'd guess it ranged between 75°F and 85°F degrees year-round in Naralina.

While the view off his balcony may be breathtaking, gazing at Akasha was more her speed. She held her hands out, even with her shoulders, and made fists. Then she brought them up over her head and back to her starting point before touching her hands together in front of her and back. She did twenty repetitions, but it just wasn't enough resistance.

She needed some kind of weights. In her condo, she'd collected various items to use, but she doubted that Akasha would be happy with her rummaging through his sparse belongings to find the perfect substitutes. Too bad he didn't have any planters on his patrio, or even a mini-statue or two. Anything hard with some pounds to it.

Scanning the barren area, her gaze landed on the cliffside. Well, hell, how stupid could she be? A rock would work, like the one she'd used to hammer at the hinge in the door. She strode toward that area of the patrio and examined the rough wall of the mountain. There had been a couple rocks that were larger than the one she'd taken yesterday.

Toni stepped onto the half-wall and stretched, grabbing a large rock. Even as she lifted it, it challenged her. Perfect. Setting it down on the wall next to her, she studied the steep grade again. If she had a wire, she'd attempt to scale down the mountain, but she wasn't stupid. If performing stunts had taught her anything, it was safety first. It might look dangerous on film, but her stunts were well choreographed when working with a *good* stunt coordinator.

Of course, standing on a wall looking straight down the side of what had to be at least a two thousand-foot drop without netting or a wire, wasn't the safest place to be, but she was careful.

Her balance was good and she knew her body's limitations better than most.

Returning her focus to the cliff side, she spotted another rock that could be the perfect mate to the one she'd already gathered. It was a bit farther away, so she grabbed hold of what appeared to be a sturdy root, protruding from the dirt. Grasping the rubbery hand-hold, she raised onto her tiptoes and reached for the rock. Her fingertips brushed it.

Well, hell. That figured. Leaning out over the edge a bit more, she worked her hand forward on the root and stretched. Her other hand latched onto the rock and lifted. As triumph rushed through her veins, the root beneath her other hand loosened. Fuck!

She braced herself with the rock in hand against the cliff wall as the root slithered from her hand. Fuck, the thing was alive!

If she was still on Earth, she could easily bring herself back to an upright position, but her core had weakened over the months and she hesitated to try. She was stretched out over the chasm, her hands against the loose dirt of the mountain and she needed leverage. Maybe she could move a leg up to brace—

An arm came around her waist and she fell backward. She landed on Akasha's chest, which was only slightly more forgiving than the stone floor of the patrio.

"Woman, is staying with me so terrible that you must risk your life to escape?" Akasha's chest beneath her pounded with his racing heart.

"Of course not!" Her own adrenaline at the scare pounded through her, and she quickly rolled off him onto the stone floor. "I just wanted this rock." She held it up for him to see.

He looked at her as if she'd just told him the sun had blown up. "A rock."

She nodded. Shit, now she looked like an idiot. "I'm not like other women here."

He rolled his eyes and shook his head as he sat up, his abs crunching far harder than hers ever had. "I know."

"No, you don't. I need to keep my muscles strong. It's what I always did on Earth and I need it like, well, like a bird needs to fly." She set the rock down next to her as she sat and faced him. "I also know how to handle myself in dangerous situations. I was fine until that damn root started to move. What the hell was that thing?"

His brows lowered in puzzlement before he looked toward the mountainside. His lip quirked up. "You mean that?" He pointed to a long brown snake with nodules every few inches that resembled the bumps on a root.

"Yes, that. What is it?" She rose to walk toward the edge as the snake burrowed into the side of the mountain again with both ends of its body.

He spoke from right behind her. "That is a fithee. They are grubbers and eat bothersome insects. They sleep during the day. The sun on their mid-section helps them digest the food they ate the night before."

She could feel the heat of his body from standing in the sun. It felt good despite her own sweat. Plus, his clove-like scent was extra strong with his perspiration, so she inhaled gladly, but kept to their topic. "Do they bite? Are they poisonous?" Those were the two most important questions regarding snakes that she was aware of.

"No, they do not. But they are also afraid of us."

She stared at the snake that now looked like any other root on the cliff. "He's pretty cool. I can't believe he held my weight for so long."

Akasha moved away. "They are very strong snakes."

She picked up her first rock from the wall and turned, only to see him striding for the door. "Wait. Don't you have to finish your meditation?"

He didn't even pause. "I'm done. I need to wash and leave." He opened the door and disappeared into his rooms.

Oh, no, he wasn't getting away that fast. They had a deal. She followed after him, walking into the bathing area when she heard the shower running. At first she just enjoyed the sight of water running down all the indentations made by his muscles, but then she remembered why she stalked him. "You promised to show me two more of your colors."

He pulled his face out of the spray. "You are very persistent."

She rested one hand on her hip. "So are you."

He seemed to think about that for a moment then nodded. "Very well, when I am dry, I will show you green." He turned around at that, but not before she saw him smile.

Now what the hell was that about? What would green light do? She watched him for a few more minutes, but he was far too enticing, so she spun away and waited in the living area. Not wanting to sit down and get any of the furniture sweaty, she perused the room a bit more and when she came to the front door, she stared.

The hinge she'd worked so hard to get loose looked as if it was repaired. She stepped closer only to find a new stone peg among the infragile vine. Score one for Akasha. The man was smart and thorough. She could appreciate that. Besides, she'd already rejected that as a way to escape since he was aware of her first attempt.

She wouldn't mind hanging with him for a while if he would just drop the spying questions and let her visit her condo. She found him far more interesting than the men she'd had sex with at the Temple. Then again, being in a Pleasure Temple meant she wasn't looking for a relationship, so there wasn't a lot of getting to know each other.

Akasha came out into the living area, his long hair still damp from his shower, his ripped body dry and yummy. "I will be gone through meal time, but I will bring you back something to eat."

She mentally shrugged off her sudden disappointment. Sparring with the man had become addictive. "Fine. I'll continue my workout and find something in here to occupy my time. But I expect a run at the stairs after you get back, not to mention another color and my pleasure." She winked. He needed to know she wasn't about to forget.

"And I will expect to hear of your plans regarding Grandall." The seriousness of his deep voice made it clear he knew how important their discussion would be. "I also forbid you to stand on the patrio wall and gather rocks unless I am here."

"Now wait a minute. We had a deal."

"Yes, and I can't fulfill my part of it if you lay broken and dead at the bottom of the mountain."

"Fine, you win. No standing on the wall."

"Good. Here is my green light." He raised his hand and green light lit up the opposite wall.

She watched, expecting something to happen, but nothing did. Maybe she just couldn't see what it was. "So what does it do?"

He closed his hand. "It makes green light."

"Of course it does, but what does the green light do? Does it help plants grow or show you what's on the other side of a wall or what?"

He shook his head. "It doesn't do anything. It's just green light."

"What?"

He shrugged. "Ever since my transition I have searched for why I can emit it, but I have found it doesn't affect anything."

She crossed her arms and squinted her eyes. "Then I'm sure as hell glad I bargained for two colors."

Akasha laughed as he strode for the door. "Toni, I would have thought you'd be more happy to have bargained for your pleasure. Guess I was wrong about you."

As she stood there trying to find a wise comeback, he slipped outside and locked the door. "Urgh." Why did she feel as if he was one step ahead of her all the time. Frustrated, she uncrossed her arms and headed back to the patrio. A little exercise should help work off some of her irritation.

Gathering her two rocks, she began her biceps and triceps exercises. The rocks' weight helped her work up a good sweat. She held onto them as she did more squats. After those, she moved to the wall to sit on it, but stopped. She didn't make promises often, but when she did, she kept them.

Going back inside, she picked up a chair and brought it outside. She'd just sat down to start her leg lifts when a shadow flew over her. Looking up, she shaded her eyes with her hand to find the bird that had caused it.

An elseire bird circled above and she stood up, excitement

causing her heart to race. Could it be? Stepping away from the chair, she held out her arm.

"Come on, you have to be Konala's friend."

The bird circled twice more then flew toward her. It took all she had not to jump up and down.

The purple bird landed on her arm, its claws biting into her skin before it caught its balance and folded in its wings, making it appear green. In its beak was a folded piece of paper. She held her other fist before the bird, opened it palm down then turned it upward like Konala had showed her.

The bird dropped the paper in her hand.

Yes! She closed her hand around the paper and despite her growing excitement, slowly lowered it. "Good job, sweetie."

The bird blinked its eyes at her then bobbed its head. She grinned. Letting the paper drop to the patrio, she pet the bird's head, a ritual they went through whenever they got to meet. Many times, it just dropped her note in the planter on the porch. There was no planter on this one. There was nothing but her rocks.

"I can't believe you found me. You are one smart bird, hon."

The bird ignored her, too busy enjoying her strokes. When it pulled its head away, she stopped and waited. It looked around the patrio, then blinked again. She held her arm rigid, prepared for the push off. Within two seconds, the bird opened its wings revealing its stunning purple plumage and flew upwards.

"Thank you!" She waved, too thrilled to care that she was talking to a bird. It might not be able to understand her words, but she had a feeling it was proud of itself as it circled twice again before flying off.

Immediately, she bent and retrieved the message.

Chapter Six

Akasha strode up the hill, his thoughts more scattered than he wanted them to be at the moment. Seeing Toni on the precipice of falling to her death had shaken him. At first he'd ignored her attempts to garner his attention. Though she disturbed his meditations, he remained focused.

When she moved out of his view, he stubbornly remained in his meditation stance, but her noises broke in and sent warning bells through him. When he'd lifted his head to see what she was doing, his heart had stopped beating, even as he ran to her. The second he had her in his arms, he felt a rush of relief and anger.

He'd never had either of those feelings toward a fellow Edenist, probably because he'd never seen one on the verge of plummeting to his death. Feeling fear and anger made sense in one who was honorable.

He liked to think he had a good essence. He wasn't perfect, but if another Kindred of Light had the ability of white light, he hoped to have it shined on himself to see his ratio of gray to white. He'd tried very hard since before he went through his transition to be honorable and just in all his actions.

It made sense that he would fear for Toni's life. No doubt he would be concerned about any man or woman's life. He needed to accept that and calm his racing thoughts. His sexual attraction to Toni was no more or less than any other female in a Pleasure Temple. He just had never spent so much time with one female and by Toni's admission, one as different as she was.

That was why he headed now to attend a Ruling Circle open session—to determine the truth of Toni's stories about Grandall. He had no doubt that she despised the man and believed what she said, but he needed to see for himself if there was a chance what she believed was true.

The Ruling Circle used to have more meetings before they discovered two of their members had planned to steal women from Earth and bring them to the city. Since then, they had few meetings, three a year considered Closed Circle and the rest Open Circle. Today was Open.

It had been years since he'd seen Grandall. He didn't attend festivities or visits from other city leaders. The only reason he'd known who Toni spied on was because he'd been on his way to find release with a woman who had given him her living quarters' number and he had followed Grandall to the third level. As he turned the corner for the room he was bound for, he'd seen Toni opening the peep hole. He stopped, backing up to watch her.

He studied her for a long while from around the corner. By the grimace on her face when she first looked through the hole, he knew she was no voyeur. Her expressions were guileless since she had no idea she was watched. He knew the moment she'd discovered something important. He didn't know if Grandall shared secret city rulings with his cythera, but he couldn't take the risk. Toni's behavior put her in the wrong.

But after more than twenty-two hours with her, he had his doubts, only because of his own visceral reaction to Grandall. He needed to cast aside his emotions and keep his mind open and his judgment at bay until he had evidence one way or another.

He filed in with those most affected by the Council's rulings. The Circle Sessions took place in a building that was part of the Ruling Circle compound at the top of the mountain, but it wasn't protected by a Crius shield like the Triad building. Only the High Hall had shield as well.

While there were two sets of laws the entire planet lived by, Dickinson Law and Cruison Law, each city created its own rules through its governing body. In Naralina, the oligarchy of five different kindreds determined what rules were needed city-wide, the punishment for those who broke the rules or laws, and if any new improvements should be approved for the city.

Everyone stood and clapped as the Ruling Circle entered. Grandall was first, followed by Algeron, Rohert, Yiting, and Maduka. The first three were of equal age to Akasha's father, but the last two were his age, having only ascended to the Ruling Circle after the two corrupt rulers had been exiled.

Grandall raised his hand, smiling as he scanned the crowd, nodding at a few in recognition. When his gaze came to Akasha, his eyes widened before his smile turned benevolent as if he looked upon a child.

Though it rankled, he nodded in return, forcing his mouth in to a small smile. It was no surprise that Grandall recognized him. As Kindred of Mind, Grandall had the ability to sense individual people around him. One of the reasons Akasha was concerned for Toni. Grandall probably knew she was outside his cythera's room unless he was too focused on her and his own release. That was Akasha's hope.

Once Grandall had viewed the large room with benches set up in levels like an amphitheater, he lowered his hand and the clapping ceased. He waited for everyone to be seated then started the proceedings with a welcome, a reading of the list of issues needing decisions, and ending with an invitation for everyone to join the Circle for ambrosia and a light repast.

"Everyone except any sentenced to exile or punishment, of course." Though Grandall chuckled, no one else did.

Akasha watched the crowd as the Circle went through a number of suggested changes for the city. Rohert led the discussion on many of those, though Algeron took the lead on the request for a new public bath. The two men could have passed for brothers. The easiest way to tell them apart was Algeron had a substantial graying beard.

The people in the room were engaged in the discussion, often standing to be recognized and to speak on the proposed change. Or rather those with the most interest in the particular topic. He spotted one older man napping in the back row, his head having fallen forward on his chest. Akasha was about as interested as the old man since none of the changes would affect the Triad.

When the changes to Naralina were approved or disapproved, Yiting stood, the soft-edged birthmark on his collarbone declaring him Kindred of Heart. He was a thin man with large eyes and short blond hair. "It has come to our attention that in the near future, we may have women who may wish to attend the Open Circle sessions."

A murmur ran through the crowd. It hadn't occurred to Akasha that women weren't there since the Triad had no women, except the one he had hidden in his rooms.

Yiting continued. "We have decided to create a rule governing the attendance of women to these sessions. It is our recommendation that women be allowed to attend providing they are accompanied by at least one agapayto and their pheromones are suppressed for the duration of the official session."

Immediately, three men stood and Yiting glanced back at Grandall, who gave the slightest nod.

Now this was very interesting. Akasha focused on the Circle as well as the crowd. It was obvious that Yiting was no more than Grandall's servant. Toni may be right. Grandall may be the only one leading Naralina. Yet he'd shown no interest in the improvement discussions.

Two men argued about the pheromones being suppressed while the third one argued that a woman shouldn't be allowed to attend at all. A fourth man stood during the discussion and stated he felt it was a personal decision best left to the filoz.

Akasha found himself wanting to ask about the women of the Pleasure Temples, but refrained. It was not his place. He was a Triad member-to-be. Still, he hoped someone would bring it up because Toni would have if he had brought her with him.

He'd never thought about whether a woman could attend the Open Circle sessions. There were definitely women at the Triad panels. Many mothers came to see if their sons would be given a chip. It was a pivotal moment of adulthood. For him that had come very early since he had learned how to use his abilities quickly after his transition at the age of fourteen.

Yiting called on the seventeenth man to weigh in on the subject. It was Naralinian Rules that dictated everyone who wanted to speak be allowed to. "Why are you considering this now? What has changed that we are even discussing this? Are we expecting a sudden influx of women or something?"

The people near him chuckled, but Akasha watched Yiting's eyes widen before he caught himself. "It has been brought to our attention and so we must address it."

The man wasn't so easily appeased. "Who brought this to your attention? I know I certainly would not have. The last thing my agapayto wants to do is sit in these chambers and listen to a bunch of men talk about city issues."

Another man spoke to those around him. "No, his beloved would rather study us for her art."

As quiet chuckles moved through the crowd, Grandall motioned Yiting to sit and stood himself. "We have been approached by a number of filoz whose women are interested in these sessions. Since that is their desire, it would be neglectful of us to ignore that. Don't you agree?"

Akasha watched as every man nodded in agreement. Since women were the most precious part of most Edenists life, whether in Naralina or another city, Grandall had used that reasoning to quiet the audience, but Akasha was absolutely sure that the man lied. The problem was, he couldn't be sure without using his purple light, which Grandall would never allow.

Despite what Toni might think about his ability to read her, he was not adept at truth-reading like some Mind Kindred were. He paused in his thoughts. Wasn't that what Nassic had been, a truth-reader? But he'd been exiled. Coincidence?

When it came to reading Toni, he had simply seen more than she realized, so it was easy to sense when she began to tell a lie. There was a looseness about her and a certain tone in her voice that made him want to smile in anticipation of what untruth might come next even before she spoke.

After Grandall's explanation, no one else spoke and he thanked them for their input. "Now we must turn to a troubling situation. It concerns one of our discoverists. Unfortunately, he is currently being seen by a healer. However, since our next session is not for another eleven days, we must decide his fate today."

Akasha tensed. What he knew about Naralinian Rules had been taught to him at school. In fact, the last Open Circle he'd attended was over ten years earlier while in school, but he did know that a man was required to be at his own judgment ruling. He also believed that was the right thing to do despite a wait of eleven days.

Another man immediately stood. "Are you saying Keeva will not be at his own ruling?"

Akasha studied the older man. He was probably over forty and looked familiar. How could that be? He didn't go many places outside the temple, so where did he know him from?

"I am sorry, Eldus, but your son was caught trying to escape through a portal this morning. We had to bring him to a healer immediately to have his chip removed and the other man who helped him is now being held for judgment at the next session."

Even as the two men argued back and forth, with Grandall showing sorrow over the situation, Akasha had the distinct feeling that the "escape" was made up and Grandall wanted the discoverist out of his city as soon as possible.

Despite Eldus' objections as well as those of the other two fathers, the discoverist was sentenced to exile which brought the session to a close.

Grandall joyfully reiterated his invitation to the Circle's repast then led the way out of the room.

The crowd split, those interested in food and those disheartened by the outcome of the judgement. Murmurings caught Akasha's attention as he made his way out.

"There is no fair judgement anymore. As soon as a man is found at fault for anything, he's exiled. What happened to reparation and retraining?" The man in his prime with a heavy dark beard shook his head.

"What are we going to tell his mother?" Eldus looked to another man. "We only have two sons and her other one lives in the Triad building. This will kill her."

Akasha stopped. Now he remembered where he'd seen Eldus before. That man had come to the Triad building when his son had been formally accepted as a member-to-be. Triad residents didn't associate with their families very often. It was all part of their training.

He tried to imagine Eldus' wife's reaction when she learned Keeva was exiled. A strange sympathy filled him, one he could only attribute to his sincere doubt as to the discoverist's guilt. For the second time since meeting Toni, he questioned his lack of knowledge regarding how Naralina was run.

He needed to remember that his only focus was on the morality of individual men and whether they deserved a Crius chip. Should morality only be judged in a vacuum? The shocking question had him halting.

Eldus and his filoz exited the room, making their way down

the cavernous hall. Akasha couldn't stop watching them, his mind going in directions he had never gone. When the three men finally exited the building, he shook his head. Better to save such complicated ideas for his meditation.

He continued toward the door where everyone else had already entered. Inside, he found a large assortment of food of which he had little interest. It appeared the others who had been invited were not attracted there for the meal either, but rather by the Ruling Circle members themselves.

Each Circle member had taken a plate of food and moved to a large round table of his own. There men gathered, some sitting and others standing. There were a few who gathered in small groups to talk, but most flocked to the five tables.

Akasha studied the body language. Yiting, who had appeared unsure in the session, now presided over his table as if he were sole ruler. A quick scan of the other ruling members showed a little less arrogance except where the largest number of men gathered. Though he appeared benevolent, Grandall's self-value was obvious to someone who took time to notice.

When had the Ruling Circle become the one to be served as opposed to the servant? Or had it always been so and what he remembered as a child was simply the teachings of his studies? He'd come to determine if Toni's feelings toward Grandall were justified and instead had only more questions.

Not willing to join Grandall's large group, he moved to the five-sided table where the repast was set. After a quick scan of the offerings, he was surprised to see honey, a labor-intensive delicacy. So as not to appear too interested in the Ruling Circle members, he poured himself a glass of ambrosia.

"Akasha." At the sound of his name, he turned to find Grandall approaching him. Beyond the ruler, he could see the men at the table frowning.

"Grandall." He nodded.

"Come, walk with me." Grandall indicated the large patrio outside the open archways in the room.

"Of course."

Grandall took slow, stately steps as if each was important. It reminded Akasha of the Triad members.

"Did you enjoy the session?"

The question surprised him. "I found it educational."

Grandall stopped and faced him. "You have not been to an Open Circle session in a very long time. Why did you come?"

Akasha smiled. "Curiosity." He always told the truth, but that didn't mean he told all there was to tell.

"Curiosity about what?"

He looked out at the view before answering. "I was curious as to how decisions were made. As you say, it has been a long time. I wished to see how it all works again so I can meditate upon it."

"Ah yes. I imagine you need more fodder for your thoughts than simply the walls of the Triad building. You are next in line to ascend to the panel, are you not?"

Akasha nodded.

"There is a good chance you will take your place there. Two of those members should be stepping down soon, correct?"

Again he nodded, curious about why Grandall was discussing the obvious.

"It would be good to have youth on the Triad panel again.

I think you could bring them a better perspective and more understanding."

"Moral worth is not about perspective, but about right and wrong." He didn't like the implication that goodness could be twisted.

Grandall chuckled. "I see you have learned your lessons well. Just keep in mind that what may be right in one situation could be wrong in another."

"But what is right will always be right." Now he definitely understood what Toni meant. There were layers under Grandall that were not as pure as he wanted others to think.

"I see you still have more to learn." Grandall patted him on the shoulder. "I requested your company out here, away from the others because I need to ask you if you know where the cythera Toni is."

Every atom of his being went on alert. "Toni? Why would I know where she is?"

Grandall raised one eyebrow. "You were seen leaving the Pleasure Temple with her."

Now Grandall had spies? "We left at the same time, so we walked together."

"I understand she had a bag as if she were changing domiciles."

Whoever had been watching had seen a lot. "Why? She did not return?"

"No, she has not, and I wish to speak with her."

"Why?" He doubted the man would tell him the truth.

Grandall blinked as if surprised by the question. "She left without letting anyone know where she moved to."

Akasha frowned. "I do not understand. She is a cythera. Why

would you be concerned about her whereabouts? Cythera are simply for release."

"You really believe that?"

"I do." *Or I think I do.* Toni had him thinking things he'd never thought before.

Grandall shook his head. "Sometimes I think the Triad goes too far. Women are the most important part of this city. They are the nurtures, the lovers and the ones that keep us in existence. They are as precious as the very air we breathe." Grandall had a gleam in his eye that did not reflect his words.

"And this is why you need to know where a cythera went?" Akasha drew his brows together in confusion.

"What?" Grandall started as if caught in a lie. "Oh, no. Um, it was Jasmine, the cythera I see at that Pleasure Temple who was worried. This Toni is her friend."

The man admitted so much in that short sentence that Akasha's stomach tightened in concern. Grandall knew Toni heard something and he was on a quest to find her. "I would suggest your cythera check the Hall of Records. If Toni moved to a filoz, they will have recorded it."

"Excellent point." Grandall turned. "Now I must get back to my other guests. Will you be staying for the entertainment? I have brought in some very talented musicians."

He shook his head. "No, I must return to the Triad building. It is almost time for our evening meditation and meal."

"Of course. It was good to see you again, Akasha. I look forward to hearing you have ascended to the Triad panel."

Grandall said the last as he strode away, his interest in how Akasha could help him at an end.

But Grandall had helped *him* in many ways. Despite not having used his light ability, he now knew that not only did Grandall know Toni had listened, but he wanted to find her. Unsettled in a way he'd never been before thanks to that knowledge, Akasha strode to the outside steps and descended.

He also learned that Toni was correct in her assessment of Grandall. There was no doubt. If Grandall found Toni and even suspected she knew something, Toni would disappear for good.

That single thought sent his blood racing and protective instincts he never knew he had, rose up to flood him with energy. He fisted his hands as he strode down the hill. No one was touching Toni…except him.

~~*~~

Toni laid out all the clothing she'd brought with her. "Now what will entice Akasha the most?" She was ready to be pleasured when the man returned. Now that she knew their hours were numbered, she wanted to get the most out of it.

She had it all planned. First, he must show her the other color he promised her. After that he could fulfill his obligation to make her orgasm. Then she'd be ready to leave with Sandale.

She couldn't believe how excited she was to see him again. The note from her bird said he was on his way to get her. She'd learned through past communications that Sandale had survived with the lawbreakers and was back at Loraleaf, but she hadn't seen him since she, Serena, Jahl and Khaos had left him bleeding from a bullet wound in the middle of the jungle.

It had to be hard for him to adjust to Serena, Jahl and Khaos being bonded. He had expected to bond with Serena, too. Now he was odd man out. He may be in need of some sexual release as well, and she was more than happy to oblige. He might even get her to stop obsessing about Akasha, something she found herself doing. She didn't like that at all.

She shook her head at the clothing on the bed. She couldn't decide what to wear for Akasha, her man for a night of pleasure. Maybe if she pulled off the items that were less sexy that would help. One by one she folded clothing and returned it to her bag.

Much better. She had two outfits left. Either the sheer harem-like outfit she'd made from material she'd told one of the Temple suppliers was for a table cover, or a brown leather halter with its very short matching skirt. She made that outfit from Feroon hide that Konala had brought her when she lived in Loraleaf. She liked that ensemble the best because it made her feel sexy and strong in a warrior princess kind of way. She wore it a lot.

She put a hand on her hip. *Eeny, meanie, miniey, oh hell.* She stuffed the leather outfit into her bag and picked up the harem set. Finding something not see-through but not heavy was difficult in Naralina. To find a table cover, as they called table cloths, made of the opaque siris webbing had been pure luck.

Naked was the order of the day on the planet, or so she'd been told, and so she'd witnessed at Haven, Loraleaf and Naralina. She didn't mind that at all since all Edenists were built like Olympic athletes and they did everything nude. Nope, she didn't mind the eye-candy in the least. The only clothing she'd seen, which was mostly wraps, was worn by older women and shy ladies.

Having already taken another shower, she quickly donned the harem pants. Buttons were non-existent in the city since pins were big, so she used ties through three holes beneath her belly button to keep the pants on. She loosened them enough to let the pants fall to her hips. Not that it mattered. There was a slit for easy access from her mons to her ass.

Next she carefully shrugged into the sleeveless vest. Sleeves had been too far beyond her sewing skill level. She pulled the vest over her chest and tied it so her entire cleavage showed, revealing the inner sides of her breasts.

Lastly, she bent over and tied the loose material at her ankles, which left two full-length slits on either side of her legs. "Fit for a harem." She scanned the room for a mirror, but finding none, searched the entire apartment. "That figures."

Akasha probably hadn't looked at himself in years, unless he used that reflecting pool she'd seen when they first arrived. She chuckled as she imagined a bunch of monks staring into the pool as if in meditation but actually checking out their reflections. If they were all as hot as Akasha, she wouldn't mind taking a peek.

That gave her an idea. It was growing dark outside, so she turned on the shiner mounted on a wall in the living area. It still amazed her that the entire planet had all the energy it would ever need simply by digging beneath the surface, chipping off a piece of energy rock and controlling the output. The eyllen mineral never lost its glow no matter how long it was used.

Once she had the room lit, she turned toward the glass patrio door. Critically, she studied herself in the reflection. She was definitely hot, but the ponytail at the base of her neck didn't work. Pulling the tie out, she flipped her hair over and tied it on top of her head.

Standing back up, she gazed at herself. "Perfect." She did a quick practice kick, happy to see the skin exposed between her legs. "Okay Akasha, let's see you talk your way out of this."

She hoped he brought the ale with him. Naralina had wine as well, but she was more an ale kind of girl. Mulled wine was good for special occasions. If he returned at the same time as yesterday, then he should be home soon. She should lay on the couch in a seductive pose, but she couldn't resist the chance to see the city at night from so high up.

Opening the glass door, she meandered out onto the patrio, but the light from inside infringed on her view. She quickly turned the shiner off and returned to the outdoors.

This high up, she could see at least half the mountain was covered in golden lights that reflected off the gold spires, domes and trim of the homes and public buildings all the way up. Akasha's rooms were on the east side, so she could see night on the horizon while there was a faint pink hue still coming from directly above. She loved city lights at night. She'd always been a city girl. Her apartment, when she lived in Las Vegas with Serena, had offered a view of the strip. Though she couldn't afford one too close, she could see many of the casinos.

Loraleaf and Haven were settlements in no man's land. They were to the west, but were completely hidden from Naralina—Loraleaf's tree settlement due to Theron's reflection abilities, and Haven behind its tall teal walls. She turned back toward the east, a view she didn't have at her condo.

Selene had not risen yet. If she remembered correctly, that moon should be about half full now. She'd never forget the first time she saw Eden's second moon, Bendis, the pink one in all its glory. She'd never forget because that was the night she completely embraced Eden as her home.

Any woman in a filoz or Pleasure Temple could visit Earth, but Toni had no reason to, except for birth control, and Jasmine supplied her with all she needed when she visited home.

As a cythera, Toni was honored and she had her choice as to who she took to her bed. The Pleasure Temples were set up the opposite of a bordello back in Nevada. Here the men interested in finding pleasure came to the Temple and relaxed in the public rooms. The cythera were able to view them from a balcony and when one took their fancy, they sent a note to him with their room number.

There were a few who only focused on teaching the younger Edenists how to pleasure a woman, and she was forever grateful to them. Eden men definitely paid attention to instruction because they knew their way around a woman's body.

In the Temple, she only had one limitation. She wasn't allowed to have sex with two or more men at a time as that could cause a bond, and she definitely didn't want that. Not that some of the other cythera hadn't bonded and left with a filoz, but that was after establishing a relationship with men from the same filoz over different nights.

Back home, if she had a couple one night stands with more than one man on set, she'd be labeled a slut. On Eden, every woman had to take at least two men as their husbands, so a word that meant slut didn't even exist. She was thankful almost every day that she'd been brought to Eden with Serena. The men practically worshipped women here…except Akasha.

She walked toward the other end of the patrio. From this

point, she could see one of the markets or what she thought of as bazaars. The square that was so busy during the day was completely dark. She grinned. That's because Edenists prized their—

"Toni?" She turned at Akasha's voice inside the apartment. Her heartbeat sped up whether she wanted it to or not. Well, hell, she was acting like a girlfriend who hadn't seen her man in a week. Pathetic.

"Toni!" Akasha's voice sounded panicked.

Oh, shit, the lights were off. He probably thought she'd escaped. She ran toward the open door just as he stepped through.

He grasped her by her arms as they collided.

She laughed. "You found me."

As he steadied her, his gaze swept over her. "Are you well?"

"I'm fine. I'm not fragile like the sherry flower."

"Why is it dark?" His brows knit. "We're you hiding? Did someone come in search of you?"

"No, I was…" She trailed off, suddenly aware of the intensity of his hold. "I was just appreciating the view. What's wrong? Something's wrong."

He stared at her but she couldn't really see his eyes in the dark. Without warning, he pulled her against him and his mouth captured hers.

His tongue thrust into her mouth as if he had been starving for a taste of her. A wave of excitement hit hard and she grasped his broad shoulders to keep her suddenly weakening legs from dropping her.

After the initial shock of desire, she pulled her wits about her and explored his mouth with her tongue. She'd just registered the spicy aftertaste of ambrosia and the hard cock digging into her belly when he broke off the kiss.

He pushed her back to arms-length and dropped his hands.

Had she repulsed him? Was he repulsed with himself? Oh shit, did he break some cardinal rule about kissing?

Though she couldn't see his expression that well, she could hear his rapid breaths. He jerked his head to the side to get his hair back over his shoulder.

She let her instinct lead her as a new awareness formed near her heart. Putting a hand on his chest, she looked in to his eyes. "I'm okay. No one came here. If they had, I would have kicked some balls all the way to Earth." She gave him a smirk, hoping he'd understand that she could take care of herself.

His other hand captured hers against his chest for a moment then he gently took hers and pulled it down, letting her go completely. "I have brought you a meal."

Oh, no, he wasn't getting away that easily. She stepped closer and wrapped her arms around his neck, letting her body get close to his without actually pressing against him. "My hunger has shifted more in the direction of one hunky Triad member-to-be."

He held himself back, but she could tell it wasn't easy. Half the fun of sex was the tease, so she didn't move any closer.

Before she could blink, he'd bent his knees, swept one arm under her legs and lifted her in to his arms, no small task with a woman of her size. A new rush of excitement at his strength spread to every corner of her being. Holding on, she kept quiet as he stepped into the dark living area and strode to his bed.

She thought he would drop her on it, but he didn't. Instead, a green glow filled the room. Now that was cool. Her monkish man set the mood. They needed no other light.

Akasha lowered her legs, letting them slide down against his body. His free arm pulled her ass tight to him. "I believe I owe you release."

Did he ever! "Yes, you do, but I believe you promised to show me another color light besides this green one."

His lips quirked up into the most devilish smile she'd ever seen and her breath caught at the desire in his eyes. Suddenly, the phrase a "wolf in sheep's clothing" came to mind.

Akasha removed his hand from her back, though the other remained splayed over her ass. "My pleasure."

Something in his tone warned her his light wouldn't be what she expected just before she became mesmerized by a purple swirl.

CHAPTER SEVEN

Akasha watched as Toni's bright green eyes glazed over. His purple light hypnotized which allowed him to make people do what he wished…within reason. His own moral compass refused to ask anyone to do something they wouldn't willingly do. *Though with Grandall I might make an exception.*

Holy Bendis! Where did that idea come from? Shaking off the disturbing thought, he focused on Toni. When he'd walked in and thought she'd been taken, his heart had lodged in his throat. The feeling, so foreign to him, had taken his breath and reasoning away.

No one could enter the Triad building without a Triad member-to-be, but he didn't doubt that Grandall could talk his way in easily. The urge to storm into Grandall's home to rip the place apart until he found her had overwhelmed him.

The strange sensations were the only excuse he could find for why he'd kissed her. The sudden relief of finding her there, safe, where he wanted her to be had wiped away the last of his reasoning. Triad members-to-be *did not* kiss women, not even in the Pleasure Temples. It was far too intimate an act on a personal level. Sex was sex for him and nothing more than release.

He stepped back to finally look at the material he felt between Toni and himself. Though she stood with no animation, her breathing parted the tiny opaque vest she wore exposing more of her breasts. The tease at what lay beneath was not lost on him.

His gaze roved over her bare rippled abdominals to the top of her leg coverings. A tie there told him that a quick pull would send the sheer material to the floor. If the idea was to tease him in to getting harder, she'd succeeded. He wanted to sink between her thighs and lose himself inside her, but his new fear was that he might very well do that.

He needed to find release before he pleasured her or he might give in to his new weakness. Anticipation flew down his back and tightened his balls. He grinned as he lifted a head puff from the bed and dropped it at his feet. "Toni, kneel on the head puff."

Obediently, she did.

He swallowed hard. Just having her in that position made his cock jump. He stepped closer and with his free hand brushed his tip across her lips. Her mouth opened slightly as if she couldn't wait.

If he thought for a moment she wouldn't want to pleasure him, he'd stop, but he had no doubts. And as opposed to bemoaning that she missed the experience, he would allow her to remember everything when he released her.

Comfortable with his decision and anxious for release, he ran his cock between her breasts, the feel of the heavy globes against him sending spikes of need shooting through his groin. Unable to resist, he burrowed beneath the vest with his hand and rubbed his thumb across her large nipple.

Her unrestrained moan had his cock jerking again. If he continued, he'd be done before he ever felt the warmth of her mouth. He removed his hand from her silky breast and wrapped his fingers at the base of his cock, waiting for the urge to lessen. It didn't help much, but it helped his focus.

He set his tip against her lips, once again. "Toni, pleasure me with your mouth until I find my release."

She didn't open her mouth as he expected. Instead, she licked at his tip, swirling her tongue around the ridge.

He forced himself not to pull away, though the agony of not shooting his seed into her mouth right then was almost more than he could bear. If only he'd found release before catching Toni, he might have more control.

Her magic tongue glided down the underside of him and every muscle in his ass tightened as excitement raced through him, leaving a drop at the end of his cock.

Ever attentive, Toni's tongue glided up his shaft and licked off his tell-tale readiness.

He *would* stay in control.

Toni wrapped one hand around the base of his cock, then opened her mouth and guided him inside.

By the Crius, it felt too good. He wrapped his hand around her highly piled hair and held her in place as he took a deep breath, his balls already tight and ready for his climax.

She locked her mouth around him and moaned, the sound vibrating up and down his cock. It was more than he could take. He loosened his hold slightly, giving her free reign.

Toni took it without hesitation. She pulled him in and pushed him out of her mouth, finding the rhythm that pleased him most without a word from him. Then again, his hand tangled in her hair may have given her clues.

She kept her mouth loose, letting his tip glide far back into her throat, tightening on it as he inadvertently tried to go farther, which sent his need spiking through him. He could feel his balls readying. She grasped his ass with her free hand, pulled him deep into her mouth and sucked hard.

He exploded, his seed squirting down her throat as she held him to her. His head fell back and a moan from the depth of his groin forced its way past his lips. He let his free hand drop to his side, the purple light extinguishing.

Toni started to pull back. He held her for a moment, the friction too much for his sensitized cock. He took deep breaths to slow his racing heart before finally releasing her.

He wasn't sure what he'd expected her reaction to being hypnotized would be, but her licking him off as she did, was not part of it. He gazed down at her. Her hard nipples pushed against the silky fabric she wore and he would guess she was as ready for release as he had been. At least now he had control of himself.

Toni stopped licking and looked up at him with a sly smile. "Neat trick. So that's what your purple light does. If your last color is even half as interesting, I may be willing to bargain again."

He chuckled, once more amazed at how different she was from what he kept expecting. Similar to when he caught her spying only to discover she wasn't the one in the wrong...or, at least he didn't believe so. Not after talking to Grandall.

Pushing the man from his thoughts, he held out his hand to help Toni rise. "But do you have anything to bargain with?"

Her sly smile said far more than words.

Now he wanted to find out what that meant as well as everything else about this woman of layers.

Toni placed her hand in his, but she rose with no help, another reminder of her bodily strength as well as mental strength. "It's a good thing you hypnotized me or I would have left you hanging like you did to me this morning."

He looked away, uncomfortable with her censure. Was it because she was right and he was in the wrong? The feeling did not sit well with him. He wanted to apologize, but his gut said it had been necessary.

"I'll give you fair warning. You leave me hanging like that on purpose again, and I will kick you in the balls like I originally intended when we first met. Do you understand?" She stood with one hand on her hip, a clear indication she meant every word.

While he doubted she could move faster than himself, he guessed that she wouldn't think twice about catching him when he least expected it…like in bed. He nodded. He doubted withholding release would work a second time anyway. "Speaking of your release, I believe I owe you one." He opened his arm toward the bed.

She grinned. "Yes, you do. But I took care of myself this morning and after that blow job, I'm ready to eat."

He blinked in surprise. Would he ever understand her? *More importantly, why do I want to?*

~~*~~

Sandale paced the confines of his parents' courtyard for the second night in a row. From all his interactions with his family, he'd discovered he had been a patient man.

He wasn't anymore.

He'd spent the day reuniting with the rest of his brothers and meeting their filoz. Those men knew more about him than he did. It wasn't hard to see that all of them were hurt by his lack of memory. One by one they'd found an excuse to leave, all except Haldone.

He didn't blame his brothers. They wanted him to be what he used to be. The problem was, he didn't know what that was.

His mom's expansive love and acceptance were made even clearer in comparison. Though he recognized the flash of pain in her eyes when he didn't remember something she cherished about their relationship, she quickly hid it, happy to explain the history of the event.

His three fathers were equally different in their reactions. Baruch was the most expressive, showing his hurt openly but rebounding when he could happily retell a past story with a few added embellishments that Ulik often corrected. Ulik took the memory loss in stride, just happy to have him back home and focused on helping to retrieve Toni.

Fripp couldn't seem to focus on any one thing for long. His mother said that was why she fell in love with him. He was so scattered, he needed her just to keep him on track. Sandale smiled as he remembered his last conversation with Fripp. He didn't even remember that Sandale had his memory wiped. In a way, that made him feel more at ease with Fripp.

This is where he needed to be if he was ever going to have a life again. Loraleaf may have been his home, but his connection to the men there was gone now. He no longer remembered the past pain he'd shared with them or even the pride they held in having created a thriving settlement.

Once he found Toni and returned her to Loraleaf, he would

return here, to his parents' home. Here he could rediscover who he had been and recapture what he could. That plan, added to his anxiousness about Toni's safety, had him wearing a path in the stone of his mother's courtyard.

At the sound of the courtyard door opening, he paused. Haldone ducked under a hanging plant and strode toward him.

He had learned over the last two days that Haldone was always doing something. He never slowed down and right now that behavior made Sandale pleased to have his company. His brother, at least, understood his impatience.

"I told Vectar we would take the next watch. You look like you need to do something."

"Yes, I do. Thank you." He smiled in relief. "Has anyone seen anything important?"

Haldone shook his head. "No, but the last thing we need is for Grandall to get into the Triad building the night before we reclaim your Toni."

Sandale frowned. "She's not *my* Toni. She is Serena's Toni, I think." Haldone's assumption did beg the question of where Toni belonged. At least getting her out of Naralina would keep her safe until Loraleaf's and Haven's leadership decided how to stop Grandall.

Haldone shrugged. "Since I don't know this Serena, Toni is yours in my head. Come. Vectar is anxious to get home to his filoz. They plan to make their initial contact with their beloved on Earth tonight."

"I am happy to help my brother in his quest for love."

Haldone raised an eyebrow at him before turning and leading the way out of the house. They strode up the street in perfect unison, an oddity that Sandale enjoyed. Something about that fact made him feel as if he belonged, even if only fleetingly.

"Do you remember what love is?" Haldone's question caught him off guard.

"I know what it is intellectually, but I can't tell you I remember loving Serena. Why do you ask?"

Haldone shrugged. "Just curious."

He laid a hand on his brother's shoulder and halted them. "No, you're not. There is something more to your question."

"Logar's ass, it figures you remember how to read me, the one thing I had hoped you wouldn't remember."

"Remember? No, it is not a memory. I think I am just in tune with you."

Haldone smiled sheepishly. "Then I guess that is a good thing, right?"

He smiled and nodded. "I think so. So why did you ask about love?"

Haldone started walking again, and he joined him. "I guess because I am not part of a filoz, I haven't had any experience with women beyond the Pleasure Temples. None of them interest me for more than pleasure. Yet I see mom and our fathers still in love after so many years."

He had noticed that too. "I am told when Jahl, Khaos and I went to Earth to search out a chosen one, Khaos fell in love instantly. Jahl and I were willing to consider Serena for his sake. I must have eventually loved her since I almost died saving her." He frowned, that strong an emotion was still hard to comprehend with his connections to other Edenists so new.

Haldone appeared to ponder that and they walked in

companionable silence, up the stone pathway toward the Triad building. They would actually watch from the balcony of Ulik's friend's home. Yet another person who would be disappointed that he was not the man they remembered. Sandale sighed heavily.

"I heard that." Haldone glanced at him.

"Just not looking forward to disappointing more people who knew me BW." He'd shared his acronym for the wiping of his memory with Haldone. His older brother was the only one he felt comfortable enough with to share that.

"Not to worry." Haldone grinned. "I'll just create a see-through ladder and we can climb onto the balcony without anyone the wiser."

The relief he felt in his chest made him aware of how tiring it was to meet people again. He would have to build some mental stamina because if he stayed in Naralina, it would keep happening, of that he had no doubt.

Haldone stopped and pointed to a walled set of stairs that ascended at least three levels. Every step was clearly illuminated in the bright white light of Selene as she peeked over the top of the mountain. "Those are the stairs to the Triad building. It is the second highest complex in Naralina."

He glanced upward. Somewhere in that large white building at the top was Toni. He didn't remember her, but Serena had shown him a photograph of her friend on her phone, which she charged when she went to Earth for a visit. Unfortunately, he didn't have Ulik's memory ability. All he remembered was the woman was tall next to Serena and had her hair tied in the back.

"This path leads to another downward route and this last path leads only to the Ruling Circle complex." Haldone pointed each area out.

"And where is father's friend's house?" He only saw one building that would actually have a view of all four paths.

Haldone spun and pointed. "Right here."

It was the building Sandale culled out as the best. It was perfect. He looked up the side and frowned. "I don't see a balcony."

"Oh, you will. Dad's friend is a Light Kindred and he has created a reflection of the surrounding walls of the house, so you cannot tell there is a balcony. Come here and I will show you."

Haldone moved his hand for a few moments then stopped. "Now follow me. You will have to feel your way up."

As his brother ascended an invisible ladder, Sandale followed directly behind. At the top, it appeared that they walked through a stone wall, but in fact, there was a small balcony just big enough for three. He would guess his father's friend had a filoz of two and a beloved female.

Three chairs were set on the balcony and he and his brother sat.

Haldone twisted his hand in the air. "Our ladder is now nothing but air." He lowered his voice. "I forgot, this reflection is not soundproof, so we need to be quiet."

Sandale nodded to show he understood. On Loraleaf, Theron had worked with another Edenist to create a reflective shield powered by eyllen that not only hid the entire settlement in the trees, but also kept any sound from being heard. Plus, it was strong enough to protect all within.

As he learned about each person's unique abilities, it made him want to master his own better. Not only did he not have the control of range he used to, but he also had to use his hand and touch a person to affect them. He'd been told that he could, with much effort, cause an entire settlement to be rendered unconscious or just asleep.

Over the last months, he'd focused more on learning about his planet, his home, and all the typical social lessons he would have received growing up. He covered a lot in a short amount of time and was sure he'd only touched the surface, but it was necessary to stay at the surface level in order to function among others.

Still, in Loraleaf, which was made up of only men in a filoz, he was an outsider. They all respected him, but each group of men, be it two or five, had been together for years. It was another reason for him to return to Naralina. There had to be other men who were yet not part of a group friendship. Men like his brother.

He leaned toward Haldone and kept his voice low. "Why are you not part of a filoz."

His older brother's face grew hard. "As my teachers would say, I do not get along well with others." He finally turned toward Sandale. "I have no patience, is what mom tells me." He shrugged. "To tell the truth, I prefer to be alone. I can make my own decisions, my own mistakes or celebrate my own achievements. I do not have to share credit, ideas or compromise when I know what should be done." Haldone's midnight eyes glowed with his emotion.

His brother's view was so opposite of any he'd encountered so far, that it took him a minute to process it. "So you are not interested in a filoz and a beloved?"

His brother's eyes lost their intensity and his lip quirked up. "Of course, as long as any other man is willing to agree with me all the time and the woman follows whatever I say."

Sandale had to choke down a laugh. "Sounds boring to me."

"Maybe, but it would make life easy and less solitary at the same time."

That his brother used the word solitary and not the word lonely was telling. Haldone was very comfortable being alone. It made Sandale think about how he felt. Because of what he learned from the men at Loraleaf, he had never considered *being alone* an option.

His brother had returned his gaze to the crossroads. Sandale viewed him with new respect. When Haldon had asked about love, Sandale had assumed he was anxious for it, but now he saw it for the philosophical question it was.

At that realization, Sandale's anxiety about getting back to his old self lessened. At Loraleaf, around all the filoz, many who were courting women on Earth, he felt like the only way to fit in was to become part of life there. Here in Naralina, being with his family, he wanted to ease their pain by returning to his former self as fast as possible. But Haldone's contrary social views gave him pause.

Maybe he could take his time. That might make learning about himself a more enjoyable task.

Haldon nudged him and pointed.

Coming down the stairs at a quick pace was a man. As he came closer, it was clear he didn't have the unique markings on his chest that Haldone had said all Triad members and members-to-be had been given as part of their initiation in to such a prestigious group. So who was it and why would he leave the Triad building at this time of night unless something was afoot?

Sandale scanned the other paths. Someone strode down

from the highest part of the city. He leaned in toward Haldone. "Someone else comes."

Haldone noticed the man and immediately raised his hand. "What did you do?"

His brother's scowl told him all was not well. "It is Grandall. He is of the Mind Kindred and can sense who is nearby even if he can't see them. I have boxed us in so he won't know we are here, but it also means we cannot hear what is said."

Now that was frustrating. There was only one reason that Grandall would be meeting a person from the Triad building, and that was to find out if Toni was there. She had been spying on Grandall and her note said she was caught by Akasha. From what Jahl had told him, if Grandall found Toni before he did, she would never be seen again.

A new urgency to protect rose hard in his gut. He may not be connected with any women except his mother, but the thought of a woman being in danger by the most powerful man in Naralina had him wanting to jump the man and render him into a permanent unconsciousness.

It was a harsh thought, and he immediately stepped away from it mentally. When such ideas manifested, he could not help but think tinges of evil had been left by the mind he'd been saddled with BW because according to his friends, he never hurt anyone, and had even kept Jahl from killing a few men during their adulthood, despite the men deserving it.

He turned his attention back to his task. He and Haldone remained silent as the two men drew closer. From where he sat, he could see that the man from the Triad building sported a Water Kindred birthmark like his father, Fripp. At least that man didn't have any mind or heart abilities that might jeopardize their position…unless he could sense men nearby since they were made up of so much water. Even so, Haldone's box should keep them from being detected.

The two men met and moved into the shadow of the building where he and Haldone sat. They both rose quietly.

Sandale studied Grandall. The older man wore confidence like Earth kings wore robes. He met the Triad man with a smile on his face and a hand to the shoulder.

The Triad man was clearly uncomfortable as he stepped back and spoke. He shook his head and opened his arms out as if to punctuate that he had no idea. Hope rose in Sandale chest.

Grandall scowled and approached the man. Whatever words he used caused the man to shake his head, his eyes widening with fear. Grandall pointed up the stairs to the Triad building.

The man backed away again, still shaking his head.

Sandale gripped the balustrade on the balcony, wanting to give the Triad man the courage to withstand Grandall. Obviously, Grandall wanted entrance into the building. If he entered before Sandale could, then Toni would be taken.

He could attempt to make them both unconscious, but to do that Haldone would have to open the invisible box. Unfortunately, he didn't have full control of that ability and he could not guarantee it would work.

As the two below them argued, Sandale's tension rose. If they headed for the stairs toward Toni, he would follow. Grandall probably wouldn't know him and if he could touch him, he could take care of their problem completely.

Then Grandall brushed by the Triad man and strode up the

stairs toward the building. Sandale moved to follow him, but was stopped by Haldone's box. His brother's hand on his arm had him turning with a snarl.

Haldone put his finger to his lips then pointed below.

The Triad man stood where Grandall had left him, smiling, his arms crossed over his chest.

Haldone smiled as well.

Sandale calmed enough to notice Grandall slowed after a couple levels of stairs, the man obviously so used to a life of leisure, he did not have the stamina of his youth. That simple fact added to the others Sandale had on the man. He looked back to where the Triad man stood, but he'd disappeared.

Of course! Grandall couldn't get in the building unless invited in by a Triad member thanks to the Crius shield. Without a Triad member, Grandall would be left outside and the man from the Triad building was gone, so not available for Grandall to threaten anymore. For a man of the Mind Kindred, the Naralina leader was thinking with his heart.

Sandale stilled. If that was the case, it meant Grandall was desperate to keep Toni from letting anyone know what she had discovered. They needed to get her out of Naralina as fast as possible.

Grandall had reached the Triad building and bent over to catch his breath.

Sandale glanced at his brother who grinned.

Then Grandall strode for the door only to bounce against an invisible wall much like Haldone's. The Circle leader stared as if he couldn't comprehend what had happened, but even from many levels down, Sandale could sense the moment rage took over.

Grandall turned to look for the Triad man he'd met and when

he didn't find him, fisted his hands and pumped then toward the sky. Then he ran down the stairs. As he drew closer, the redness in his face made Sandale think the man might very well collapse. His loose skin, due to age and luxury, jiggled as he raced downward, but even though Eden's gravity helped him, he still slowed before reaching the paths crossed.

Grandall searched the entire area for the Triad man before finally giving up and slowly making his way back up the hill to the Ruling Circle compound, but his shoulders did not slump in defeat, which put Sandale on edge.

Haldone waited until Grandall was almost to the top before eliminating his invisible box. "Tonight has turned much more enjoyable than I thought it would."

"I agree, there was humor to be found, but I think this event made things worse for Toni."

Haldone stopped smiling. "Yes. A man of Grandall's power in Naralina will do everything to protect it, using every available resource and he has many."

"I will need to get her out of Naralina as quickly as possible." He paused, not sure how his next request would be taken. He didn't yet want to reveal that he no longer had a Crius chip. "Would you be willing to help me transport her?"

Haldone's eyes shone with excitement. "You mean into the jungle to the hidden settlement you told me about?"

"Yes, but we would first have to walk to a city wall before portaling out. It wouldn't take long and I do not think anyone will miss you."

Haldone held up his hand. "Say no more. I am anxious to learn about this place you called home. I also want to know more about the lawbreakers who held you."

He hadn't expected Haldone to be so willing, but then again, the man had no ties to Naralina except their family and his work. His excitement was a little unsettling, but since Sandale had no portal chip, he couldn't ask for a better person to help him. "Thank you."

Haldone winked. "That's what brothers are for."

A warmth entered his chest as he smiled back at Haldone. Slowly, he was starting to reconnect. He just had to be patient, not his strong suit.

"Tell me more about the jungle, so I am not ignorant and get myself in to trouble."

Sandale nodded and sat again. Haldon did also and he spent the next few hours explaining what life outside a city was like.

At eleven, the hour that marked the middle of night, Haldone stood. "There's been no one about. I suggest we return home and sleep. We will want to be among the first to enter the Triad building tomorrow."

Sandale stood as well. Though telling his brother about Loraleaf and explaining Haven and the lawbreakers had kept them occupied, he was anxious to get to Toni. "That is imperative."

Haldone moved to the edge of the balcony and raised his hand. When he put it down, he smiled. "Follow me." Then he jumped over the edge and slid down an invisible ramp before landing on his feet.

Sandale shook his head. In some ways, his older brother seemed so much younger than himself. After he jumped onto the slide and stood at the bottom, he clapped his brother on the shoulder. "I am glad I have you by my side."

"It is good to have you back, little brother."

CHAPTER EIGHT

Toni sat on the couch, sipping her ale as she watched Akasha take her empty plate and rinse it off. The man's taut thighs and ass were enough to get her wet. Everything about him physically was exactly her type on Earth, but everything about his personality was just the opposite.

Well, there were a few exceptions. One of them was the way he'd kissed her on the patrio. The force of his need had been both a surprise and welcome. She liked that in a man. At the temple, sex was always gentle and reverent and while she appreciated that more than anyone would ever know, it did get boring sometimes.

The other way he was like some of her Earth lovers was in his lack of politeness. Unlike all the other men she'd met on Eden, they always said "please" and "thank you" and were courteous to the hilt. Even Jahl, who she'd always thought of as the roughest and most damaged, was polite in that way, but not Akasha. It was almost as if what he asked was to be expected and fulfilled. She balked at that, but when it came to sex, the purely feminine side of her practically fainted over it.

Akasha turned around and faced her, leaning his handsome

ass against the wall. "I have shown you two colors and brought you ale, but I have yet to hear your plans now that you learned what you wanted to from Grandall."

Well, hell, she'd thought she might be able to put that off until, well, until after she left with Sandale. She gave him a sly smile. "Yes, but I have yet to be pleasured or run the stairs and the stairs were part of our first bargain."

He frowned, his eyebrows lowering. "I have shown you all my colored lights except one and brought you ale. You have only told me why you spied on Grandall. Now I want to know what you will do with the knowledge you have gained."

"Fine. Fine." She looked away for a moment to gather her thoughts. The man knew the second she lied, but would he know if she didn't tell the entire truth? It was worth a shot. She met his gaze full on. "I don't plan to do anything myself. Though if I could get near him, I'd castrate the bugger with a hot kafez pot. Or if you were with me I'd use that orange light of yours."

His face relaxed but he wasn't distracted. "But you are not simply keeping this information you gathered to yourself, are you?"

"Shit, no. What good would that do? I passed it on to my friends who will figure out what the next move should be." There. That's all there was.

"What friends?" Akasha pulled away from the wall as if he was ready to go find Loraleaf and bring her friends up before Grandall himself.

No way she'd let that happen. "Are you sure you want to know?"

"Toni." His deep, scolding voice sent a hot shiver racing down her arms and her stupid nipples hardened.

What the hell was with that? "Hey, just checking. Sometimes ignorance is bliss, especially when you keep yourself secluded from society and ignore what's happening beyond your isolated mission of judgement on morality in an ideal world, which by the way, doesn't exist."

"Toni."

Shit, he refused to be distracted. Then he asked for it. "Grandall's oldest son."

Akasha's eyes widened. "Jahl? Jahl disappeared."

"And if you know Grandall at all, you suspected he killed him, right?" She smirked.

"No." Akasha's response was quick. "We don't kill each other here. Not since the Fullamush."

She had to admit she hadn't heard of a single Edenist being killed by another since she'd arrived, but her gut told her, if anyone had the capacity, it was Grandall. The image of her worst stepfather floated before her and her body froze with rage for a moment before she kicked the memory away. "And I'm telling you, Grandall has it in him."

Akasha shook his head. "His essence would have to be all black and if that were the case, he would have never been given a chip. Those with black essences eventually succumb to their nature and are discovered and exiled. It is how our society survives. We don't elect leaders with that kind of morality."

"Black essence? What's that?"

He relaxed against the wall again and crossed his arms and legs. "Every Edenist has an essence." He looked away. "If you could see it, it would be shades of black, white, and gray based upon the morality of the person. Most Edenists are a mixture of white and gray, but some, those not worthy of society, have black patches. The black eventually takes over the man's essence. At some point during this progression, he breaks the law because his black side cannot accept the limitations of living among others. It consumes him." Akasha looked back at her. "Those with this black essence are eventually discovered by their actions."

Wow, that was a theory she'd never heard before. It sounded like a man was predetermined to be good or bad. Was that Akasha's take on it? The Triad's? All of Eden? More importantly, was it true? "So others can't actually tell what color another person's essence is, right? That's just a way to look at it."

He nodded.

She dodged a bullet on that one. Her guess was she had a rather large black patch on her "essence" and the last thing she needed was for someone to decide she was fated to be a lawbreaker. She hadn't actually met a lawbreaker, but in one note Serena had said they had problems with them and Sandale had been captured by them.

Akasha dropped his arms to wave away their tangent. "You say you told Jahl. Is he here?"

Time to tiptoe through the tulips now. "No." That was the truth.

"Then how did you tell him what you learned?"

"I sent a message." Another truth. She mentally patted herself on the back.

Akasha studied her, but accepted her response. "Is he coming here to do something?"

"I don't know." That was technically the truth, though knowing Jahl, she'd bet he would, especially if he and Khaos told Nassic and

Wareson. Nassic wanted back in Naralina in a bad way. He'd always been angry that Wareson had accepted their exile without fighting it.

"Why don't you know? Because you haven't received a message back or because Jahl hasn't decided yet?"

Now things were getting tricky. She did receive a message, but it was only about Sandale coming for her. "Because Jahl hasn't decided yet as far as I know."

Akasha didn't nod or shake his head, as if he was still judging the truth of her statement. He crossed his arms. "After Jahl takes action, if he does, will you remain in Naralina or leave for another city?"

The question surprised her and she let it show. "I have no idea. I hadn't thought that far. Originally, I planned to stay, but that was before I got caught." She gave him a resentful look, squinting her eyes as if to say, *we all know whose fault that is.*

"You should be glad I caught you. Anyone else would have taken you straight to Grandall." He was back to scowling. He really shouldn't do so much of that. It would give him wrinkles early.

"Anyone else wouldn't have decided I was spying. They would have accepted that I was getting turned-on by watching and listening to another couple have sex." She folded her arms to mimic him.

He remained silent.

She had him there. Score one for Toni Reid! She relaxed back against the cushioned couch and picked up her glass of ale to finish it off. "So how about your side of our bargain? I've been waiting all afternoon for your company and seeing you all naked and hunky has me ready for a little activity."

She winked to make sure he understood her implication.

Sometimes Edenists didn't understand Earth innuendo, though she was constantly surprised by how much they did know. From what she'd learned, they studied Earth, and particularly their city's assigned countries, from a very early age.

And to think everyone on Earth was clueless that Eden existed.

"Then why do you cover yourself?" Akasha raised his eyebrows as if he'd caught her in a lie.

But this was one of her favorite topics. "To entice."

He lowered his brow in puzzlement. "But is not the female body enticement enough?"

She gave him a sultry smile. "It's about the foreplay, the anticipation of fulfillment." He still looked unconvinced. "For example, these siris-webbing pants show you a vague outline of my legs, but only where there is a slit in the material can you really see them. So when I move," she straightened the leg she had crossed over her other one, "your eyes and your appetite automatically seek out my bare flesh."

"Like a tease."

"Exactly. If I have nothing covering me, then nothing is hidden and there is nothing to anticipate. Now if I uncross my legs…" She moved her leg to the side, revealing the split in the material at the juncture of her thighs and then crossed her other leg over. "You can see my bare pussy for a moment."

A zing of pleasure raced from her chest to her groin at the look on Akasha's face. His gaze was riveted to the area she'd just covered again, his nostrils flaring and his mouth slightly open. Great, she could feel moisture there already. Foreplay *did* go both ways.

He pushed away from the wall. "Show me."

Again, no "please" or "if you don't mind" which would normally piss her off, but his light blue eyes had darkened to the blue of deep ocean water. Besides he'd promised her fulfillment this time, so why not.

Slowly, she uncrossed her leg and re-crossed it.

"Again." His command, and that's what it was, came out husky.

She liked husky. This time she moved even slower, spreading her thighs before re-crossing her legs.

He pushed the small coffee table aside, his cock hard again at her little show.

She licked her lips at the remembered feel of it in her mouth.

He knelt in front of her. "Again."

Well, hell, when he told her like that all breathy and intense, what else was she to do? She uncrossed her legs and spread them, but faster than lightning he grabbed each thigh and held her knees apart.

Her first reaction was to force them closed, but she stopped pressing against his strength when his cock jumped. She wanted to feel that slide inside her. Now would be a good time.

He didn't say anything, just stared. It wasn't as if he hadn't already seen her opening as he already cleaned it and inspected it. Obviously, she'd made her point.

She smiled slyly. "See anything you like?"

He finally looked her in the eyes and without blinking let go of one leg only to hold it open with his own as he buried two fingers inside her.

"Oh wow. That's one way to get a girl's heart racing." Her whole body was primed for him. How did he do that?

"I promised you pleasure." Akasha's voice had turned less husky.

Was putting his fingers inside her enough to give him back his control? "Yes, you did." Now if she could get him to replace his fingers with his hard, thick cock, her pleasure would be perfect.

But before she could make the suggestion, he lowered his head and licked her clit.

Oh, the big man knew what he was doing. She closed her eyes as he tongued her sensitive nub with hard and soft pressure, circling it, stroking it, causing her sheath to tighten around his manly fingers.

She moaned, freely enjoying Akasha's attentions when he stopped tonguing her though his fingers remained inside.

Opening her eyes, she found him staring at her breasts. "What?"

"I almost forgot. You haven't shown me why you cover your nipples."

Fuck. Did the man have any idea how hot it was to hear him talk about her body like that? "I guess I didn't." She moved one hand to trail her fingers along her cleavage, then she pulled the tie that held the vest together. It pulled away, scraping across her hard nipples, but it didn't reveal them.

Akasha hadn't moved a muscle, his gaze still on her chest.

She moved her finger under the material of her left breast and pinched her nipple. The shot of excitement ran from her nub to her sheath which tightened of its own accord.

"You like your nipples pinched." Akasha's eyes darkened even more.

She removed her hand. "If you continue your task, the

material of my vest, may or may not slide to the side, depending on our movements. That's the tease."

He shook his head briefly before leaning forward and pushing the material from her right breast with his fine nose so he could latch onto her nipple. He took it between his teeth and pinched, causing her sheath to tighten again.

Then he let go. "Interesting." He blew on her now wet nub, before lowering his head again to suck hard.

She arched into his mouth and let out a loud groan.

He licked her nipple as if soothing it before he sucked it hard again, causing her to come away from the couch in absolute bliss. He repeated the process twice more before sitting back on his haunches.

She gulped in much needed air, her body wound so tight in preparation for her orgasm, she was surprised she could even breathe. Maybe if he had removed his fingers, she'd be able to delay, but they were inside her and her body wasn't letting them leave anytime soon.

"If I release your leg, will you leave it there?" He looked at her in expectation.

Well, hell, of course she would. That would give him another hand to play with her. "I will." Any sarcastic comment she might have made was gone along with all the blood in her brain since it moved south.

He grinned. "Good."

Was he kidding? It wasn't just good. It was fucking hot as hell.

Akasha didn't waste time with any more preliminaries. With his free hand, he spread her labia apart to better access her clit and licked upward. A few more strokes up and down had her panting for breath.

As his lips covered her excited nub, he moved his free hand to her right nipple and pinched.

Excitement raced from there to her sheath, causing her to tighten again. Fuck, her orgasm was so close.

Akasha made a sound deep in his throat just before he started to nip at her clit. She let her head fall back against the couch and closed her eyes as streaks of pleasure shot through her. *Yes.*

He played her like an expert, bringing her to the edge of orgasm only to keep her there before backing off. She was frustrated and excited at the same time. The sensations were intense and sustained as he alternated between pinching her nipple, nibbling her clit and stroking.

She panted for air, but beyond her moans, she wouldn't ask him to finish it. It was too fucking amazing.

As if he sensed her stubbornness, he stopped pinching and instead rolled her nipple between his thumb and forefinger, changing the pleasure that flooded her from her chest to the spot where his mouth covered her clit.

Then he sucked, pushing her clit with his tongue at the same time and her hips rose as she grabbed his head and pulled him closer.

It happened. Her orgasm sneaked up on her, pushing her into another state of being as it balled her up and splintered through her.

She yelled at the eruption of exquisite pleasure just before Akasha moved his fingers out and then in again. It was like another volcano of ecstasy flowing from her as he continued to pump into her until she released his hair and gasped for air.

The man didn't stop, though his fingers slowed and his mouth left her sensitive clit to lazily play with her neglected left nipple. The tiny zings he sent through her wiped her out.

When she opened her eyes, he met her gaze, a smirk on his face. "Did I fulfill my part of our bargain?"

She laughed though it came out choked as her breath still wasn't under control. She waited a few more moments then nodded. "For…today."

He chuckled at her response and slowly removed his hands from her body. He raised one and flooded her in red light. It had the softest touch, almost like a siris-webbing blanket, which she'd never seen as that would be far too time-consuming to make.

When she could breathe normally again, she pulled herself into a more upright position. "For a Triad member-to-be, you certainly know your way around a woman's body."

Akasha lowered his hand, extinguishing the light then he rose and strode into the bathroom. His lack of response was strange. When he returned from washing up, she noticed his cock was no longer rigid. As much as she wanted to feel him inside her, she didn't have the energy for another orgasm. Maybe tomorrow.

"Are you ready to run the stairs? I believe I owe you that as well." Though he didn't smile, it didn't take a genius to figure out he thought he'd escaped his agreement.

"I think I'll take you up on that in the morning after a good night's sleep."

He shook his head. "I cannot take you then. Tomorrow is a Crius chip panel and we will be eating our meal early. Then I must supervise the entrance of families and friends into the building."

She rolled her eyes. "Really? What are you going to do, hold their hands and walk them in?"

"Yes, though not me. The other Triad members-to-be will. Usually, they link arms with those wanting entrance."

"Why?" This had to be some kind of ritual.

His eyes widened for a moment as if stunned by her lack of knowledge. "To get them through the Crius shield that surrounds the building."

Crius shield? "But you didn't—"

"Yes, I did. I made sure I had your wrist."

She'd completely forgotten that. "So how does you holding me allow me through this shield?" And how the hell was she going to get out if that was the case. She was sure that Sandale wasn't part of the Triad thingy.

"You asked me about the markings on my chest. They are more than a representation of my essence and my place in Naralina. They also contain the elements needed to allow me to pass through the Crius shield. When I touch someone else, that extends my opening to include them. This is why Grandall cannot come for you unless he is with a Triad member or member-to-be."

Wow, she learned something new every day with this man, and this particular tidbit would make her escape a lot more difficult unless Sandale knew someone in the Triad building.

As for Grandall, the man was an idiot. He had no idea they were on to him. She waved her hand dismissively. "Grandall doesn't even know I exist. I'm not worried about him."

"You should be." His face was far too serious.

Either he knew something she didn't, or miracle of miracles, he believed her about the Ruling Circle scum. "You figured out I was right about Grandall?"

"I fear you have more insight into his character than most

men." He paused as if he wasn't sure how to say what he needed to say. "Grandall is aware that you were listening to what he said to his cythera."

"What? He can't. I made sure no one saw me." At his look, she amended her statement. "Until you did. How could he possibly know?"

He shook his head at her. "Did you not know that the man you spied upon was Kindred of Mind and can sense who is nearby? I can understand not knowing how far Grandall's senses can reach, but *everyone* knows of his ability."

Well, fuck that pivotal piece of information. Why didn't Jahl warn her about his dad's ability? When she saw that man next, she planned to give him a piece of her mind in a tone that would make him deaf for days. She'd as soon kick him in the balls, but Serena would never speak to her again. "Well, that sucks, doesn't it?"

Akasha's lip quirked upward. "I would not have put it quite that way, but I agree with your general sentiment."

"Right." She rose from the couch, too much new information in her head for her to sit still. "So I'm relatively safe in this building unless Grandall cons someone into letting him in."

Akasha nodded. "Tomorrow, anyone with an interest in the eleven candidates for a Crius chip will be walked into the building. I will know if Grandall comes in."

She strode to the glass door that led to the patrio. "Then what? If he comes in, you'll let me leave?" She turned to look at him. "Or will you hand me over to him?"

Akasha strode toward her, the flash of anger in his blue eyes caused her to steel herself for his response. Instead, he grabbed her to him and wrapped his arms around her. "I will not let that man near you."

The intensity in his tone combined with his strength surrounding her was far more than she ever expected…from anyone. She swallowed hard and wrapped her arms around him as well. She'd never expected to have a champion in her corner as it was, but for it to be Akasha, the monk, the lover, the commander, the distant, had her fighting watery eyes. Since when the hell did she cry?

Akasha had no idea why he wanted to protect Toni, but he always had good instincts and despite the evidence to the contrary, in this case, his instinct screamed that Toni had far more white in her essence than Grandall.

That such a thing was possible was far beyond his power of explanation, but he was as certain of that fact as the rising of Helios every morning. He had never felt the need to protect a woman, not even with his own mother, but that could be because she had two powerful husbands to do that for her. He always knew she would be safe. His mother would never put herself in danger and since she loved his fathers so much, she did anything they asked.

Toni, on the other hand, needed someone to protect her, even from herself. Whoever tasked her with spying on Grandall had made a serious error. Toni was worth far more to Naralina than Grandall, in his opinion, though when that belief shifted, he couldn't quite pinpoint.

She lifted her head from his shoulder to tilt it back very slightly since she was almost his height. "Is your offer to run the stairs still open? I'm so energized right now with anger that I need to work it off."

He kept one arm around her as he opened the door to the patrio behind her and checked the sky. Selene had started her descent. "If you can wait another twenty minutes or so, we can go out. I want to make sure Selene has set and it is very dark to keep you from prying eyes."

"Good idea." She disengaged herself from him, and he had to keep himself from grabbing her back, which made no sense at all.

"I'll change into my work-out clothes." She winked. "I wouldn't want to turn you on by running in my split pants."

He watched her saunter into the sleeping area. Her hips swished, revealing slivers of skin on her legs. Her quick recovery from his devastating information had him admiring more than her hips. She was a strong woman who made a lot of sense when she wasn't lying.

He could feel himself growing fond of her, making a connection to her that would impede his judgment. This was not good for either of them. Once the problem of Grandall was solved, she would return to her Pleasure Temple. If it couldn't be solved, then she might leave Naralina and return to Jahl.

At the thought of her with another man, his entire body froze. Anger at the prospect filled him, which made no sense. It was not as if he could keep her with him. Triad members did not bond with women.

Shaking his head at himself, he stepped outside on the patrio. He looked up at the sky, the stars muted by the soft glow the Ruling Circle building gave off at the top of the mountain. Below, very few lights remained on.

He would use his green light so Toni could see the steps clearly. She didn't need to complicate matters by hurting herself.

What concerned him more was what she'd heard from Grandall. What was it that would have her contacting the son? There were far more questions now that he'd learned more from her. If he was to help her, she would have to tell him everything. And if she didn't want his help?

He pushed the idea away. She did and she would. His last bargaining chip was his final color. He'd prefer not to reveal that. Very few people were aware of his white color ability, and it would be best if he kept it that way.

Maybe their bargaining days were over. It was time to work together to solve the issues surrounding the day Toni came into his life.

"I'm ready." Her voice behind him pulled him from his thoughts.

He turned around to find her striding toward him in the same outfit she'd worn this afternoon. He hadn't missed any of her curves then and it took all his effort to keep his body from reacting now.

When she reached him, she looked at the sky. "I don't see the white moon. That means we can go, right?"

"Yes, but we need to be very quiet for many reasons."

"Especially if Grandall has someone watching the building." They stepped into his rooms, and she stopped him. "I really appreciate this. I know it's a risk." She paused to take a deep breath. "If you think we shouldn't go, I'll skip it."

His immediate reaction was to tell her to forego her exercise, but he had no idea how long he would need to keep her and he didn't want her to lose her mental capabilities because she was locked in his rooms for days.

That she understood the real danger she was in and was

willing to make the sacrifice told him she could be depended upon when necessary. That was reassuring and validated his faith in her.

Maybe it was weakness on his part, but he couldn't deny her this chance when the risk was the lowest it could be. "As long as we're quiet and you don't try to run anywhere else, I feel it would be acceptable to go."

Her relief at his answer filled him with pride, though why he had no explanation.

"Then let's do this." She strode to the door and waited for him to unlock it.

He wasn't oblivious to how closely she watched him maneuver the mechanism. Once open, he took her hand and led her through the hall, then outside the building and through the Crius shield to the top of the stairs. The Crius shield only kept people from gaining entrance. Anyone could leave, so he didn't need to hold her hand, but he wasn't in a hurry to release it.

She lifted onto her toes and whispered in his ear. "It's really dark."

He grinned, then turned his palm to the ground. A circle of green light lit the stone beneath their feet, encompassing at least six stairs below.

She smiled, her joy at being able to run a set of stairs that even some Edenists found difficult, filled him with pleasure. That didn't make sense either. He lifted their clasped hands toward the stairs.

Toni nodded and without another word bounded downward with him at her side.

Their footsteps were silent since neither of them had donned their footwear. He matched his pace to hers, pleased to be able to do such a simple exercise with her. When they reached the bottom, he extinguished his light and examined the area around them.

Here, if anywhere, was the perfect place to wait and watch. Luckily, they were still far enough from the cross paths that unless a person in the house across the way at the point of intersection was vigilant all night, no one would see them.

Toni let go of his hand and shook out her arms as her breathing returned to normal and she looked up to where they'd been. Her face held both determination and excitement.

When she grasped his hand in hers again, his heart warmed in a way it hadn't since he'd been a child. Strange.

He nodded that he was ready.

Toni took a few more solid breaths then started up the stairs. Again, he matched her pace. When they were halfway up, she disengaged her hand from his to help her propel herself better.

He understood why she needed to do so, but he found he didn't like it nearly as much. As she reached the last level of stairs, she slowed considerably, but still pushed onward until they made the stone patrio outside the Crius shield.

She fell to her knees and slapped her hands on the ground, taking deep breaths. After a few minutes, she turned over on to her ass and leaned back on her arms, her breathing still labored.

He crouched down in front of her, wishing he could help her breathe somehow.

She rolled her eyes at him and gave him a self-deprecating smirk.

That eased his mind regarding her condition, so he rose and waited patiently for her to calm.

Toni held her arms up and looked at him.

He kept his smile to himself and pulled her to a standing position.

She leaned forward and kissed him on the cheek before she turned to walk into the building. He made a grab for her shoulder but missed.

She bumped into the Crius shield face first. "Ow." She rubbed her nose before she scowled at him.

He shook his head and took her hand, leading her through the shield and into the long two-level corridor. As they approached his door, she tried to pull him past it.

"Toni, we need to go inside."

"I know, but I want to see the meditation pool first."

As far as he knew, a woman had never set foot in that area. Not that there was a rule about it. It just wasn't done. He started to shake his head, but stopped. It was past the middle of the night and no one would be there, plus it would be a good show of faith in working together with her.

He gave a quick nod and led the way. His rooms were the closest to the pool so even from his doorway, the golden glow of a hundred and eleven tiny shiners could be seen. He dropped her hand and wrapped his arm around her bare waist. "This is a sacred place. No woman has ever been here before."

She stared at him with wide eyes. "Really?"

He nodded.

She moved away from him and walked to the edge of the pool. Some of the tiny shiners were set beneath the water, while other's dotted the columns on either side and still more were embedded in the stone patrio itself.

Toni sat on the edge of the pool which rose no higher than

her knee. "It looks like fireflies." Her voice held awe. "I only saw fireflies once as a kid when my foster family took a vacation to Iowa. There were hundreds as dusk hit."

He tried to imagine Toni as a child and couldn't. As for fireflies, he would research that. Eden might have something similar that he could show her.

"Can I touch the water?"

No one ever did, but that didn't mean she couldn't. He gave her a nod, and she immediately trailed her fingers through it.

"It's really warm."

He motioned to the area surrounding it. "The pool is under Helios all day. The Crius designed it that way."

She ignored him as she scooped her hand in and dribbled the water on her legs.

He turned to glance at the windows on the second floor where the Crius chip reviews would take place. No one should be up there now. The area had a direct line of sight to the reflecting pool.

A splash alerted him that he'd taken his eyes off Toni for too long. He spun at the sound. "What are you doing?" He kept his voice low.

She grinned as she lay back in the pool, the water covering her to her neck. "Relaxing. This is almost hot tub temperature. It feels great. Too bad it isn't deeper. At least as high as your waist would be perfect. It soothes your muscles, especially the day after a particularly strenuous workout."

"You need to leave the pool. It is not for bathing."

"This isn't bathing. It's relaxing. You should try it." She swished her feet back and forth, opening her legs and closing them.

He wasn't immune to the blurry image of her breasts as the

moving water swept her top up. He had to concede that her ideas regarding minimal clothing were valid. Luckily, no other woman in Naralina went about as Toni. If they all did, nothing would get done in the city.

He crouched next to the edge. "Come. It is not right to be in there."

She cocked her head. "Why? Is this water blessed?"

When he hesitated to answer her, not sure exactly what she meant, her eyes widened.

"Holy, hell." She rose quickly. "I'm sorry. I didn't know." She stepped out of the pool faster than he could stand.

She backed away. "Fuck, I really messed that up."

He stopped her retreat by grabbing her shoulders. "It is not awful. I don't know what you mean by blessed."

Her relief was complete. "Oh, well, it's like when a priest, who is a man of God makes a sign over the water. It kind of connects the water to God."

He frowned. "As I said before, we do not have gods anymore. We have only what is good and what is bad, what is right and what is wrong. An ideal to reach for." He pointed to the pool. "The water frees our minds to discover the truth of all."

Though he only came to the mediation pool occasionally since his white light ability showed him the difference without his human side getting in the way, he understood its importance to the other members.

"It seems like this Triad place is very similar to our religious places."

From what he remembered of his school days, his impression of religions was that there were many different ones and each one thought they were right and others were wrong. "We do not have religion. We are respected because we determine morality. That is all."

She wiggled her brows. "In that case, why don't we both enjoy the warm pool?"

She raised her foot to enter it again, but he grasped her arm. "No. It is time to go inside. I do not want anyone to see you."

Her smile left and she nodded, understanding the risk once again.

Taking her hand, he led her back to his door and guided her inside.

She headed straight for his cabinet. She pulled out a glass and poured herself water. After swallowing half of it, she turned toward him. "Would you like some?"

The glow of the shiner fell on her body, showing him that her nipples were hard beneath the wet material clinging to her breasts. Water rivulets dripped over the ripples of her abdomen before adding their wetness to the cloth plastered to her mons.

He forced his cock not to respond and quickly turned toward the sleeping area. "No. I will have a glass of ambrosia before sleeping." As much as he wanted to bury himself in her strong body, he would not until he could be sure that everything he had observed and deduced about her was true. There was only one way to do that, and he was not ready to reveal it yet.

As he gathered a head puff from his bed, he heard her go out onto the patrio. He returned to the living area and placed the puff on the longseat that Toni called a couch.

The patrio door opened and he looked up.

Toni came in completely nude. He wished that her theory of

being slightly clad was absolutely true, but seeing her naked still had his cock hardening.

"I left my clothes outside to dry." She glanced at his puff. "Are you sleeping out here again? I thought since we know each other so much better…" Her gaze slipped to his hard cock.

He turned away from her and sat. "No. It is important that I sleep. By the time you awake, I'll be gone."

"Oh, right, I forgot you have that panel thing tomorrow." She padded over to him. "Don't forget my breakfast." Her grin was sultry. "I worked up a big appetite tonight."

He didn't look at her and simply nodded.

She leaned over and kissed him on the cheek. "Thank you for taking me out tonight. I can't wait to do it again."

He snapped his gaze to hers, but she'd already turned away, a soft smirk about her lips, and a jiggle in her stride.

By the Crius! The woman was trouble.

CHAPTER NINE

Sandale moved up in the line of people entering the Triad building. He watched each marked man, wishing he knew which was Akasha. Ten men escorted people inside while one man oversaw the others.

Haldone leaned toward him. "This is supposed to be a joyous occasion. Your scowl looks a bit out of place."

He snapped his gaze to his brother and forced a smile.

Haldone laughed, causing Ulik to turn around and frown at them. That simple look from his father had Sandale's heart easing. He felt like he was part of his family, and it felt good.

When Ulik came to the spot between two large potted trees. A marked man stepped next to him, linked his arm around Ulik's and walked him through.

Haldone nudged him. "Go ahead."

He kept a soft smile on his face as he stepped between the trees and another marked man with short blond hair linked his arm around his and walked him through.

He stood next to his father until Haldone had joined them. Then the three of them followed the family they were supposedly there to celebrate with.

As they entered under the two-level arch, Sandale glanced down the long corridor with doors on either side before they turned left toward a set of stairs that led to the next level. He was anxious to find Toni, but they had had to make it look as if they really were there to cheer on their father's friend's son. The stairs brought them almost to the ceiling of the second level, where everyone turned to the right. About halfway down the wall were two open doors.

They followed the crowd into a large room with rows and rows of seats in a semi-circle along the entire length. Opposite was a raised dais with three large intricately ornamented chairs. His father had informed him earlier that the chairs were left in the building by the Crius. There had been more but they'd been distributed to other cities. Apparently, a lot of sharing took place after the Fullamush.

Between the crowd and the dais was a single platform with two steps up to it. Everyone filed into the seats around the room. Most people rushed down toward the bottom and the front rows, but he and his father and brother found seats near the entrance to make it easy to leave.

By time the room was full, every seat was taken and a few people sat on the center stairs. As soon as the doors closed behind them, a soft melodic tone filled the chamber and a door opened opposite where they entered. Three men filed in, all with long white hair tied in the back. The first was the tallest and youngest, the next was a bit shorter and older and last came the shortest and oldest, sporting a long white beard.

These were the Triad panel members. The markings across their collarbones were similar to the ones he'd seen on the men outside, yet each was slightly different.

With no preliminary, one of the younger men from outside stepped up and called the first name.

The young man to be judged strode to the small center platform. The entire room went silent. The music that had heralded the entrance of the Triad ceased as well. Ulik had told him that each Triad used their unique abilities to determine the worthiness of a man to receive a Crius chip.

The first man, the tallest of the trio, was Kindred of Heart and like Rekah could read the candidate's emotions. The second man was Kindred of Light and he could produce images that allowed him and his two fellow members the ability to actually see an event from the candidate's life. The events he produced were brought about by the third man's ability. The oldest man, who was Kindred of Mind, was a truth-reader like Nassic, or so Khaos had told him. The candidate would be forced to tell the truth about certain times in his life.

A bell rang and the Triad began questioning the candidate.

He leaned closer to his father, keeping his voice soft. "How do they know what to ask?"

"The members-to-be, who walked us in, do the research on each candidate and give that to the Triad in advance. The Triad then determine how to approach the revelation of the candidate's morality."

Sandale found the entire process intriguing. What would the Triad do about him? Could a truth-reader make him tell about an event he didn't remember? Probably not. It wasn't as if he'd forgotten. His memory had been wiped clean, leaving a large void in his brain.

As much as he wanted to watch and learn, he became anxious

for the first break between candidates. He needed to find Toni before Grandall did. The man could already be inside, but sitting in the back as they were, he could only see the back of men's heads.

Haldone nudged him in the side. "There."

He looked to his right to see Grandall walking down the center stairs. Another man slid over as he approached, and the two immediately started whispering.

Sandale studied the man. He was obviously not interested in the proceedings either. Luckily, Sandale had never met him, so he wouldn't be able to sense him. Even so, he pretended to focus on the candidate's evidence.

Ulik leaned toward him. "You will need to exit immediately. I will attempt to interfere if I see him head out."

That his father didn't use Grandall's name made him too aware of the trouble his actions could cause for his family. "Please. I do not want any repercussions to fall upon you."

Ulik smiled at him with such love that his throat closed.

"For my sons, I would do anything." He winked. "Besides, if I ever find myself in trouble, I now know where I can go."

At his father's reference to the jungle, he tensed. He obviously needed to explain a bit more about what life was like out there. Without that knowledge, his family could fall into more trouble there than within Naralina's walls.

Despite the panel discussion continuing, he rose and headed for the door. As quietly as possible he opened it and slipped outside, only to have it pulled from his hand.

Haldone gently closed the door behind him. "Don't look so surprised. I didn't come with you to watch young Edenists receive their chip."

He grinned, happy to have his brother's company. They headed to the stairs and Haldone held up his hand. "A slide is faster."

Within seconds they strode down the resident corridor and stopped at the first door. Sandale pointed to the three on the opposite wall. "What if she is over there?"

Haldone shook his head. "Those are the quarters of the Triad members. Over here is the members-to-be. This Akasha will be on this side."

Sandale tried the door. It was locked. "How will we know which one is Akasha's?"

Haldone grinned. Then he placed his hand over the locking mechanism and a whirring sounded from within. He removed his hand and lifted the latch.

Sandale didn't think twice about his brother's ability to use hardened air to unlock the door. Instead, he ran inside. "Toni?"

No one was there. He checked the space thoroughly. With no doors in the rooms, it was quick work.

They exited the space and Haldone relocked it.

Sandale glanced at the next ten doors. "This could take too long."

Haldone was already unlocking the next door. "We have no choice. This time, don't run in. Triad members-to-be have abilities like the rest of us. You could get yourself killed if they strike you down with fire, or throw you across the hall with air."

Scrat, he wasn't thinking straight. "You're right."

Haldone raised one eyebrow. "Can't you use some of that calming ability on yourself?"

He frowned. "No. Now please open the door."

Toni sat on the couch enjoying the unique pastry and henny eggs

Akasha had brought her. She took the glass of ambrosia from him and drank. "I have to say this is the best breakfast yet."

He sat down across from her on a straight back chair, his legs spread wide, showing off his package. Her gaze flicked there. She had one hot jailer.

Akasha's fingers under her chin lifted her head. "I will keep my promise to you later. I need to get back before I'm missed."

She winked. "I'm looking forward to 'later.'" Then she scooped more henny eggs into her mouth. The spices they used on Eden, minus sugar, were addictive. Then again, so was Akasha's spicy scent.

She'd smelled his deep clove scent the minute he'd walked in with her breakfast, before becoming aware of the food smells. She must be really attuned to him already if his scent could wake her even when the door opening and the food didn't.

Akasha bent forward, his elbows resting on his knees, his hands clasped. "Grandall did not enter with this morning's crowd. That surprises me. I thought after his questions to me yesterday, he would have been here."

She paused, her food halfway to her mouth, having forgotten for a few minutes that Grandall knew she'd spied on him. "And now for indigestion."

"What is that?"

She waved off her comment. "Never mind." Resting her plate on the coffee table between them, she leaned forward like him, though her wrap covered *her* body. "I can't stay here forever, but if I go back to my rooms, he'll easily find me. Maybe you should let me return to Jahl."

"No." His answer was so fast, she widened her eyes.

He sat straight again. "I don't think that is wise."

Cocking her head, she studied him. The man was not only hotter than hot, he was smart. Something was going on in his head. "What are you thinking?"

He finally met her gaze. "I think you need to tell me what you heard from Grandall."

Well, hell. She wanted to, but how would he take it? He'd think she lied. She didn't like the hurt that thought sent through her, so she pushed it aside. She gave him her best seductive grin. "What's it worth to you? Can you offer anything besides your last color? Because you know it's worth more than that."

He dropped her gaze as if she'd disappointed him somehow. "I think the time for bargaining is over." His gaze came back to her. "You are in danger. I cannot help you if I do not know what it is you heard."

At his reproach, she sat back to give the knot in her stomach a chance to go away. "You won't believe me, so why bother?"

His blue eyes appeared to lighten, but it was the flash of hurt she saw there before he rose that had her heart skipping. "I believe you when you tell the truth and I don't believe you when you lie." He turned away and walked to the glass door of the patrio. He half turned back and stared at her. "I know the difference."

This was getting far too serious. They were supposed to have a lighthearted captor to captive relationship until Sandale came to take her to Loraleaf. They weren't supposed to be tackling city corruption and moving their relationship past sex. "I thought you were Kindred of Light not Kindred of Mind."

Akasha's speed caught her off guard. He'd moved to the couch and grasped her shoulders to haul her against him. "You can't brush this aside, Toni. This is your life we are talking about. A life I want you to continue."

The last was said with a growl, sending a strange excitement through her chest that had nothing to do with sex. No man had ever cared if *she* lived or died.

She stared into Akasha's eyes, the turbulent blue colors reminding her of a storm at sea. *He cared.* But a monk—

His mouth came down on hers, hard, possessive, angry, as if he fought his feelings for her.

She should push him away. He didn't need her messing up his life or his calling or whatever the Triad was. Too bad her generous thoughts disappeared under the onslaught of his kiss.

She wrapped her arms around his neck and pressed her body against his, wishing she'd left off the wrap. She tangled her tongue with his, searching out his taste and revealing in it. Her pulse began to pound as a need grew to get as close to him as possible.

Akasha grabbed her hands from his neck and pushed away, stepping back three steps. "Tell me what you learned from Grandall."

Of all the dirty, rotten tactics to pull on her. "Why? What will you do? Go tell your precious Triad? Confront Grandall? What fucking good will it do you except to tangle you up in this serious mess?"

His biceps bulged as he lifted his fists as if he were doing biceps curls. "How can I know what I would do if I don't have any idea what the issue is!" He stalked back toward the glass door, but he didn't enjoy the view. Instead, he stared at her, his breaths as fast as hers.

Great, now they were both fucking angry. Not exactly productive. "You may find this hard to believe, but the less you know, the better off you'll be." Hell, did she really just say that to the hulking man with a gazillion light abilities? She needed to have her head examined.

Akasha's scowl was deep, forewarning her that whatever he said next would not be sweet nothings. "You leave me no choice." He unfurled his fist and raised his hand. Her instinct was to block a hit, but he was too far way for any physical contact.

Oh shit.

The next few seconds were a blur. Just as Akasha's purple light emitted from his hand, the door behind her slammed open and she turned, the light hitting the back of her head. "Sandale!"

The blond man strode to her, and she jumped onto him in a bear hug, the scent of apples engulfing her, triggering memories of him. Another dark-haired man continued in, his hand raised much like Akasha's. At first, she couldn't figure out why it was so hard to hold on to Sandale. Her legs were wrapped around his waist and her arms around his neck.

She dropped her feet when his lack of return hug became apparent and she let go. "Aren't you glad to see me?"

He nodded, staring at her as if he'd never seen her before. She put one hand on her hip and cocked her head. "Come on, it hasn't been that long. Don't you remember me? I'd know you anywhere even if you did let your hair grow into a beautiful golden mane."

He shook his head. "I have no memory of you."

"Can we do this reunion somewhere else? I think we found Akasha, too."

She turned to find Akasha pushing against some kind of

invisible wall. She grabbed the other man's arm. "Are you doing that?" She pointed at Akasha.

He nodded.

"Wow."

The dark hair man grinned. "Your lady has good taste, Sandale."

"I told you, she's not my—"

"Sons, we have to go, now." Another man appeared at the door.

Toni preened. Well, talk about the cavalry coming to the rescue.

Sandale looked at his dad. "We are."

The older man shook his head. "No, I mean now. Grandall just asked one of the Triad members-to-be where Akasha was."

They all turned to look at her monk. He had stopped trying to escape from the invisible box, but instead of showing his rage, he seemed almost calm. Maybe he was really rather happy to be rid of her after all. No more Toni, no more problem, and life was back to normal.

"What do I do with him?" The dark haired man pointed to Akasha.

"We leave him here." At Sandale's words, they all heard a muffled "no" come from Akasha.

"He must have some pretty strong lungs on him to get sound through my box."

Sandale's dad stepped into the rooms and closed the door. "I think it was more than lung power that caused that. Haldone, lighten the walls enough for us to hear him."

Well, hell, if Grandall was on the way and they wanted to converse with Akasha, she would grab her bag of belongings. She ran to the bedroom and hooked it over her shoulder. When she returned, she found Akasha had followed her with his gaze.

"Take me with you." Akasha's tone was calm, but his eyes were dark, reminding her of when they had sex.

Seriously? How was she supposed to resist that?

"We can't." Sandale grasped her hand. "They will be looking for him, and if he is gone, Grandall will demand a search and make something up that will sound ominous."

He was right. She was about to shake her head when she remembered that they needed Akasha to leave the building. She tugged on Sandale's hand. "We need to take him with us."

Haldone laughed, but Sandale's brows drew together before he looked at the older man. "Father?"

The older man strode to the box. "Will you promise not to compromise the safety of Toni and the rest of us?"

Akasha nodded.

Sandale shook his head. "He could betray us anyway."

Toni grinned. "No, he can't. He's next in line for a Triad position. If he gives his word, he will keep it. It's like he can't help it."

Sandale's father nodded and Haldone dropped his hand. As soon as he did, Akasha stepped to her side and grasped her other hand. Hmmm, a girl could get used to this. As long as there was no fighting like back at Libations in Loraleaf when she'd first arrived there.

"Haldone, you and dad open a portal. We can travel to the market square then walk to the next one and portal home. That way no one will be able to trace us, since all portal openings look the same and there will be plenty in the market."

Both men listened to Sandale and stood about six-feet apart. Then they each reached under their arms and pressed their Crius chips. When the opening shimmered into a clear view of the market, she and her two Edenists stepped through.

~~*~~

"Don't tell me to calm down." Sandale's mother faced off with Ulik. "I just got my boy back and now you're telling me he is leaving again and taking another one of my sons with him?"

Her angst hurt him, so Sandale stepped closer to calm her.

"Don't you touch me! I'm upset for a reason. And it's a damn good reason." She glared at him.

He did not move closer, but did not move away either.

Toni walked in. "What's all the yelling?"

His mother turned on her. "I'll tell you what all the yelling is about. It's about you. Because of you, my son wants to take his brother into the jungle."

Toni elbowed his dad out of the way and took his mom's arm. She walked her to the couch and sat down with her. "Pam, I'll take the blame for a lot of things, but you cannot lay this at my door, or Sandale's or your husband's. This lies firmly with the leader of Naralina."

His mom opened her mouth to object and Toni raised her hand. "No, what I said is correct. Grandall *is* the leader of this city and because this populace, you included, turned a blind eye to what was happening in the Ruling Circle, his son and yours are now required to fix this."

His mom actually looked a little guilty. "I understand all that with my head, but my heart hurts."

Toni grasped his mom's hands. "But you should be proud, not hurt. He will be back. He has to be because the only way to fix this is for us all to return."

His mother just shook her head.

"And you can help us."

"I can?" At the light in his mother's eyes, he felt some of his own tension leave.

"Yes." Toni looked at him and winked then returned her gaze to his mother. "We need you and your friends and all your husbands' friends to start questioning Grandall's every ruling, every statement, every visit to someone. You don't have to insinuate anything, just speak to another person be they known or a stranger and ask 'Why is Grandall there?' or 'Why did he not speak against this?' or 'I heard Grandall proposed that someone be exiled. Do you know why?'"

Toni paused and looked at Ulik. "Grandall needs to be the topic of every conversation so there is no starting point to the unrest and doubt, but it is there anyway."

His father nodded. "That is a good plan. You are a smart woman."

She looked away. "I had a little help."

Sandale glanced toward the room where Akasha voluntarily stayed after Toni had protested keeping him in Haldone's box. There was more between her and Akasha than it had first appeared. He wanted to learn about the man because in the short time he'd been with Toni, he was impressed.

She wasn't like any other woman he'd met so far. In fact, she was not what he expected at all when he thought of someone who would be friends with Serena. Toni was brash, extroverted, even a bit confrontational. Her "clothes" were unlike any he'd seen worn by women on Eden as well. Her brown leather top and skirt made him think of the Amazon princesses of Earth. She was ready for battle.

Yet despite her confidence and strength, she didn't want Akasha to be harmed, imprisoned or left out.

As she continued to give his mother a mission for while he was away, he quietly slipped from the room and entered the reading room. It was where his parents would read or research topics of the day. At the moment, it would seem that Akasha was content to do the same.

"Is that a classic or something more current?"

The marked man looked up from his book. "A classic. I find they impart the most insight on life as an Edenist." He set the book aside. "It sounds like you were able to calm your mother."

He smirked. "I can take no credit for that. Toni has convinced her that not only is it necessary I leave, but that my mom has an important role to play as well."

"I'm not surprised. Toni is…"

"Unique?"

Akasha nodded. "Exactly."

Sandale moved farther into the room, finally taking a chair opposite Akasha. "You realize by being with us, you risk your own position. If we left you at the Triad building, no one would have been the wiser."

"You are correct. But I cannot leave Toni until I am satisfied that she is safe. With Grandall still in power, she is not, nor are you or your family."

Sandale nodded. It was true and something that worried him.

Whatever Jahl and Khaos planned to do would need to be done soon. "What about your family?"

At the surprised look on Akasha's face, it was clear he hadn't considered them.

"You do have family, correct?"

"I do." Akasha moved his gaze to the small statue of a layfeenya, the closest thing Eden had to the Earth Dolphin.

The statue, according to Haldone, was their mother's favorite species. "And are you worried for them?"

"I am, of course, but we are not close like yours. Since my transition, a distance has formed between us, which is good. A triad member cannot have close ties with anyone, even family."

Sandale barely contained his snort. If this man thought he didn't have any close ties, he was blind. Akasha's concern for Toni was far more than an Edenist's concern for an Earth woman, but if the man refused to see it, it wasn't his place to point it out.

"How long have you known Toni?"

Akasha's question caught him off guard. "Not long. I saved her and Serena from danger when I was part of a filoz, but I was wounded and dragged off by lawbreakers."

"You lived with lawbreakers?" Akasha's eyes widened.

He stood, needing to pace. It was too hard to discuss while sitting still. "I do not remember it. I was rescued and my memory wiped. My guess is you know her far better than I."

"I am sorry to hear of your trouble. That cannot be an easy thing to overcome."

He stopped and looked at the man who had kept Toni safe. In Akasha's eyes, he saw true understanding of his difficulties for the first time. There was something unique about this Edenist.

"It is difficult, but I have a warm family and good friends to help me."

Akasha nodded as he looked toward the door. "I noticed."

There was a singularity about Akasha that was different. It wasn't that he exuded loneliness. Sandale doubted the man even understood that feeling. But Akasha did distant himself from others. His emotion was always well controlled, except with Toni. He grinned. Then again, it would be very difficult to not react to Toni.

He found himself attracted to her as well, and not on simply a physical level. There was a confidence and strength in her that he hadn't seen before. Then again, since he was new to his own life, he may very well have known others like her.

"Is what Toni discovered about Grandall a threat to Jahl and the city he lives in, or is it only a threat to Naralina?"

Sandale raised his brows at the question. "She didn't tell you what she heard?"

Akasha shook his head, frustration obvious in the set of his jaw.

His admiration grew with that knowledge. Toni had spent at least two days with Akasha and had managed to keep from telling him what she'd learned even though it was clear they had been intimate.

That in itself surprised him because Ulik told him that Triad members-to-be only sought out release at the Pleasure Temples when absolutely necessary and never with the same woman. They "avoid connections at all costs" mentality.

A yearning inside him to be in their presence when she told Akasha the realities of Grandall suddenly flared to life. Since he was no longer his former, patient self, he strode to the doorway and stepped into the living area. "Toni, we need you in here, please."

She gave his mom a quick hug before she rose. "Well, when you ask so nicely, how can I resist?" She sauntered past him, her stride strong, her hips swaying.

"That's one you don't want to let get away." His mother nodded sagely.

Why would she suggest that? He wasn't even part of a filoz. He didn't respond to her. Instead, he turned and followed Toni into the reading room. When he stepped inside, he closed the door behind him. The less his family knew, the safer they would be, if that was even possible anymore.

Toni hopped her butt up onto his fathers' desk. "What do you need me for? If it's sex, I think we should do it in a more private place. I'd rather not have your mom hear me because with you two," she waved her hand toward him and Akasha, "I know I would make way too much noise."

His balls tightened at her bald statement. He'd visited a Pleasure Temple when he first arrived to practice sex, since his memory on that was gone as well, but he had little confidence he could satisfy someone like Toni. That didn't mean he didn't want to.

He glanced at Akasha, who stared at Toni with darkening eyes. He didn't doubt the man had enough ability for both of them. An image of Akasha coming into Toni on her hands and knees while she sucked on his own cock flashed across his mind, just long enough for his body to take notice.

Sandale turned away from both of them, pretending an interest in a row of books.

"I don't think that's why Sandale called you in." Akasha's voice was a lot calmer than Sandale felt.

He spoke over his shoulder, not happy that his cock was still hard. "I think it's time you tell Akasha what you learned about Grandall."

Toni snapped her head around to look at him. "Are you sure? I don't want Jahl getting pissed at me."

He nodded. "I'm sure. I'll tell him I asked you to."

"Cool." She turned back to face Akasha, whose interest in her was absolute.

And the man thought he had no connection? Sandale rolled his eyes. Akasha was clearly denying his feelings.

Or Akasha had no idea what those feelings were. The idea surprised him, but at the same time took up permanent residence in his in his head.

Toni crossed her legs. "I'm not sure you will believe me, but trust me, Jahl does and so does Sandale." She glanced at him for confirmation, and he nodded.

As if that was all she needed, her face became serious and she looked Akasha in the eye. "Grandall has been working on a portal that can span a much larger space than between two Edenists."

"But a portal any larger than two men is unstable."

She nodded. "Yes, a portal opened by two Crius chips by two men, but Grandall has been working with his discoverists to combine abilities to build a stationary portal that will enhance the chips of two men and enable many people to transport through it."

Akasha leaned back in his chair, his body language saying he doubted her information already. "Why? Why would we need to transport more than one or two people?"

Toni looked back at him, and he nodded for her to continue. It wasn't important that Akasha believe her, but he deserved to know.

She grasped the edge of the desk as she leaned forward, clearly anxious to have Akasha's trust. This was important to her. "Grandall wants to bring many Earth women to Naralina at once."

"That doesn't make sense. Every filoz is free to find their mate already. Is this for the Pleasure Temples?"

Toni relaxed. "You believe me then?"

Akasha lowered his brow. "I believe that you believe what you are saying."

"Seriously?" She looked at him for help.

Sandale moved to stand next to her, his cock finally back to behaving. "We also believe what Toni is saying."

"Why?" Akasha shook his head, his hands coming up, palms up. "What possible reason would Grandall have to bring crowds of women to Eden faster than they already are?"

Toni jumped down from the desk and put one hand on her hip. "Because he plans to trade them to other cities either for those worthless rancels you use for money or for goods and services. That's why."

Akasha rose. "That sounds like slavery."

She stepped closer to him. "It does, doesn't it? The women won't have any choice in where they go and who knows how the other cities will disperse them?"

Sandale stepped closer in case he needed to protect Toni. What she told Akasha clearly shook some of his beliefs.

"Again, I ask you why? Why would Grandall do something—

something so against Dickinson Law? This could cause another Fullamush."

Toni laid her hand on Akasha's chest. "Exactly. From what I've gathered, Grandall isn't happy with just ruling Naralina. Based on what I've heard him tell Jasmine, he wants to rule the entire planet."

"That's impossible." Akasha backed away, pushing the chair behind him backwards until he could step away from them. "No one can rule the planet. That is against Cruison Law.

Toni opened her mouth to speak, but Sandale set his hand on her shoulder. When she looked at him, he shook his head before he met Akasha's troubled gaze. "A man who would break Dickinson Law won't stop there. For every success he has, he wants more. I know this is difficult to accept. We will leave you alone to think about what we said."

He looked to Toni and she understood, stepping past him toward the door. He followed. After she exited, he looked back. "Remember, Grandall's own son, a man who knows him well, believes his father capable of this."

When he closed the door behind them to give Akasha privacy, Toni took his hand. "I feel sorry for the big guy. He's so assured, but I think a lot of that is because he doesn't take everything into account."

Sandale agreed. He also felt empathy for the man and would have calmed him, but sometimes the mind worked better when a little tension motivated it. "We will give him some time to see we are right. We need to confer with my fathers and brother as to how to leave."

She lost her seriousness and gave him a wink, even as she

wrapped her other arm around his arm, pressing her body close. "I get to spend time with you and four other men? What are we waiting for?"

He grinned, enjoying her quick change of mood. "We are waiting for this."

He grasped her head with his free hand and kissed her like he'd wanted to since she'd walked into the reading room.

Her mouth opened under his, her tongue seeking out his own, as her cinnamon scent surrounded him. He let go of her hand to press her closer. At the feel of her breasts crushed against his chest, he moved his hand down from her bare waist to her leather covered ass and pressed her hips against his hardening cock.

"Sandale?"

Startled, he broke off the kiss and blinked at Vectar over Toni's shoulder. "Yes?"

His younger brother frowned, his blond hair almost reaching his eyebrows. "We're waiting for you."

He loosened his hold as Toni grinned at him before turning to walk by Vectar. "Some things are worth waiting for."

After she passed into the meal room, Vectar approached. "What are you doing?" His voice was low and upset.

Sandale smirked. "What do you think I was doing?"

His brother shook his head. "That's not like you." Then he followed Toni into the other room.

The censure skittered under his skin, irritating him as he joined his family.

CHAPTER TEN

Toni's mind drifted from the conversation, Sandale's kiss affecting her more than she'd expected. Probably because it was so out of character. She'd literally known him only a few minutes, but everything Serena told her had her expecting a completely different person than he actually was. He was edgier, quicker, more enticing than Serena had made him out to be. Serena had described a man who was calm, gentle and patient.

He was none of those now and he intrigued her.

"What should we do with Akasha? If we release him, he may lead Grandall back to us."

Baruch's question brought her mind back to their escape. "If we can get him to promise not to tell, he won't." The thought of leaving him behind bothered her. He'd protected her and deserved to see this out to the end. Besides, he was learning a lot from hanging out with her. She liked that she could show him the other side of his Pollyanna city. No one should be ignorant of corruption.

"Do you really think he will? It's one thing for him to stay in the reading room, but another to keep this whole problem a secret." Vectar received a number of nods from those at the table.

They just didn't know Akasha. She'd miss having sex with him, but she would be back…hopefully. It was that sliver of doubt that made her decision for her. "I think we should bring him with us."

"What?" Sandale stared at her as if she'd fallen off the highest spire of Naralina and just stood up and brushed herself off.

She didn't blame him. She wasn't sure why she suggested it either. "It would solve the problem of him leading Grandall here. Plus, if we couldn't trust him, that would mean you'd have to lock him up here, where again he could be discovered. Unless you want to kill him."

"No." This sentiment was voiced by all three fathers.

Now that she'd started, she could think of lots of reasons to take him with them. "He also has some pretty incredible abilities that could be very helpful outside Naralina."

Sandale spoke up. "I noticed from the perpendicular lines and three dots that he is Kindred of Light. What is his ability?"

She grinned, unreasonably proud of Akasha's power. "He has a different ability for each color in the light spectrum."

"Each?" Ulik stared in surprise. "That is unheard of."

Well, maybe his green light didn't do much, but he still could produce it. She nodded. "Yes, and they could all come in handy."

"What are they?" Vectar studied her as if he guessed she was really just thinking up excuses for keeping Akasha around.

"His yellow light lights up like a shiner. His blue light will show you what you can't see with your naked eye like amobes."

"Those really exist?" Sandale's mom shivered.

"I saw one when Akasha showed me his light. I know, it's a little creepy, but at least they do their job." She laid a comforting hand on Pam's hand across the table from her. She liked Sandale's mom.

She was warm and accepting, something Toni hadn't experienced from many women, if any.

"That's only two."

Sandale's younger brother was wound too tight for her taste. "You didn't let me finish. His orange light—"

The front door opening and loud footsteps running through the living area had them all turning toward the kitchen doorway.

Haldone stopped on the threshold. "We have to leave now."

Toni stood. "Why? What's happened?"

He looked at her for a moment before addressing his parents. "It's Grandall. He came into the market square where we portaled into earlier today and took away two men. He claimed they had abducted Akasha."

Sandale stood as well, his body barely touching the back of her shoulder as if to say he was there to protect her. She liked that. She was no sissy, but Grandall didn't play fair, and she'd already had a run in with someone very like him on Earth. She didn't want to repeat that experience.

Ulik looked at his family. "They finally tracked the portal opening to the square. It will only be a matter of time before they figure out those men were the wrong ones. Haldone's right, you need to leave now."

Toni headed for the door. "I'll grab my bag and Akasha."

Haldon grabbed her arm as she strode by. "Akasha?"

She gave him her best stare down. "Yes, Akasha. He can help us and if he doesn't come, then I stay here."

Haldone looked behind her and she turned her head to see Sandale nod. The dark brother, as she referred to him in her own mind, let her go and she continued out of the room. Part of her bristled that Haldone wouldn't listen to her and had to get it from Sandale.

The other part of her, the weak part, melted at Sandale's support. She really needed to get her head on straight. Toni Reid did not melt for men.

She stalked into the reading room to find Akasha standing, waiting for her. "We leave now?"

How did he do that? "Yes. Grandall actually had the portal trackers track the portal we used into the market and took the wrong men."

"Then we must hurry. He, or rather the Ruling Circle, has the authority to suspend portal openings for up to twenty-two hours."

"Well, hell. Has it ever been done?"

He nodded.

She grabbed her bag from the floor. "Can't people open them anyway?"

"Yes, but if they do they risk exile."

She stilled. "Just for opening a portal?"

He took her bag from her. "Yes, because portal use shutdown is only instituted in an emergency for the safety of all within the walls of Naralina."

Just her luck. She headed out the door only to run into Sandale. "Whoa."

He grabbed her arms to keep her from falling. "We still must be careful. Don't rush too much or we will draw attention outside." He looked over her shoulder. "You told him he's coming?"

She glanced behind her to find Akasha not a foot away. She

raised her eyebrow at him. "He's a smart man." She turned back to Sandale. "He figured it out."

"Then we go." He grabbed her hand and moved into the living room.

Toni's throat turned scratchy as she said goodbye to Sandale's mom and fathers. Vectar had already left and Haldone was going with them.

"Take care of my boys." Sandale's mom stood with her three hulking husbands behind her, tears cascading down her cheeks.

Toni gave her a salute. "You bet. You think I'd let anything happen to such gorgeous hunks?" She gave a quick wink before she was shuffled out the door by Akasha.

Now was the hard part. Pretending to enjoy the company of three men without giving away the fact that they were headed for the nearest wall. She walked between Akasha and Sandale, Haldone next to his brother.

Men stared at her attire, but that was nothing new. She winked at them as they went by.

Sandale squeezed her hand. "What flower do you wish us to buy you this time?"

She laughed gaily as if she was thrilled by some stupid flower. "I don't know. I'm torn between the sherry flower and the bonabus vine."

Akasha chimed in. "I think the bonabus vine because it is like you, clingy with just the right amount of scent."

She laughed loudly, her nerves getting to her. Three men walking by frowned at her.

Sandale leaned in. "It's fine."

She thought he meant the choice of flower in the pretend

conversation, but then she felt a calmness fill her and she understood. He'd used his ability to calm her. "Thank you."

"My pleasure." He gave her a devilish grin that she was one hundred percent certain the old Sandale had never used because if he had she would have fought Serena for him.

They turned down a narrow alley which forced their foursome to break into twos. Akasha stepped forward to walk with Haldone while Sandale kept hold of her hand.

It was strange to be nervous and yet completely calm.

They turned the last corner to the path that would lead them to the wall, only to find it blocked by two men. They were in a heated discussion and didn't see them.

Akasha grabbed Haldone by the arm and forced all of them back around the corner.

Toni whispered. "What is it?"

"That's Yiting, one of the Ruling Council."

"Scrat." Sandale looked at his brother. "We need another path."

Haldone scowled. "We will have to go out to the main one and walk farther down the mountain."

"Wait." Akasha made sure he had their attention. "Stay here."

She looked worriedly at Sandale, but quickly returned her gaze to Akasha's back. She grinned as she stared at his birthmark. *Of course.*

Purple light filled the area where the two men were. Akasha turned back to them. "It's safe now."

She stepped forward first, but as soon as Sandale joined her, he pulled her back. "They're watching us."

Akasha shook his head. "They will forget they saw us. Go."

At his nudge, Toni led the way past the two men, even

waving at them as they slipped by. Once they were all around the corner, Akasha went back. "When you awake, you will remember nothing of the strangers who passed by here." Then he rejoined them.

Haldone finally spoke. "How long will they remain hypnotized?"

"Only until I'm too far away to hold it, but they shouldn't follow us because they won't remember we were here."

They strode quickly the few yards to the wall. Toni could see why Haldone chose this spot. The windows of the houses faced the view, the back sides faced the wall and had no windows at all. Even if people were home, they wouldn't see them.

Sandale pointed to his brother. "Stand as close to the wall as possible." He turned to Akasha. "I will need you to be the other side of the portal. The lawbreakers took my Crius chip, so I cannot open one. Can I trust you with our safe passage?"

She and Akasha stared at him in shock. Suddenly, the reality of his experience filled her. She turned to Akasha, not willing to let Sandale see how much she hurt for him. "Will you help?"

"Where are we going?"

At Akasha's question, Sandale looked at her. As if he'd made up his mind, he answered. "Just the other side of this wall."

"But what about the lawbreakers?" Toni could feel her tension rising now that she had an inkling of the lawbreaker danger. "We could be jumping from the frying pan into the fire."

"I doubt that." He shook his head. "Lawbreakers don't generally wait right outside the walls unless they hope to catch an exile and that always happens on the south side. Our first priority is to leave Naralina."

What wasn't he telling her? "I told you Grandall is no longer working on the tracking device for portals outside the city walls, so why can't we just go directly to—"

"It is not safe." He turned away from her. "Akasha?"

Now she wasn't just nervous but pissed off as well.

Akasha moved to stand six feet from Haldone. "You can trust me with Toni's life."

"Good." Sandale reached for her.

She stepped away, crossing her arms over her chest. "I'm not going anywhere until you tell me why we can't simply—"

Voices coming down the path around the corner behind them had her shutting her mouth. "Well, hell." Grabbing Sandale's hand, she strode toward the now shimmering opening between Akasha and Haldone.

On the other side of the wall, she dropped his hand and moved to a tree with a large trunk. Crossing her arms once again, she planted her ass against it as Akasha then Haldone stepped through. They stood on either side of the portal and pressing their Crius chips, closed it.

They were safe now and she wanted an answer.

"It's so thick." Haldone looked around at the dense jungle they'd walked into, his dark eyes excited by his new surroundings.

She'd forgotten that most Naralinians never left their city. What a limited world view…so to speak.

Sandale grimaced. "Yes, it is right here, but there are many places where you could find yourself in the open and an easy target for lawbreakers."

"There is a lot of life here." Akasha had his blue light shining over the ground where dozens of various creatures crawled.

Okay, she wasn't a germ-a-phobe, but that was just eerie. "Akasha, can you douse the light please?"

He looked up from the ground and closed his hand. "Of course."

Sandale moved closer to her and lowered his voice. "I think you will agree that it is best if Akasha not see where Serena lives unless we are sure we can trust him."

"That's why you wanted to portal here."

He nodded.

Maybe she'd overreacted. "Next time, give me some warning, okay?"

One side of his lip quirked up. "Agreed."

Akasha's attention had strayed from his surroundings to her and Sandale's conversation though Haldone seemed inordinately fascinated by a tree.

She raised her voice to her normal tone. "So what do we do now?"

"I have an idea." Sandale spoke to her, but his attention was taken by Haldone's odd behavior.

His back was to them as he looked at something in the undergrowth. He lifted one hand then put it down. Then he lifted both hands and waved before he put them down.

Toni pushed away from her tree. "Haldone, what are you doing?" She walked toward him.

He started at her question and snapped his head around to face her. "There's some kind of reflection wall here." He pointed past a salis bush.

She continued toward him until she could see what he saw. "It *is* a reflection." Her pulse started to race. "No way."

Sandale and Akasha moved behind her to see what the object was.

Hell, did they look awesome. Tall, dark and tattooed on one side and tall, blond and smooth on the other. She looked at Sandale in the reflection. "Could it be Theron?"

"It could." He frowned. "Or it could be a lawbreaker."

At his words, Akasha grasped her arm. "Reflections are created by Kindred of Light."

"I know. Our friend Theron creates reflections." She didn't pull her arm away. Male egos could be so fragile sometimes. If her good boy in bad boy tats wanted to play protector, she wouldn't hurt his feelings. She looked at Sandale. "You said you had an idea?"

"I do, but I don't think it a good idea to discuss it so close to this reflection. It may be that a lawbreaker is nearby creating it to distract us."

Haldone elbowed Sandale. "Then he did a good job. Look."

The vegetation moved not twenty yards from them.

"Haldone." Sandale's voice was only a whisper.

Without a word, Haldone lifted his hand. "Done."

She whispered in Sandale's ear. "What is done?"

Akasha stepped around to face them both. "He formed an invisible box around us."

Cool. She had to admit she liked hanging out with Edenists in the jungle. They used their abilities a lot more here than in the city.

They all faced the threat even though they were relatively safe. Toni allowed herself a smirk at what the men had done. Haldone stood in front of her though a bit to the side. Akasha stood next to her and Sandale was so close behind her, she could feel the heat of his body on her bare back. For the first time in her life, she felt short.

Whatever came their way was large. Could it just be a feroon? Those lumbering extra-large bull-like creatures with tusks were very docile…unless it was mating season.

Finally, the last of the tall foliage parted, and she laughed. She knew the tall large man that moved toward them. He was the gentle giant. "Rekah!"

She patted Haldone on the shoulder. "It's okay. Sandale and I know him."

Rekah paused and another man stepped from behind him. "Toni?"

She laughed again and shouldered Haldone out of the way. "Theron, what are you two doing here?" She strode forward only to slam in to the invisible wall. "Ouch, fuck that hurt."

Immediately, Akasha grabbed her wrist. "Let me see."

She rubbed at her nose. "Is it bleeding?"

He frowned as he examined her face. "No, I don't think you damaged it."

"Well, good." She turned on Haldone. "What are you waiting for, take down this box."

Again, he turned to Sandale, infuriating her further. What an ass. He and she needed to come to an understanding soon or he was going to lose his ability to procreate.

Sandale nodded his approval, and Haldone raised his hand to form it in to a fist.

She glared at him. "Are we good?"

He stared at her uncomprehending. Sometimes talking to Edenists could be frustrating. Instead of explaining, she put her hands in front of her until she passed the place where the invisible wall had been.

Once clear, she ran to the smiling Rekah, and he lifted her into his arms. She lowered her head and gave him a kiss on the lips. After all, they had been lovers when she'd been at Loraleaf last.

When he put her down, she turned to give Theron a hug, but was grabbed about the waist from behind. "What the hell?"

She looked behind her to find Sandale scowling at Rekah. "Sandale, what are you doing? I want to say hello to our friends."

"I don't think he approved of your kiss." Theron chuckled.

"Neither did I." Akasha stepped next to Sandale.

If she didn't know better, she'd say the two men behind her were jealous, but that was impossible. "Okay, okay, no kisses. Now will you let me go so I can give my friend a hug? Because if you don't, I can't guarantee I won't do some permanent damage to your person."

Akasha's lip quirked at her words, and Sandale's hold loosened. Still, she had to forcefully pull away from him to greet Theron. She gave him a hug and whispered in his ear. "Seriously?"

He chuckled as he let her go. "It would appear so."

She stepped back and made the introductions. "This is Rekah, Kindred of Heart and Theron, Kindred of Light." At Akasha's nod, she continued. "Yes, you and Theron have your kindred in common."

She motioned to her companions. "This is Akasha, Kindred of Light and Triad member-to-be, and this is Sandale's brother, Haldone, Kindred of Air and you just saw a perfect example of what his ability is." She rubbed her nose again. The bugger still throbbed.

She didn't miss the surprise in Theron's and Rekah's faces when she mentioned Akasha was part of the Triad group. Their smiles at Haldone though were very welcoming. Must be a testosterone thing.

Sandale grasped her hand again. It reminded her of Jahl with Serena. She hoped it didn't mean he was as messed up as Jahl had been.

"Theron, how did you find us?" Since he asked exactly what she wanted to know, she kept quiet.

"I set up reflection panels around the walls of Naralina when Konala's bird came back to tell him where Toni was. Then we simply took turns monitoring them through an open portal until you arrived." Theron looked at Rekah. "Once we portaled nearby, Rekah said he sensed someone was very excited."

She winked. "Of course they were. I'm here." She opened her free hand wide and laughed. It felt good to be free of the threat of Grandall for a while.

Rekah shook his head. "No, it was this one, Haldone."

They turned to stare at him where he had hung back. He shrugged. "I've never been in the jungle. I'm excited to learn about it."

Rekah gave him an odd look before turning back to them.

Akasha grasped her arm again, a habit she really needed to break him of. "What bird? I saw no bird."

She grinned slyly. "You were out. The elseire bird visited me on your patrio while you were away."

"You didn't tell me."

The disappointment in his eyes made her uncomfortable. He may be a saint, but she definitely was not. She had a hunch that if she were to head over to Dante's vision of the afterlife, according to the horror movie she'd worked on, she wouldn't even make Limbo.

There was a pretty good chance she'd be in the eighth circle of hell. She stared Akasha in the eye. "You didn't ask."

Rekah laughed. "I guess you don't know Toni very well yet."

She wiggled her brows at her friend.

Akasha would not be distracted. "How did the bird communicate where you were?"

Oh, shit. She didn't want to explain Konala's abilities until she was sure Akasha was on their side. He saw everything as either good or bad. Most of the people at Loraleaf fell in the "both" category.

Theron took the decision out of her hands. "One of the men in my filoz is Kindred of Eden. He can talk to animals."

Akasha looked at her with new understanding. "This is how you communicated with Jahl." He turned back to Theron and Rekah. "Do we now go to your city?"

At the men's confused faces, she squeezed Sandale's hand. "Where are we going to go? I'm guessing you don't want us all to go to Khaos and Jahl's." She purposefully left out the name of Loraleaf, hoping Akasha hadn't noticed the one time she slipped.

Sandale caught on immediately. "No."

"But you need to confer with Jahl." Theron stepped forward as if he could make Sandale understand.

"I know. We do, but Akasha is not convinced we are in the right and the less Haldone knows about our home, the safer he is until we neutralize the threat of Grandall."

Neutralize? Now she *did* feel like she was in one of the science fiction movies she and Serena used to work on.

Rekah shook his head. "You can't go to Nassic and Wareson without talking to Jahl and Khaos first. They would be furious."

"Khaos?" Akasha looked at her for explanation.

She leaned over to whisper. "Part of Jahl's filoz."

He nodded.

Now that she thought about it, all this had to be pretty weird for Haldone and Akasha, especially for Akasha. Haldone may have never visited the jungle before, but Akasha barely visited anywhere even within his own city. His life at the Triad building was sheltered in more ways than one.

"So what do you propose?" Theron made a wide sweep with his arm. "Stay out here with the lawbreakers?"

"What I propose is that we go to your cave. It is a good neutral spot."

Theron's eyebrows rose. "That's true. But there are four of you and my cave is small. If we add Jahl, Khaos, Nassic and Wareson, plus you know their agapaytos, Serena and Erin will want to come, then we won't fit."

Rekah stepped forward. "But there is more to the cave than just your living space." He looked at them. "If you can modify it, everyone can fit."

"We can." Haldone joined the conversation. "My ability to make air hard allows me to shape it into whatever we need. We can dig, cut, build anything. With a little eyllen, I can even create a window, furniture, doors."

"There's plenty of eyllen in there, but there is also—"

At Rekah's sudden pause, Toni rolled her eyes. "Also what?"

Rekah dragged his thumb across his chest, the usual sign for *be quiet*. "I'm sensing anger from more than one man. We need to leave."

Sandale's hand in hers tightened and Akasha wrapped his

arm around her waist. She didn't see herself as some simpering wimp, but the men's immediate need to protect her had her feeling pretty damn special.

Theron and Rekah stepped apart and pressed their Crius chips. As soon as the portal opened, Sandale pulled her with him and Akasha and Haldone followed. When they were on the other side, they stood in front of a rock the size of a garage back home, but there was no opening.

"Well, hell."

CHAPTER ELEVEN

Akasha stared at the impenetrable wall and wrapped his arm around Toni again. If this was a trick, he would keep her safe. He glanced at Sandale who had let go of her hand to walk around the area with Haldone.

Theron and Rekah joined them and closed the portal.

"Come. It is not safe out here." Theron strode toward the mound of solid rock.

There must be an entrance they could not see. He urged Toni forward when Theron disappeared into the rock. "Holy Bendis." He halted and looked behind them at a smiling Rekah.

"Theron's pretty good with his reflection abilities. Go ahead. Just step where he stepped."

Toni pulled away, excitement in her green eyes. "Come on. Let's check this out." She headed for the rock.

Not anxious to lose sight of her, he followed close behind until he too walked into what could only be considered the living area of a cave.

"Hey, Akasha, this place is not much smaller than yours."

Toni was right. The set-up was similar except he saw no bathing area and it had doors. Doors were considered barriers to free-thinking in the Triad building. There were three doors across the living area.

"Come check this out." Toni had opened a door and walked into another room. From where he stood, he could see it was a sleeping area. He followed her, her enthusiasm rubbing off.

She opened a door opposite the one they walked in. "Hey look. It even has a flushing toilet." She grinned at him as she pulled a lever and water flowed into the basin below, while an opening beneath let water out.

What interested him more was the large bed in the sleeping area. While here, he would not sleep somewhere else. He would stay as close to her as possible. Everyone seemed to be on friendly terms, but he did not know Nassic and Wareson or Jahl and Khaos, and for that reason, he would remain vigilant.

Sandale stepped into the sleeping area. He too looked at the bed. "It looks big enough for three, but someone will need to sleep in the living area."

"I'm sure Haldone won't mind that." She'd noticed there was no couch. Let the man sleep on the floor.

Sandale nodded in agreement before he turned to follow his brother through another door back off the living area.

Akasha breathed easier. He had no doubt of Sandale's dedication to Toni. He would make a good ally in keeping her safe…even against her own wishes.

Once she checked out the running water in the stone sink and open rainbox, she walked back into the bedroom. He blocked her way with his body.

She looked up at him, a seductive smile curving her lips. "Did you want to try out the bed?"

He did. He wanted her. He wanted to be inside her. But he couldn't. Not until he knew the color of her essence. He could not risk his position on the Triad, which he felt became more important every day as his knowledge expanded.

He had gone beyond the meditative walls of the Triad complex, even beyond the city. His presence on the Triad would benefit Naralina perhaps more than any other member had in centuries.

Toni wrapped her arms around his neck and pressed her leather clad body against his. "As soon as Rekah and Theron leave, I'll be happy to satisfy all of you."

He pulled her hard against him. "No. Not Haldone."

She raised her eyebrow. "Oh, really. So you're okay with Sandale?"

He liked Sandale. Maybe because his memory had been wiped or it could be because he protected Toni as he did. "I am."

Her eyes widened. "Good, because I'm not particularly happy with Haldone either and didn't really plan on having sex with him." She rose up on her toes and gave him a kiss on the lips.

He should have let it go at that. Kissing her went beyond mere sex, but a man would have to be dead to ignore her appeal.

He moved his hand behind her head just as she started to pull away and brought her mouth back to his. Within seconds, he breeched her lips. Her cinnamon scent filled his nostrils and tightened his balls.

She needed no encouragement, pressing her abdomen against his growing erection as she tangled her tongue with his own.

He moved his hand beneath her skirt and cupped her smooth ass cheek, wanting more than ever to pleasure her there as well.

"I can take out this doorway and make it an arch. It will be a long narrow room, but could certainly fit all of us." At the sound of Haldone's voice in the next room, he loosened his hold on Toni and she lowered her heels, the scrape of her leather skirt against his cock causing him to moan.

"I guess we should be sociable." She stepped away but ran her hand across his chest, hitting both nipples before trailing it down toward his cock.

He grabbed her hand before she touched him. "You are right. You join them. I need to use the bathing area."

"Of course you do." She winked before brushing by him and giving him a slap on his ass.

He held himself completely still to keep from throwing her down on the bed and fulfilling his own need. After a couple deep breaths, he walked into the bathing area. When he discovered there was no cold water with which to bathe his cock, he groaned.

Toni's essence needed to be revealed soon, or he would be in danger of corrupting his own. And what if hers was black? What if he was completely wrong about her?

Then he would be forced to take appropriate action.

~~*~~

Sandale poured himself another glass of ale. Theron and Rekah had brought them a complete meal, a longseat for Haldone and provisions for a couple days until a meeting could be arranged, though Toni had argued strenuously for something sooner. He had a feeling she hadn't told them everything and he planned to discover what else she knew.

The food wasn't as good as his mother's, but Toni loved it. Wasn't she given whatever she wanted at the Pleasure Temple?

Haldone stood. "Now that I have been nourished, I'm ready to tackle this expansion."

"That is a good idea." Sandale grinned at his brother. "You know what needs to be done. Tell me what you'd like from us." He waited, happy to do whatever was needed.

Haldone frowned. "What I would like is for you to stay out of my way."

Akasha spoke before he could. "You wish to do this all by yourself? It is a large task in a short time."

"Which is why I don't want you three involved. I have experience at this. You do not. You'll slow me down like you did when I made that window for Theron's reflection wall."

Sandale glanced toward the reed covered window. Haldone was right. Their abilities did not extend to building or reconfiguring a home. "Agreed. We will stay out of your way. Do you need anything to begin?"

Haldone had already opened the middle door in the living area. "Not now. Once I have the basics done, I will need more eyllen than what's in this shiner, but Rekah told me the cave is full of it." He gave him a look his father would be proud of. "I will find you if I need you, so don't come in."

Sandale smiled. "We promise."

After the door closed, he turned to his companions. Akasha sat on the couch next to Toni. The space on the other side of her was now vacant as that is where he had sat. He liked how comfortable he felt around Akasha, much like he felt around his older brother.

And Toni…he wished he remembered Toni. Her personality

spoke to him in a way no one else's did and her clothing had his sexual need rising to the surface, but he no longer had the experience he once had.

Akasha stood and walked toward him. "Something is troubling you."

The man was quieter than most, but more observant as well. Since Sandale didn't want to talk about his lack of expertise in the bedroom, he chose his other problem. "It is. I am concerned about what Toni has not told us."

Akasha turned from him to look at Toni. She appeared as surprised as he, but Sandale had begun to sense her nuances.

"What I haven't told you? Well hell, there's lots of things I haven't told you. I haven't told you my favorite color is green or that I don't ever need to go back to Earth except for birth control. I don't even think I told you how hot the two of you look standing next to each other like that. One dark and one light." She cocked her head and gave them a sultry look. "I don't have to settle for one side, but get to eat the whole enchilada."

His cock reacted to her words and her gaze as it swept down him and then Akasha. The woman was born to have sex, but he refused to be distracted. "I meant that you haven't told us everything you know about Grandall's plans."

She sighed, sat back and crossed her legs, teasing them with a brief view of her bare, shaved pussy. "There isn't much else to tell. He's building a huge portal to transport women to Naralina and then will use them to trade with other cities. I would think that's enough."

"Then why were you so insistent that Theron and Rekah set up the meeting for tomorrow instead of the following day?"

She rolled her eyes. "I would think that's obvious. The sooner the better. This man is totally high on his own power. He's addicted to it. He can taste it. He's going to move ahead as fast as possible."

"Is something standing in his way that he hasn't completed the project?" Akasha low voice held none of the edge Sandale heard in his own.

Toni looked away. "He's had a lot of problems trying to create this thing. It still needs two men with Crius chips so he must have taken some people into his confidence."

"He has." At Akasha's words, they both looked at him.

Sandale beat Toni to the question. "How do you know?"

"I attended the last Open Circle session. It is obvious that Grandall is in charge. No member did or said anything without first looking to him."

Toni shot up from the couch. "Do you mean the whole Ruling Circle is involved?" At Akasha's nod, she strode toward the door, as if she was ready to tackle the entire Ruling Circle itself. "Well, fuck. That makes our job even harder." She turned and faced them. "How are we supposed to take down the entire Ruling Circle without the whole city coming to the rescue? Grandall has everyone snowed."

He frowned at the term. "Snowed?"

"Yes. It means everyone believes he is the benevolent father who will take care of them while underneath he commits heinous acts that are against the law, but when you try to prove it, no one will listen to you." Her chest rose and fell with her agitation.

Sandale took the few steps he needed to touch her and help her calm. "Are you still talking about Grandall?"

She blinked. "Grandall? Yes, of course." She pulled her shoulder from his grasp and flopped down on the couch. "Grandall is the worst kind of snake. He's infected those around him. The only thing stopping him from succeeding right now is the time to complete the final changes." She looked up at them. "There was a discoverist that was causing some problems. I'm not sure what, but Grandall said once that was taken care of, he only needed forty-four hours before he could test the portal."

"A discoverist?" Akasha's blue eyes had grown even lighter as his gaze on Toni turned intense. "Did he mention the name of the discoverist?"

She crinkled her brow. "I'm not sure."

"Think. You must know."

Sandale sat next to Toni and took her hand. Calming her so she could think. Akasha's intensity wouldn't help her remember, but it certainly had his own tension spiking again.

"It was something like Meena, Seeda." She looked at Akasha. "Edenist names are weird-sounding to me. I don't know." At her look of failure, Sandale lifted her hand and kissed it. She turned a half-hearted smile on him.

"Was it Keeva?"

Her gaze snapped back to Akasha. "Yes! That's it. How did you know?"

He looked away, his brow furrowed.

Sandale's gut tightened. "What is it?"

Akasha faced them. "Keeva was exiled yesterday."

"Fuck." Toni expressed what they all felt.

Silence filled the room. All of them lost in their own thoughts. Sandale had less to think about then the other two since his mind had such a limited number of memories. But he had learned enough to know that if Grandall was successful with his plan, even the jungle wouldn't be safe from the planet-wide war that was sure to follow.

He caught Akasha's gaze and shook his head. There was nothing they could do until tomorrow. The exile ceremony occurred in the evening. That meant they had until tomorrow evening to stop Grandall.

Akasha seemed to understand his silent message. "We are not defeated yet. We must move forward as planned. For all we know, your Jahl, Khaos, Wareson and Nassic are creating their own individual plans as we speak. I doubt they will want to wait."

Toni perked up. "You're right. Nassic has wanted to return to Naralina and rule on the Circle again since the night he left. And Jahl would do anything to take down his father." She smiled at both of them. "My guess is we will have early morning visitors."

Sandale nodded as he stood. "I agree about Jahl and I trust your judgement on Nassic."

She sat a little straighter at his words. Did no one realize how dependable she was? She acted as if no one trusted her.

"Thank you." She turned her head and batted her eyelashes at Akasha. "See you can trust me."

The man laughed. "Sandale, you need to know that Toni did nothing but lie to me from the moment I caught her spying until the day you came."

"Hey, that's not true." She stuck her bottom lip out. "I told you truth after both our bargains."

He nodded. "Yes you did, but only what you wanted to tell, not all there was to tell."

She shrugged. "You didn't ask for all of the truth." She raised her brows and gave him a stern face. "You need to learn to be more specific."

Again he chuckled.

Rather than feeling like an outsider, Sandale enjoyed the banter. Being around two people who didn't know him BW was refreshing.

Toni sprawled out on the longseat. "If I remember correctly, you still have a color to show me."

Akasha lost his smile. "I thought we weren't bargaining anymore."

"We're not. I've been open and honest about everything. It's time you were too."

"I'm always honest."

She waved his comment away. "I know you are better than I am. I'll give you that, but you still should show me your last color."

At Toni's assumption that Akasha was better than her, Sandale frowned at him.

Akasha frowned back. "I think we need to show Toni exactly how good she is."

Now this was interesting. Sandale asked before Toni could. "How?"

Akasha looked at her. "I will show you only because I trust you and Sandale not to tell anyone, not even your family members about my final colored light."

Toni reacted by sitting up, all teasing gone. "I promise."

Akasha took a deep breath before explaining. "My white light reveals a person's essence. A pure white essence, which doesn't exist among men, is a man free from all wrong doing. A black essence can be seen on those who only do wrong—"

"Like Grandall."

At Toni's interruption, Akasha shook his head. "No. Most men have white areas, black areas and gray areas. It is simply a matter of the size of each. What happens with lawbreakers, or so the discoverists tell us, is that the black area grows."

Sandale couldn't resist asking a question. "Is the essence a reflection of actions we've already taken or something we are born with?"

Akasha looked him in the eye. "Your essence is a reflection of your decisions, so you are free to choose how to live your life."

"In that case, I'm not sure I'd want to know what color my essence is. That other mind that took mine over did some unspeakable things according to what I said BW."

"I do not know what your essence would look like since you were not in complete control of what you did." Akasha put a hand on his shoulder. "But know this. All that matters is how you act now."

He fisted his hands to ignore his need to pace. It was a small space and he had to share it. From what his family told him about the way he was before, he'd guess he had a white and gray essence, but from their reaction to his actions now, he had to assume it was mostly gray unless it was black from the other mind.

In an odd way, he felt as if he had to live up to his old self, yet his new self didn't have the benefit of those other experiences. By the Crius, it frustrated him!

"Sandale, what's wrong?" Toni's voice brought his attention back to his companions.

He crossed his arms over his chest as if he could guard against any future disappointment on others' faces. "I'm not sure you'd understand, so it's probably better I keep silent."

"No." Akasha's quick response surprised him. "You are among friends here. Among others who only know you as you are now in whatever light your essence may be. Tell us what bothers you."

He had seen Akasha hypnotize Yiting and his companion with purple light back in Naralina yet despite their being no colored light, Sandale felt compelled to speak. "I doubt you can understand." He moved his gaze to Toni. "Either of you."

She leaned forward. "Try us."

He hesitated. He didn't want to see disappointment on these two faces. He felt a certain kinship with Toni and Akasha.

Neither of them spoke, waiting patiently for him to share his concerns.

He nodded. "Very well. This discussion of essences and what I might have done in the past doesn't just bring to mind the evil I perpetrated while influenced by another. It also conjures up a blank wall in my brain when it comes to those actions I made that were for the good of others and myself."

He paused, picking his words carefully and thankful they didn't interrupt. "The fact is, no matter what I do now, what I learn now, I will never be the Sandale that people remember. I can spend the rest of my life learning about how I was, but that won't make me be that way. Those experiences that made me in to who I was are gone. Now I can do nothing but go through life disappointing those I am coming to love. I see no end in sight."

Akasha frowned, offering no words to lighten his mood.

Then Toni stood up and sauntered toward him. She wrapped her arms around his neck and gazed into his eyes. "I want you to listen to me."

"It would be difficult not to with you so close." He could feel his body responding already, so he wrapped his arms loosely around her waist.

She smirked. "Now that's perfect. That response is just right for who you are today. You need to stop trying to be your old self. As you just pointed out. You can't. So you have a golden opportunity here."

He raised an eyebrow in disbelief. He didn't see anything positive in his situation…except maybe her and Akasha. "I do?"

"Yes, you do. You have the opportunity to make yourself into whatever type of person you want to be. Back on Earth, I know dozens of people who would like to be able to do that, to start over again with a clean slate."

"I do have that."

"Exactly. You can be whoever you want. And just for the record, I wasn't in the least bit attracted to the calm Sandale. However, this edgier Sandale is freakin' hot." She pressed her hips against him as she said it.

Both his mind and body came alive. To no longer attempt to act as he used to but embrace his future with an open mind and a sea of endless possibilities? It was like Helios shining through clouds after days of rain. He could be whoever he wanted to be.

He looked over Toni's shoulder to see Akasha smiling. There was approval in his gaze, and as he moved it to Toni, Sandale saw pride. He returned his gaze to Toni's beautiful green eyes. "You have the insight of a wise man."

She pushed away and waved her finger at him. "Oh no, don't be associating me with some smart guru. That's Akasha's job. I just call it like I see it."

Akasha stepped behind her. "Sandale's right. You have a wisdom beyond the norm."

She spun around as Akasha grasped her hips. "Let's just say I don't think along the normal lines of thought. I think they call it being a rebel."

Sandale grasped her waist, letting his face fall into her hair, the cinnamon scent of her filling his nostrils and contentment seeping into his heart.

She moved her hips back and forth against his hard cock then pushed her pelvis into Akasha. "I'd love to hop in the sack with you two, but I still want to see Akasha's colored light."

Sandale smiled even as Akasha chuckled.

She pulled away and faced both of them. "And here you thought I had a one-track mind." She let her gaze sweep over their cocks.

"Very well. Stand in front of the longseat."

Toni had just moved into place when a loud bang was heard behind the door where Haldone had gone. Sandale looked at the other two before striding toward the door, concern for his brother taking all thoughts of sex from his brain.

He opened the door and found the interior completely dark. "Haldone, are you hurt?" He took two steps in before light filled the space and he saw his brother on the ground. "Haldone!"

Haldone waved him away. "I'm fine. I'm fine. Don't come any closer or you'll hit the table like I did."

Table? Suddenly the scene made sense. Haldone ran into his invisible table and dropped the shiner, causing him to trip. "Are you sure you are well? Can I get you anything?"

His brother stood and set the shiner on the table, which made it look like it hung in midair. "I'm fine." He brushed off his thighs and ass. "And what you can do is leave. I told you if I needed you I would come get you."

Sandale held up his hand. "Very well." He backed out of the room and closed the door. Akasha and Toni looked at him expectantly.

"He's fine. He just bumped into his own furniture." He couldn't help smirking. It made him feel better that he was not the only one who had trouble with his abilities. "I believe Akasha was going to show us his light that reveals a person's essence."

"Yes, do me first." Toni paused then winked. "I mean with the light. You can do me as well, afterward."

Since he hadn't had time to study all Earth expressions, he assumed Akasha would know what she meant.

The man looked blankly at her as well, but obviously decided to ignore her comment. "I must remind you both that you cannot tell anyone about this part of my abilities."

They both nodded.

"As I said, my white light will reveal the color of someone's essence. Are you ready, Toni?"

"Will it hurt?"

He smiled gently. "No, not at all, but you won't be able to see your own essence colors."

"What? Wait. I want to see them."

He shook his head. "It doesn't work that way."

Sandale grasped Akasha's forearm as he started to raise it. "What if we had a reflection in the room? Could she see it then?"

Akasha lowered his hand. "I don't know."

Toni pouted. "Theron's not here so it's not like we can conjure up a reflection at will."

Sandale grinned as he headed for the sleeping area. "No we can't, but we are in Theron's home and I believe…" He glanced around the bed, sure he had seen a reflection, or mirror, as Toni would call it, hanging somewhere.

Scanning the room, he didn't see it at first until he looked back toward the door he'd come through. It hung on that wall. He unhooked the reflection then brought it into the other room and leaned it against the cabinet Theron used to store food. "Now we will discover if your light on a person's essence can be reflected."

Akasha stood for a moment staring at the reflection. He'd turned thoughtful and very serious. Finally, he glanced at them both and nodded. "Let us see what happens."

"Great, so what do I do?"

Akasha raised his hand. "Close your eyes."

She cocked her head. "Seriously? Then how am I going to see the reflection?"

Sandale chuckled at Akasha's confused look. "What if Toni stands in front of the mirror and you shine your white light on her back?"

"As I said, we can see what happens, but I still suggest closing your eyes to start."

Toni nodded excitedly and moved in front of the reflection. He and Akasha stepped behind her.

Akasha raised his hand and Toni closed her eyes.

A bright flash lit the room as pure white light emitted from Akasha's hand. Sandale had to close his eyes and open them slowly.

Toni was surrounded by the light, but an amorphous oval cloud at her center blocked any view of her body.

"Try opening your eyes." Akasha's voice was barely a whisper. Sandale moved his gaze to him. The man stared not at Toni, but at the reflection where her essence was visible.

"Oh wow, that's so cool. Hey look." She pointed at the reflection. "I have a hell of a lot more white than I expected."

Sandale laughed. "That makes two of us."

"Hey." She gave him a fake scowl before her lips twitched upward.

"You have black in your essence." Akasha's accusatory words brought Sandale's attention to the lower part of the oval. It was blacker than a night with no moon. At least the night had stars.

"Yeah, well, I told you I wasn't as good as you, so don't act so surprised." Though she tried to make light of it, he could tell the reality of that color bothered her. What had she done that was so horrific that it stained her essence? He expected it in his, but she was not an evil person.

Akasha curled his hand into a fist and the light disappeared.

Toni stepped away from the reflection. "That was cool. So who's next?"

Akasha didn't say anything, his gaze on Toni, a frown on his face.

"I am curious how much of what I did while under the influence of another mind has corrupted my essence. Maybe I am too far gone."

Toni sashayed over to him. "Tell you what, if you are, then maybe we can hang out together. You know, birds of a feather and all that." She rested her hand on his chest and wiggled her eyebrows.

He captured her hand. "If that means living with you, I can think of no one I would rather have."

A fleeting look of fear flickered in her eyes before she laughed. "You are a charmer."

"I too would be curious as to the state of your essence." Akasha's deep voice was serious, completely opposite of Toni's attempt at levity.

A person's essence was very important to Akasha. That made sense since he was of the Triad. Sandale had learned about the basic structure of Naralina and he would guess that Akasha had the purest essence of any of them.

At Akasha's raised brow, Sandale stepped in front of the reflection and closed his eyes. As the light hit his back, he felt as if he floated just inches from the ground, but as he opened his eyes, his feet were still on the floor. The feeling of weightlessness was odd.

"Well, hell." Toni's words had him focusing on his essence.

It was completely different from Toni's. Hers was layered, white on top, grey in the middle until it gave way to black. His was different. He was completely white, but in the background was a dark cloud. "Akasha, what does this mean?" He looked at the man behind him in the reflection.

"I have never seen this before." Akasha studied him. "It appears your essence has been split in half. Your purity is probably because of the shortness of your life since your mind was erased. As we are all born like this, or so I'm told, and as we act our goodness remains white, but the more immoral we are, the grayer we get. You are like a newborn."

"See Sandale, I told you." Toni grinned. "You get a do-over. You can be whoever you want."

"And the dark cloud I can see around it?"

Akasha shook his head. "I am only guessing, but I would surmise it is the blackness of the essence of the mind that took claim to you. This means the man who had that mind died when he was transferred to you. That essence is trapped with you."

Sandale felt his blood turn cold. "Does that mean it can influence my actions?"

Akasha shook his head. "Honestly, I do not know."

"Fuck. Are you saying that Sandale still has to worry about that other person even though he's sacrificed the memory of his life to be free of it?" Toni stepped up to Akasha as if she would force him to separate the essences.

Sandale couldn't breathe at the thought that his sacrifice had been for nothing and he would soon succumb to evil intention again. Better not to live than that.

Akasha's eyes widened as Sandale's own essence sparked a bright white light with his thought.

He pointed to the reflection. "What was that?"

Akasha smiled. "I do not know what you were thinking, but whatever it was reaffirmed your white essence. I do not think you will have any problems with the other one unless there is an Edenist who can reach it and manipulate it. I have never heard of such an ability."

That did ease his mind. "Thank you." In fact, he felt joy filling him.

Toni sighed. "Now you're going to have to do a couple bad things if you want to hang with me. Right now you are way too good."

He looked at Akasha and smirked. The man nodded, closed

his hand and Sandale spun around. He took the two steps to Toni, fell to his knees, and before she could react, he lifted her leather skirt and licked her bare mons.

"Well, hell, I guess I know what to say next time I want you to do dirty little things to me."

He laughed then rose to his feet and raised an eyebrow. "Dirty?"

"Just an expression back home for kinky sexual actions."

He looked at Akasha to see if the man understood "kinky," but he wasn't paying attention.

Toni also glanced at Akasha. "What's wrong?"

He was so lost in thought, he didn't respond. Sandale reached over and touched him on the arm.

"What?"

"Is something wrong?"

Akasha stared at him uncomprehendingly for a moment, before answering. "No, I was just pondering your essence."

"Good." Toni leaned against Sandale. "Because we want to see what your essence looks like." She wiggled her brows, clearly enjoying the experience.

Akasha shook his head. "I cannot shine the white light upon myself. It doesn't work." He sighed. "I've tried."

"That's a bummer, but the good news is, of the three of us, yours is the least we have to worry about."

Despite Toni's banter, Akasha's brow did not lighten. There was something else bothering him. Sandale was about to ask when Toni stepped between them and ran her hand down their torsos, stopping at the hair just above their cocks. "Well, if we can't play with essences anymore, how about if we play with bodies?"

Sandale caught her hand at the same time Akasha did. He nodded to the other man who seemed to understand him somehow and without a word to each other, they picked Toni up and strode to the bedroom, her laughter louder than the banging coming from the cave.

CHAPTER TWELVE

Toni pushed away the anger at the blackness on her essence and focused on how much white there had been. All this time she would have thought her willingness to share her body with Edenists who had no beloved would have turned her essence completely gray, but it hadn't.

She saw it as doing a service, but on Earth she could think of a number of derogatory words that would be used for her. Her past had left her feeling like a rebel and just a bit like she was in the wrong, despite her reasons for joining the Pleasure Temple. The revelation of the white in her essence relieved her of a burden of guilt she hadn't even known she had…and she owed it to these two men.

They lowered her to her feet, and she stood between them. Sandale turned her to face him. "I want you naked."

That worked for her. Lifting her arms wide she grinned. "I'm good with that."

Sandale brushed her hair back over her shoulder before his blunt fingers found the ties that held her halter vest together. He paused then ran one finger down the crease of her cleavage. "I do not understand why you cover your breasts."

She looked over her shoulder at Akasha, whose gaze was on her ass. "We'll have to show him."

He looked up and over her shoulder. "She does it to entice. It makes an odd kind of sense."

She turned back to watch Sandale untie her laces. He was almost done, the leather halter starting to part, when Akasha's hands glided up the back of her thighs and over her ass, pushing her leather skirt up as he went.

Her sheath began to moisten at his touch, but before she could guess what he'd do next, Sandale was pushing her vest aside, his hands brushing her hardening nipples as he went.

Shit, it had been so long since she had two men that her entire body was sensitive. Not knowing what each man would do when, just added fuel to the fire burning in her abdomen.

"Beautiful." Sandale's breathy response to her breasts caused her throat to tighten.

No one had told her that before. Her nipples and areolas were unusually large, something a couple of her Earth lovers had pointed out. Eden men were far too polite to do so, but none had gone out of their way to say they were beautiful.

Oh, hell, what if Sandale thought that because he didn't have anything to compare them to. "You have had sex with other women since your brain wipe, right?"

He grinned, still staring at her nipples. "I have. I've seen others and I like yours best."

If the man kept talking like that, he was going to worm his way into her heart, something she wasn't ready for anyone to do.

Akasha's hands on her ass distracted her as he spread her cheeks. A soft touch over her anal hole told her he was using his red light. It didn't matter one wit. Her pussy tightened at the feeling. Something about her ass being penetrated always made her a simpering idiot.

Sandale pulled the vest down behind her back, but held it there, trapping her arms. Her gut reaction was to bring her knee up to his crotch, but luckily his mouth came down to lick her nipple and she was able tap down her instinct. The vest was loose and she could remove her hands if she wanted to.

Akasha took the opportunity to push his hard cock between her spread cheeks.

Her knees threatened to weaken, but she refused and braced herself even though she let her head fall back.

He must have thought that an invitation. His lips came down at the spot where her neck met her shoulder and he started to suck at the exact moment Sandale took her nipple into his mouth.

"Oh yes." Pleasure raced to her core as her blood left her brain for her labia. This would be good.

Sandale moved to her other nipple and played with it before taking it into his mouth.

Akasha let go of her ass, allowing it to capture his cock as he wrapped one hand around her waist to keep them close, pushing her hands and Sandale's into her back. With his free hand he lifted the front of her leather skirt and cupped her pussy.

She held her breath, hoping he'd move one of his fingers into her entrance.

Sandale's bite on her hard nub had her expelling her breath in a moan. She'd swear they'd talked to her former lovers to find out what she liked most. Either that or it was what they liked too. At that thought, her excitement doubled.

Sandale left her hard nipples and pulled his hands from behind her, but her own remained pinned by Akasha. "Your scent has kept me in an excited state since I found you. I cannot resist tasting you another moment." With his words, Sandale dropped to his knees.

As if they had planned it, Akasha's hand left her pussy and pulled her skirt up. Sandale's fingers explored her wet folds before he leaned into her and lapped her clit.

Fuck, that was good.

Sandale continued to lap upward, circling her and blowing on her, keeping her toes curled and her sheath tight, while Akasha moved his hands to cup her breasts, occasionally flicking a nipple with his thumb then pinching it, causing a wave of heat to speed down to her core.

Akasha growled in her ear. "Kiss me."

As soon as the shiver finished racing down her spine, she turned her head. He captured her mouth in a demanding kiss and Sandale inserted two fingers into her sheath.

She came up on her toes as the sensations caused by the two men converged faster than she expected and her orgasm hit hard. Akasha wouldn't let her mouth go and Sandale pumped his fingers as he brought her to a new height of ecstasy with his tongue.

Her whole body seemed suspended as satisfaction burst through her like fireworks, Sandale's tongue forcing every spark to its final end. She pulled her head away from Akasha and gulped in much needed air. Then before she was aware of it, both men turned her and set her on the bed.

"I think she needs ambrosia." Sandale stepped back and at Akasha's nod, he left the room.

She wanted to tell him she'd prefer an ale, but she *did* crave the coconut-mango drink with the spicy aftertaste, or rather her body did. She definitely needed something more nutritional than ale.

Once her breathing had returned to a more normal rate, she cocked her head at Akasha. "Did you and Sandale know each other before now?"

"No, why do you ask?"

"I don't know. It seems pretty strange that you work so well as a team for two men who just met."

He looked toward the open doorway. "Sometimes there are people you meet that you have an immediate understanding with. Almost as if you have known each other for a long time and are completely comfortable with them. Granted it doesn't happen often, but I felt it with Sandale."

"That's weird, that's exactly how I felt when he came to get me. I feel very comfortable with this new Sandale. Do you think it's because he doesn't have that long history without us, so we are in sync with him? Or maybe that he's more relaxed with us?"

"I am." Sandale stood in the doorway. "And I know part of it is because you two do not expect me to be someone else. You accept me as I am now." He strode in and handed both she and Akasha the drink.

She took a couple sips. "Back on Earth when people go through a disappointment or tough spot in their lives, they will often say *that everything happens for a reason*. I always thought of that has a copout for accepting crap instead of fighting against it, but in your case, and after what you went through, and also after having Akasha catch me spying, I think there might be something to that idea after all."

Akasha frowned. "You mean like there is a greater force arranging our lives?"

She laughed. "Not at all. More like we are being guided in the right direction by nature and time and the universe." She shook her head. "I guess I'm not making sense. Like I said, it's just a saying."

Sandale sat on the bed next to her. "I can see where that belief would be a great comfort. If I believe that my experience with the lawbreakers and consequent memory loss happened for a reason, that reason might be so that I could later protect you from Grandall.

"Exactly." She took a few more sips, already feeling her energy returning.

"And what reason would there be for me catching you spying?"

She turned toward Akasha, who stood in front of them. "Well, I would first think it was so we could have some fantastic sex." She winked and his lips lifted a bit. "But I really think it was so you could learn more about the people of Naralina and those outside its walls so you can be a better leader."

"You are confusing the Triad with the Ruling Circle. The Triad does not lead Naralina."

"I know, but I think you are destined for greater things."

Akasha's brows lowered. "There is no greater calling than the Triad."

It sounded as if he'd said that a million times, almost like he'd had to defend his decision to join the Triad for decades. After seeing how they lived, she wasn't surprised, but she didn't like that he felt he had to defend himself from her

She shrugged. "And maybe you'll be the better Triad member for it because of this."

"I agree." His face lightened and he finished his drink.

She didn't like the idea of him going back to live within that mausoleum of a building. He would be so less accessible, and she wanted to be able to see him more…once they ousted Grandall.

Well, hell, a lot could change in the next twenty-two hours. Who knew? Maybe she could be sitting on the Ruling Circle instead of Grandall. She chuckled.

Sandale pulled at the tie that kept her hair in a ponytail. "What do you find so humorous?"

She looked at him and then Akasha. "Not humorous, just happy. In the Pleasure Temple, we are only allowed one man at a time. We don't want to accidently bond. We are very careful not to have sex with more than one man a night. Can you imagine if two men from different filoz were to come inside me one after another? That could really mess things up."

"I had not thought about that."

"Of course you didn't, Akasha. You didn't use Pleasure Temples." Or did he? "Hold on, you were at my Pleasure Temple. Did you go to them often? You must have learned how to pleasure a woman at some point because you can't tell me all those moves of yours are instinct."

He quirked his lips. "I can't?"

She gave him a sidelong look. "No, you can't. Inspect me to make sure I'm clean enough? You are so full of shit."

He chuckled. "I do go to Pleasure Temples when I must have release, but I use them rarely and a different one each time and a different woman."

Of course. He didn't want to make connections with anyone. He was lucky she wasn't interested in a long term relationship, but a short term one would be a nice change. She turned toward Sandale and ran her hand through his hair. It fell almost to his shoulders now, but she liked it better that way. "And we already know you've been to a Pleasure Temple since you already compared me to your other lovers. Besides how else could you be so good with your tongue?"

He stuck his tongue out and flicked it.

She laughed, loving this side of the new Sandale. He seemed more likely to enjoy himself rather than hold back all the time. "This is such a treat for me. As long as you are careful not to bond with me, we can have some fun tonight. And I do believe it's my turn to pleasure you both."

She moved her hand from Sandale's hair to his cock and reached out to grasp Akasha's with her other.

Both men sucked in air before holding themselves still for her. She loved that about men on Eden. They considered themselves to be of service to their women. It did get old on occasion, but in this case with two at her disposal, she wasn't going to complain.

She stroked her hands down and up the hard cocks next to her, stopping to run her thumb over the tips and against the ridges before stroking down again.

Sandale found his voice first. "What did you have in mind?" His violet colored eyes had darkened to almost black, which sent a thrill up her spine.

She pretended to ponder the question, but she knew exactly what she wanted. The question was, who would take what. "There's only a couple ways for me to pleasure you both at the same time. That's what I want. I'll leave the details to you." She wiggled her brows, curious to see what the two men, who were not of a filoz but who could read each other so well, would come up with.

She watched as they looked at each other as if they were Kindred of Mind and had some special telepathy. Then at the same time, they pulled their cocks from her hands. She pouted.

But they ignored her and moved into the living area.

She couldn't hear what they said, but just knowing they discussed the best way for them all to orgasm at the same time had her sheath moistening again. They would probably want her to suck on one as the other entered her sheath.

Then again, the way Akasha had snuggled his cock between her ass cheeks could mean a double penetration. Well, hell, just that thought had her pulse speeding up. She had shilla in her bag. It couldn't hurt to have it out, just in case.

Standing, she scanned the room for her bag. It was in the corner. Quickly, she rummaged through it. "Ah-ha." She palmed the small bottle and set it on the table by the side of the bed.

"What are you doing?" Sandale strode toward her, his eyes alight with deviltry.

Uh-oh, what were they up to? "I was just seeing what I had in my bag for toys and ointments. That's all I brought." She pointed to the small bottle.

Sandale shook his head in mock disappointment. "You should know better than to ask us to pleasure you and then try to control it."

Wow, this was a side of Sandale she didn't know at all. She liked it because it was different from the normal Edenist. She gave him a sultry smile. "I was just being helpful."

He took her by the shoulders and turned her toward Akasha. "I found her trying to control our sex play."

Akasha raised his brows. "Truly. That is unfortunate. Now we will have to use our alternate plan."

"What? No, the first one is fine." She really didn't want to miss out on something awesome. She was just playing. Weren't they?

"I agree." Sandale stepped against her back and wrapped his arm around her waist.

She tried to look up at him. "How about we go with whatever will feel the best?"

Akasha took her hands and looped them around his neck as he crushed her between himself and Sandale, pressing his cock in to her as hard as Sandale's pressed against her ass. "We will do what we wish as you requested." He raised his brow as he grabbed her hips and held her against him. "Unless you rescind your request?" His blue eyes were dark with the promise of exquisite pleasure.

"Well, hell, when you put it that way, go ahead and have your way with me, whatever you like." She didn't want him to hold back. After all, he was like a monk, so she licked her lips in invitation.

He broke their eye contact and looked at Sandale over her shoulder. "She taunts us."

"Good."

Good? Her breath hitched at the word.

Sandale backed away, but when she turned her head to see what he did, Akasha used one of his hands to turn it back.

"Uh-uh, you look at me."

She grinned. "I'm more than happy to." The promise of sex already had her hot, so she pulled herself up and licked at Akasha's lips.

He continued to hold her tight, but he didn't break down and kiss her. The man had some serious control.

Just as she lowered her heels back to the floor, Sandale covered her eyes with a piece of cloth. She let go of Akasha to make a grab for the material.

"Do not touch the cloth or we will tie your hands as well."

She stopped in mid reach. Securing her hands was out of the question. She'd barely held her self-control earlier when they trapped them behind her back. If they tied them, she would freak for sure. "I guess I did give you freedom to do as you liked."

Sandale lowered his lips next to her ear. "Yes, you did." He gave her a love bite on her ear that sent a thrill down to her very toes.

Akasha took her hands and had her take two steps forward. "Now I want you to climb on the bed and ride Sandale."

Was that all? She could do that.

He let go of her hands, and she moved toward the bed. When it hit her legs, she bent over and put one knee on the sheet. Akasha's hands on her shoulder stopped her from continuing. "Slowly. We want to see you move like the graceful woman you are."

Nice way to couch a command by adding a compliment. Good thing this was just sex play because if they tried to tell her what to—oh.

Akasha's hands had left her shoulders and ran over her breasts. He smoothed his way around her hips and over her ass until his finger swiped past her clit and opening.

Okay, she was totally onboard now. She moved her other knee onto the bed slowly and as she moved one hand forward, Akasha swept his hands over her body again.

She crawled toward the center of the bed, Akasha's strokes making her feel sexy as hell. When she touched a thigh, she smiled. Sandale lay on his back, waiting for her.

Slowly, she lifted one leg over his as she turned her body. Akasha rewarded her slow movements with an extra stroke over her clit. Then she lifted the other leg so that she knelt between Sandale's knees. With her thighs touching, Akasha took a different route and after stroking her breasts and hips, moved one finger down her crease.

She let out a hiss at the touch.

Akasha's low voice came from behind her. "How are you to ride him if you kneel between his legs?"

"I want to lick him and make sure he's ready for me."

Sandale's bark of laughter and the slight shaking of the bed made her smile.

The bed dipped as Akasha knelt on the mattress and his hands came around to her breasts. This time he pinched her nipples. His hair brushed her back just before he breathed into her ear. "More to the point, do we need to make sure you are ready?"

Her sheath tightened, telling her she was more than wet, but perversely she nodded.

"Then go ahead and lick Sandale's cock."

She ran her hand up the strong thigh beside her and cupped Sandale's balls. They tightened in her hand. Then she moved one knee closer, exposing her pussy and allowing her to use her other hand to hold the hard cock that waited for her.

Lowering her head, she licked across the top, thrilled to taste the pre-come that coated it. But that was nothing to the feel of Akasha's finger gliding along her folds before sliding into her wet sheath.

Sandale grabbed her wrists and pushed them to either side of him, bringing his cock to lie against her cheek and leaving her ass in the air. "Suck me."

It was the huskiness in his voice that motivated her even more than his words. Without hesitation, she took him into her mouth as far as she could. She swallowed and his hands left her wrists to bury themselves in her hair.

She raised her head slowly then glided down. It was then she felt the lube gliding along her crease. She wanted to shout with joy, but Sandale's cock hitting the back of her throat had her swallowing.

Akasha's finger followed the cool shilla down to her anal bud. Reflexively, she pushed upward toward his touch. He hesitated before stroking the tight opening with his finger.

She moaned against Sandale's cock. He held her head down, his own groans reaching her ears.

Akasha pushed harder against her hole until his finger slipped in.

Yes! Every muscle in her body wanted to collapse, but she held herself in her position to enjoy every second.

As Akasha pulled his finger out, she rubbed her teeth against the base of Sandale's cock as a warning to let her move before she pulled her head up to lightly scratch him all the way to the tip when his hold loosened.

Akasha pushed again against her ass hole, and she stretched as two of his fingers slid inside. She couldn't hold herself up and lowered her head onto Sandale, swallowing against his base as her hips fell to the side.

Akasha spread her cheeks with his other hand and pulled out his fingers. She felt him lean over her before he spoke in her ear. "I'm going to take you there."

She pulled her head up and off Sandale. "Yes."

She wished she could see Akasha's face. She was sure his eyes were the deepest blue. And Sandale's? From his rapid breaths, she would guess his violet eyes would look completely black by now.

Akasha lifted his weight from her just as Sandale pulled at her shoulders. "Come. Let me inside you. I have waited long enough."

His words sent a spike of desire straight to her core, and she happily moved her body up until she straddled his hips. Blindly, she found his cock and lifting herself, she positioned him at her entrance.

Akasha's hands grabbed her waist. "Remember, slowly."

Ugh, it was so hard to move slowly when she wanted to come in the worst way. Still, she did as he instructed, again with no please or thank you. This is why she lov—liked this guy. He was straight forward about what he wanted.

Despite her weakening muscles, she lowered herself slowly, letting Sandale's wide cock spread her and push into her until he could go no farther, then she tilted her pelvis and brought him in deeper.

"Holy Crius, you feel good." Sandale words were said with awe, and a warmth settled around her heart. He really knew how to make her melt.

Akasha's hand on her back urged her to lean forward. Happy to give her arms a rest, she lay flat on Sandale, his heartbeat as fast as her own. She brought her hand up between them and pinched his nipple. He grabbed her hand away. "I will have to return the favor."

His words sent moisture filling her sheathe again just before his hand pushed between their bodies and he pinched her hard nub, but as he did so, more lube flowed over her crack.

The bed moved as Akasha positioned himself behind her.

Shit, this was really going to happen. Two men at once like she'd always wanted. She couldn't wait and her hips rose of their own accord.

Akasha's hand came down on her ass and pushed her back down. "Keep Sandale deep inside you. Understand?"

His words reminded her of the first time she heard his voice, and like then she nodded, but unlike then, she was perfectly happy to obey.

Akasha spread her and the blunt tip of his cock stroked against her hole.

She was thankful she rested on Sandale because her muscles felt like honey. As Akasha's cock pushed against her ass, her sheath tightened and Sandale moaned.

Akasha stopped. "Sandale, your calming."

Sandale touched her hip and her muscles loosened.

Akasha again pushed against her hole, but despite the excitement filling her veins, she didn't tighten, just lay there and took it with Sandale's help. It was a whole new feeling for her as if she rode a wave of excitement like a surfer.

Akasha slowly slipped all the way in then pulled back, sending a new wave of pleasure through her lax body. After three more thrusts, he spoke. "Whenever you want."

She felt the hitch in Sandale's breath, but he only moved his hand to the side of her waist. The calming continued as he pulled his hips down and thrust upward hard. Spikes of excitement flew through her and her brain wanted her to tense, to reach for them, but her body remained loose.

As she comprehended the strange state of her pleasure,

Sandale's hips lowered a couple inches and this time when he thrust upward, Akasha thrust down.

"Holy fuck." The words exploded from her mouth as thrills buzzed through her body, ending in her core, but she still couldn't reach for them. If they continued with her this way, she could be here for an hour.

Even at her own thought, pleasure flowed over her, despite Sandale and Akasha pulling out. When they thrust again, the excitement sparked along her sheath, close enough to build an inner tension. They repeated their thrust, perfectly in sync as her pleasure built beyond anything she'd ever had.

"Holy Bendis, you are tight." Akasha said as he sunk into her ass.

Sandale groaned louder as they thrust again. "Not long."

"More." Akasha commanded.

She was too far beyond speaking, her entire body vibrating with building pleasure, filling her loose nerve-endings to the point she didn't have to tense to be ready for her orgasm. But Sandale's hand remained on her waist as both men thrust again, causing her to whimper her joy.

"I can't." Sandale's voice set her on edge, her pussy waiting though it couldn't contract.

"One more." Akasha's ground-out words told her even he was struggling to hold back.

They thrust again, bringing her to the edge of the precipice to hang in mid-air with every nerve quivering with excruciating heat. When they pulled out, Sandale's hand slipped to the bed.

Her muscles woke, tensing at the extreme excitement coursing through her just before both men thrust.

She screamed, her body vibrating with her orgasm as both men filled her with their come. All she could do is lie between them, her body pulsing with joy, her mind grasping for thought and her heart an emotional pile of mush. Her ecstasy went on and on as if she had been filled and now it must all push its way out wherever it could.

She gasped for breaths, afraid to move. Every part of her from her sheath to her skin was sensitized like a downed electric wire.

Akasha bit at the nape of her neck and her pelvis ground down on Sandale, hitting her clit and causing her to moan. "Fuck, don't move."

Sandale's chest beneath her vibrated with his chuckle.

"I said don't move." She ground her teeth against the pings of fire hitting her over-satisfied libido.

The men remained still while she took more deep breaths. It wasn't working. "Sandale, I need that calming touch you have."

He set his hand on her waist and immediately the sensitivity lessened. Thank the stars for that.

Akasha lifted the blindfold from her face.

She blinked. The room was bathed in a soft yellow glow from a light ball Akasha must have set on the side table. "I'm wiped. I'm not sure if I should thank you or scold you."

"Neither." Akasha braced himself and slowly pulled out. With less pressure inside her, the sensitivity lowered to a dull awareness.

"I suppose I should get up." She lifted her head to see Sandale staring at her. There was a strange look on his face almost as if he'd just found Nirvana. She grinned. Maybe he did. After all, she was one of his firsts since his memory wipe. She liked that.

"You don't have to get up."

Though he said "up," he clearly meant off. His hand still rested on her waist while the other lightly stroked her hair as if he didn't realize he was doing it. His eyes had returned to a deep purple that was so attractive with his tanned skin and blond hair.

She could have fallen asleep right there, but his gaze bothered her. It was if he loved her, but that couldn't be. As far as he was concerned, they had just met.

She lived on a planet of naked hunks. It made her too nervous to think about settling on just a couple. How would she know there wasn't someone out there better suited to her? Sandale was probably experiencing the rush of a crush. After all, she was pretty hot.

Lifting herself off him, she rolled to the side, grateful that her body had come down enough that when Sandale's hand slipped from her, the sheets didn't send her into another orgasm. "Sorry big guy, but the bed is softer than you, not that I'm complaining." She stroked her hand over his biceps. Seriously, they were hard.

Akasha strode in from the other room. "Here. You need to eat and drink."

Hell, a girl could get used to this. She forced herself to sit up and lean against the wall. "What am I eating?" She recognized the ambrosia and took a sip.

"I believe it is feroon ribs in a sauce and dally greens." He handed her the hot plate.

A spicy scent filled her nostrils. "How did you heat this? That was too fast for Theron's mini stove-like thing. I saw it."

He moved to the side of the bed and sat next to her. "My orange light."

Of course. She'd already forgotten exactly how many abilities he had. Theron was Light Kindred too, but he could only create reflections, yet Akasha had more than half a dozen abilities.

She took a bite of the meat. It was a barbeque sauce of some kind, but it didn't have the grilled flavor like Earth. Instead, there was a unique crunch on the outside. That was the feroon skin. Like chicken skin, it was loaded with flavor. "This is seriously good."

Sandale sat up and took a rib from her plate. "This is Rekah's specialty."

Akasha took one as well. "It did smell good."

She looked at Sandale then at Akasha and finally at the two ribs left on her plate. The men's actions were so opposite of Edenists in general that she laughed. "I do enjoy your company." Then she finished off her rib and dug into the greens.

How lucky was she to find two Edenists who were so unique and so her type? Maybe things did happen for—

"Sandale!" Haldone's yell had them all jumping out of the bed and running to the door in the living area.

Sandale threw it open and pitch black greeted them. What the hell happened to the shiners? "Haldone! Where are you?"

"Back here."

Akasha held up his hand and light filled the empty cave.

Sandale started for his brother and ran into something. "Scrat, what's here?"

"It's the table." Haldone's voice sounded less pissed, but also farther away then she thought he was.

Sandale moved to the side and she followed him, not wanting to hit the invisible table. Once past it, she could tell when Sandale strode down the center of the long cave, the path curved. It felt as if they were going downhill and it was growing colder.

Great, the one time she actually needed clothes, she didn't have any on.

"Haldone, what happened?" Sandale ran ahead then crouched down next to his brother, who sat on the floor of the cave holding his head.

"That's what I want to know. I was just about to dig out a small piece of eyllen from this wall when something hit me over the head. I must have lost consciousness because when I opened my eyes everything was dark except the glow of the eyllen."

"Glow?" Akasha stepped forward making the area brighter.

"You can see it when there's no light."

She knelt down next to him and batted his hand away from his head. "I didn't see any shiners by your table. Where are they? I thought you had three."

Haldone grimaced. "I did, but I used the eyllen from two of them and just had that one there."

The shiner was on its side but closed. She gently touched his head with her fingers.

"Ouch." He pulled his head away. "You don't need to tell me I have a bump on my head. I already know."

She counted to ten before she stood up. "Haldone, you have more than a bump. My guess is you have a concussion. You were hit by something big."

Akasha held his light higher as Sandale helped his brother stand.

Haldone swayed and she stepped next to him and wrapped her arm around his waist.

"I'm fine."

"No, you're not. Sandale, steady your brother, please."

Sandale wrapped his arm around Haldone, and she stepped away to face the man. "Let me explain what a concussion is. It's basically your brain hitting your skull hard. That means it could be damaged or it could just swell, either way you could have long term effects if you don't rest."

Haldone scowled. "How do you know? Are you a healer?"

She grimaced. "No, but I've had a few while practicing stunts for a movie. Trust me, you don't want to mess with them."

"There are no loose rocks here." Akasha interrupted her tirade. They all looked at him.

"How could Haldone have been hit with a hard object if there are no rocks?" Sandale's question was exactly what she was about to ask.

She closed her mouth and scanned the area. "Do you think someone else is in here?" She glanced at Sandale. "Could it be lawbreakers?"

His whole body grew taught. "Only if they found another entrance."

"We should investigate. We cannot have a meeting with your leaders if it could endanger them." Akasha's observation chilled her.

She hadn't thought about how advantageous it would be for lawbreakers to capture all of them here. Fuck.

Sandale scowled. "If they are in here, they already know we're here."

She walked around Sandale and grasped Akasha's arm. "Maybe you can tone down the light a little?"

No sooner had she said that then they were all bathed in green light, her personal favorite. "Much better."

Haldone, still being held by his brother, turned toward her and Akasha. "I think we should search now, before they leave and we can't find them."

She looked up at Akasha. "What about your blue light? Maybe we can see footsteps or something."

He nodded and the light changed.

Toni stared in shock at what it revealed.

Chapter Thirteen

"Well, hell. We *do* have company." She stared at the beautiful woman with long hair down to her knees. She appeared to be in her late twenties and was completely naked. She had a body any man would want in bed. Long toned legs, hips rounder than Toni's own, a small muscled waist and breasts to fill a man's palms.

Toni was happy with her overflowing bosom, but other than that the woman was perfect, except her face. She looked ready to bite one of their heads off, maybe all of them, and she held a large rock raised above her shoulder. With her other hand, she shaded her eyes, which made them invisible.

"Hey, we aren't the bad guys." Toni opened her arms, palms up. "We are trying to *get* the bad guys."

The woman's attention, which had been on the men, swiveled at the sound of Toni's voice. Her brows knit with confusion as she swept her gaze over Toni. Then she looked at the men then back to Toni. With her free hand, she motioned between them.

Oh shit, was the woman deaf? Toni had no clue about sign language. She nodded and pointed to both of them. "Yes, we are the same. Women." She pointed to the three men. "They are men." She wiggled her brows. "They can give pleasure."

The woman's frown deepened when she looked at the men.

"Do you understand what I'm saying?"

The woman nodded.

That was a huge relief. "Good. I'm Toni. Who are you?"

The woman made three hand gestures. Hell. She shook her head. "I didn't understand."

The woman repeated the gestures.

"She's spelling something out." Sandale's observation made sense.

Toni motioned to her. "Do it again."

It looked like the letters were M-Y-A, if the woman spelled in English like all the Edenists. "Is your name Mya?"

She nodded enthusiastically then glanced at the men as if to make sure they remained where they were.

There was definitely a fear of men there. Toni could relate to that. It would have been her predicament too if she hadn't taken matters in to her own hands when she was younger. "Do you speak?"

The woman shook her head.

Guess she couldn't get that lucky. "Mya, it's important that Haldone retrieve the eyllen. We have to have a meeting tomorrow to capture a bad man." She pointed to Sandale's brother, who continued to stare at Mya in utter disbelief. Come to think of it, Akasha seemed to be in a trance, too. Did she have some magic powers? Was she from Eden or some other alien creature?

Mya shook her head and lifted the rock.

"No." Toni held both her hands out and shook her head.

"Don't hurt him. He's a pain in the ass, but he doesn't deserve to be hurt."

Mya squinted her eyes and Toni had to laugh.

The woman stared at her in surprise.

Shit, had she never heard a laugh? How long had she been in here? Toni had about a thousand questions she wanted to ask, but squashed her need to know. "Mya, we just need a little of that rock," she pointed to one of the small red glows in the cave wall. "Then we will leave your space."

The woman lowered the rock, but didn't look convinced.

"Then tomorrow there will be a lot of people in there." She pointed back toward the curve in the cave. "But after tomorrow we will all leave. You do not need to fear us." She swept her hand toward the men. "Right, guys?"

They nodded, though Sandale was the only one with a soft smile on his face. Seriously? Either he was the only one savvy enough to be friendly or he wanted a piece of the young woman. She didn't like that thought at all.

Toni returned her attention to Mya who continued to give the men the evil eye. "If you agree to let Haldone retrieve the glow from the wall, I'll have Akasha turn off the blue light and then we won't be able to see you anymore. Would you prefer that? And will you agree?"

Mya studied Toni's face before doing the same to each man. Luckily, Akasha had snapped out of his trance and gave her a gentle smile as well.

Mya's too young for them. Why was she suddenly feeling territorial? It wasn't like they were a filoz or anything. "What do you say Mya? Truce?"

The woman's gaze snapped back to Toni at her impatient tone. Finally, she lowered the rock, but she didn't drop it. Mya nodded.

"Thank you. This won't take long. It's dangerous for the glow to be exposed to air, but Haldone knows what he's doing." At least she hoped so. If he blew up Mya's home, she had a funny feeling Mya would track him down and make him pay.

Toni grinned. Maybe she and Mya had more in common then she first thought. "Akasha?"

He switched the light back to green. In that instant, Mya disappeared. Toni glanced at the ground, but the cave floor was solid rock. There was no way to tell Mya was there. She'd bet anything the woman wouldn't leave them alone until they returned to Theron's part of the cave.

She walked to where Sandale steadied Haldone, his eyes no longer glazed now that Mya couldn't be seen. "You do know how to extract the eyllen without blowing us up, right?"

He shrugged off Sandale and scowled at her. "I know what I'm doing. I create a small, airless box around it and set it in the shiner. I close the shiner before releasing the box. My way is probably the easiest method. Satisfied?"

Some people just rubbed her the wrong way, and Haldone was one of them. "Yes."

Akasha placed his hand on her shoulder. "Come, let Haldone complete his task, so we can leave Mya alone."

She nodded and let him walk her a few feet away. She wanted to talk about Mya. Something about the woman tugged at Toni's heartstrings and that was a rare occurrence. Maybe it was simply that she reminded Toni of her younger foster sister.

"I have it." Haldone lifted the shiner in triumph. "This is

all I need to finish the room." He looked toward where Mya had been. "Thank you for allowing me to take this." Then he turned and strode back up toward Theron's part of the cave, refusing his brother's assistance.

Toni looked over her shoulder, wishing she could reassure Mya that they wouldn't bother her again. But the fact was, she couldn't. If she knew Jahl, he'd want to know a lot more about an invisible woman in Theron's old cave home.

Once inside the new room with the long invisible table, she shut the door. She looked at Haldone. "Do you wish to lock it?"

The man didn't look at her. "No. I don't think she'll want to come in with all of us in here. It will be tight and I think multiple people makes her nervous."

Toni stared at the shiner. It appeared to float in mid-air, but Akasha had directed her away from the invisible table, so she wouldn't run in to it. "Is there any way to make this table visible? I have a feeling we all are going to have bruises from bumping in to this thing."

Haldone frowned. "I can only work with what I have. I still need to make chairs as well."

Great. Invisible chairs to match. "How will we find them?"

"You can feel for them. Don't bother me with stupid questions."

"Stupid?" What a fucking asshole. She'd show him who was stupid.

Akasha grabbed her arm, keeping her from throwing herself across the invisible table to tackle Haldone. "I might be able to help with this."

Haldone raised one eyebrow. "Really?" The word was said with utter disbelief.

She tried to tug away from Akasha, but he held on. How the hell did he have so much control? Must be all that meditating he did.

Akasha spoke in his usual low tone. "Yes, 'really.' Can you lessen the density of the table to about seventy-five percent?"

"Of course." Once again, Haldone went out of his way to be condescending.

"Then do it."

Still skeptical, Haldone placed his hand on the invisible table. "Done, but don't bump it or you'll dent it."

"How the hell is anyone going to know if—"

Akasha squeezed her arm harder, and she stopped, taking a deep breath at the same time.

He laid his other hand on the table and created his green light. The light filled in the table, making it visible. Without taking his hand away, he nodded to Haldone. "Solidify it again."

When Haldon finished, he lifted his hand then Akasha lifted his.

"Wow, that is one awesome table!" She ran her hand over the shimmering green piece of furniture. "Instead of the Round Table of King Arthur's knights, we have the Green Table."

Haldone shrugged. "It is just a table."

She shook her head. "No, it's not. Not only will important things be discussed here, but it will bring together people who have never worked together before, all for a greater purpose. Besides, now we can see the lines of this table. It is really beautiful."

Haldone ignored the compliment and looked to his brother. "How many chairs?"

That would teach her to be nice to the man.

Sandale thought for a moment. "Ten."

She counted in her head. Good, that would include the women, too. She *knew* there was something about Sandale she liked.

"Will you help me with the chairs?" Haldone looked at Akasha.

"I will." He nodded to Sandale, who took her hand and they exited the room.

Sandale closed the door on his brother. Something was wrong with Haldone. Ever since they'd arrived at Theron's, he'd been too quiet and too serious.

Maybe if he still had his memory, he would have an idea of what Haldone was thinking, but he didn't. It was one thing to embrace his new self but another not to have the instinctual knowledge of his past. He would simply ask his brother when he finished the room.

Toni sauntered to the cabinet and found the cold box. "Oh good, we have ale. Would you like one?"

That was exactly what he needed. "Yes."

Toni grabbed two ales and handed him one with a glass. "Rough day or celebrating?"

He frowned. "Neither. Why?"

"From what I learned about you, you rarely drank ale. You preferred the Apple Fire at Libations."

"It is all part of the new me. You did tell me I could be who I wanted."

She laughed. "Yes, I did. And to be honest, I'm glad you want to drink ale. It's more common, like me, not stuffy like you used to be." She lowered herself on to the longseat, tucking her legs under her.

He widened his eyes. "You are anything but common." Sitting next to her, he took her hand. "You are vivacious and strong and insightful."

She tossed her loose hair over her shoulder. "Not beautiful? I should be insulted."

Placing her hand on her own chest, he smiled. "That is not as important as your other strengths. It is your heart I am more interested in." From the moment she threw herself into his arms, he'd been taken with her like Khaos had been when he'd first seen Serena, and like Konala had with Jaelene.

Around Toni, he felt normal, free, like a man in charge instead of a man floundering to figure out who he used to be.

She pushed his hand away and grimaced. "Trust me, the outside is the better part. You aren't turning stuffy on me, are you? I hope you aren't going to start reciting Emily Dickinson poetry like you used to."

He grinned. "*Has sated flame's conditions, its quivering substance plays without a color but the light of unanointed blaze.*"

"Hey, that sounds like you're talking about Akasha and his light ability."

That was odd. He hadn't thought of his new favorite poem in that vein before.

"At least it's more interesting than the one you used to quote about lips being like a fainting bee. Ugh." She stuck out her tongue. "Definitely too high brow for me."

Her constant reference to his new interests and likes as better than he used to be made him want to discover his new self even more, especially if she could do it with him. He was well aware that he was half in love with her already, but he hadn't expected to feel so…happy.

He wiggled his brows. *"Least village boasts its blacksmith, whose anvil's even din stands symbol for the finer forge that soundless —"*

Her hand over his mouth stopped his recital. "No, no more, please. Remember, you're going to be common like me, only more fun."

He grasped her wrist and licked the fingers she held over his mouth.

Laughing, she pulled her hand away. "Exactly like that. Perfect."

He smiled as she took another gulp of her ale. Did Akasha see in her what he saw? Was that why he'd gone so far to protect her, or was he merely following his own moral dictates? No, the man was definitely taken with Toni, too, he just did not realize it yet. That moment would be a significant realization for someone planning to ascend to the Triad panel. Those members were not allowed a filoz.

A sadness crept into his chest. He would have liked to form a filoz with Akasha. Despite his focus on morality, there was an empathy towards others that Sandale appreciated.

"What are we going to do about Mya? I know Jahl is going to interrogate her. It's probably none of my concern, but there was something in her body language that made me want to step in front of her and protect her."

He was happy to have his thoughts redirected and he nodded. He'd felt the same way, once he'd overcome his shock. There was no such thing as a female Edenist, yet what other explanation could there be for her being invisible except that she was Kindred of Light?

"Do you think she's an alien?" Toni's eyes had grown round.

"What?"

She placed her hand on his forearm as she leaned toward him. "What if she is a Crius?"

Holy Bendis! He hadn't considered that.

She cocked her head. "I didn't see a Kindred birthmark on her, not that she could have one anyway with only males being born on this planet. She has to be an alien."

"It could be that—"

"Oh, shit. What if she's from an ancient race that no one on the planet realized was still here."

"There is no ancient—"

"Or what if one of the other cities has figured out how to do test tube babies?"

He smiled, putting his finger against her lips so he could speak. "What if we ask her?"

She nodded before her mouth opened and she sucked his finger inside. The sensuous action was very Toni, but sex was a distraction from what he was most interested in. Or was it a defense? The thought made him pause.

"Sandale, you still with me?" She pulled his finger from her mouth and gazed at him.

Her green eyes were as lush and bright as new born leaves in the morning dew with the bright light of Helios bursting over them.

He nodded.

"Good. I have to tell you, I don't want to tell Jahl and Khaos about Mya."

It took him a moment to switch his mind back to Mya. "Why not?"

She took another sip of ale before answering. "It's just a gut feeling, but I don't think Jahl is the right one to initiate contact with her, and we both know he would insist on being the one. Besides, we have bigger fish to fry in Naralina first. I was thinking maybe we wait until all that is over with and then we come back here and talk to her, find out more."

She talked about not having a heart, yet it was bigger than the city of Naralina. "If you are asking me not to tell anyone about Mya until you are ready, then you have my promise. But you will have to convince Akasha and Haldone."

She waved away his comment. "Haldone I'm not worried about. He was in so much shock, I'm not even sure the man believes what he saw. Akasha, though, may be tough."

Again his mind drifted off the topic. Toni was intelligent, brave and very caring, no matter what she said about herself. She cared for many, but who did she love?

She frowned. "Are you okay?"

"I am. I was thinking."

"Thinking instead of feeling? Be careful, don't let that become a habit." She smiled crookedly as if she hoped he wasn't really bothered by something.

But he was. He took her hand. "Toni, do you miss your family on Earth?"

"You're kidding, right?"

He shook his head.

"Sorry, I forgot for a minute that you know nothing about me." She looked away.

She was wrong about that. He understood more than she could guess.

"I was raised in foster families. Had about four growing up. I'd try to be good, but eventually, they lost patience with me." She returned her gaze to him. "One benefit was I had a lot of sisters and brothers, so to speak. They were good kids. Far better than me."

"Do you miss them?"

She frowned. "No, I don't. We were like friends that drifted apart. By the time you, Jahl and Khaos rescued Serena and myself from those scumbags, I had lost touch with all of my foster-siblings, except one, and she and I only saw each other once a year."

"Then you like living on Eden?" He held his breath.

"Are you kidding? What's not to love? I'm one of few women in a place that worships them and allows me to have a taste of as many men as I like or I can settle down into a filoz of two to five, but I don't see that happening ever." She winked before finishing her ale.

Elated and then stunned, he swallowed hard. "Why not a filoz?"

Toni shrugged. "I would always be worried that there was someone out there that was better for me."

"And if you fell in love?"

"You mean like Serena did?" She pondered that a moment. "I'm not sure I'm capable of that. Don't get me wrong, I think it's a beautiful thing, especially here with the bonding and stuff."

His heart stalled at her words. It took him a moment to start breathing again. It was obvious she was quite capable of love and loyalty. He just needed to show her that.

Toni yawned. "Is your brother going to work all night?"

"I do not know. I have not known him long enough to guess at his motivation or stamina. But if you are tired, we should go to bed."

"Now those are words I love to hear from a well-built Edenist." She winked as she rose, setting her empty glass on a small stump that served as a side table.

He stood as well. "After you."

She sauntered into the sleeping room, her hips swaying proactively, but he would not give in to his sexual desires. He was not interested in sex. He wanted the relationship he could see building between them.

She stopped at the bed, turned and fell back on it, her arms outstretched. "I'm all yours." She winked. "And that's saying a lot in Eden."

He smiled in response and lay down next to her. "Good. Then come here."

She turned her head to look at him. "I am here."

"No, lay your head on my chest."

"Okay." She scooted over, resting her head on his chest, her arm across his abdomen. She threw one leg over his own. "This is comfortable. If you're not careful, I may just fall asleep on you."

He wrapped his arm around her, resting his hand on her waist. "That is fine. You have had a very eventful day."

She looked up at him confused. "You mean you don't want to have sex?"

He shook his head.

Her brow furrowed before she rested it on his chest. "I thought you wanted me here for sex." She lowered her hand down to his cock and cradled it. "Are you sure you know what you want?"

He grabbed her hand, bringing to back to his stomach. "Yes, I'm sure. I like being close to you like this."

She was silent for a few minutes, then lifted her head. "I don't like it."

"Why?"

Her gaze skittered away from his. "It's too…I just don't like it."

"Tell me, Toni, why don't you like it."

"I don't know. It feels like you want something from me I can't give. I can't explain it." She pulled away, leaving a space between their bodies.

His disappointment was keen. "But we were closer than this while having sex."

She moved farther away. "No, we weren't. I mean, physically, maybe but not whatever this is."

"What are you afraid of?" He probably should let it go, but he couldn't. He'd seen what Jahl and Khaos had with Serena and what his fathers had with his mother. He wanted that too, and he wanted it with Toni.

She scowled at him. "I'm not afraid of anything. I just know what I want. Do you want to have sex or not?"

"Not."

"Have it your way. I'm going to sleep." She rolled over, facing away from him.

Her rejection caused his patience to flee. He rolled on to his side and pulled her against him. "Good."

"What are you doing?" She struggled to get away, her arms trapped against her body by his hold.

"I'm going to sleep." He held on, determined to show her it was better to be close this way.

"Fuck, let me go."

It took him a minute to recognize that her body quivered beneath all her contortions to get free. When he did, he immediately let go.

She scrambled off the bed, her body shaking. "Don't you ever hold me like that again." Her words came out between gritted teeth.

Her anger hit him like an enraged Tigran. By the bowels of Bangley! The woman really despised him. How did he not see that? He rose stiffly from the bed. "I will remove myself from your presence so that you may sleep in peace. I was wrong about you after all."

He strode to the door, his need to get away from her as strong as his need to get closer was just a few moments earlier. That he had been so mistaken and such an ithio made him want to hit something.

"Sandale."

He paused, not wanting to hear what other hate she might spew. "Have a good sleep." He slammed the door shut behind him. He stalked across the living area and pulled open the outside door. Without another thought, he slipped outside.

~~*~~

Akasha moved to the other side of the table where Haldone worked on the second to the last chair, his movements jerky like those of a person who was so angry he couldn't quite control his actions.

"What is it that concerns you?"

Haldone stilled. "What makes you think I have a concern?"

Akasha barely kept from smiling. "You have reworked that chair three times and it still is not right. Also, I have noticed you do all in your power to make Toni feel inferior, and you watch your brother as if he will disappear at any second."

Haldone's shoulders sagged. "My brother was just returned to us, but I see him growing closer to that woman than his own family. He has not had time to regain his old life and already he is moving away again."

Akasha shook his head. "You do not need to worry about Toni. She has no interest in a relationship." Was it no interest in, or a fear of? Did she lie and joke to keep people at arm's length? He needed to observe her more to be sure.

"How do you know? My brother appears to be very interested."

He agreed. Sandale was very interested in Toni even though she had a black area in her essence. He didn't understand how Sandale could overlook that.

That Toni had kept the blackness as small as it was impressed him. It could be why she didn't want a filoz, so she wouldn't disappoint those she cared about. "Yes, I'm sure."

"What about you? You appear to appreciate her as well."

He grinned. "I do. She is very resourceful, blunt, willing to take risks, but she also lies more than she tells the truth and she has something in her past that is unacceptable."

"What is it?" Haldone's curiosity was too intense.

"I do not know."

Almost as if disappointed, Haldone turned away. "I'm sure whatever it was, it couldn't be worse than what the lawbreakers did to Sandale. They should be made to pay for that."

Akasha studied Haldone. "That is the problem with living in the jungle. There is no law here. If someone maims or kills, no one is held accountable. Every law abiding citizen lives safely behind the walls of a city."

Haldone returned to the chair he had been working on then stepped aside and indicated the chair was ready for green light. "But doesn't that mean that we are restricting those who are decent and freeing those who break the law?"

Akasha shook his head, but he could understand how it could be viewed that way. He lowered his hand and filled the chair. "No. We are a civilized society while the jungle is not."

"That's true, but it is one thing for lawbreakers to prey on each other, but to attack those who are innocent is wrong, and they need to pay." Haldone slammed his hand on the chair they just finished.

Akasha laid his hand on the man's arm. "I fear you want revenge. Be careful. That is a downhill slope."

Haldone shrugged off his hand. "I was just making an observation about what is right. As a Triad member-to-be, I figured you would agree, that is all."

"I do agree, but we have to take into account the fact that Sandale lived outside the city walls. The jungle belongs to lawbreakers."

Haldone glared. "It doesn't belong to them. They make no attempt to live peaceably or to build a community. The jungle belongs to all the cities."

He could see that this was a debate he could not win. Haldone spoke from the heart, from the love he bore his brother. "Yes, that is essentially true."

Haldone gave a curt nod before reaching for the last chair. "You can fill this one and retire. I need to make some last adjustments to the room."

Akasha placed his hand on the chair and let his green light flow, happy the color had become so useful. When he finished, he scanned the room. Toni was right. The shimmering green table and chairs was an important part of Naralina history, or it would be if they succeeded in stopping Grandall from creating the next world war. "This looks right."

Haldone turned around to view his own handiwork. "It's just a table and chairs."

Akasha looked at the man, but could see the pride in his face. "It is more than that."

Haldone met his gaze. "Yeah. It is."

He laid his hand on Haldone's shoulder for a moment then moved to the door. "Good sleep."

As Haldone nodded, Akasha left the room.

The living area was dark and the door to the bedroom closed. He was alone. He should take the time to meditate. The path his mind had taken after seeing the essences of Sandale and Toni had been too complicated to be attempted without meditation and for him to do that, he needed to be alone.

Knowing he could never enter Toni's sheath because of the black area in her essence, and his subsequent acceptance that it would grow, had been hard. He was glad he had been able to give her a pleasurable experience now, while she was still acceptable. That she would become a lawbreaker had hurt, which didn't make sense. That wouldn't affect him in any way as long as he didn't enter her sheath.

He'd been shocked by the blackness in her essence, his instincts usually very good when it came to a person's character. He had, in fact, expected more gray, but to see so much white and yet black in the same essence had amazed him. He needed to know what had caused it. What could Toni have done? The more he thought about it, the more his need to know grew.

It could be very important to what was decided tomorrow. What if she betrayed them? Or what if she harmed one of them? She was definitely strong enough.

He hated that he had to prepare for such heinous acts on her part. It didn't seem right, but a person's essence didn't lie, even if the person did.

He stared at the reflection left in the room. Sandale's essence had also surprised him, but only at first. The man was like a newborn in that he had not enough time to make poor choices yet. He had essentially started his life over just a few months ago and spent that time learning to function again in his society.

That had to have been difficult. Probably no more difficult than to decide to have his own mind wiped. What torture he must have been in. Akasha's heart beat with empathy for Sandale. If he wasn't bound for the Triad panel, he could see them being good friends.

But he would be ascending to the panel soon, and all ties to others would be completely cut off for him, except for the members-to-be. He needed to remain unbiased and to keep his essence pure.

He glanced at the reflection again. Would he be able to see his own essence? It was something he'd always wanted to know but no one he knew could emit the white light. The temptation was too great to ignore. He stood in front of the mirror and emitted his white light at it.

Blinding light hit his eyes and he quickly closed his hand. Blinking in the darkness, white blotches impaired his vision. His disappointment was heavy. Would he ever get to see his own essence? To see if his lifelong work toward his calling had been successful?

He clenched his fists in frustration. One side of him was angry while the other tried to tell him that knowing the color of his essence was an experience no other triad member-to-be could have. He should always act by the highest standards for the sake of being good, not for the reward of seeing it reflected in his essence.

Yet Toni, who had black on hers, and Sandale with his pureness had been able to see theirs.

He stilled. When he shined his light on them he had directed it at their body and they looked in the reflection to see the result.

He had shined his light on himself in the wrong direction!

Anticipation had his heartbeat racing as he positioned himself away from the reflection, but still directly across from it.

With the longseat touching his calves, he twisted his arm behind him and emitted the white light from his palm onto his own back. In the reflection shone his essence, an amorphous oval at the center of his being.

It wasn't white.

He stared in disbelief. At least a third of his essence was gray. How could that be? How could he have worked so hard for so long only to have so much gray? He didn't understand.

Instinctually, he balled his hands into fists, eliminating the telltale light. Shaken by the revelation, he sat and stared at the reflection opposite him. Though the light was gone, he could still see his essence. His *gray* essence.

All his life. All his sacrifices. They only added up to two-thirds pure essence?

He lowered his head and stared unseeing at the floor, his mind replaying every harsh step taken to follow his calling. The distancing of his mother's love, his friendships ending, the limitations of moving into the Triad building, the hours of meditation on what was right, the lack of emotional connections with anyone, the limited ventures into the city. All of it, like self-flagellation, to pursue the truth and purity of essence. And he had failed.

The Triad!

He snapped his head up and looked at himself in the reflection. How could he ascend to the Triad knowing he was unworthy?

Chapter Fourteen

Toni paced the living area. Her mind was clear, but her heart was blurry, so she ignored it. The only thing that mattered was that they find Sandale. It was her fault he was missing. She was sure of it.

She kept her eyes on the view outside. The sun was bright, leaving the clearing where the cave stood bare. Anyone for a mile would be able to see her if she walked outside. Then she'd catch hell from all three men currently combing the bush for the kindest man she knew.

He didn't let her explain. He held her arms pinned and without the sex as a reward, she'd lost it. She wanted to tell him the truth, but it might be better if he continued to think she couldn't stand to be near him unless they had sex. It would make it a lot easier on him after they finished with Grandall and all went back to their lives, or in his case, started his.

Movement on the south end of the clearing had her stopping. Akasha and Haldone would just portal into the cave. Fuck, what was it now?

The leaves swayed madly like a feroon was charging through

the bush, or maybe it was one of those boaroxes she'd heard Jaelene had encountered near here. Finally, enough greenery separated to reveal Rekah with Theron behind him.

She chuckled. "I should have known." Striding to the door, she threw it open. "Where's everyone else?"

"Good morning to you, too, Toni." Rekah kissed her on the cheek as he bent to walk inside.

"Whatever. Theron, Sandale is missing. He left the cave sometime in the night and hasn't come back. Akasha and Haldone are searching for him."

Theron shook his head. "No, Sandale came home last night. He will return with Jahl and Khaos."

"And Serena, right?"

Theron grinned. "Yes, and Erin."

"Good. Now we have to find Akasha and Haldone. You'd think Sandale could have left us a note. What if Akasha is captured by lawbreakers?"

Theron frowned. "And Haldone?"

He was Sandale's brother and she did care about Sandale. She waved off the comment. "Of course, him, too."

"What happened here last night, Toni?"

She refused to look Theron in the eye. "Haldone built an amazing meeting place. Akasha showed us our essences, and we went to bed." She winked at him. "After some amazing sex, of course."

Theron raised his eyebrows. "You bonded?"

"Shit, no."

Theron gave her an odd look. "I thought…never mind. Rekah and I will use a portal and his ability to sense emotions to find the other two. You stay here and wait for the others to arrive."

Once again she had to play the little lady and stay home and wait for the men to take care of things. She hated that, but she wasn't stupid. They knew the area and possessed a few cool abilities she didn't have. "Of course, but they better all get here quick. We may only have until Helios descends before Grandall starts up his machine. And that's if we're lucky."

She ignored Theron's widening eyes and spun on her heel to fetch Rekah. "Hey, big man, you still have one more errand to run."

After shooing him out the door, she pulled out a glass and filled it with ambrosia. She'd rather have an ale, but there was too much riding on today. Part of her was excited to finally take the scumbag down and part of her was worried about her friends, specifically Sandale and Akasha.

Akasha had been even more quiet this morning than usual as if he was preoccupied. Discovering the ruler of his city was corrupt had to be a shock to him, but he'd figured that out before they escaped the city. Something else bothered him.

A shimmering outside caught her attention and she set her glass down hard.

As the portal cleared, Jahl stepped out followed by Serena and Khaos.

Toni's heart leapt. She hadn't seen her best friend in months. She ran to the door and straight outside. "Serena!"

"Toni!"

She grasped her friend in a tight hug before letting her go. "Well, hell, don't you look healthy." Serena wore a wrap that only came down to her knees. Her hair was past her ears now and she had a nice tan.

Serena laughed. "I should. I have these two men spoiling me.

I think I've gained twenty pounds. But you look pretty fit as usual. I love that leather outfit on you."

Toni shrugged. "It's hard staying in shape when they wait on you hand and foot." She grimaced for good measure.

Serena laughed. "It is so good to see you. I worry about you every day."

"She does, but I tell her all is well." Khaos stepped forward and opened his arms.

The dark-haired man with gray eyes had a new confidence about him that hadn't been there before. She liked to think she had something to do with that. Stepping forward, she gave him a hug. "It's good to see you."

"What about me?" Jahl frowned, which was so typical of him.

She scowled at the Edenist who looked most like a military man of all that she'd met. "What about you? I'll tell you what about you. You never told me your father could sense those around him. He knew I spied on him!" She stalked toward Serena's agapayto, her hands balling into fists. Friend or no friend, he'd set her up for failure and that feeling was too old and angry to ignore.

Jahl didn't move away, but his eyes widened in surprise. "He could sense *who* was near? He never told me that. I thought he could sense a person was near." Jahl frowned. "I apologize. If I'd have known I would have never sent you."

Well, hell, how was she supposed to stay mad at him after that confession. His father was a slimeball. He's the one she needed to stay mad at. She shrugged. "I can't really blame you for what you didn't know. So you're off the hook." She grinned and opened her arms. "So do you want your welcome hug?"

"No, I was thinking more in the way of a feroon steak with

tyree sauce. Of course I want a hug." He broke into a smile which set her back a second before she stepped forward and gave in to his request. He'd never been so quick to smile. Being bonded obviously agreed with him.

After a strong embrace by Jahl, she stepped away. "Come inside. It's not safe out here. Wait until you see the meeting room."

"Is it green?" Khaos asked.

She cocked her head. "You've seen something?"

He gave her a soft smile. "No, just the color green."

She led the way through the invisible entrance. "You're right as usual." Khaos could see snippets of the future, which reassured and drove him crazy at the same time. She led them inside and showed them the room. As she expected, they were duly impressed. The table Haldone built was amazing with the shimmering green light inside, but with all the chairs, it made her think of a sci-fi Robin Hood movie she'd worked on a couple years back.

Jahl grumbled. "There's no head of the table."

She grinned. "Nope." Haldone had made it in the shape of an oval only with a blunt point at each long end. She saw the wisdom of his design now. Jahl would have taken the seat at the head and lorded it over all of them like a general.

Khaos walked to the door at the end. "What is through here?"

"Nothing." She tensed, but looked away so he wouldn't think anything about it. "Just more cave."

Serena grabbed her by the arm. "You men do what you need to do. I'm catching up with Toni until the others get here." Serena pulled her through the doorway and into the living room. Spotting the bedroom, she led the way in there and shut the door.

Toni finally pulled her arm from her grasp and plopped on

the bed. "So what's up? Do you still have Wally? How's your sister doing? Any more women come to Loraleaf yet?"

Serena stood in front of her with one hand raised. Her other hand ticked off one finger. "Sandale comes home last night." She ticked off another finger. "He was supposed to be here with you." She ticked off yet a third finger. "And I arrive to find the other two men gone." She dropped her hands. "What did you do to them?"

"Me? Nothing." The last thing she'd expected was the third degree. "Well, not exactly nothing. Sandale, Akasha and I had some amazing sex."

"Shit, Toni, did you bond?" The hopeful gleam in Serena's eye rubbed her the wrong way.

"No. Why does everyone keep saying that? We had sex. That's all. That's the best part."

Serena sat on the bed next to her, shaking her head. "No, it's not. It gets even better after the bonding."

Well, hell, no one ever told her that juicy tidbit. Then again, maybe Serena was lying. "How?"

"It depends on the men. For me, thanks to Jahl's ability to control dead nature, he makes toys out of rock and wood and manipulates them leaving his hands free."

"That's cool." So even though Serena only had two men in bed, it could be like three. She liked that.

"Plus, because of the bond, I can see whatever Khaos is looking at while we make love."

"So if he's playing with your pussy, you can see what he's doing?"

Serena blushed. "Yes."

"No shit. Talk about an erotic experience. And it's this way for everyone who bonds?"

"No." Serena shook her head. "It depends on what the bond is. We didn't know how I would be connected to Jahl and Khaos for a good twenty-two hours. It has something to do with their abilities and my body."

She'd already experienced what Sandale's ability could add to sex. Could Akasha get creative, too? What was she thinking? Bonding for the sake of heightened sexual experiences was stupid. It meant being forever attached to the same men.

Serena grabbed her arm. "What are you thinking? Maybe about bonding with Sandale and the other man?"

Toni pulled away and stood. "No, that would be stupid. You and I both know my ability to stick with one man for long is pretty pitiful. I gave up on love a long time ago."

"But what if a man loved you, like Sandale. He wouldn't say anything to us, but it was obvious he was hurt. Did you tell him that, that you can't love him?"

Toni started to pace the small bedroom. "No, I didn't say that. He just wanted more from me than I can give. Then he tried to hold me and trapped my arms."

"Shit, and he thought you broke away because you didn't want to be close to him."

Toni halted to nod. Serena was one of two people who understood. "Then he left the room and slammed the door. I decided not to explain. Why hurt him again. His feelings for me are new. It's better this way. He'll get over me and move on."

Serena's amber eyes took on a telling glint. "But how can he move on when he's not part of a filoz?"

She started to pace again. "He can make friends in Naralina once we get Grandall."

"*If* we're successful and *if* he wants to stay there."

She didn't respond. Just the mention of Grandall had her itching to get her hands around the man's neck.

"Sandale didn't say anything about you last night except that you were well, but he did talk about a man named Akasha?"

"Akasha. He's a Triad member-to-be. Next in line, in fact, to sit on the Triad panel." Now why was she so proud of that? It wasn't her accomplishment.

"Sandale seems to have formed a friendship with him."

She stopped. "I see what you're doing here, but it won't work. If those two want to form a filoz, then great, but I'm not bonding with them. I'm pretty sure that Akasha isn't interested anyway. He saw my essence."

"Your essence?"

She leaned back against the wall. "Yeah, it was eerie. Your essence is like the manifestation of your soul or something. I'm not entirely clear, but mine had this big black section at the bottom. We know what that was all about."

Serena nodded.

"Akasha is like a monk, only I guess he's allowed to have sex. Otherwise, he's all about what's right. I have a whole lot of what's wrong going on." Though she still felt fucking good about all the white her essence had. How much was normal, she didn't know, but that she even had any had made her stupidly happy.

"Then maybe—"

"Where's Toni!" A feminine voice in the living room had them both rising.

Serena laughed. "That's got to be Erin."

Toni strode for the door. Throwing it open, she yelled. "Erin!"

The short blonde woman, clothed in what looked like a replica of Toni's harem outfit only it covered everything, threw herself at her. "It's been too long."

She hugged Erin back with enthusiasm. "Yes, it has."

Serena stepped forward. "It's good to see you again."

Erin gave her a hug as well. "It seems like forever. I'm getting bored. The security system at Haven is rudimentary at best, and I've organized everything. From the library, such as it is, to the bath house, I've got that place in order. I even developed a training for women coming to Haven that your sister let me practice on her, but only two women have arrived. I need more company."

Serena grimaced and glanced at the man standing in the doorway of the meeting room. "If only our agapaytos would let us visit more often. They are too protective."

Toni glanced at Jahl who was busy scowling at Nase. Seriously? Still? She turned back to Erin. "How did you figure out how to get in the door? It looks like solid rock out there."

She hooked her finger over her shoulder. "Khaos was outside waiting for us."

Toni glanced outside to see Khaos talking to a man with long black hair. Her attention reverted back inside to the mounting tension and she strode between Jahl and Nassic and gave Nase a hug. "Good to see you."

He absently hugged her.

Fuck that. She pulled away and stood in his line of vision. "Hey, I'm over here."

His brown eyes finally settled on her and he grinned. "I'm glad you made it out of Naralina alive."

She nodded. "Yup, and you are going to prove to the whole city what a scumbag Grandall is before I strangle him."

He laughed. "You never change."

"Remember that." She turned to Jahl. "You two make nice-nice or I'm going to kick you both in the balls and your beloveds will not appreciate that."

Jahl's lip quirked and she blinked. Obviously, married life agreed with the man. Last she saw him, he was still scowling most of the time despite having won Serena back.

Toni sauntered outside to greet Wareson. No sooner had she'd given the man a hug than a shimmer appeared behind him.

Akasha stepped through first and frowned at her before Haldone followed. Sandale's brother barely spared her a glance. Seriously, what was up with that man? What did she ever do to him?

She'd just let go of Ware when Akasha grabbed her wrist. "I want to talk to you."

"Really? Now? We're about to plan the take down of Grandall. This is Wareson by the way."

Akasha nodded at Ware then tugged. "Yes, now."

She rolled her eyes at Ware and let Akasha pull her into Theron's cave, past those in the living room and directly into the bedroom. He closed the door and let her go.

Maybe she'd finally find out what had made him so quiet when they woke up. As opposed to Sandale, Akasha had slept in bed with her though he hadn't tried to get close.

"What caused your essence to be black?"

Fuck, he wanted to talk about that of all things? "Why? Are you going to suggest I be exiled from Naralina when we get back?"

He stared uncomprehending for a split second before he stalked to her and grabbed her shoulders. "No, that's not why. I want to know because I deserve to know."

"Now you wait just a minute. Who died and made you king? I don't owe—"

His mouth came down on hers and his tongue dominated her mouth, even as he pressed her against him.

She relaxed and laid her hands on his waist as she teased him with her own tongue.

Abruptly, he pushed her away. "Tell me."

"What is wrong with you? This is not the calm, confident Akasha from yesterday."

He crossed his arms. "No, it isn't. I want to know why your essence is black before we enter Naralina."

Well, hell. He didn't trust her. After everything they'd done together. Too bad. "Again, I ask you why? Is it that you don't trust me? Are you afraid I'll hand you over to Grandall? If you think that, you don't know me very well."

"Does anyone? Do you let anyone know you? I don't know what you did to Sandale, but my guess is it has something to do with the blackness in your essence."

What a lucky shot. Tangentially, it did. "Why do you think I did something? Maybe he did something. Did you think of that?" She stepped closer to him and rose onto her tiptoes to get in his face. "You need to get your act together. I did nothing to you this morning and yet you act like I sold you and your family out to the lawbreakers. I don't have to tell you anything. Now get out of my way."

The last came out in a growl, her whole body pissed off at the man. What a difference twenty-two hours made.

He opened his mouth, but a knock at the door stopped him.

"Hey, you lovebirds, Sandale, Konala and Jaelene have arrived. Time to get to work." Serena's voice sounded overly bright.

Toni stepped away. "You heard her. We have work to do." Stepping around him, she threw open the door and stalked into the living room.

~~*~~

Sandale didn't look at Toni sitting beside him. Her rejection stung. It was easier to focus on the meeting and what needed to be accomplished than to delve into his feelings for her.

He'd thought Jahl would dominate the conversation, but Wareson had taken over as a firm, but respectful leader. Then again, he had once served on the Ruling Circle, so he had experience.

Every chair at the table was taken, each filoz with their woman between them. Though he and Akasha were not a filoz, Toni sat between them. Haldone on Akasha's right. He sat next to Jahl in case he needed to calm the man down. Besides, he used to be part of his filoz BW.

Toni jumped in to the conversation. "This is all great, but if Grandall lives through the capture, how are we going to convince the rest of Naralina that he's the bad guy and we're the good guys? Not to be rude, but everyone here except Akasha and myself were exiled or abandoned Naralina. Your credibility with the populace is not exactly high."

"That's where I come in. Since I'm a truth-reader, I can make

Grandall confess all he's done in front of everyone." Nassic grinned, obviously looking forward to that moment.

"What about the rest of the Ruling Circle?" Theron's question caught them all by surprise.

Akasha added to it. "Are we orchestrating an entire takeover of the Naralinian government?"

There was silence at the realization of what they were about to do.

"No." Wareson looked at each of them. "We allow the people to decide as it should be."

"Wait just a minute." Toni's tone was far more furious than the moment called for. "Are you saying we allow the Naralinian people, who have been completely snowed by this scumbag, choose who stays and who goes?"

"I have to agree with, Toni."

Akasha's statement surprised him. They had all heard them yelling at each other before the meeting. "You do?"

"Yes. We need to expose Grandall to the people, but the others of the Ruling Circle must step down as well. Either they turned a blind eye to what he did or they supported it. Either way it makes them unfit."

Wareson nodded. "I agree. I just believe we need to get the Naralinians to agree."

"Whatever. My biggest concern is getting that bastard out of there. Exile would be too kind for him. What you politicians do after that is your business."

"Toni," Jaelene spoke up for the first time. "Even if there is a decision whether or not to have a woman sit on the Ruling Council?"

Sandale smothered his smile at the shock on all faces but his and Toni's. As a mother-to-be, Jaelene was treated with great deference, so for her to suggest such a radical idea was like having the ice from the polar freeze dropped on them.

Even the diplomatic Wareson seemed at a loss for words.

Sandale stepped in. "I think that is definitely a direction the Circle needs to go, but I do agree with Toni. This is a discussion for after Grandall is captured and his portal destroyed."

Something hitting the door to the cave had Konala rising from his seat, since he was closest.

Sandale craned his head to look through the open doorway into the living area, but he couldn't see anything. Lawbreakers? Trouble at one of the settlements? He glanced at Rekah and Theron across from him, who could see into the next room and out the new window Haldone created. They didn't appear concerned, so he sat back.

Konala strode back in. "I'm afraid we need to leave as soon as possible."

Khaos' eyes turned an eerie silver before he stood. "He's right. Someone's life is threatened." He looked at each one of them then stopped on Sandale.

Scrat, what else could go wrong? Sandale tensed.

Khaos pointed at him. "It has to do with your family."

"What?" The tension inside him spread to every muscle in his body.

Konala faced him as well. "I sent my friend the elseire bird to check on the status of the city. Your three fathers have been taken to the Ruling Circle complex to await the next Open Circle session to be considered for exile."

He stood, his hands fisting of their own accord. "What are the charges?" He wouldn't lose his family again. He'd just started to be a part of them.

Konala shook his head. "The kidnapping of Akasha and Toni."

"What?" Toni rose next to him. "That's crazy." She turned her head toward him, sorrow and anger clear in her eyes. "Grandall must have eventually tracked the portal-opening to your house."

Akasha stood as well and faced those on the opposite side of the table. "We need to change our plan."

Everyone rose and Wareson quickly reassigned people to new tasks.

He and Haldone would focus on freeing their fathers as it should be, but he didn't like that Toni and Akasha planned to use themselves as bait to discover where Grandall's machine was located.

Once everyone filed out of the cave, the women said their goodbyes to each other. Only Toni would be going to Naralina. She should stay in Loraleaf where it was safe, but Sandale knew better than to attempt to argue that point. Her forceful personality was what attracted him to her in the first place, but at times like these, he wished he had some influence over her actions.

That was not to be. She'd made it clear his attentions were unwanted, but he couldn't simply close off his heart and not be worried. It angered him that Akasha had no qualms about Toni helping to ensnare Grandall. It was as if the man pushed her toward it, instead of wanting to protect her. He was either completely wrong about Akasha, or Akasha thought because he would be with her, she would be safe.

With Erin, Serena and Jaelene gone, the rest of them grouped themselves together and one after the other portaled to a spot just outside the city walls. Toni stepped through her portal without a backward glance and his stomach tightened. He did not like how spread out they all would need to be.

"Ready, brother?" Haldone waited in front of a portal opened by Rekah and Khaos.

"Yes." Without another word, he stepped through.

~~*~~

Akasha and Konala followed Toni through the portal on to the patrio before the Triad building after their quick hop from outside the walls. "I'm sure we will be seen very soon. Come." He placed a hand on Konala's shoulder and took Toni's wrist.

Once inside the corridor to his rooms, she twisted away.

He ignored her and led them to his door. It stood open and he cautiously entered.

Konala followed. "I'll go out to the patrio so Khaos knows we made it. He, Rekah and Nassic should have their portal hovering above the city, but they will need to move it every quarter of an hour or get caught by the portal trackers."

Toni picked up a chair that had fallen over in their rush to leave. "I can't believe no one came in here while you were gone."

He closed the door before he lifted his hand and emitted his blue light. There were hand prints on everything except the cabinet where he kept his food. The amobe was busy cleaning it. "Someone did enter and they looked at everything."

She walked over to where he stood. "Did they find anything?"

He scowled. "There is nothing to find. Who I am is who you see."

She backed away, her two hands raised in the air. "It wasn't an accusation."

The color of his essence was eating away at him and without meditation to find his center again, he was off balance. As much as he'd like to take what few moments they had to meditate, there was more at stake than his personal doubt. "I ask you again. What did you do to cause the black stain on your essence?"

Toni waved off his comment. "That again. Listen, I'll tell you during the next blue moon."

He stalked toward her. "There is no blue moon on this planet. Only white and pink and you know it. You need to tell me now."

"And if I don't?"

"I'll hypnotize you and ask you that way."

"Well, fuck. That's not playing fair."

She continued to move away from him, frustrating him more. "Toni!"

She froze, and he grabbed her arm.

"Tell me now before they come for us. I must know in case we are separated."

"Why? So you can decide who to save, me or yourself? I can tell you right now, saving yourself would be the best decision. I doubt you have any black on your essence."

He barely kept his anger in check, between listening for the sound of footsteps outside, his own questions about his calling and his sorrow over Toni's fated future. "I don't. Now tell me why you do."

She glared at him, her eyes brighter than he'd ever seen them. "Fine. If you want to know so bad I'll tell you. Just remember you asked for it."

He held his breath.

"I killed a man."

It left him in a whoosh of surprise. That was the last thing he'd expected, and the tiny glimmer of hope he had for her died. His heart constricted to know she would be lost.

"I bet you want details, too. I'll be happy to give you those." She twisted out of his grasp. "I was seventeen and the fucker I killed tried to rape me. When I punched and screamed, he tied my hands behind my back and put a sock in my mouth. But I got away by kneeing him in his balls as hard as I could. He limped around for days. Even went to the doctor about it. I told my foster mother, but she wouldn't believe me. So I told my teacher, but my pig of a foster-father was a pillar of society, and my teacher couldn't believe it." Toni took a deep breath.

As much as he didn't want to hear it, he didn't stop her.

"I told two more adults, but they didn't believe me either. Finally, I gave up trying to tell anyone, but I told *him* if he touched me again, I'd kill him. I never thought he'd take me seriously. I was fucking seventeen. But the bastard did. That's when he decided my fifteen-year-old foster sister was easier prey."

He tried to grasp what she said. Rape was such an old word, it took him a moment to remember what it meant, but as the meaning became clear, he felt his body turn cold.

She stood next to the longseat, her hand grasping the back like a lifeline. "He'd been raping her for about a month, but she didn't say anything because the pig told her that no one would believe her."

Toni snorted and pointed to her chest. "I would have. I would have stopped it. I did stop it. I skipped school one day and came home to steal some cash from the bastard's desk drawer, only to find his car in the driveway. I heard him doing it in the living room and thought I'd catch him cheating on his wife, but when I walked in the door, I found my foster sister laying on the floor, her eyes resigned while the bastard fucked her. She just lay there with her eyes glazed over."

Toni's own eyes held tears, but they didn't fall.

"I lost it. He hadn't seen me yet, so I ran back out and around to the back door. Upstairs in his bedroom, I grabbed the gun he kept in his nightstand drawer. When I got back to the living room, he was just standing up to zip his pants. I didn't even warn him. I just pulled the trigger."

"Toni, you—"

"Don't! You wanted to know, so you *listen*. I didn't just pull it once. I shot him until there were no bullets left, no chance he'd ever get up and walk again. I had to be sure he would never rape another girl. My foster sister grabbed the gun out of my hand and wiped it clean. She pushed me onto the couch then she stood next to the body, the gun in her hand."

Toni shook her head and wiped her eyes with the back of her hand. "Those few minutes of complete quiet before the sirens sounded bonded us. Within seconds, we agreed on our story. She didn't want me to go to jail. I was too close to being an adult and I wasn't the one attacked. At least not that time."

Akasha wanted to take her into his arms, tell her she was justified, but it *was* murder.

"The court said it was self-defense and she got off, but the town still refused to believe what was splayed on the front page of the paper. Rumors started that she had enticed him then killed him. I couldn't stomach it. I got us a couple of bus tickets and one night the two of us left. We never returned."

She held her arms to the sides. "So there you go. I killed someone and never paid for it. That's my black stain. I hope knowing that frees you from feeling any responsibility for me. I can take care of myself just fine, thank you." She turned her back on him and went to the cabinet.

Movement in the doorway to the patrio caught his attention. Konala stood there with his mouth open, obviously just as stunned by Toni's story. The ironic part for Akasha was that he didn't doubt a word of it.

Konala put his finger to his lips then strode in. "Khaos said Grandall's men are on their way. Since I'm supposed to help after they take you, where would you like me to hide?"

Toni turned to face Konala. "What? You don't want to be brought before the all mighty Wizard of Oz?"

Konala grinned. "I don't know about a wizard, but if Grandall is truly the snake you call him, I'd be able to handle him by myself."

Akasha stared. Toni chuckled as if she hadn't just told him of the day she killed a man. How could she do that? Switch so quickly?

She pointed to the patrio. "Then you better hide outside. They won't expect anyone but him and me." She waved her hand in his direction, but didn't look at him. "If they try to go outside, I'll distract them." She wiggled her brows at Konala for emphasis.

The man sighed. "Are you sure you want to let Grandall capture you? Jahl may have already breached the walls of the High Hall."

"Ah, but if he had, Khaos would know and would have told

you." She shook her head. "I now know the High Hall is protected like the Triad building with a Crius shield. Turns out anyone can come out, but getting in will be tough. That is if that's where the machine is. Akasha and I are the only sure way we can get to Grandall and find out. We have to stick to the plan. My gut tells me the portal is in that building, but that doesn't mean I'm right."

Footsteps in the corridor warned him. "They come. Konala, go."

Toni poured her ale into a glass and took a gulp.

Akasha stared at Toni. She was so strong. No wonder her blackness hadn't corrupted the rest of her essence. She'd gone through so much. While he had not. He had not lived because he had his calling. Serving the city was far more important than his life.

Just as Toni tainted her essence for her foster-sister, he gave up his life for the citizens of Naralina. The comparison was valid, yet it didn't help the uncomfortable feeling he had in the pit of his stomach. So much about Toni made him question all he believed.

When the door to his rooms burst open and three men ran in, the first grabbing Toni and two other grabbing his arms, it took all his concentration not to fight them. "Why are you here?"

The man holding Toni had an Eden birthmark which meant he could probably control plants or animals. He turned at Akasha's question. "We must take you directly to Grandall. He wants to know where you've been."

Toni had sweat running down the side of her face, probably from not struggling against the man that held her arms behind her back.

Akasha lowered his voice. "We are happy to come with you.

Do not hold the woman like that or public reaction will be bad. She will promise to obey."

Toni gave him a puzzled look before the man holding her nodded and took her by the arm. "Aw, and here I thought things were going to get kinky."

Akasha stifled his grin at the man's look of shock. Only Toni.

He let them take him out of the Triad building and a portal was opened to the Ruling Circle compound. Their plan was working. Konala would send his bird to follow them and report back where Grandall was.

Chapter Fifteen

Sandale held his mother tight, her tears wetting his chest. He had brought this on his family and he needed to fix it. He wouldn't tell her it would be far more than a simple rescue but an entire overthrow of the government. She was upset enough as it was.

"Do not worry, mother. Haldone and I will find our fathers and bring them home."

Vectar scowled at him. "Then what? They will just be taken again." He crossed his arms over his chest.

He'd had it with his younger brother. Releasing his mother, he grabbed Vectar by the arm and forced him from the room. Since the man's ability was to levitate, Sandale didn't worry about bodily harm.

Once in the den, he closed the door and turned on his brother. "I do not know what makes you look at the worst side of every situation, but in this instance, you will refrain from making our mother more unhappy than she already is. Do you understand?"

Vectar's eyes widened before his brow lowered. "Who put you in charge? You leave for five years, come back not knowing any of us, then get our fathers taken away. What gives you the right?"

He took the two steps to bring him directly in front of his brother. "I have the right because I know what is happening and you don't. Now you either support our mother or I'll render you unconscious until this is all over."

Vectar stepped back. "You *have* changed."

Sandale ground his teeth. "No, I haven't changed. I have become an entirely new person with new knowledge and experiences and this is the person I will be from now on. You decide whether you can live with that or not, but this is who I am."

Vectar shook his head. "I liked the old Sandale."

"And I do not care a rhybat's whisker what you like. Now are you going to comfort our mother and give her hope or are you going to sleep through all of this?"

"What am I supposed to tell her? What hope can there be?"

Sandale took a deep breath. He probably should just put his brother to sleep, but his mother would not be able to handle that as well. "Tell her we have evidence that will prove our fathers innocent."

"How can you have evidence if they *are* guilty. I don't know for sure but I—"

He held up his hand. "They are *not* guilty and we can prove it. That is what will release them. Now go." He gave his brother a push toward the door, not quite hard enough to knock him off his feet.

Vectar gave him one more scowl then pasted a smile on his face and whispered. "For mom."

Sandale rolled his eyes. How could he have two brothers so incredibly different? If Vectar was always such a logar's ass, he was glad he'd lost all memories of his childhood.

He strode into the living area to find that Konala had arrived. That meant Toni and Akasha had been taken. His gut tightened.

He wanted to save her, but his fathers were a part of him and he had put them in danger for her.

Konala, as if reading his mind, laid a hand on his shoulder. "The plan is working. Have faith."

He nodded, but didn't say anything. Instead, he gave his mother another hug. "I promise. Our fathers will be home after the setting of Helios."

She nodded, her eyes filled with tears. "I will believe that because you say it is so. You have grown into a stronger person. I know you will succeed."

His mother's simple words shoved away Vectar's, soothing his psyche, and he turned to Haldone. "Let us go."

Once outside, he, Konala, and Haldon strode purposefully higher up the cobbled pathways of Naralina. They had agreed walking would give them a better chance of not being noticed. A portal opening in or near the Circle Session hall would be reported immediately.

Ulik had explained to him the layout of the hall. There was the Open Circle Session room, a Closed Circle Session room, the reception area, a few small meeting rooms and the vestibule. The vestibule was a room no bigger than his family's house with 11 individual rooms inside for those waiting to be judged lawbreakers or free to go with restitution and retraining.

His fathers would be housed there. The easy part about that building was it had no Crius shield, having been built after the Crius left. But it was part of the entire Ruling Council compound at the top of the city. That included Circle members' homes, recreational facilities, longhouses for trackers and keepers, a community dining hall, the discoverists' building and the High Hall.

There was a chance Grandall had Akasha and Toni brought to the vestibule rooms and was questioning them there. His stride lengthened, but Haldone grabbed his arm.

"Do not to be too hasty. You will draw attention."

He slowed his walk. That he was preoccupied with Toni's safety was abundantly clear if his rash brother had to hold *him* back. He needed to remember she didn't want him in her life.

They reached the bottom of the single level steps to the compound when a purple winged bird flew by. Despite other men brushing past them to ascend, Konala stopped and held out his arm. The bird returned to perch on it, folding its wings in until it appeared completely green.

Konala stared at the bird who cocked its head. Obviously, there was a silent conversation going on. Finally, Konala nodded, then holding his arm straight out, the bird unfolded its feathers and launched into the air.

Sandale was too impatient to wait. "Where did they take Toni?"

"To the High Hall."

"Scrat. That means we will have to be invited in. If Grandall is there, I doubt very much that he will have the doors wide open."

Haldone tugged on his arm. "We have a more important task to complete and standing here isn't going to get our fathers released."

No, it wouldn't. Nor would it get Toni released.

The three of them started up the steps. His anger at Akasha for agreeing to be taken with Toni as bait grew with every stair. By time they reached the main square of the compound, he wanted to storm into the High Hall to knock Akasha out and save Toni.

"I need to relay this information to Jahl, Wareson and Theron."

Konala's voice brought Sandale back to his reality. He had to save his fathers first. At least he was assured that his love was reciprocated there.

A new calmness filled him. He had begun to love his fathers again. His life was starting over. He was building connections. The realization gave him patience he didn't know he had. "Go. We will free our fathers. At least the Session building has no Crius technology."

Konala nodded and strode off toward the High Hall.

Sandale glanced at the towering white, steepled structure before turning toward his anxious brother. "Let's retrieve our fathers."

They strode across the square to the Session Hall. People went about their daily work as if nothing momentous was about to happen. Excitement sped through his veins. He was about to be a part of a new era, just like he had started a new life. Anything was possible.

Just as Toni had said.

"This way." Haldone pointed to another side of the Session building and they walked down an open arched corridor. Two men patrolled this side of the building. They moved sedately from the middle door to the ends, one passing Sandale and Haldone.

Sandale scanned the "keeper" at the center door for his kindred. Spotting it, he leaned toward his brother. "He is Kindred of Light. Let me precede you."

Haldone nodded, and as they approached the keeper at the door, he fell behind.

Sandale pasted on a smile. "Excuse me, I was told that my

fathers might be inside. May I see them?" He placed his hand on the man's arm. The keeper opened his mouth then his eyes rolled back and he slumped to the savinstone floor. Sandale looked at Haldone. "Get our fathers and when the other two keepers leave, I'll let you know it is safe to bring them out."

Haldone nodded and rushed inside.

Sandale had no doubt that if there were any other keepers inside, Haldone would "box them up." He glanced both ways to see the patrolling keepers had almost reached the end of the building. It was good that Naralina was so civilized. No one, but lawbreakers, would ever rescue people from holding for a Circle session.

He crouched next to the door keeper. "Help, someone! He has collapsed."

The two others keepers spun and ran toward him.

"What happened? What did you do?"

"Me? I did not do anything. I am Kindred of Heart. I think he may have died."

One keeper crouched and felt the fallen man. "He breathes."

Sandale widened his eyes. "That is good. Do you have a healer nearby?"

"We do. I'll get him." The man who still stood turned and ran.

Sandale waited for him to run out of sight then touched the other man and he crumpled, too.

He was lucky that neither were Kindred of Mind. Deception was difficult around those who could read minds.

Opening the door, he stuck his head inside. "Haldone?"

"Here." Haldone turned a corner and Ulik, Baruch, and Fripp followed.

Success felt good. The five of them meandered away from the

Session building toward a larger one not far from the High Hall. It was the library of ancient texts, and they quickly slipped inside. They moved into an alcove off the lobby, away from any curious men.

He turned and gave each of his fathers a hug. "I cannot explain everything right now, but I have to go to the High Hall and save Toni."

"What about us?" Ulik took his arm. "They will only bring us back to holding if we go home."

He looked at his brother, who nodded. Quickly, he explained what they were about to do. "This is serious." Fripp frowned. "Are you absolutely sure this is what Grandall is planning?"

Was he? Toni was not known for telling the truth, but he had seen her essence. She was good at heart and she was smart. He had complete faith in her information. "Yes, I am sure. Even now, we have others attempting to get into the High Hall to stop him."

"Then we need to help." Baruch looked to Ulik and Fripp. Both men nodded.

This he had not anticipated, but having his fathers and brother with him, having that kind of support, filled him with confidence.

"Then let us go."

Toni stared at the gold arch that spanned at least fifty feet and had to be about thirty feet high. It was overkill, or Grandall really didn't know what the hell he was doing. Either was a plausible explanation for the huge monstrosity in the middle of the room.

The entire High Hall was one large space that towered upward four stories at least. The only windows were those at the third story and higher. There did seem to be round turret doors in various places, so maybe there were small rooms in them, but generally it was a big empty space the size of a castle. It made all the men working in it look like ants to her. There had to be at least a couple dozen.

At one end of the giant arch, two Edenists tinkered around a square box with a door on it, almost like a witness stand. There was a similar one on the other end. That is where Grandall stood pointing at something and talking to another man.

The plan was for her and Akasha to go quietly and find the giant portal. They had succeeded in that. Now they were to either keep it from starting or capture Grandall, which meant all bets were off.

The man that held her arm had stopped just inside the double doors of the High Hall, so she looked behind her to see the other two tying Akasha's hands behind his back. Well, hell. She'd bet that was infragile vine. One of the men was Kindred of Water and the other was Kindred of Air. She'd seen what Haldone and Wareson could do with their air abilities, so she didn't doubt that man was pretty powerful.

When the two guards finished that, they wrapped material over Akasha's hands and knotted it between the ties. How was he supposed to use his light ability if his hands were covered? Fuck. Looked like saving the city was up to her.

The Kindred of Eden man that held her arm started forward now that he thought their one threat was taken care of.

She smirked. Men could be so stupid sometimes. They were halfway to the machine when Grandall looked up. The smile that lit up his face was anything but friendly. It was evil triumph if she ever saw it.

He started toward them. As he came closer, she had to wonder what Jasmine saw in him. Was it his power? It had to be because the man was old and hadn't taken care of his body like most of the other older men she'd seen in Naralina.

He opened his arms wide. "Toni, Akasha, how glad I am that you are both safe."

"Seriously? Why wouldn't we be? The only one who would hurt us is you."

Behind her, Akasha made a low noise deep in his throat, but she ignored it.

Grandall lost his smile and looked at their guards. "You can leave us now."

She kept herself from chuckling. This was perfect.

"Why have you brought us here? Why am I tied up?" Akasha played the baffled Triad member-to-be really well.

Grandall's gaze switched to him. "Because you lied to me."

"I never lie."

That he was affronted was obvious in his tone. It took Grandall back a bit. Ah, so the man thought he had it all figured out, but now he wasn't sure. She couldn't let that go.

"This is how you plan to flood our Pleasure Temples with women?" She pointed at the gold arch. "Did you ever think about how those of us in the Temples would feel about that? Did you?" She took a step closer to him.

His confusion over her questions was exactly what she had hoped for.

"Of course you didn't. You just thought more women for you. Well, let me tell you something." She advanced on him. "I don't want any more competition than I already have. It's hard enough finding Edenists who don't want frail little flowers for bedmates. If you bring more women, I'll be lucky to have sex once a week."

"That's what you think I plan to do?" Grandall's brows were drawn together. "You stupid woman. You drew a perfectly good man into helping you because you thought I would flood the Pleasure Temples?"

She kept her temper under control. "Of course. Why else would you build this thing?"

He didn't miss a beat. "So every filoz could have a beloved." He swung his arm to the side to indicate the machine. "This will allow eleven women at a time to enter our fair city and be chosen for bonding."

Even the way he stated it told her it was a form of slavery, even if the women were lucky to have a couple Edenists or more worshipping them. They would be prisoners here. "What's wrong with the way men find women now?"

Again, Akasha's made a low warning sound in the back of his throat, but she didn't care. He could play good cop and she'd play bad cop. That's what they were anyway. Or rather she was the bad person. She'd seen the look in his eye when she told him she'd murdered a man.

Grandall sneered. "I'm not discussing this with you. You don't know anything about our ways. You even came from a different city. I have a portal to open." He started to turn away, dismissing her like a bothersome mosquito.

Fuck that. This mosquito could sting. She took one step toward him and sent her foot into his ass.

He stumbled before turning toward her with rage in his gray eyes.

Too late she remembered what the man had done to his son. She glanced around to see two men staring in surprise. Grandall's other sons had helped hold Jahl down when he burned his birthmark. But no one was close enough to stop her.

Adrenaline rushed through her as she felt success within her reach. She sent her foot up again and connected with his balls.

He yelled and crumbled to the ground.

"Toni, no!"

She ignored Akasha and jumped on Grandall. She pummeled him with her fists, letting out her rage at him, her step-father, and the hurt she felt at Akasha's judgement. She would kill him.

Suddenly, she was levitated off him at least twenty feet in the air. "What the hell?" The next thing she knew she had slammed back to the ground, a loud crack coming from her shoulder before heart-stopping pain hit her.

She screamed.

"Toni!" Akasha knelt next to her. "Toni."

She grasped her shoulder, tears running down her cheeks. "Fuck! That hurt."

"Take them to the observation area." Grandall spoke from behind her, his tone much higher than usual.

Good, she hoped he felt worse than her. She'd broke her arm before. Twice to be fair, but she was a hundred percent sure her shoulder was shattered. A guard grasped her and made her stand up, sending new pain powering through her body. The edges of her vision started to go hazy.

No way was she fainting now. Not with Grandall still alive.

The guard pushed her in the middle of her back to make her follow Akasha to a platform that looked like a bandstand only without a roof. It was placed opposite the center of the machine. At the front of it were three steps covered in a white cloth runner that ended about ten feet from the arch.

Seriously, Grandall had such huge visions of grandeur that he expected the women to come to his dais and kneel at his feet or something?

When they were pushed to a corner of the platform, Akasha leaned toward her. "You could have been killed."

She started to shrug when the pain almost sent her to her knees. She grabbed on to the half-wall of the platform with her good hand to stay upright. "It would have been worth it if I had killed him."

"No, it wouldn't."

Akasha's tone had her turning to look at him. "But I have black in my essence. I'm expendable, you're not. Not that I have a death wish or anything."

The guard standing in front of them, the one with air abilities and probably the one who had slammed her to the ground, turned around and scowled at her. She blew him a kiss and winked.

His confusion eased her tension.

Akasha didn't whisper any more sweet nothings in her ear, so she watched the proceedings. There had to be a way to stop this thing. She looked at Akasha, who was also studying the activity. His green, white, blue, and yellow light wouldn't do them any good, unless Edenists were afraid of amobes, which she doubted.

Purple had real possibilities, but his hands needed to be free. Red might be able to distract a guard, but she couldn't see that helping much. His orange light would work great. Maybe he could burn the sucker down.

She looked behind the platform to see if anyone was watching and a man with a swirl on his chest stared at her. Fuck, a Kindred of Mind. Could he read her mind?

She looked at him and didn't move a muscle. *Oh, now you are one handsome man. I don't think I've had a cock that big inside me in three cycles of Selene. Hell, my nipples are hardening at just the thought of you thrusting into my wet pussy.*

The man raised an eyebrow and his cock hardened.

Too bad you're on the wrong side. Did you know Grandall plans to sell the women he brings to Eden to other cities? Did you know he burned the Kindred birthmark on his own son because he didn't like his son's ability?

The Edenist scowled at her.

Don't get mad at me because you don't want to hear the truth.

"What are you doing?" Akasha had leaned in again.

She turned back to the front, careful to whisper. "The man behind us is Kindred of Mind, so I told him what Grandall is planning to do. He doesn't want to hear it."

Akasha looked over his shoulder. "There's no one there."

She glanced back and scanned the area. When she faced forward she grinned. "Guess he couldn't handle the truth."

CLEAR THE PORTAL

The voice was so loud she cringed, which sent more shooting pain through her body. "Shit, they're going to try it." She glanced at the high windows. The light was fading. "Can you hypnotize anyone without your hands?"

He shook his head.

She hated standing there and doing nothing. "I could make a run for the doors and let the others in."

He frowned at her. "That would do no good. You need the mechanism to walk through the Crius shield."

"Okay, what does it look like? The mechanism?" She could always get close to one of the guards and take it from him.

"I don't know."

"What?"

"Shhhh."

She clamped her mouth shut as the guard in front of them turned around and glowered at her again. She didn't bother to ask why Akasha didn't know what the mechanism looked like. She was pretty sure it was because the man just didn't get out much.

So now to plan C. Too bad she only had plans up to B.

Sandale forced himself to stand still, though what he wanted to do was pace. "What if we each took on one?"

He stood with his fathers, Haldone, Jahl, and Wareson. The others were in groups around the building. Since the patrio gave them nowhere to hide, they were supposed to look like they were busy conducting business.

Wareson responded. "That might work. The five keepers patrolling the outside are of no use to us because they have no key. It is the three inside the shield we need to get to, but the ones outside will stop us if they know our intention."

He fisted his hands in frustration. "We only need one key, correct?"

Ulik nodded.

Sandale looked at Jahl. "We just need to figure out how to get one of the inside guards to let one of us in. I think the rest of us can take care of the others in whatever way they feel fit."

"I can help with that." Baruch smiled. He was probably the only man of their group who looked like he was having a casual conversation.

"You can? How?" He was happy for his fathers' help, but worried as well.

"I can flood a man with so much sorrow that he will happily allow me in."

He stared at his dad. "That is exactly what we need. Are you sure it will work?"

Baruch's eyes took on a devilish gleam. "Absolutely."

Why did he have the feeling his father had done this before? It was a question he would definitely ask if they all managed to stop Grandall and have a normal life.

Jahl gestured toward the High Hall. "I will go with you to handle the three inside." "Wareson, have the others take the five outside." At Wareson's agreement, Jahl turned back to him. "Konala can send his bird around the building. When we see it, we move in."

"That should work." After Wareson left to tell the others the plan, Sandale talked with his family. They would go with Baruch and once inside, Sandale would put the keeper to sleep. Then Haldone would take care of one inner keeper and Fripp and Baruch the other. He would leave the key with Ulik, who would make sure everyone else made it through.

He didn't like involving his family so much, but he had no choice. He needed to get into the hall.

A shimmering behind his father Fripp heralded a portal opening.

Khaos stepped through and it closed. "We will be too late."

Fear raced through him. "Too late? What do you mean too late?"

Khaos pointed to the High Hall. "The machine. I saw it work."

"Fuck."

They all looked at him in surprise.

He shrugged. "It is what Toni says when things are the worst they can get." He spoke to Khaos. "We are about to enter. We will just have to take this one step at a time."

"I'm going in with you."

He was grateful for the added support. Khaos may not be a brother of his heart anymore, but they were still friends and on the same side.

"There's the bird." Haldone pointed to the purple elseire flying by the front of the hall.

Sandale didn't have to say anything. They all turned and walked toward the keeper at the front of the hall. When they arrived, the man folded his arms. "No one is to enter the High Hall today."

Baruch stepped up, tears in his eyes. "But I must go inside. My son is working in there and his wife sent me. She fell off their balcony and the healer says there is nothing more he can do."

The man looked stunned. "I am very sorry but—"

Baruch had tears running down his cheeks now. "Please. It took my son three years to woo her here to Eden. She's trying to hang on just to see him."

"I—"

"What if this short delay is the difference between him seeing her before she dies and not?"

The man's eyes were starting to water. "Very well. But just you."

"Of course, but hurry."

"Take my hand." The keeper reached his arm out.

Seeing the band around the man's wrist, Sandale grabbed it and stepped through.

"Wait!" The keeper crumpled to the ground.

Sandale yanked the band off and pulled his father in. "Here, put this on and help everyone get through. I'm going in."

Before he could open the doors, Jahl had joined him. "I've waited a long time for this. It's time for my father's reckoning."

An Edenist stepped into the box on either side of the gold arch. Akasha tried to focus on his task, but Toni's pain and anxiousness was distracting him. He glanced at the keeper standing in front of them and leaned toward her. He kept his voice low. "Be still."

"I can't. Grandall is going to win." Her eyes were bright green and they glistened with unshed tears.

He couldn't be sure if it was due to frustration or pain. Knowing Toni, it was both. "If you can be calm and silent, I may be able to help."

She looked at him with a hopelessness that had his heart tightening.

He raised one brow.

Finally, she nodded and returned her gaze to the activity before them. She continued to hold her shoulder with her other hand, but she didn't move.

The machine started to whirr, filling the hall with a low vibration and a steady sound. It was just what he needed. Carefully, he moved his finger within the material around his hands. He emitted a small beam of orange light toward the floor.

The smell of burning fabric and the wood floor beneath them floated upward. He glanced at Toni, but if she smelled it, she didn't move.

He stopped the light and worked at the charred edges around his hands. He needed his whole hand to actually have any effect. The material was strong. He moved his finger as a high-pitched sound filled the hall then disappeared.

He burned more of the material and the gold arch shimmered. Forgetting to be careful, he gritted his teeth as part of the orange light hit his calf. He stopped it and worked his hand through the hole.

"Aw, fuck." Toni's dejected exclamation froze him.

Eleven women from Earth stood in the hall blinking in confusion.

Grandall's head snapped toward the entrance. "You three, lock the doors." He must have sensed the others had breached the shield.

Akasha needed to move.

Grandall stepped off the platform and proceeded down the white material on the floor as if he were an emperor.

"If this wasn't so disheartening, I'd find this funny." Toni looked up at him. "They aren't too impressed with Grandall."

A few of the women had recovered enough to chuckle at Grandall's aging body. The older man paused.

Akasha took the opportunity to ram the keeper in front of him. The man went toppling over the half-wall, giving him the opening he needed. Twisting his body and bending his arms, he opened his hand and let his orange light streak from the opening in the platform to the side near the box containing an Edenist.

That man yelled, jumping out of the box. Women screamed as they ran away from the orange beam.

Akasha kept his concentration on his orange light. If anyone ran into it, they would die. The wood support for the arch caught fire just as the doors to the hall banged open.

"Finally, the cavalry is here." Toni's voice, though excited, was edged with pain.

He wanted to help her, but he couldn't take his eyes from the machine. Once sure the machine was burning well beyond repair, he closed his hand.

Akasha turned to help Toni, but was shoved to the side as Grandall grabbed her.

"Ow!"

Grandall backed into the corner of the platform, his arm around Toni's waist and a stone dagger pressed against her chest. "Stay where you are if you value her life."

The collective gasp of the men in the room gave him hope. Grandall had gone too far.

Sandale took in the chaotic scene in an instant. Everything was almost slow motion for him from the women heading for the doors to the burning machine to the shock of Grandall's men. But as soon as he saw Toni at Grandall's mercy, everything inside him went cold.

He didn't take his eyes from his enemy, except to glance at Akasha, who stood on the other side of the platform, his hands behind his back. "Ware, Haldone, close the doors. Ulik, Khaos, gather the women. Fripp, put out that fire." He quickly assigned the appropriate man for each task, especially his father Fripp who could produce water from the air.

Jahl moved past him. "By the Crius, father. You go too far!"

Grandall's lip curled in to a sneer. "So you still live. What bog did you crawl out from?"

"Your time in control is over." Jahl stopped halfway to the platform.

Grandall laughed. "Why, because of you and a handful of men? I'm disappointed in your choice of company. Then again, you always disappointed me. Look around. I have many more men than you, and I have just proven to them that I can bring every filoz and Pleasure Temple women. What can you do for Naralina?"

Jahl circled to look at every person in the room.

Sandale forced himself to stay where he was. Jahl deserved to have this moment, but if it endangered Toni in any way, he would put Jahl to sleep in an instant. He stared at Toni. She was hurting, but she was furious. Another reason why he loved her.

Jahl finished his circle then waved his arm.

"What?" Grandall looked down at his feet. "What's this?"

Jahl shrugged. "You are now held by the wooden platform you stand on. Did you forget so soon that I can control anything in nature not alive. Every one of your men is now held to the floor by the very material it is made of. Just because you burned the birthmark from my chest does not mean my 'paltry' ability, as you called it, disappeared."

"Release me at once."

"Release the woman."

Grandall's gaze flickered over Sandale and his men. Was that a glimmer of uncertainty? Sandale strode forward and stood shoulder to shoulder with Jahl. "He said to release her."

"I do not take orders from a son who abandoned his family." He spoke to the entire room. "*I* am the ruler of Naralina. With this golden portal, we can rule all of Eden."

Jahl smirked. "A ruler of Naralina who was not even granted a Crius chip by the Triad?"

Sandale froze. By the Bowels on Bangley! Grandall had no Crius chip? He looked to Akasha whose brows had lowered. Anger radiated from the Triad-member-to-be.

"You lie." Grandall's gaze flicked to the room. "He lies."

"Tell us the truth, Grandall!" Nassic's voice came from behind as he strode to stand next to Jahl. It was only seconds before Wareson was by his side. "No more lies, Grandall. No more exiling those of us who would reveal your intentions. Tell us, do you have a Crius chip."

Sandale's heart swelled with unity. They stood shoulder to shoulder against the most powerful man in Naralina. Nassic's Kindred of Mind ability to force people to tell the truth would shift public opinion in their favor.

Grandall's face twisted as if he was in agony, and his hold on Toni tightened, causing her to wince in pain. "I have no chip. But I do not need one. Look at all I have done for the best city on the planet!"

At Toni's expression, Sandale couldn't hold back any longer. He strode toward the platform, his anger fighting with his fear for Toni. He would not let her die. No matter how much she'd hurt him.

"Do not take another step unless you want to watch her bleed." Grandall's voice was desperate and cruel. His face contorted with rage.

Sandale stopped. If he could just touch the man, but there was no way Grandall was going to let him close enough for that. His gaze moved to Toni just as she spoke.

"Give it up, Grandall. Your master plan is trashed. Try to go out with a little class. Oh, that's right, you don't have any class." She breathed heavily. "One reason Naralina won't miss you."

"By the Crius woman, close your mouth or I'll cut out your tongue."

"Oh really? You and what army?"

Grandall tightened his grip.

"Ouch! You logar's ass."

Grandall's eyes turned to slits.

Sandale raised his hand as Grandall pulled his arm back to plunge the dagger into Toni's chest.

It was the moment he needed. Without warning, Sandale let his calming flood the hall. The dagger dropped as Grandall and Toni crumpled to the floor. So too did Akasha…and everyone else in the room.

Chapter Sixteen

Sandale ran up to the platform and gently pulled Toni's limp form away from Grandall. Even in her unconscious state, she twitched as if in pain and his heart constricted. Carefully, he laid her down near Akasha. Touching his friend, he withdrew the calming to wake him.

Akasha blinked. "What happened?"

"I put everyone to sleep."

"Everyone? How?" Akasha sat up.

He grimaced. "I have little control over my ability when I cannot touch a person, so if I use it in that way, everyone within the area is affected."

Akasha turned. "Can you untie me?"

Sandale brushed away the charred remains of material and untied the infragile vine. Now he knew how the fire started.

Akasha rose. "Holy Bendis. Every single person in the hall is asleep."

Sandale brushed Toni's hair back away from her face. "Not just asleep, but unconscious. Tell me, was Toni hurt."

Akasha crouched down beside him. "She was. I am sorry. I could not stop her."

Anger surged through him, and he glared at Akasha. "What happened?"

"She kicked Grandall in the balls then started beating him."

He widened his eyes and a slight smile curved his lip as he imagined the scene. Then his humor vanished. "Then?"

"One of the keepers with levitation ability lifted her off him and slammed her to the floor. She's been holding her left shoulder."

His gut twisted in pain that she'd been hurt. Keeping her unconscious was the best plan until he could find a healer. He rose and scowled at Akasha. "You were supposed to protect her."

"I know. I failed."

He wanted to hurt his friend, but the admission took the impulse away. "I will find her a healer."

Akasha nodded. "Yes. But first, while she is not in pain, we need to wake our people up."

He didn't want to wait, but they had to take action for the people of Naralina, the city he would call home from now on. "You are right. Come help me."

Akasha helped Rekah and Konala to stand.

"What happened?"

He answered as he had with the others he'd helped after Sandale woke them. "Sandale made everyone unconscious so he could save Toni."

Both men nodded. "He always was one step ahead of everyone."

Again, Akasha felt a pang for the man he had come to admire.

How much of his past self would meld with his new personality was a complete unknown. He sincerely hoped Sandale's old friends would learn to accept him as he was. After all, the man was morally ahead of them all.

He stilled at that thought, his own tainted essence still eating at him. He pushed the thought away for a time when he could meditate on it. "Jahl has taken Grandall to holding and will take responsibility for this overthrow. Khaos, Wareson, Nassic and Theron have gone to capture the rest of the Ruling Circle to put them in holding as well."

"What can we do?"

Akasha looked to where Sandale was. He had finished waking up the rest of the women and now strode toward Toni. Akasha wanted to join him, but his responsibility to her was over now. He needed to ignore his instinct to help her. She was in good hands. He knew that, but it didn't take away his urge to hold her again.

"Akasha?"

He blinked before responding to Rekah. "Sandale needs you to return the women to Earth. He said there is a Kindred of Mind here who can erase their memories of this place and of this place only."

"You are troubled." Rekah studied him.

He turned away. "Just concerned with how this will end."

"Come, Rekah. The women are confused and scared." Konala pulled the brother of his heart away.

Akasha was thankful. He did not need help sorting through his thoughts. He was trained to do so. It was his feelings that were affecting his thoughts. All he needed was time to think and put his new experiences into perspective.

"Oh, my God, I know you!" The woman's yell caught his attention and he spun.

A woman with long bright red hair and green eyes like Toni pointed at the Rekah and Konala.

"Star?" Rekah's eyes were wide.

"Oh yes! You remember me! You came back for me! I had hoped and waited and—so I'm really on another planet? Are you all nudists?"

The two men looked uncomfortable, so he stepped in. "Yes, you are on another planet and we do not wear clothes here. But do not worry." He raised his gaze to include all the women huddled together. "These two men will bring you back home and you won't remember any of this."

The woman, Star, grabbed his arm. "Can I stay? Please."

There were only two options for women on Naralina, a filoz or a Pleasure Temple. They came to the planet as chosen ones of a filoz, not as single women looking for a filoz. "I don't think you understand."

She let go of his arm and grabbed Konala's. "But I know them. They know me. I have wanted to go to another planet ever since I was born. I'm meant to stay here."

He looked to Konala, who appeared guilty. There was a story there, but he had more important matters to attend to. "I leave it up to Konala and Rekah." If they had made a mistake in the past, it was their responsibility to make it right. He turned and headed toward the gold portal. And it was his job to finish what he'd started.

"So that's your names. I love them." At the woman's words, Akasha smirked. It was good to know he wasn't the only one who made mistakes. Konala, Rekah and Theron's beloved may not be too happy with theirs.

~~*~~

Toni carefully lifted both arms above her head, then to the side. Exercising without weight of any kind was boring, but the healer told her she needed to do it that way for a cycle of Selene.

She shouldn't complain because Earth had nothing on Eden when it came to the medical field. It amazed her that the Edenists had figured out how to mend the body through their abilities. It was only four days since her injury and she was exercising!

She'd been right, her shoulder had shattered, yet here she was working out as usual, or almost as usual. She brought her arms down. "Face it, woman, you're bored to tears." She picked up the towel she didn't use yet and brought it inside.

Dropping it on her table, she moved to her cold box and pulled out an ale. Maybe she should design a new outfit. She flopped on her couch and took a sip. Maybe something else in leather. If she asked real nice, she might be able to get more feroon hide. Or she could try—

A knock on her door interrupted her musings. She hadn't been to the public room of the Temple to pick out any men, so it had to be a friend. "Coming."

She ran to the door and threw it open.

"Whoa, Toni. Put some clothes on."

She laughed. "Come on in, Erin. I can't believe Nase and Ware let you come to a Pleasure Temple."

Erin walked in and looked around. "I told them I needed to

know every part of Naralina if I was going to be the agapayto of two Ruling Circle members."

Toni grabbed a wrap from her room and came back out. "Does that help?"

"Much better. Now all I need is a glass of ambrosia and I'll be perfect."

"Not a problem. Have a seat." She poured Erin her drink and found her out on the balcony.

"Thanks. You have a lovely view."

Toni sat next to Erin and raised an eyebrow. "Okay, cut to the chase. You didn't come here to enjoy my view. Not when you'll have the best view on the mountain in a few days."

Erin smirked. "True." She took a sip of her drink. "You're right. I'm here on a mission."

"I'm pretty good with missions."

"That you are." Erin chuckled. "Have you been keeping up to date with the fallout from the coup?"

She grimaced. "The last I heard, Jahl took the blame or credit for ousting the entire Circle and he was calling for a special election of a new one. I heard Grandall is in holding, waiting for the new Circle to decide his fate and on a personal note, Jahl and Theron won't allow Serena and Jaelene to come to Naralina until everything is settled. Did I get it all?"

Erin's eyes twinkled with amusement. "Almost. Four of the Ruling Circle members to be voted on have been announced."

"That *is* news. I'm assuming that both Nase and Ware are in, especially after all that dirt came out on Grandall."

Erin rolled her eyes. "Honestly, it's a good thing the man is in holding for his own protection. Between Nase making Grandall confess and then Ulik viewing it and teaming up with a Kindred of Light man to show the confession all over the city, people want his head."

"If anyone gets his head, it should be me. He took up a lot of my time when I could have been having fun."

"Is this fun?" Erin motioned with her glass to the balcony as a whole.

"You mean having a drink with a friend? Absolutely."

"No. I mean the Pleasure Temple and having sex with whichever hunk turns you on that night."

"Or day." Toni winked. Not that she'd had sex since her night in the cave with Sandale and Akasha. She just hadn't felt like it, which scared the hell out of her. She wanted to ask the healer about it, but she didn't. Maybe she should ask Rekah. Maybe it was a mental block like she was afraid that after those two, sex with one man wouldn't be able to compare.

"Toni?" Erin waved her hand in front of her face. "You with me?"

She blinked. "Well, I'm certainly not with anyone else."

Erin squinted. "Do you want to be?"

"What do you mean?" She took another swig of ale.

"I mean do you want to be with Sandale and Akasha?"

She waved off the comment. "Why would I want to be with them? They have their own lives and I have mine."

Erin didn't say anything, just took another sip of her ambrosia. "What?"

Her friend shrugged. "I just thought you might be a little more interested in Sandale since he saved you and is going up for election to the Ruling Circle."

"Seriously?"

Erin grinned. "Yes. He's one of the four."

Well, hell. Not only did he come in and save the day, he would be running the whole city. The old Sandale wouldn't have done that. She couldn't help but remember how hard her heart was pounding while Grandall held that dagger to her chest. Then Sandale strolled in, all in charge of everyone and her heart did a joyful leap. Somehow, she knew she'd get out of there alive.

"There's another man too, named Eldus, who was announced. I met him yesterday. He seems very level headed. I feel bad for him though. Grandall falsely accused his son, Keeva, and had him exiled."

"Did you say Keeva?"

Erin nodded.

That was the discoverist who had planned to turn in Grandall but was found out and exiled. "So who are they thinking of for the fifth person. Oh wait, that's why you're here, isn't it? They want me to be a Ruling Circle member. You can tell them no way. I'm done playing with politics. It doesn't sit well with me."

Erin laughed. "No, they weren't going to ask you. I don't think Naralina is ready for you quite yet."

"Hey, I heard they're calling me a hero."

"Yes, they are, but last I heard they were still deciding whether or not women would be allowed to go to Open Circle sessions."

Toni widened her eyes. "This place is so backwards in some ways."

Erin nodded. "Yes, and so forward in others."

"Then who are they looking at?"

"Akasha."

Toni's heart skipped over that. "He won't. He thinks the Triad is better than the Ruling Circle."

"That's what Nase and Ware are worried about. They really want him on the Circle because of his abilities, his level headedness, and they think having him as a moral compass would insure the Circle of being elected."

Toni took another swig of ale. Akasha would make a great Ruling Circle member. She'd always thought so, but he was probably too pure for that. "So did anyone ask him yet?"

Erin put down her drink.

Toni tensed. "Shit, no. Don't look at me like that. I'm not asking that man to do anything. He wouldn't care if I ceased to exist. You'd be sinking your own ship with me."

"Please Toni. We need you. Akasha was just called up to be on the Triad. His ceremony is tomorrow. We have to get to him first."

"Tomorrow? His dream comes true tomorrow?" She was thrilled for him. It was what he'd wanted since he was a boy. She should be bursting with joy like she was when she found out Theron, Rekah, Konala and Jaelene were having a baby.

The Triad was like that for Akasha. But instead of joy, her heart ached.

Sandale strode up the hill from his parents' house. If he was elected, he would have his own home in the Ruling Circle compound and a new purpose in life.

He already liked Nassic and Wareson, and Eldus was a smart man, who was anxious to learn about the jungle and organize a search for Keeva. His maturity would be good for the oligarchy and Naralina.

There were only two things standing in the way of his happiness—convincing Akasha to join the Ruling Circle instead of the Triad and forgetting about Toni. The first he had hope of, but the second he doubted he could accomplish. Forgetting Toni would be like forgetting Eden had two moons. Every time Bendis rose in all its pink glory, he would be reminded it existed. He foresaw a similar occurrence happening when he was with anyone who knew Toni.

He paused at the bottom of the stairs to the Triad building. Did Akasha have any idea why he asked to meet? He started up the steps. The man was smart, if limited, in his experiences.

That Akasha had been called to the Triad panel so soon had surprised him. He had a gut feeling it was the uncertainty of who would be put forth to rule Naralina that had caused the oldest of the Triad to step down. There were rumblings that the entire panel was going to as well.

Jahl looked like a tyrant for ousting his father, even though Grandall's crimes had been well documented and distributed. That didn't matter. The peace-loving people of Naralina were horrified by the overthrow.

But Jahl was happy at Loraleaf and had no interest in ruling Naralina. He seemed very satisfied that he had been able to take his father down and give him over for the punishment he deserved. Soon the lawbreakers would have another in their midst.

Sandale reached the top of the stairs and stepped onto the patrio in front of the Crius shield and waited. Within moments, Akasha himself strode out to meet him.

"It is good to see you again." Akasha's smile was warm.

"A lot has happened in the last four days."

Akasha nodded and gestured toward another side of the patrio that had benches scattered about.

They were still outside the Crius shield, which Sandale found interesting. Did Akasha not want their conversation to be overheard from those inside? "Do you know why I am here?"

Akasha sat. "Not specifically. Please, sit."

Sandale sat across from his friend. He was far more comfortable with his family now, or rather with his mother, fathers and Haldone, but he missed talking to Akasha. "We want you to join the Ruling Circle."

Akasha's eyes widened. "But I am to ascend to the Triad panel this afternoon."

"I know. But we think you would better serve the city by helping us to rule."

Akasha looked away. "This has been my calling since I was a boy. To keep the city safe by assuring good men thrived here."

"I understand that, or I think I do." How could he really know what it was like to long for something his whole life when his had just started again months earlier? "But we are hoping to change the Triad's duties as well, and we think that your insight would be particularly helpful for the transition."

Akasha's gaze snapped back to his. "What do you mean, change duties?"

No one besides Nassic, Wareson, Eldus and himself had discussed this. If Akasha told the Triad too soon, there could be serious repercussions. "I must ask you as a friend, to not divulge this to anyone, even within your Triad members."

Akasha hesitated then gave a quick nod.

"We want the Triad be the ones to judge those in holding."

"Holy Bendis."

"I know it sounds impossible, but hear me out. The Triad is already an expert on morality and being unbiased. The Ruling Circle has too much power and could become self-serving as we have seen. We do not want that to happen again."

Akasha remained quiet. Finally, he spoke. "You would need to train the Triad members. Right now they operate within a vacuum of right and wrong, with no firsthand experience."

Maybe Akasha's adventures with Toni *had* widened his view. He didn't dismiss the idea outright. "Would you help us with this? Could you support the Triad in the transition if we can get this to pass?"

"Yes. It is something I have been thinking about also, but you do not need me to be a Ruling Council member to help. Would I not be more beneficial working from inside the Triad?"

With one argument out of the way, Sandale faced the hardest one. "The fact is, we want someone of Triad caliber on the Ruling Council. We know those who step-up among the Triad members-to-be, are well trained to do what is right. The rest of us have multiple agendas and we want to be sure we always keep Naralina as our first priority. We have faith that you will make that so."

Akasha's brow furrowed.

That was not a good sign. "I have a personal reason as well."

"And that is?"

"I admit I have fallen in love with Toni." He raised his hand as Akasha opened his mouth to speak. "I know it is not reciprocated. She can't even stand for me to touch her. However, I still want a filoz to search out another love. I doubt anyone could ever erase her from my heart, and only you would understand that because you know her like I do."

Now Akasha looked as if he were in pain.

Had he mistaken Akasha's sympathy for more than it was? Maybe the man did not feel the camaraderie he felt.

Akasha stood. "You have given me a lot to think about. It is time for my meditations, so I must go. I will let you know my decision."

Sandale nodded. He tried to ignore the defeat in his heart and gave his friend a smile. "I know you will do what it best. Thank you for meeting with me."

Akasha stepped forward and gave him a hug, which he returned. He couldn't be wrong about their friendship.

When they parted, Akasha simply opened his arm toward the top of the stairs and they walked together in silence.

Before taking the first step down, Sandale faced Akasha. "Whatever you decide, I hope we can remain friends."

Akasha smiled sadly and nodded.

It was not what he'd hoped to see. With resignation, he turned away and strode down the stairs. When he reached the bottom of the five levels, he stopped to look back. Akasha remained at the top and on seeing him, waved.

A glimmer of hope kindled inside him. At least Akasha would think about it. He would tell the others to wait on identifying anyone else until the afternoon. Looking up at Helios, he estimated they had six hours before the proposed Ruling Circle could be announced. It was also the amount of time before his own life would be decided.

Akasha watched Sandale leave then turned back and entered

the Triad building. His heart was torn in too many directions to count, and he craved time for meditation. As soon as he entered his rooms, he strode outside and stood with his legs apart, his arms outstretched and tilted his head back.

Closing his eyes, he searched for peace and calm. He waited for the usual suspended state to come over him. He breathed evenly, focusing on his breaths, his heartbeats, his oneness with the air around him. He embraced the light within him. Calm.

He waited…calm.

Peace…

He snapped his head up.

It was unreachable…again. His peace was gone. Was it because so too was his innocence and ignorance? Ever since he came back, he'd been unable to meditate. He had hoped, after hearing what Sandale had to say, it would bring him the focus he needed.

It did not.

He stood straight again and meandered to the edge of his patrio to look out over the city. He was meant for the Triad, but either he'd been corrupted by his experience or the Triad was not perfect. Both concepts were hard to accept.

Had he been wrong his entire life about the Triad?

Had his connections to Toni, Sandale and the others of the jungle made him too tainted to ascend?

Every time he tried to envision sitting on the panel now, he couldn't do it without feeling like an imposter. Would he have felt this way if he had never seen his own essence? Would he have ascended in ignorant bliss? And was this a flaw in the Triad system?

He stalked to the other end of the patrio, to where Toni had once leaned across the cliff face. Was she to blame?

His mind yelled, "Yes!" But his heart told him his blame was in the wrong place. The fact was, he felt something for Toni. He felt love like he hadn't felt for another Edenist since he was a boy who adored his mother. He hadn't even thought himself capable of it after years of keeping himself apart.

Now Sandale had offered him everything his heart wanted. If they formed a filoz, then Toni could be theirs. Sandale may think Toni didn't care about him, but he was wrong. He'd seen her reactions to Sandale when he walked into the High Hall. Pride had shone in her eyes and worry built on her brow as Grandall spoke.

Even he had been surprised, but as he looked back, he could see he was in no state to judge her actions, especially when he didn't understand love himself.

Now he did, and everything fell into place.

For Sandale to offer the Triad the added duty of judging men accused of transgressions, it was as if he'd reached into his mind and discovered his deepest thought. An idea Toni, in her sharp observations, had suggested.

To be with his friend and Toni was the strongest temptation he ever had to leave the Triad.

Yet all his life he knew he was meant to ascend. How could a lifetime of sacrifice and training be wrong?

"Fuck."

He spun and strode into his rooms, straight to the cold box. Opening it, he grabbed an ale and drank.

Toni sauntered through the market square. She was nuts, but she had to tell Sandale the truth about why she rejected him. Maybe then she could get back to her life of enjoying sex with the many

Edenists who came to the Pleasure Temple. Her guilt over hurting him stood in the way. Every time she surveyed the men in the gathering room, none appealed to her and she went to bed alone.

This *had* to be the way to get back to normal. The Edenists she passed admired her in her new leather outfit. Instead of a halter, she'd sewn leather straps to cross her breasts, wrap around her back and tie in front. The leather skirt was tight instead of flared like her other one. The whole ensemble was to entice. It was her back-up plan to convince Sandale by having sex. Then he'd know she didn't dislike him.

Arriving at the door to his house, she knocked.

"Toni!" His mother answered. "How lovely to see you. Come in. Come in."

She relaxed and gave the woman a heart-felt hug. "Is Sandale here?"

"He is. That boy is wearing a hole in my patrio with all his pacing."

She walked with Pam through the home. "Is something wrong?"

"I'm not sure yet. He asked Akasha to join the Ruling Council. He is waiting to hear if Akasha ascended."

"Well, hell. That *is* nerve-wracking." Her own stomach tightened. It was what Akasha wanted, but she hoped Sandale was successful. Why was beyond her.

Pam opened the door. "Go ahead. He will be thrilled to see you."

She wasn't so sure, but she gave the woman a kind smile before slipping into the courtyard.

Sandale didn't see her, completely involved in his own

thoughts and pacing. She stood still, admiring the movement of his thighs as he walked, the muscles tightening and loosening clearly visible. His broad shoulders, brushed by his longer hair, also revealed the sinews moving as his arms swung. He was a sight for sore eyes.

Well, hell, she'd missed him. "Sandale."

At her voice, he stopped in midstride and his gaze snapped to her.

"Toni?"

She smiled. "In the flesh." She posed, one hand on her hip, the other behind her head like a pin-up girl.

He remained frozen in place as his gaze feasted on her outfit. "I thought you were a figment of my imagination. I did not expect to see you again."

Oh shit, now she felt like an asshole. She'd really hurt him. She sauntered forward. "I had to come. I wanted to thank you for saving me."

He shrugged and turned away. "It was all part of taking down Grandall."

She grasped his arm. "Still, you saved me when you weren't very happy with me."

He still wouldn't look at her. "It is not your fault you cannot stand my touch."

"Now that isn't true. You never let me explain. I had an experience in my past where my hands had been tied and a man tried to rape me. Your hold sent the same fear through me. It's just something I can't seem to shake."

He finally looked at her, his brows angry. "Did this man succeed?"

She laughed it off at his look. "With me? Not a chance. But he did with my foster sister and I killed him."

"Good."

His acceptance of her actions was like a balm to her soul. So different from Akasha's.

"Sandale, if you want to have sex, I'm totally game. I've missed you."

He wouldn't look at her. "I don't want to have sex with you."

The hurt that statement sent through her heart made no sense at all.

"I want to make love to you. And I want you to love me." His violet eyes were dark with intensity.

She lifted her hands to the side, her palms up. "I don't know if I can love. Besides, what good would it do? You are not part of a filoz."

He stopped looking at her again. "I have asked Akasha to be a part of a filoz if he doesn't ascend."

Holy fuck! Akasha and Sandale as a filoz. What woman wouldn't jump at the chance? Those two would be bonding with someone within a week. She hated that idea.

"Your mom said you're waiting to hear. Can I wait with you?"

He glared at her. "Why? What do you want, Toni?"

Good question. She placed her hand on her hip. "Who the fuck knows? I just came here to thank you, apologize, and have sex. Now my mind and my heart are a tangled mess. Plus, I'm horny as hell. No one is turning me on besides you."

He didn't touch her, but at least he was looking at her again.

"Sandale, you have another visitor." Sandale's mom's voice stopped them from breaching the chasm between them.

She turned and Akasha strode forward. His face was serious until he spotted her. "Toni?"

Great, another man that didn't want to see her.

"I was just leaving." She started by him, but he hooked her arm in his.

"No, this concerns you."

She looked at him and her gut tightened. Did he ascend? Was he among the untouchable now? She walked with him back to Sandale and only let go when Sandale reached out his arm and Akasha grasped it.

"You made your decision." Sandale's face could not have been any more tense.

Akasha nodded. "I did. I have decided to accept both your offers."

Her heart squeezed as Sandale's expression relaxed and he laughed. Then he pulled Akasha in for a man hug before letting him go. "This is cause for celebration."

Akasha turned to stand next to Sandale. "Not yet. We need to complete our filoz with a beloved and I know exactly who it should be."

Both men looked at her, one set of blue eyes filled with mischief, the other set of violet eyes filled with hesitant love.

Now, how was she supposed to resist that? She tried to think of all the reasons she had for not bonding with a filoz, but every one of them paled in comparison to what her life would be like with the two naked hunks in front of her.

Akasha kept his grin. "Toni, will you be our beloved?"

Could she do it? "Seriously?"

Both men nodded. Shit, if Akasha could give up the one goal

he had in life to bond with her and Sandale could commit so soon after starting his life over, she'd be damned if she copped out now.

She threw up her hands. "Well, hell. Let's do it!"

Sandale's heart filled with joy. He strode forward and grabbed Toni to him, lifting her off the ground. "I knew you would see it our way."

"What?" Toni started to struggle.

He laughed and pushed her away into Akasha's waiting arms.

Akasha caught her and wrapped his arms around her bare waist, pulling her ass against him. He spoke into her ear. "He means, he had confidence you would open your heart to the love we both bear you."

Toni stilled. "Well, when you put it that way." She wiggled her butt.

Sandale stepped closer. His parents' courtyard was probably not the typical place for a bonding, but his mother loved Toni and he had no doubt that Toni could care less who saw her.

With confidence, he ran a finger beneath the leather strapping that covered her nipples then grasped the straps and pulled her toward him, pinching her hard tips between his fingers. "We will not wait to make you ours."

Her sudden intake of breath was all he needed. He took her mouth with his own and swept his tongue inside to claim her. Opening his eyes, he raised a brow to Akasha.

The new brother of his heart reached beneath Toni's skirt, no doubt to finger her opening.

When she moaned into his mouth, he broke off the kiss. "We are going to take you right here."

She opened her eyes. "You better because I am so wet right now, I could hump the fountain."

Sandale looked at the statue in doubt.

Akasha backed up and sat on the half-wall. He waved Sandale toward him.

With quick understanding, he forced Toni to step back until she was directly in front of Akasha. "If you want the fountain so much, you can have it." With his hands still grasping both her straps and nipples, he pushed her down until she fell onto Akasha's lap.

The man caught her, slowing her descent and protecting his hard cock at the same time.

She laughed. "Ah, the best of both worl—oh."

Akasha pulled his cock up against her pussy. "You are mine now. All of you, good, bad, and in between."

"Don't forget in bed and out."

When she winked at Sandale, he pinched her nipples again then pulled her forward so Akasha could find her opening.

"She is as wet as the fountain." Akasha's words came out husky.

She looked back at him. "You aren't going to tease me this time, are you? Remember what I told you."

Akasha grasped her hip with one hand. "No. I've wanted this for too long."

Had he never entered Toni's sheath? Sandale was impressed. He would not have such self-control.

As Akasha pulled her back toward him, Sandale kept his fingers on her hard nipples.

At the first touch of Toni's hot, wet softness on his cock, Akasha closed his eyes. All his senses tuned to the feel of her. With patience born of long training, he slowly pulled her closer.

As his head slipped into the entrance of her tight sheath, every thought, doubt, and concern fled. He pulled her farther down, his cock pushing against her inner tension until her sheath sucked him in. Gliding deeper, he revealed in every inch of the silkiness surrounding him.

Then as she sank fully onto his lap, he let out the breath he'd been holding. Peace flooded him. This was where he was supposed to be, with Toni and Sandale, connected.

Toni adjusted her hips, and he pushed his cock upward.

"Oh. Oh, that's good."

He looked at Sandale who nodded, their ability to read each other already growing.

Sandale pushed Toni upright so she sat straight on top of Akasha.

Akasha could tell every time Sandale pinched her large nipples because her sheath tightened around him. He moved his hand from his cock to her mons and slid one finger down to stroke her clit.

"Oh shit." Toni's whispered expletive echoed his own feelings.

His body was primed. The need to spill his seed inside her more than he could control now that he had succumbed to her seduction. He gritted his teeth and looked at Sandale.

Sandale's smirk told him the man knew what to do.

As soon as Akasha increased the speed with which he rubbed Toni's clit, he felt the responding tightening in her sheath as Sandale rolled her nipples between his fingers. Akasha quickly thrust his cock upward, pushing Toni higher.

"Fuck." Toni's word was barely understandable and he pulled back and thrust upward again, driving his cock to its hilt, forcing her sheath to accept all of him.

Toni started to moan with pleasure.

He thrust again, keeping her clit sensitized with his finger as her sheath contracted.

He thrust again and then again, his hold on his body slipping, his balls tightening until he couldn't tell where he ended and she began.

His seed burst from him just as her scream filled the courtyard, her sheath sucking him, pulling all he had from him as her body vibrated with aftershocks.

Akasha looked at Sandale and nodded.

The man immediately pulled Toni off.

"Well, hell, don't fight over me."

Sandale laughed. "We aren't. We are bonding. Bend over and brace your arms on the fountain wall."

Toni leaned over as instructed, and Akasha immediately sat on the patrio ground beneath her. Tilting his head back, he sucked her nipple and half her breast into his mouth.

"Oh." Her body still hummed with the remnants of her orgasm, and his mouth sent new zings of excitement straight to her pulsing sheath. Her legs felt weak, but she locked her knees, refusing to buckle before her two strong men.

Then Sandale's cock spread her labia. Already?

Akasha's mouth slipped down until he held her nipple in his teeth.

Oh, shit.

Sandale didn't hesitate. He grabbed her hips and thrust his cock into her until his balls slapped forward.

Her core lit up like a meteor shower, and she grasped the edge of the fountain wall to keep from falling into it. She expected him to savor the moment, but instead, he pulled out and rammed himself home again, setting off fireworks inside her.

Almost as if Akasha waited to catch the rhythm, the next thrust of Sandale's was met with a bite on her nipple.

She yelled her pleasure, unable to keep it inside and not caring who heard or saw her reach her climax with her two hunky men.

As Sandale pulled out again. Akasha switched breasts, but his fingers found her clit as Sandale thrust again.

Her body wound tight, every nerve-ending filling with pleasure. "I'm going to come." She gasped.

Sandale pumped back in, faster and harder this time. Then again. And again.

She screamed as he pushed in deep and held her hips tight to him, his own shout of pleasure ringing in her ears. She splintered into a thousand pieces, her body singing with joy.

When she opened her eyes, she found herself held up by Akasha. She grinned. "Now that was amazing."

Sandale wrapped an arm around her and pulled her upright. Akasha quickly stood and caught her as Sandale pulled away from her.

"Aw, too fast." She pouted after Akasha helped her sit on the fountain wall, her body still humming with happiness.

Each man sat on either side of her.

Sandale took her hand. "It is necessary for the bonding that our seed mix inside you."

"But I can't get pregnant." She had an implant that was good for three years.

Akasha took her other hand. "That is of no matter."

She looked at the large hands grasping hers. How the hell did this happen?

Akasha lifted her hand to his mouth and kissed it. "You are our beloved now."

Shit, she was, wasn't she?

Sandale lifted her other hand and kissed it. "Are you happy?"

She gave him an open honest smile. "More than I thought possible." Then she raised her brows and looked at both of them quickly. "Maybe we should to do that again. I want to make sure it worked."

Both men laughed and her heart filled with satisfaction. Finally, she had her own family.

EPILOGUE

Toni gave Serena a tight hug. She wouldn't see her for who knew how long now. Finally, she let her friend go. "I still find it hard to believe that I'm the one on top of the city and you're the one living in the jungle." She waved her hand toward the large foyer of the giant house she now called home.

Serena laughed. "I wouldn't want it any other way. I'm so psyched that you found your own agapaytos."

She wiggled her eyebrows. "Well, hell. I'd be stupid to let these two hunks go."

"Absolutely." Serena moved toward Sandale.

Jahl grasped Toni in his arms. "I'll be sure to contact you, if I need any more information on Naralina."

Toni laughed and pushed him away. "Shit, no. I'm done with that. Besides, you had your crowning moment when you portaled your dad outside the walls of the city. Just watch your back out there."

Jahl shrugged as if exiling his father personally hadn't been the best moment of his life and as if he had little concern about the man who was now stuck in the jungle of Eden. "I have not feared him since I left his home. I certainly will not start now."

She nodded in understanding. Somehow, witnessing Grandall being found guilty in the first Open Circle session of the new Ruling Circle had finally put to rest her own troubled past. It was as if she needed to see the public turn their backs on him. They had even suggested a death penalty, a punishment that had never before found so much support since the restructuring of the city after the Fullamush.

That the new Ruling Circle did not agree was a testament to how they would handle all future sessions. Not only would they stick to both sets of laws, but they would be completely thorough. She was proud of her two men for keeping everyone on track. She'd already killed one slimeball. She was glad they wouldn't taint their own essences with the blackness she carried.

Sandale turned from Serena to face Jahl. "Thank you for looking out for my brother. I tried to dissuade him, but he is bent on revenge."

"I promise to teach Haldone all that we know." Jahl placed his hand on Sandale's shoulder. "Or rather, I'll have Theron teach him. I cannot say I am that patient."

"Anything you can do to keep him alive…do not hesitate to find me if I am needed."

Jahl nodded.

Khaos grabbed her to him before she could chime in. "Toni, all is as it should be." Giving the man a hug, she waited until he released her before raising one eyebrow. "Have you seen something?"

He laughed. "No. I don't need my ability to see that you have made a good choice. I am elated that Sandale has found you and Akasha. Now my heart can finally be at peace with what happened to him."

"Don't worry about him. He's a completely different man now."

"I noticed." Khaos winked, and she grinned.

Arms wrapped around her, and she inhaled the heady scent of clove. "As you can see, I am also in very good hands. No need to worry about us." Akasha squeezed her a little tighter at her words.

"Come on, Khaos. We still need to say goodbye to Nassic, Wareson and Erin." Serena looked over Toni's shoulder to Sandale.

Jahl scowled. "It is not necessary."

Serena grabbed the man's hand. "Yes, it is." As she pulled him toward the door, he looked back at them and winked.

Well, blow her over with an air blast. The man had developed a sense of humor after all.

After saying their final goodbyes, Akasha closed the door behind their guests.

Toni slipped out of Sandale's arms and headed straight for the meal room. They'd had company for four days now. She was anxious for some uninterrupted time with her hot hunks. The house was huge, and she had a goal to make love in every room by the next rising of the pink moon, Bendis. Not that she'd told her beloveds that.

Before she could open the cold box, one of her men caught her hand and spun her around. She fell against Akasha, laughed, and wrapped her arms around his neck. "Hello, bad boy."

He smirked, now that he understood it was a term of endearment. He'd been so affronted the first time she called him that to his face that she'd had to explain exactly what she meant. It took a while, but he eventually accepted it.

"It is time for us to take you. A full day is far too long to wait."

Sandale pressed against her back and licked the side of her neck. "Far too long."

Oh, she liked this. "Any chance I can have a sip of ale before we get started?"

Akasha's blue gaze went over her shoulder then came back to her. "No."

A zing of desire went straight to her core. Suddenly, her Amazon leather outfit was too much clothing. Though she'd hoped they could have sex in the music room, maybe on the piano-like instrument, the kitchen was just as good a place to start. She ground her hips in a circle, pushing against Sandale's hard cock then Akasha's. "And if I suggested we move this to the music room?"

Sandale gave her a love bite on her earlobe before moving his lips to her ear and whispering. "No."

Her sheath contracted. Her men had already figured her out. The more they denied her wishes in sex, the more excited she became. Hmm. "So will it be the floor or the counter?"

Again her men had that silent communication as they looked at each other.

Her heart sped with anticipation. In the next instant, Akasha had unwrapped her arms from around his neck and pulled her to the low butcher block work area in the center of the large kitchen.

Sandale followed and bent her over it, pushing her feet farther apart. It was low, leaving her ass in the air when he flipped up her leather skirt to lay it on her back.

She swallowed a moan, not willing to let them know yet exactly how ready she was.

Akasha moved a chair to where her head was and sat. He pulled at the tie that held her vest over her breasts. "Lift."

She started to rise, but he pushed aside her leather and clasped her nipples, stopping her from going farther. The tug sent more moisture pooling toward her entrance.

"Lower yourself again."

She did so. Though he still held her large nipples, he lowered with her until her breasts hung over the other edge of the square piece of wood.

Akasha let go and moved his chair closer until his cock was under her chin. "Open your mouth, now."

Cool liquid hitting her ass had her turning her head to look back and up.

Akasha caught her ponytail and pulled her head to face him again. "I said, now."

Holy fuck. Her entire body vibrated with need. She opened her mouth to protest, but his cock head stroked her lips, and she forgot what she'd planned to say.

When Sandale spread her cheeks and let the shilla flow between her crack, her body tensed. She hadn't felt him there yet.

Akasha's cock pushed against her lips and she opened wide even as Sandale's finger ran down her crease and found her anal hole. His fingers fluttered around it, just before his calming radiated from the hand holding her ass.

Oh, shit. He hadn't used that ability on her since their time in the cave. Then again, neither had come in her ass since then either.

Her body relaxed despite the heady feelings of excitement flowing over her. She sucked harder on Akasha's cock in her mouth, still able to use her tongue to stroke him as Sandale replaced his fingers with his cock, running it up and down her crease.

Akasha pulled back, and she stroked him lightly with her

teeth, even as she caught his balls in her hand. He pushed her hands away. "No."

She bit lightly on his cock, well aware that his balls were tight and ready to release.

He got back at her by taking each nipple between his thumbs and index fingers and rolling them before giving them a good pinch.

She groaned against his cock as it slid to the back of her throat, causing his hold on her hard nubs to tighten.

Sandale's cock stopped stroking and paused at her anal hole. One of his hands move from her ass to cup her between the legs. He slipped two fingers into her sheath.

Fucking A, she was ready to come, but the calming kept her body loose. It was the hottest torture she'd ever endured. Far worse than having no sex for a month, which happened just before she'd been brought to Eden.

Sandale's cock pushed into her ass and her thoughts fled as excitement rifled through her and her sheath contracted around his fingers.

At the pinch of her nipples, she sucked Akasha's cock harder, wanting him to feel what she felt, hot, ready, close.

Then Sandale slipped his other hand around her to play with her clit while the calming center switched from her ass to her sheath. Her body tightened and Sandale moved his cock slowly.

The friction on her nipples and her clit combined with the feelings of two cocks pumping into her and her body wound up, even with the calming running through it. The feelings fought against each other until the calming suddenly stopped.

Her orgasm took over and she screamed against the cock in her mouth as Akasha came, his fingers pinching her nipples while Sandale's shout joined hers, his hand slipping from her clit to grab her hip and hold her tight to him.

Akasha's hands dropped from her breasts and he stroked her jaw until she released him.

She felt light headed. White flashes clouded her vision even behind closed eyes. If the wooden block wasn't beneath her, she would collapse. Then Sandale slowly pulled out his fingers and cock, and she moaned.

Without a word, he helped her to stand, but her knees gave way. She opened her eyes in time to see Akasha kick the work table out of the way. He scooped her up into his arms and carried her to their bedroom.

"I'm fine. Just need a minute."

As Akasha gently laid her on the bed, Sandale came in with ambrosia.

She happily took the glass from him and drank. In no time, she was feeling like herself and she stared at the empty glass. "There is more to this drink than I thought, isn't there?"

Sandale grinned, but didn't say anything. Well, hell. All along she thought it was a wimpy drink. She should have known something called ambrosia had to be special.

Sandale jumped on to the larger than king-sized bed and lay on his back next to her, taking her hand in his. She smiled at him in the mirror above their bed, an addition she had Theron make to their room.

Akasha joined them, his broad body on her other side and she took his hand.

She stared at her two men, one dark and blue-eyed, one light with violet eyes and herself, brown-haired and green-eyed. What a mismatched group of individuals and yet, so in-tuned and made for each other. It was hard to believe she was bonded with two of the most respected men in Naralina.

She frowned at that thought. "I hope you two know that I'm not going to be the typical wife of a statesman. I can't pretend to be something I'm not. There is a good chance I'll piss off some dignitary from another city."

Sandale chuckled. "You don't have to worry about that. Remember what happened during Grandall's session?"

She thought back to her testimony. Every word out of her mouth had been eloquent. Even when she thought she swore, it didn't come out that way. "What was that?"

He squeezed her hand while he looked at her in the reflection. "That was me, speaking for you."

"So the bonding really worked? Why didn't you tell me?" She sat up and looked at Sandale directly.

"I was waiting to see what the bonding had done for you and Akasha."

She turned toward Akasha. "Do you have any idea?"

He shook his head. "No, but we will discover it eventually."

"You're too patient."

"I agree." Sandale pulled her back down to the bed. "Maybe we need to bond again."

She wiggled her eyebrows in the mirror at them both. The bonding never worked with just one, so it was obvious they had bonded, but she was always up for more sex. "I think you're right. Let's give it another try."

Akasha's lip quirked up. "You do not need an excuse to make love."

She shrugged. "I know, but it's fun making them up. Now, set the mood, bad boy."

He lifted his hand and a green cloud of color floated before them.

"Hey, I can't see the reflection. Try another color." She waved at the green cloud shimmering between them and the mirror. It immediately dissipated. She glanced at Akasha. "You're fast. I like that."

He stared at her. "I did not do anything."

Sandale grinned at her in the mirror. "I think we just discovered what your bonding connection is."

"Seriously? You mean I can get rid of Akasha's green light?"

Akasha frowned in concentration. Then he raised his hand and the green light appeared again. "My light has changed. It is no longer clear green. It is as if it can hide us. Wave your hand again and dismiss the light."

She waved her hand at it, wishing it away and it disappeared. "Well hell, will you look at that." She examined her hand, but it didn't look any different.

Akasha's blue eyes were bright with excitement. "Raise your hand and wish the green light would cover you."

She did as he asked. The green light appeared directly above her. Fuck! She could make green light! She waved it away. "That's amazing!"

Akasha grinned. "I always knew there had to be a reason for my green light. Now I know." He paused, his face growing serious. "If I had not met you, I would have never known what that reason was."

She winked. "Good thing you met me then, huh?"

He nodded, the love shining in his eyes filling her with happiness.

Sandale rolled onto his side, wrapping his arm around her waist, but he spoke to Akasha. "We already saw what your white light could reveal about our essences, but we never saw yours. Would it be possible for us to see it now that we are bonded together?"

"What a great idea." She looked at Akasha who was back to frowning. "Come on. It doesn't hurt. I promise."

His lips quirked up on one side. "I know. I had thought to keep it private, but since I am no longer a Triad member…"

She laid her hand on his mounded chest. "I hope you don't regret leaving the Triad. I know you will serve Naralina with honor, and I have to say, I'm very happy you are with me." She really meant it, which in itself was a new feeling.

He let out his breath. "I am happy to be with you as well. It just takes time to get used to the fact I am no longer of the Triad."

Sandale's voice passed by her ear. "I am also glad you are here instead of there."

"Thank you. This feels right here." Akasha laid his hand over his heart. "My mind is just slow to adjust."

Toni moved her hand over his. "It feels right because it is."

Sandale laid his hand over both of theirs. "We are a filoz now, connected and bonded."

Toni wiggled her hips. "You bet." She pulled her hand out from the two men's and waved it, covering them in green light. "This is so cool." She waved it away again. "That could come in handy for hiding."

Sandale moved his hand to her hip. "Akasha is still hiding his essence from us."

"Not hiding. Delaying."

Toni frowned at him. "Come on, time to come clean, as if your essence isn't already clean. I bet it's whiter than Sandale's. I guess I'm the black sheep, so to speak." She winked.

Akasha grasped her hand in his. "You are perhaps the purest of us all. You have been tested by the white heat."

"White heat?"

He moved her hand across his tattoo. "That is the meaning of my markings, but I have never been tested. I thought I had, but you and Sandale have shown me that I had not. I have learned more from you than years of meditation afforded me."

Her heart felt full at Akasha's thoughtful look. Had *she* actually helped him? "Then let's see your essence."

Akasha nodded, his shoulders a little less tense. He burrowed his hand beneath his back.

Toni moved her gaze to the mirror above them just as his essence emerged. "Wow. You have more gray than I thought. How can that be? You don't even lie."

She looked at him in the reflection. Akasha stared as if he hadn't see his essence before. Was it his first time?

Sandale spoke. "You are almost all white. Is it your lack of experience that has caused the gray?"

"I do not know for certain." Akasha brows drew together. "I believe it was my refusal to be tested that has caused the gray."

"You look confused." She was still impressed by how white his essence was.

He gaze moved from his essence to her. "I am. When I viewed my essence in the cave, there was not as much white."

Sandale grinned. "You have been tested in a very significant way. You were challenged to give up your life-long calling and you made a difficult decision. That had to count for something. *Least village boasts its blacksmith, whose anvil's even din stands symbol for the finer forge that soundless tugs within.*"

"Ah, a line from our first High Poetess. You believe that choosing you and Toni over the Triad increased my white area?"

"Of course." A new feeling of rightness settled inside Toni. "It was the ultimate sacrifice."

Akasha pulled his hand from behind his back, extinguishing the light and he took her hand in his again. "It was a sacrifice, but it was for something I wanted."

Sandale shook his head. "It doesn't matter. You could have ascended, but my gut tells me, your gray would have dominated then because you would have avoided the hard choice. *Refining these impatient ores with hammer and with blaze, until the designated light repudiate the forge.* You were tested by the basest of trials—love."

Akasha's frown disappeared. "Love? Yes, my connection to us is bound by love."

Her heart filled with joy at Akasha's confession. Despite having avoided the feeling her whole life, she had to voice it. "I love you." She looked over her shoulder at Sandale. "I love you, too."

He opened his mouth, but she set her free hand over his lips.

"Don't get all sappy on me now."

Akasha pulled her hand to his mouth and sucked in one of her fingers.

She snapped her head around as a spike of desire sped to her core. Sandale grasped her wrist and nipped at it, causing another spike of excitement to rifle through her body.

She laughed. "Much better. Words are one thing, but actions are so much more convincing."

In the next moment, she was sandwiched between her men, protected, loved, and oh, so horny.

If you enjoyed this story, please leave a review at http://amzn.to/2oqGop0

For free books, updates, sneak peeks, and special prizes, sign up to receive the latest news from Lexi Post at http://bit.ly/LexiUpdate

Eden – English Dictionary

agapayto – wife, but more, woman has a connection with every man in the filoz

amobe – invisible to the eye flat blob like creature that cleans places by eating dirt, including skin, hair, fur and dried stains

ambrosia - mango, coconut tasting drink with a trace of spice in the aftertaste

baka bun – Similar to a jelly donut only filled with citrusy fruit jams like lemon and orange

Bedia – endearment meaning "beloved"

beloved – less formal name for agapayto (wife), a woman can refuse to be a beloved

Bendis - the large moon with pink light often called the second moon

blood sign - marking of lawbreaker band - a circle of blood with an x over it.

boarox – as big as a bison with no hair and black splotches on its legs, large droopy upper lip that covers mouth full of white shark teeth

bonabus vine – a leafy vine with small flowers like bluebells

bonding – the sexual act that connects a beloved with her filoz if she is on Eden

breast binding – bra

brother of his heart - best friend who he will share a beloved with

burning ceremony – celebration of an Edenist's life with everything the deceased liked from food to songs to favorite free time activities. Then the dead is placed on a pyre and burned. People take turns watching the fire so the man is never alone as his spirit rejoins Eden

caball - bird with blue feathers

chosen one - like fiancée, but the Edenists choose with no agreement from the woman

cold box - refrigerator

Criuson Law - law set up by the original settlers of Eden

crossover - the first time the chosen one goes through the portal to Eden

cyndistone – teal, granite-like stone

Cythera or Cys for short- women of the Pleasure Temples

daemond - honey bee

dally greens – similar to brussel sprouts but with an overtone of onion

decods - like leagues (3 miles are a decod)

Depoteese - Director

Dickinson Law – laws instituted after the Fullamush when the men fought over women

direlot - ferocious and cunning animal most closely resembles a wolf

Dirgon – mythical creature

discoverists – scientists but not only in the scientific field

Eden day - 22 hours

Eden month - 40 days

elseire - Bird with purple wings when in flight but folded up looks green

eyllen - energy rock source

feroon - big beast with tusks, furry and as large as an elephant but no trunk, fairly docile

filoz - group of men (2-5) who are close like a family

Fithee - long brown snake-like creature that burrows into mountainsides with both ends.

Fiya – endearment closest to sweetheart

Fullamush - the great war that almost destroyed the planet but the women and Emily Dickinson brought peace (story in Unexpected Eden)

grapet - purple vegetable that havling pigs like (used as bait)

grendal – like a wild boar but larger, has tusks and squeals, travels in herds

Haven – new walled settlement founded by Nassic and Wareson who escaped Naralina and gathered other "lawbreakers" who were falsely accused to form a society

havling pig – Smaller pig-like animal that wanders alone

head puffs - pillows

heat top -stove

Helios - Sun

henny - chicken like bird

Hermday - Wednesday

hestas – blankets made of see through material that is very thin, but quite warm

High Hall – center (highest) building in the Ruling Circle complex

Holy Bendis - expression of surprise, frustration, anger, etc.

Holy Crius - expression of surprise, frustration, anger, etc.

idonee – nightingale

inducer - microwave

infragile vine - unbreakable a day after it's cut from its live piece

ithio - idiot

jump-off ledge – in Loraleaf where men pick up the vines left on a hook to swing across or down.

kafez - coffee but stronger

keepers - guards

kerasi – mild sleep inducing fruit (cherry flavored) red

Khityki - kitten

Kif - Capital of Eden

Kindred – a broad group that every Edenist is born into but doesn't know his specific abilities until his transition. A family will have multiple kindreds within it.

Latzeran Sea - large body of water known for its depth

lawbreakers - what the Edenists call criminals – those exiled from cities

layfeenya - dolphin like creatures with much bigger tails

liquidator - bartender

living area - living room

logar - horse

longseat - couch

Loraleaf – an older settlement in the trees founded by Jahl, Khaos and Sandale as an alternative to the city of Naralina which contains men who followed them from the city

meal room - kitchen

Naralina – white and gold walled city that men of Haven and Loraleaf hail from

pander bush – bush with large dark green leaves

patrio - patio

pecone rolls – cinnamon pastry with tiny nuts

racide - poisonous plant

rainbox – shower

rancels – exchange token backed by the city's largest export most commonly used between cities (only used between individuals when bartering, giving, or owing won't work)

rhoade -like chicken with chickpea, a mild curry, mild garlic, coriander maybe, a strong flavored potato and a tinge of hotness, maybe a tiny amount of red pepper

rhybat - small rodent with super large ears - afraid of its own shadow

Ruling Circle of Naralina – the oligarchy government of 5 for the city of Naralina

sable worm silk - thread

salis bush - looks like a small weeping willow

Samuvian desert – large cactus filled desert

savinstone - gold

Scrat – swear, like "shit"

Selene - moon with silver light

sherry flower - light pink flower with strong scent that grows on a thin stem (very fragile)

shilla - lube

shiner - lantern powered by eyllen

siris webbing - silky soft webbing made by large caterpillar type creatures often used for head puffs - pillows

sitki - barn

Stass! - whoa!

table cover - table cloth

Talia - tigran Theron befriended while living in his cave

tigran - sabretooth sized cat with chameleon abilities, loves to be petted

tyree – dairy product like cheese with less salt and each type with a different spice.

villain's mark – blood sign

waterhole - swimming pond or stream

walstone – white stone they built walls of Naralina with

Read on for an excerpt from *Masque*.

Chapter One

Cape Breton, Nova Scotia

People. Living, breathing people.

Synn MacAllistair grasped the embrasure of the parapet, his heart thudding as he stared at the vehicle crossing the stone bridge over the moat. It came to a stop at Ashton Abbey's massive gate.

He waited. The great iron grille, chained and padlocked against intruders, would be considered a significant deterrent to entering. *Open it. Damn it, open it!*

The vehicle remained stationary. No one exited the large red monstrosity.

Impatiently, he pushed away his hair as the breeze whipped it across his view. What were they waiting for? If they needed an axe to break the chain, he'd gladly provide them with one.

Another smaller vehicle rolling parallel to the west wall caught his attention. It crossed the bridge and parked behind the larger one. More people?

A man stepped from the small conveyance and shuffled to the gate. Synn leaned farther over the battlement, anxious to see if their time had come. The joyful sound of clanking chains floated up to him on the breeze.

Finally! About bloody time. He swallowed hard to keep the yell of triumph from escaping his throat. No need to scare their new guests.

The man below hurried back to his transport and, without hesitation, backed across the bridge and left faster than he'd arrived.

Synn peered down at the red vehicle, still as a brick, its black windows making it impossible to see inside. A door opened and a woman burst onto the cobblestone entrance. She bent over and spoke to someone else still inside. Her blonde hair hid her face, but her ass, covered in men's trousers, was small, her legs lanky. A woman? A woman dared enter a haunted abbey? He tried to grasp the concept.

His plan was to convince a man to enjoy the pleasures of the flesh, but there had to be a man to convince…unless a couple entered the Abbey. Couples enjoyed the Pleasure Rooms as well. If he could persuade a couple to participate in the Masque then his companions could still be freed.

Peering hard, he watched and waited. After what seemed another decade, a door on the other side of the red contraption opened. He held his breath, willing the occupant to have broad shoulders, a beard, anything to indicate a man.

A long, slender leg stretched out, a black high-heel shoe of delicate design at its end, and a feminine hand grasped the side, but remained stationary.

He growled with frustration. "Bloody hell. What am I supposed to do with two women?" He hadn't expected women. The Abbey overflowed with spirits. Only men should dare enter. How were blasted women going to help him? He paced away from the wall, but quickly returned. Could there be more people inside the vehicle?

He waited, his patience long gone, not that he ever had much, but damn, it'd been a hundred and fifty years. That would strain the patience of an archangel, something he definitely was not.

He glared as the leg moved and within a moment's breath, the woman unfolded herself from the conveyance.

Synn stared, frozen in time for once, drinking in a beauty far surpassing any painted Aphrodite he'd ever gazed upon. Her long, wavy brown hair captured the sun, shining like fine brandy. Her figure, as lush as any Greek goddess, swayed sensuously in her short dress. Her arms were bare and the smallest of noses held her dark glasses in place. He stepped back, away from the crenellation, his heart racing, his mind whirling with ideas.

He paced the length of the wall. A vision was about to enter his stone prison. A woman fit to be worshiped with every salacious touch he'd ever learned. His cock hardened beneath his pantaloons. Amazed, he stopped and looked down at it. After so many years of having no needs—for food, for sleep, for relieving himself—the last he'd expected to feel was the need for a woman. He shook his head. It defied logic. But if his body could respond, then he could participate, guide a woman through the Masque.

The creaking hinges of the gate brought him back to the wall to see the backs of the two women entering the Abbey courtyard. Two women. Vivid memories of his happier days with the prince caught him by surprise and gave him hope. As he strode across the wall-walk and down the stone staircase, his mind raced with possibilities. One after another they were discarded as he floated to the landing on the second floor. But a new plan began to form as the great pine doors opened.

If she hadn't been in heels, Rena Mills would have jumped over the threshold as she and Valerie pushed open the twelve-foot doors of Ashton Abbey. Their creaking sound didn't bother her. In fact, she'd be sure those hinges never saw oil for the rest of their days. They made a perfect first impression for a haunted bed-and-breakfast.

Valerie shook her head. "You love that noise, don't you?"

Rena grinned sheepishly as she stepped into the two-story stone entry the size of her parents' house and spread her arms wide. "It's perfect. I can't believe it. I'm actually going to make this happen. Can't you see it, Valerie?"

Her friend raised her eyebrow. "If you say so."

"I do." She examined the stone floor beneath her feet before touching a wall. The hard rock under her fingers was cool and rough. Her stomach somersaulted as success filled her veins. She could do this. Ashton Abbey resembled a castle and tourists would love staying here. All she needed was a little plumbing, a little electricity, a functioning kitchen, and a few ghosts. "Seriously, Val. You can see the potential, right?"

Valerie gave her a hard look. "You don't have to do this, Ree. You don't have to prove anything. That jerk is full of himself. So all your success has come while working at your family's company or at Bryce's. That's simply because you are a good event planner. Look at me. I've worked for my dad's company all my life. That doesn't mean I don't know my shit."

"It's not about Bryce. I have to prove this to myself." She wished Valerie could understand.

Her friend threw up her hands and stalked away. The woman was too confident to have any idea how it felt to be unsure. Rena sighed. The fact was, her ex-fiancé had a point. All her jobs had been obtained through her parents or him. After two months of being out of work, this was her only option. Now she had to make her new haunted abbey into a successful bed-and-breakfast, not simply to prove she could, but because she had every last penny on the line.

As she perused the large entry with its double staircase leading to the next floor, her jubilance returned. The abandoned building was so much more than she'd expected for the price. She looked up at the semicircle windows near the ceiling, which let in sunlight, but she didn't see any spirits. "I hope the real estate agent hadn't exaggerated about the ghosts. If this place hasn't sold because it's haunted, then I better see some dead people pretty darn fast."

"Uh, Rena?"

She glanced behind her to see Valerie had stepped into the next room. Turning, she strode through the doorway to find a grand dining room with green-and-gold paisley wallpaper. She stopped and smiled. "Oh, this is too good to be true." Valerie had pulled aside one of the curtains from the fifteen-foot windows to let in the sun, and it reflected off an elegantly set table.

"Over here." Her friend stood at the head of the table, a deep frown on her face.

"What is it? Did you find something?" She started down the length of the long table set to feed twenty-four. Her stomach twitched with excitement at the sight. She stopped to look at the place setting Valerie stared at. "What am I looking for?"

Valerie shook her head. "Do you see anything unusual here?"

She peered at the setting. The silverware had an elaborate P etched into it, but other than the fact it had multiple plates as if set for a formal occasion, she saw nothing out of the ordinary. "No. Should I?"

Valerie sighed and crossed her arms over her small chest. "How long has this place been empty?"

She shrugged. "I don't know. Over a hundred years or so? From what I hear, colored lights can be seen shining from the windows at night, but there's no electricity. I guess the Abbey got lucky with ghosts and I'm going to make that work for us."

"And is there a caretaker of some sort?"

"There is one family here who has taken care of the grounds for eons. I can't remember their names, but it's an old widower and his son. Why?"

Valerie dragged her finger across the plate. "Do they take care of the inside as well?"

"No, we are the only ones to enter inside these walls in a hundred and fifty years. Isn't that amazing? Why, what are you getting at?"

Valerie lifted her finger in front of Rena's eyes. "Then why is there no dust?"

Her brain came to a halt as she grasped Valerie's point. Taking another look around the room, she saw no cobwebs, no dust, not even a chair out of place. She returned her gaze to Valerie. "Clean ghosts?"

Valerie raised her brow. "Did you read about that in your research?"

Rena picked up the plate and examined it, not comfortable meeting her friend's eyes. "No, but I didn't exactly do research. I watched a few shows on television and discovered people will pay to go to a haunted hotel. There has to be an explanation. Maybe someone has been living here and no one realized it."

Valerie crossed the room to the windows. "You mean behind the padlocked gate?"

She joined her friend, puzzled, ready to believe in ghosts who cleaned. "What are you looking at?"

"These curtains. If they're a hundred years old, shouldn't they be dry-rotted and in shreds?"

A shiver ran across Rena's skin. "Oh, damn. This is stranger than a simple haunting." She ran her hand along the forest-green velvet of the curtain. The material, strong and thick, had a beige cotton backing. This didn't make any sense. She turned to examine the rest of the room. The chairs around the massive table also had velvet in their backs. She stepped closer to one and ran her hand over the material. The softness was irresistible…and new.

She paused. "It's as if time has no meaning inside these walls. I wonder if the place is bewitched as well as haunted!"

Valerie gave her one of her deprecating smiles. "And why is it haunted?"

She grinned. She couldn't help it. The more she saw of the Abbey, the more convinced she was that she could make it profitable. "It had something to do with the Red Death that swept through this town around 1861. I read that it could take a life within thirty minutes of exposure."

"Hmmm, that would explain a haunted town." Valerie ran her hand along the fireplace mantle. "But why is the Abbey the only place haunted? There has to be more to it than that. Maybe a monk bargained for a life and they all ended up dead?"

Even more sure now than the night she'd watched the documentary on haunted hotels, Rena headed for the door at the end of the room, the clacking of her heels echoing across the room.

"I don't know, but I plan to find out. I will need a history of this place to put up on the website."

Valerie followed. "That will work. It's a good thing you're rid of Bryce. He'd find a reasonable, logical explanation for this and take all the fun out of it."

Rena stopped in her tracks, causing Valerie to bump into her. "Ugh. Thanks for ruining my mood again, Val."

"Hey, it's true. You are so lucky to be rid of him. Are you ready yet to tell me why he broke off the engagement? There's no one to overhear but the ghosts."

She faced her friend, aware that her heartache shone in her eyes, but it was too raw, too humiliating still. "I can't. Not yet. Okay?"

Valerie gave her a quick hug. "Of course. But remember, I'm your best friend and you will have to tell me eventually."

She nodded, but her excitement for the Abbey had left. "Why don't we bring our luggage in and find bedrooms? If we have to buy blow-up mattresses, I'd rather know now instead of tonight when the place is pitch black and all we have are our lanterns."

"You got it. And maybe we'll run into a ghost in the process."

Valerie's smile was contagious and Rena grinned, her upbeat spirit making a quick return. "We better, or this haunted bed-and-breakfast idea will be a complete bust."

Synn ducked around the doorway as the ladies turned toward the entry once again. He let the slender blonde pass through, but he couldn't resist touching the other one. Lightly, so as not to frighten her, he brushed his fingers across her bare shoulder.

"What?" She turned, looking about.

The scent of dusky, tart pomegranate wafted by his nose. His body responded with an overwhelming need to touch her again. He craved her smoothness like a pickpocket coveted a half-dollar. When had he last craved anything? He tamped down his own interest. It was of little importance. This woman would be their freedom.

"Rena, are you coming?"

With her smile wide and full of joy, she followed after her friend. "You are not going to believe this, but a ghost just touched me."

That she hadn't run in fear confirmed his belief she could be the answer. Rena. He liked her name.

Her hips swayed with her quick pace, her energy palpable. Would she have that kind of liveliness in bed?

As she crossed the threshold to the outside, his gut tightened in panic. She couldn't leave. Not now!

Synn ran to the open door and stopped, the memory of his last venture outside freezing his limbs in place. He couldn't leave the Abbey or he'd cease to exist. He needed to calm himself. Too much was at stake.

The women pulled belongings from their conveyance. They should have allowed the servants to do that kind of work. When they turned to enter again, he blended back into the wall, his stomach relaxing at their entrance.

The blonde dropped her bags. "Okay, I'll take the stairway to the left and you take the one on the right."

Rena glanced upward. "Great. If you see anything unusual, yell. I want to see a ghost."

"Believe me, you'll know if I see one."

As the two ascended the grand stairways, Synn followed.

He glanced around, surprised Mrs. McMurray hadn't appeared yet. Not that he minded. Their two guests seemed to be open to the spirits who lived here, but he hoped they could settle in first. At least until he introduced himself, and the way he wanted to introduce himself had his cock paying attention.

Rena headed down the hallway on the second floor, opening doors and looking inside. Her mumbled words made her opinions of each room clear. Everything from "hideous" to "extraordinary" passed by her lips. Lips, full and red, with no rouge, begged for a kiss.

When she had passed judgment on all the rooms, she returned to the one second from the stairs. He tried to ignore the fact she stood outside the bedroom next to his. It appeared fate continued to play with him.

He followed her inside as she gave the bedroom a thorough inspection. He could not fault her taste. Decorated in pale yellows and deep purples, it suited her. When she moved next to the large four-poster bed, he couldn't resist standing behind her, inhaling her unique scent. Her hand touched the quilt, and he ran his fingers along her bare arm, wanting more than anything to turn her around and kiss her.

She stilled but didn't pull away. "Is there someone here?"

He remained silent, but placed his hands upon her arms and let his breath brush by her ear.

A shiver ran through her body and Synn grinned. A responsive woman was exactly what he needed. Triumph filled his heart and he brought his chest in contact with her back.

Her breathing grew rapid, but from sexual excitement or at being touched by a ghost? He bent his head to kiss her neck when a scream rent the air.

"Reeeennnaaa!!!"

She pulled away and ran across the inside balcony that connected the two stairways on the second floor.

Irritated, he tried to ignore his reborn need for a woman. Adjusting himself within his pantaloons, he followed. Who was causing problems now?

Rena came to a halt before an open doorway. Inside, the blonde stood with a candelabra held before her like a Roman shield.

"What is it, Val?"

She pointed to the corner of the room. Before the open wardrobe doors stood Mrs. McMurray. Synn silently sighed. At least Mrs. McMurray was a kindhearted soul who wouldn't hurt a three-legged cat.

Rena clapped her hands as she joined her friend. "It's a ghost. A real, live ghost."

She probably wouldn't appreciate him correcting her oxymoron, so he remained silent and invisible. He leaned against the doorframe behind the women, but where Mrs. McMurray could see him. The older woman's expression turned from concerned to relieved.

Rena approached her. "Hello. I'm Rena and this is Valerie. We are pleased to meet you."

Mrs. McMurray gave her guests a deep curtsy.

Rena turned back to look at Valerie and smiled. She had the whitest teeth he'd ever seen. She mouthed the words "she has no legs", her eyes wide with surprise.

Valerie glanced toward the older lady and sucked in a breath before nodding.

Facing Mrs. McMurray again, Rena addressed the spirit. "Can you tell us your name?"

Mrs. McMurray shook her head then lifted her gaze to him. Her pleading look had him cursing inside. He had wanted more time, but he couldn't ignore his friend's request. She wouldn't be able to vocalize until closer to the full moon. Blast.

Allowing himself to materialize, he answered for her. "Her name is Mrs. McMurray."

Rena spun at the deep voice that caressed her senses. Before her stood a woman's wet dream come to life, though as a respectable woman, she shouldn't be having wet dreams, or so she'd been informed.

The man looked as if he'd stepped out of a nineteenth-century drawing room, except his coffee-brown hair hung loose about his shoulders. She was pretty sure it should have been tied in a queue to be proper. His entire demeanor projected upper class from his sharp nose, to his angular chin outlined by a neatly trimmed beard, to his broad-shouldered stance. A rather tall stance it was too, with one snugly encased leg crossed over the other. But his eyes stupefied her. They appeared gray, ancient, yet flickered with bright shards of blue.

Valerie recovered first, brandishing her tightly held candelabra as she stepped forward. "Who are you and what are you doing in here?"

He straightened and gave them a formal bow. "My name is Synn MacAllistair. That is Synn as in S Y N N. I'm the caretaker of the ghosts."

Rena took a deep breath. She could feel her cheeks heating as his voice reverberated through her body. Sin fit him. When he moved his gaze from Valerie to herself, his intense scrutiny warmed her. She swallowed. "Uh, I didn't think anyone lived here."

His stare held hers captive. "I do."

Valerie retreated to stand next to her. "Oh really. With a padlock on the outside of the gate?"

He raised his right brow, the look of arrogance worthy of Mr. Darcy. "There is a postern gate."

Rena racked her brain. She'd heard that word before. Oh yes. "I thought only the owners of a castle knew the secret to that rear exit."

He raised his brows together. "That is true but I desi—discovered it while following a small boy around the Abbey."

Valerie crossed her arms. "A small boy?"

"Yes. The children in the neighborhood dare each other to get close to the Abbey. They want to see the ghosts, who are quite harmless to humans." He gestured to the housekeeper. "Mrs. McMurray here will become more solid as the full moon approaches and will be pleased to help you in any way she can."

They turned and stared at their ghost, having forgotten her. The older woman nodded vigorously, her white cap covering her gray hair falling to the side. Mrs. McMurray's plump frame included pudgy arms sprouting from a short-sleeved blouse and a white apron that protected her skirt, but from the knees down, she didn't exist at all.

Rena's heart pounded. A real ghost. If what Synn said was true, that the ghosts would become solid, the possibilities for her new venture were endless. Could the ghosts serve breakfast to the guests? How would she pay them? She couldn't resist asking. "Are you the one who keeps it so clean in here?"

Mrs. McMurray blushed and nodded again. She actually *blushed.*

Synn clarified. "She and a dozen maids have kept this place

clean for centuries in the hopes that someone would come here to live. Do you plan to stay?"

She turned to answer him, but Valerie gave him a disapproving look. "The real estate agent didn't say anything about anyone living here."

He sighed, clearly bored. "No, I imagine he didn't. He is what we refer to as a lickfinger."

Rena chuckled at the strange word. She couldn't help it. It sounded backward.

Valerie didn't find the expression funny. "Well, you need to know, Rena owns this castle now, abbey, whatever you want to call it, and she has the right to throw you out."

Rena grabbed her arm. "Valerie." She changed her warning tone to a more pleasant octave as she addressed the sexy man in front of her. "You are of course welcome to stay, Synn. Perhaps you can help us understand the ghosts, the history of the Abbey and anything else that might be helpful." She smiled encouragingly. She didn't want him to leave.

He gave her an arrogant nod. "I would be happy to be of service. Perhaps I should start by helping you to bring your personal items upstairs as the footmen will not be solid enough to lift anything for another week."

Another week? How strange. She didn't remember seeing anything on television regarding ghosts changing with the moon. "Thank you. That would be perfect." She could tell Valerie didn't trust him. She, on the other hand, was thrilled to have him in the Abbey. Anyone who could help her succeed was welcome. The fact that the man was incredibly hot didn't hurt either.

He nodded once and held his arm out to her. She looked at

her friend and shrugged, then looped her arm with his. The second they made contact, a sizzling sensation raced across her skin.

He didn't move. Did he feel it too? He gazed down at her, his face serious. "Shall we?"

She nodded, her throat having closed at his look. There was something sensual about his lips. They were strong, full and serious and made her want to taste him. Sheesh, hadn't she learned anything from her failed engagement? She needed to keep her libido under control. Men like Synn wouldn't appreciate her scandalous thoughts. Besides, who used phrases like "shall we"? He was too far out of her league. Probably from an old Nova Scotia family who could trace its ancestors back to King Robert the Bruce of Scotland.

As they descended the stairs, Rena could picture herself in a beautiful ball gown entering the foyer to meet her beau. The image was so powerful, she stopped. Could this have happened here? In an abbey?

"Rena?"

Synn had covered her hand with his and the sizzling sensation started again, but there was more warmth to it, like the tingling gel she'd bought once and threw away before Bryce discovered it. She lifted her gaze to Synn's. His intense focus unnerved her, and she looked back down at the entryway. "I can picture grand ladies descending these staircases in beautiful gowns, but that couldn't be, because this was an abbey, right?"

She chanced a quick look into his face and caught a glimpse of pain and anger in his eyes before he masked it with a matter-of-fact look.

"Actually, women did descend these staircases in grand ball gowns. The structure was built as a Pleasure Palace. The name Ashton

Abbey was added as a bad joke, but there is a beautiful chapel in the back, so it couldn't have been all licentiousness and depravity."

"A Pleasure Palace? That sounds decadent." They continued their descent. Maybe women came to show off their costly dresses, play poker, and, heaven forbid, smoke cigars. "I think it would be lovely all lit up. Maybe for a charity dinner. Oh, are there any charities in town?"

As they reached the bottom, Synn unlinked their arms and faced her, his look condescending, like the ones Bryce used to give her.

From habit, she straightened herself to her full height.

He must have noticed because he quirked his brow. "I think, perhaps, you should learn a bit more about the Abbey before throwing a ball as there are many who reside here."

Her shoulders fell. He was right, of course. She hadn't seen the entire place yet and already her event-planning instincts were sending her off in another direction. She came to open a haunted bed-and-breakfast, not throw parties. She looked up into Synn's face to apologize, but his gaze made her catch her breath. Admiration shone in his eyes before he turned away to pick up her suitcase.

Stunned and baffled, she hesitated before grabbing her laptop. "I'm sorry. You're right. I need to get a feel for the place first. I hope you can help me with that."

He was already striding toward the stairs when he stopped, but he didn't look at her when he spoke. "It will be my pleasure to help you feel this place."

Masque (http://amzn.to/1NVsW8f)

Also by Lexi Post

Sci-fi Romance

Cruise into Eden
(The Eden Series: Book 1)
Unexpected Eden
(The Eden Series: Book 2)
Eden Discovered
(The Eden Series: Book 3)
Eden Revealed
(The Eden Series: Book 4)
Avenging Eden
(The Eden Series: Book 5) *Coming soon*

Paranormal Romance

Masque
Passion's Poison
Passion of Sleepy Hollow
Pleasures of Christmas Past
(A Christmas Carol Series: Book 1)
Desires of Christmas Present
(A Christmas Carol Series: Book 2)
Temptations of Christmas Future
(A Christmas Carol Series: Book 3) *Coming 2017*

Contemporary Cowboy Romance

Cowboys Never Fold
(Poker Flat Series: Book 1)
Cowboy's Match
(Poker Flat Series: Book 2)
Cowboy's Best Shot
(Poker Flat Series: Book 3)
Cowboy's Break
(Poker Flat Series: Book 4)
Christmas with Angel
(Last Chance Series: Book 1)
Trace's Trouble
(Last Chance Series: Book 2)
Fletcher's Flame
(Last Chance Series: Book 3)
Logan's Luck
(Last Chance Series: Book 4) *Coming 2017*

Military Romance

When Love Chimes
(Broken Valor: Book 1)
Poisoned Honor
(Broken Valor: Book 2)

About Lexi Post

Lexi Post is a New York Times and USA Today best-selling author of romance inspired by the classics. She spent years in higher education taking and teaching courses about the classical literature she loved. From Edgar Allan Poe's short story "The Masque of the Red Death" to Tolstoy's War and Peace, she's read, studied, and taught wonderful classics.

But Lexi's first love is romance novels. In an effort to marry her two first loves, she started writing romance inspired by the classics and found she loved it. From hot paranormals to sizzling cowboys to hunks from out of this world, Lexi provides a sensuous experience with a "whole lotta story."

Lexi is living her own happily ever after with her husband and her cat in Florida. She makes her own ice cream every weekend, loves bright colors, and you will never see her without a hat.

www.lexipostbooks.com